Realm Award: Fantasy

Alliance Award: Reader's Choice

"Swanson introduces a modern sensibility and maturity in this thoughtful revisiting... an intriguing experience."

— PUBLISHERS WEEKLY

"Delightfully twisted... a charming and engaging read."

— LOREHAVEN

"A vibrant, mesmerizing storyteller and original voice in young adult fiction."

— TOSCA LEE, *New York Times* best-selling author

"*Dust* sparkles with hope, magic, and a little bit of pixie dust. If you loved Peter Pan as a child, you'll devour every gorgeous page of this romantic adventure! I can't wait to see what happens next!"

— LORIE LANGDON, award-winning author of *Olivia Twist* and the Doon series

"A whimsical imagining of the dark side of Neverland. *Dust* takes readers beyond the fairytale and, if possible, brings even more enchantment to the already beloved story."

— NADINE BRANDES, award-winning author of *A Time To Die, Fawkes,* and *Romanov*

"Kara Swanson's *Dust* will send you soaring above the bounds of this tired world to a Neverland you've never seen before and won't ever forget."

— WAYNE THOMAS BATSON, best-selling author of
The Door Within Trilogy

"*Dust* is pure magic! Fans of Peter Pan will be delighted to fly off on this journey sprinkled with faith, trust, and pixie dust! Kara Swanson is an author to watch. Her tale is a fantastical spin on a beloved classic."

— SARA ELLA, award-winning author of *The Wonderland Trials*
and The Unblemished Trilogy

"*Dust* is a soaring adventure that taps into the darker themes of J.M. Barrie's original tale while still giving the reader an entirely new and magical journey. If you loved Peter, this book is for you."

— SHANNON DITTEMORE, author of *Winter, White and Wicked*

"With vivid descriptions, conflicted characters, and spirited pacing, *Dust* has it all. Swanson's captivating sense of wonder makes this novel an immersive journey into a land you've visited in your dreams—and sometimes your nightmares."

— CHRISTOPHER HOPPER, best-selling author of
Ruins of the Galaxy

Books by Kara Swanson

The Girl Who Could See

Dust
Shadow

Dust

KARA SWANSON

Escape

Published by Enclave Publishing, an imprint of Oasis Family Media, LLC

Carol Stream, Illinois, USA.
www.enclavepublishing.com

ISBN: 978-1-62184-126-5 (printed hardback)
ISBN: 978-1-62184-129-6 (printed softcover)
ISBN: 978-1-62184-127-2 (ebook)

Cover design by Kirk DouPonce, www.DogEaredDesign.com
Typesetting by Jamie Foley, www.JamieFoley.com

Printed in the United States of America.

Thank you Alysia Maxwell
for contributing to so many of the elements and ideas
in this story—your sweet heart is the fairy dust
sprinkled all over this novel.

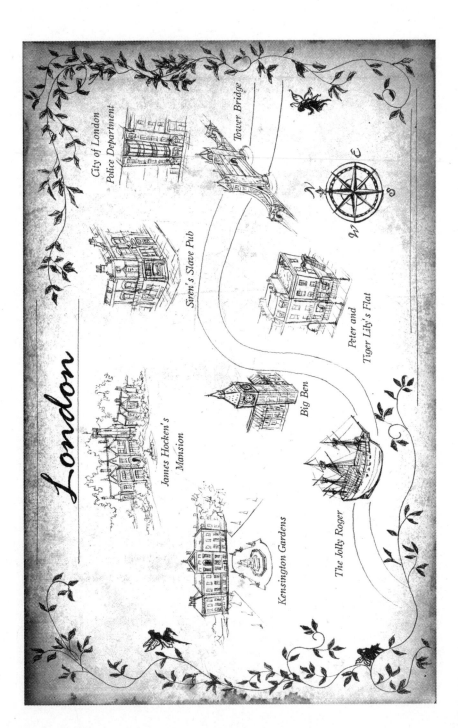

Some day you will be old enough

to start reading fairy tales again.

— C. S. Lewis

1

CLAIRE

Wildomar, California

When did this fairy tale become a nightmare?

I slide my fingers over the worn little book, and the question surfaces again. Each textured hollow in the cover is as familiar as my own lightly freckled skin and chipped nail polish. How many times have I searched this storybook for answers?

But all I've ever found is a myth. A lie.

Something at the far side of the convenience store clangs. Loud. I glare at the wall of refrigerators opposite my cashier counter. They're on the fritz *again*? Oh well. Duty calls.

As I reach for a wad of paper towels, I lay the book beside the small rack of Little Debbies. A few pale, thin specks drip from my fingertips. My dust—the strange, lightly colored, scentless flecks that no number of doctors and needles and scalpels have been able to diagnose. A skin disorder was all they said.

Code for: you're a freak of nature.

I blow the haunting, sandy flecks away from the book, as the mocking green eyes of the boy who never grew up peer up at me from the cover. He's there in watercolor, perched on the edge of a window seat, sporting a jaunty green cap and a pair of panpipes.

This book is the favorite bedtime story of my twin, Connor. An innocent fairy tale, I once thought. But it isn't a story, it's a curse— just like the flakes that drip from my fingertips.

Shoving up the sleeves of my wool cardigan, I step out from behind the counter and around a stack of dollar DVDs, heading for the wall of humming fridges. I need to keep up with this job. Being broke won't help me find him any faster.

Not to mention that work allows me to drown out my mind, something especially needed today.

The anniversary of Connor's disappearance.

I trot down the line of smudged glass refrigerator doors and finally find the culprit eliciting the racket. The tall fridge sports rows of Coca-Cola products and some foggy-looking plastic bottles of water, but nothing is leaking like last time.

"I told them we needed a handyman in here, so they better not blame me for this." I aim a solid kick at the fussy refrigerator. The machine gives a wheeze, but the hissing clatter stops.

Feeling almost triumphant, I turn back, unused paper towels in hand. Then I hear a telltale drip-drip-drip.

I groan. "Fine, fine. Nothing can ever be easy, can it?" Oh boy, two hours into my shift, and I'm already talking to inanimate objects.

Figures. At least they're good listeners.

I drop down to wipe up the gathering pool. As I sop up the mess, the bell at the front of the store dings. I'm half-tempted to stay put and see if the customer walks away. *Really, Claire?* Pathetic. This is my job, and I can't afford to lose another one. Not as a poor nineteen-year-old financing her own search for someone everyone else has forgotten.

Two girls appear in front of the cashier counter—their glistening hair falls in waves, their fashionably ripped jeans and tank tops showing far more skin than I'd ever dare. They're both well cared for, put together. Things I've never been that set my nerves on edge. *Take a deep breath.*

I can't let my insecurities hurt them. Can't let my emotions leak out in burning dust. I've never been able to stop or understand it, only bury the flecks and pray they stay locked away.

The girls glance around and spot me, still by the refrigerator. One of them, a brunette, lifts a hand in a half wave. "The bathroom at Starbucks is broken. Can we use the one here?"

This Circle K doesn't seem like their kind of place, with its cheap knickknacks and dented soda cans and paint peeling from the walls. Not that it's my first choice either. But I've always had to scrape by—thanks to the mother who abandoned my brother and me as babies without even bothering to leave a blanket.

As I rise from my knees, I stifle the urge to hide my chipped nails in my jeans pockets. My comfortable, faded teal cardigan suddenly feels like a shapeless sack that will do nothing to hide the scar-laced skin that could betray me and start leaking the taunting, pale flecks again. Dust that could turn toxic if I don't keep it together.

I muster a smile. "Uh—yeah. The bathroom is in the back right corner. I'll get you the key."

The brunette raises her finely penciled eyebrows. "Oh, it's all right! You look busy. Is it here . . . ?"

She attempts to reach over the cashier counter, and I pick up my pace. "Ah—actually, it's better if I do it."

But I'm too late. She's already fumbling for the key and knocks over a small plastic cup of water I had balanced on the edge of the counter. The liquid flows toward the *Peter Pan* book I had set beside the register.

Hot panic flashes through my limbs.

"*No!*" I hurry to get behind the counter, grasping for the book. As the water soaks through a corner, I grab it. But I'm too late.

My vision blurs as I snatch another paper towel and pat at the cover. I hate this storybook—but it's all I have left of him.

"*Peter Pan?* Isn't that a children's book?" The girls are still standing there. The brunette glances down at the book. "Sorry. Ah, I can give you a few bucks to buy another copy?"

I shake my head. We may have been fourteen when he vanished, but Connor had never outgrown fairy tales—while I learned far too early that there is no magic left in the world. Only the kind you make for yourself by working your fingers to the bone.

The short redheaded girl looks at me quizzically. "Do I know you?"

Tucking the book under my arm, I dry the counter with more paper towels, avoiding eye contact. "I don't think so."

I fight to concentrate on the task at hand, despite the way my breath shakes. Losing control, even for a moment, could risk so much—my job, the money I desperately need, even these girls' safety.

Tossing the soiled towels in the trash, I form another smile and reach for the bathroom key. "Wait," the brunette says. "You were in my freshman English class at McKinley for a few months."

I groan inwardly. Of all the schools I've bounced around in Southern California, they have to be from McKinley. Not that I recognize them, but that was the year Connor disappeared. I'd rather not make another trip down memory lane—especially with how uneasy I am today.

The other girl jumps in. "Weren't you the girl who dropped out before the end of the year because . . ." Her eyes widen. "Your brother is the one who disappeared, isn't he?"

I drop the key to the counter with a metallic clatter and nod, face tense.

If they know about Connor, what else have they heard?

About the fruitless doctors' tests? Or about my hospital visit six months ago? The memory may be distant, but the twinge of the scars lining my back is a painful reminder.

The dark-haired girl leans on the counter. "I'm so sorry. They still haven't found your brother?"

I hate the way the tears sting my eyes. Staring down at the smudges on the counter, I shake my head.

No. Not a single clue has turned up.

Just breathe. Just get through today, through work.

Through this moment.

The girls seem to take my wordless reply as a silent plea for help, and the brunette reaches over to put a gentle hand on my shoulder. That warm touch is enough to cut through my resolve, and a single tear leaks down my face.

"Oh, honey." She squeezes my arm, her manicured nails unwittingly digging into my already raw nerves. Bringing back the drowning ache that fills my lungs. Breathe, breathe, breathe . . . I force myself to keep from wrenching away. She might be sorry, but she doesn't understand. Not really.

And I've had far too much suffocating pity.

My panic swells. I'm usually so good at locking it away, stomping it down—but this time, I can't stop the shaking. The grief is back in horrific Technicolor.

Turning away, I twist my fingers in my cardigan. I need to pull myself together.

Clenching my hands close to my aching chest, I try to focus on just pulling air in—letting a breath out. But when I rub my hands together to work some warmth into my chilled skin, my fingertips come away thick with pale flecks.

Tiny, yellowed specks seep from my skin, covering my fingers. Oh no! Not now!

I shove my quaking fists into my pockets.

Connor said it was magic. That I was special. But he was wrong. The dust isn't magic—it's poison.

So I try to repress it now, fists balled tight. Through the pounding staccato of my heart in my ears, I can just make out the hesitant voices of the girls standing opposite the counter.

"Is everything all right?"

The dust is building inside me, a volcano hammering against my ribs. Calm down! They're customers—just do your job.

They don't wait for my response. "Uh, we'll come back later."

Leaving the bathroom key forgotten on the counter, they flee the store.

Thank God. They probably meant well . . . but today I can't take talking about him with strangers.

Or watching those girls react like everyone else when they see the flakes that leak from my skin—confused, shocked, even angry. People are rarely kind about what they don't understand.

With the store finally quiet again, I sink against the wall behind the cashier counter.

Why can't I just have a day without this pain tearing me apart? A day to function like a normal person, instead of shutting down. Instead of having every breath be a reminder that I let him slip away. Every ache of my heart a testament that no matter what I do, I can't find him.

But I must try.

I stare down at the dust coating my hands and sticking to my cardigan's sleeves, and I shake it off. But even with the dust dislodged, the strange, glistening substance continues to seep from my fingertips, and I tighten my fists to push it back. To push away the panic and the thrum of electricity in my veins.

I close my eyes, muscles taut, and try to ball up the memories and that strange whisper in my core and shove them down as far as I can. I suffocate that spark of warmth in my veins, that part that has never belonged, no matter how desperately I try.

But he can't be gone forever. He can't be dead. He can't.

My breaths come in tight sobs—the dust building with each one. Layering my skin, coating my sleeves and slipping into the air. Pale and glistening and catching on the faintest whisper of a breeze. They swirl around me like taunting specks of tarnished sunlight.

A curse that no one can explain. A curse that threatens to drown me now.

Air—

I can't breathe!

My throat is thick with it, my eyes red, blurring. My pulse drowns out the sound of cars outside as the world grows shadowy. The dust starts to darken, crinkling around the edges like burning ash.

No! No, please, no—

All it takes is one person walking in, or a security camera catching sight . . .

My phone buzzes in my pocket. I'm still trembling and it isn't until the last vibration that I manage to dig out the device. I wipe at my face, clearing my vision enough to make out the one-letter name displayed on the cracked screen. *N*.

N wouldn't call unless it was important. I take a long, ragged breath. N is a friend. One of the few people I can call that anymore. The outpouring of dust ebbs, and the thundering in my chest starts to diminish as I try to focus on the glint of stability he brings to mind.

N is the computer nerd who befriended me in my search for Connor, and although he's never gone by anything more than the one-letter name, he's been there to help in far more ways than my court-assigned foster parents bothered to. The one time he'd visited, it was during my lowest point that landed me in a hospital for two weeks, and the smile that met me on N's dark face had been just as genuine as I'd always hoped.

I'd only known him for a few weeks, but that cemented our friendship. The reason why over the past several months N became one of the very few people I trust. He's an ally, and I know how rare those can be.

I hold the phone against my ear and manage a cracked, "Yeah?"

"Claire? Where are you?" The strain in N's voice sends goosebumps up my arms. But I focus on him, on his words, and watch the dust slowly return to its usual pale color. The flood stops abruptly and starts to fade from my cardigan sleeves.

I force my tone to remain steady. "I'm at work. Why? What's wrong?"

A computer mouse clicks on the other end. "I'm sending you a link—you're gonna want to see this."

I brush away the flecks skimming my palms. The chipped phone shakes beside my ear. "Does this have to do with . . . ?"

"Yes. It's about Connor," he says with a hint of excitement. "It's taken weeks to hunt down, but I found an image cut from a feed at one of the LAX terminals six years ago, just after your brother went missing."

The *clack, clack, clack* from N tapping fills the silence, and a few seconds later it pops up on my phone. My hands go numb, but I manage to tap on N's video, and it fills the screen. The playback is grainy but shows white walls, a security checkpoint, and a smattering of blurry people, most facing away from the camera.

Two people are in the forefront of the image. One a tall, shadowed, masculine silhouette, while the other is as familiar as every tattered pulse of my heart.

My knees almost buckle, and I reach for the edge of the counter, holding myself up as I stare at Connor's image on my screen.

Tall for his age, shoulders beginning to taper out, wearing his favorite threadbare Captain America shirt. Shaggy, wheat-blond hair falling to his shoulders, a shade darker than mine.

Connor.

"Dear God . . ." The words come out like a prayer.

It's Connor. My sweet Connor.

The tears are warm as they roll down my cheeks. Heavy with relief.

I half expect Connor to glance over his shoulder and lock those blue eyes with mine, to once more see that playful gleam and that shadow of an old soul reflected in his gaze. But my twin brother never turns. I don't get a last chance to see his face. Only his receding back as the larger figure guides him away from the camera, through a security checkpoint, and to a boarding gate on the other side.

But it's still him. The first real look at Connor I've had in six years.

"I don't know who the man is." N's words are rushed. "Or what was happening. But I know that Connor got on a plane. And I know where they took him, Claire."

My lungs have practically shriveled in my chest, eyes still blurred as I look at my brother's faded silhouette on my phone, replaying those words over and over again in my head. "Y-you do?"

"Yes, but you're not going to believe it."

A break. One break. That's all I'm asking for. "Where is he, N?"

There's a rumble of static as he shifts the phone. "They made several layovers, but their end destination was out of the country."

Where could he have . . . ?

My eyes drift to the edge of *Peter Pan* just sticking out of my purse and a dark suspicion starts to surface.

No—please tell me he didn't do it. Please tell me I'm wrong. That this strange man hadn't used the bedtime story I'd read to my brother as bait to steal Connor from me and drag him halfway across the planet—practically to another world.

All this time, a part of me has secretly hoped that one day Connor would appear on my front step. Say he ran away to join a circus. Reassure me he'd been fine. That no one had taken him. That no one hurt him . . .

But suddenly, the consequences of this video crash over me. The truth that all this time, when the police stopped looking, when the newspapers said perhaps he just ran away, that the girl with a record of clinically proven delusions was just crying wolf—*I was right.*

Connor hadn't left me. He'd been stolen away.

"That man took Connor to London, Claire."

And with one sentence, my nightmare becomes a reality.

2

PETER

London, England

You know that feeling between falling and flying, frozen midair, heart in throat, pulse pounding so loud it drowns out everything but that small voice screaming—*don't die?*

Yeah. That's where I'm at.

And I love it. The adrenaline, the weightlessness—the freedom.

Even though the ground rushes up at me at a breakneck pace as I launch over a towering brick wall.

Focus, Peter!

I bend my knees as the air rips past my dropping body—and then, *thud!*

I land on both feet, one hand pressed against the asphalt, unable to fight the smirk. Ha! That wasn't so hard. If only Tink could have seen—

I cut off that thought before it can bring a swell of regret. Reminding me again why I'm stuck jumping over blasted walls instead of soaring through the air. Why I'm grounded.

I fling reddish hair out of my eyes and quickly take off down the shadowed side road leading away from the brick wall I just vaulted over. That should give me at least a bit of a head start as a sliver of afternoon sun warms my well-worn green jacket.

As I run, each step feels heavy compared to free falling. Muscles fighting through gravity, my feet squarely against the earth, the buildings rising all around me like towering monsters.

I hate this weighted feeling. The sky pressing down on my shoulders.

But all thoughts of being grounded fade away as the thud of footsteps sounds across the asphalt.

They've finally found me.

The cool London mist swells through the arching cityscape, and I grin. I've been waiting for them to catch up.

Now for some fun.

With its winding alleys, gloomy skies, and brick buildings, London is practically a maze to the swarms of tourists. But not to me. Today, this game of cat and mouse is mine—and I never get caught.

"Let's get started, shall we?"

I spin on my heel, taking off down another side street. I whip past a sidewalk littered with Londoners carrying umbrellas. Trotting past a tiny green scrap of a park, I throw a quick wave to blokes resting there before ducking into an alley. My pursuers' footsteps come faster.

Feels almost like old times, eh mates?

These boys were once like brothers. Now they hunt me like dogs.

But they're the only ones who can give me a chance to find Claire and set everything right that has gone so bloomin' wrong. When I whisked her brother off on an adventure, I had no idea how much it would make a mess of everything, leaving her behind.

I'm already stuck here, grounded in London for three dreary months because the pixies can't risk helping me—thanks to

Hook's hold over them. Claire has to be the piece I'm missing. With her dust, I can fix this.

I can go home.

Not to mention finally fly. Cripes, it's still annoying how blasted alike everything looks down here. Everything is easier to navigate when you're off the ground.

But, even as the Lost Boys draw near, the rhythm of my pulse becomes a message repeating over and over again. Starting beneath my ribs and spreading through my whole body. An acute knowledge that despite everything I've lost, despite having my magic stolen, despite the danger Neverland is in, one thing hasn't changed. I may be outnumbered but there's one thing these boys will never be: *me.*

I quicken my pace, ducking through the towering buildings that pierce the cloudy skies. And then I see the fire escape at the end of the alleyway. One rung of the metal stairs hanging just low enough for me to grab. We're about a half mile from where I told Tiger Lily I'd meet her, and even closer to finally getting the information I need.

By trapping one of the blokes who think *they're* chasing *me.*

I grin. Knew this would be a jolly time.

My feet pump against the asphalt, faster and faster. I near the lowest hanging rung of the fire escape, and leap—

My fingertips barely circle the thick steel, but it's enough.

I scramble up, pausing only long enough to glance over my shoulder at the crowd of boys that have burst into the alley below me.

Their features are hidden behind dark hoods, but I know half of them by the sets of their shoulders and the weapons glinting out of their sweeping coats.

The boys are out for blood. They aim to drag me back to him. Back to the man who wants to rip everything away from me, carve out my very soul.

Nice try, chaps.

I can feel their steel eyes boring into my back as I reach the top of the fire escape. The metal stairs creak and sway as the gang of boys climb up after me.

My vision blurs for a moment. I remember another lifetime, when I desperately climbed salty rigging to escape another group of bloodthirsty vagabonds. Only those pursuers held shimmering sabers between their teeth.

"Focus!" my instincts scream at me. Right, the game at hand. I can hear the heaving breaths and creaking metal of their gang climbing, but I don't look back—only at the rooftop ahead.

I pick up the pace, across the shingles and near the edge.

Then the rooftop is gone, and I'm vaulting through the air. Weightless.

Cor, I've missed this . . .

For those stretching seconds, everything is all right. I'm lighter than pixie dust.

Then I hit hard on the shingles of the next roof, feet first, hands down to steady myself. I race over the ridge of this rooftop and leap to the next one. When I peek over my shoulder, I find only three boys have managed to keep up.

Not for long.

The distance stretches out between us, and in moments only two are still attempting to give chase.

My muscles burn, but I'm grinning wider than a hungry croc. For the first time in the months I've been trapped in this blasted city, I almost feel like myself. The damp wind in my hair, my feet dancing across rooftops, the threat of death always at my heels but never catching up.

I almost feel as if I could fly.

All I'm missing is that certain spark of light hovering at my side and the chime of her voice. I try to ignore the burn at the back of my throat at the memory of her, of flying together, Tink always at my side. I vault off another rooftop, reaching for the next one—and miss.

My hand grapples for the shingles, the gutter, anything. But I come up short. The distant rooftop sliding right past my fingertips . . .

I fall.

Something cold and hard rams into my chest, and my knees collide with a grated metal surface. The air is wrenched from my lungs. A thick metallic taste lies heavy on my tongue, and my vision spins.

Blast it all!

My forehead throbs almost as much as the sting of the scrapes covering my palms. Pulling myself to my feet, I lean against the metal bar. I've fallen into the balcony at the top of a block of flats with a fire escape running up from it. As the world slowly comes back into focus, I look over the low wall to the ground far below. It's covered in rigid pavement.

Overhead, I can hear the distant scramble of the boys still searching.

What am I thinking? The fall could have killed me. I couldn't catch myself. Couldn't fly. My light *this* close to going out.

This chase is no game. Just like my hunt for Claire is no game.

Just like what happened to Tink was no game.

My head explodes with a splitting ache. Somewhere deep

inside me, dark, spindly fingers shove down my sense of adventure with the pressure of drowning in the Neversea. Suffocating the very spark that makes me . . . *me*. That gravity-defying sense of adventure. That boyishness.

I'm shaking now, and it won't stop. I thought I was over this. These charred memories that Neverland locked away—but the beastly things have started to resurface. Memories of losing Tink, of having my island ripped away by Hook and . . . darker things. Things that are beginning to emerge now that I've been cast out of the island. Now that everything has become so twisted. And good gad—it *hurts*.

Spewing curses, I grab the cool metal rungs of the fire escape, clamber off the balcony, and let myself down. My bones feel as though they've been filled with concrete.

I need to get away, need to get to Lily . . .

I'm panting, the thoughts in my head spinning. The minute I hit the asphalt, I duck into another alley and slump back against a molding wall. My chest heaves as I hold my throbbing head.

It's all wrong. Something has shifted deep inside me. Like how my body has started to . . . to . . . Blast!

Twisting, I ram a fist into the wall behind me and wince at the impact.

I'm getting . . . *old*. There, I got it out.

I've started to age.

Everything is whirling out of control and my own body isn't playing fair anymore.

Just like those boys hunting me. They used to be like a tribe of my own, always having my back and on my side. Not anymore.

Now they are a threat to everything I care about.

And thinking of them always leads me back to her. To Claire.

The girl I lost. The girl I can hardly remember, thanks to the island that has buried my memories deeper than the roots of a spritewood tree. Memories of Claire and . . . darker things.

I close my eyes and focus hard, finding she's there in flashes. Her sun-gold curls. Her stubborn refusal to believe that fairy tales were anything but stories.

I press a fist to my forehead, angry at myself for caring so much, but even more angry that I forgot her in the first place. I have no blasted idea where she is—just that I need her. I only hope one of the Lost Boys may have more information on her whereabouts.

I've got to find her. And soon. Before whatever is happening to my body grows too crippling for me to track her down—or before someone else finds her first.

Someone with a hook and beastly intentions.

Letting out several curses that would impress a pirate, I shove off the wall and dodge through shadowed alleys to cross Copperfield Street.

I glance over my shoulder one last time and see that I've lost all but one of the dark-coated boys following me. And just ahead, tucked between a noisy pub and a quirky little gallery, is the meeting place where a certain warrior princess waits.

I've walked into enough of Hook's ambushes. Creating one of my own? *Easy.*

My quick steps carry me to the edge of a building, and I duck around the corner of the raucous pub to come face-to-face with a pair of intense, earth-brown eyes.

Tiger Lily's gaze darts past me, then back again. "You made it. Everything okay?"

The clank of bottles and muffled voices from the pub rumble

at my back—providing the perfect cover for the kidnapping we're about to attempt.

"Just dandy. One of them is on my heels and should be here any second."

She nods, ebony hand tightening around the ruddy, spritewood staff she managed to smuggle with her from Neverland. Lily's hair is pulled into a dark braid over her shoulder and streaked with teal strands that match the brightly patterned trousers beneath her leather jacket. "All right, what do you say we grab him quick and keep him from screaming—we don't want a scene. Sound good?"

"Fantastic."

We move silently toward the entrance to the alleyway, sharing a quick smile—and it almost feels like old times. Like when we'd run through the vivid jungle, racing circles around the pirate crew tromping through the underbrush. Toying with them, our laughter filtering through the trees.

Tink's glimmer of light darting around me.

Only this time, there's no Tink. No glimmer of magic.

And we're trapping one of our own.

I hold my breath, my back pressed against the dusty wall as the hooded figure of the Lost Boy rounds the corner. I leap at him. There's a flash of metal, and something sharp slices across my arm.

Gritting my teeth against the sting, I kick at the hand holding the weapon. He groans as the knife tumbles from his grasp. Tiger Lily pounces on the fallen blade, and before the Lost Boy can reach for another weapon, I wrestle his wrists behind his back—amazed to find that my newfound height has apparently increased my strength.

Brilliant.

The Lost Boy attempts to kick me, but I dodge out of his way, still clamping his arms behind him. There's something very familiar about this chap, but I can't quite see his face.

"Y-you'll regret this!"

He spurts the words out, struggling against my grasp—but then Lily's there, standing in front of him, staff aimed at his neck, applying enough pressure to make the chap quiet.

"And you'll regret following us." She wrenches back his hood with her free hand.

My eyes go wide. "*Slightly?*" I don't know who I'd expected—but not him. Not Slightly, one of the first Lost Boys. One of my oldest mates.

The gangly bloke twists around to me. "'Ey there, Pan. Been a while."

His face is still the same thin, freckled thing it's always been, only this time there's a lumpy scar on his cheek and a sharp gleam in his brown eyes. But worst of all . . . Slightly is not a boy anymore. His shoulders are broader, eyes more calloused, more grown-up. He's aged even faster than I have—but something tells me that was his own blooming choice. Just like he chose to betray me and Neverland and the whole lot of it.

My grip on his arms falters. "What happened? Why you, of all the boys?"

Slightly never quite had the imagination of other Lost Boys and was always prancing around like he was bloomin' royalty, telling us about the family he was certain he'd had before I found him. Once, he'd issued me a friendly challenge as the leader of the Lost Boys. And sure, when everything fell apart I knew that most of the boys changed sides, joining up with that blasted old codfish. But Slightly was one of my oldest mates.

I never expected him to be a traitor.

Slightly turns his gaze on Lily and spits at her. She merely wipes the saliva from her dark cheek with a free hand, her staff unwavering against his throat. She could crush his windpipe with a single jab, and I see the handle of the knife she confiscated from him sticking out from her jacket pocket. "You were one of the first ones. Like family to Peter, a friend to me and my people—why would you do something like this? Why would you join *him*?"

Slightly pulses with anger. "At least you could face me like a man, Pan!"

I roll my eyes. "Oh, I could beat your measly hide with one hand behind my back." My eyes thin into slits and I bark a bitter laugh, the sound echoing in the narrow, damp alleyway. "But you know better than most that I'd rather die than do anything like a man." Like the men I'd seen—drab and selfish and absent. And angry. So very angry.

My eyes flick to Lily, and she nods, tightening her grip on her staff. I let go of Slightly's arms, crossing to stand in front of him. Hands on my hips, meeting his vicious stare unflinchingly.

"Not like a man, but I will face you like me—*Peter*, the boy who used to be one of your best mates."

His thin lips curl into a snarl. He slams his hand against Lily's staff. I'm ready to have a good ol' romp like we used to, but before I can blink, Lily's blurring into motion.

She swings the thick rod around, ramming her staff into Slightly's kneecaps hard enough I hear the crack. He gasps, dropping to the ground, clutching at his knees.

"Oh, drat. I wanted a go." I pout.

Lily just shakes her head. "We have to get this done fast, remember? Before the rest of his gang catches up."

"Blithering ninny . . ." I mutter, not about to admit aloud that she's right.

Lily nods to the knees Slightly is cradling. "Don't worry, they're not broken." She holds fast onto the colorful threads woven into a grip around the middle of the staff. "But if you don't cooperate, next time it'll be your head."

He curses, but acknowledges the threat. Groaning, he pulls himself back to his feet and glares at me. "You say you're my mate? More like my slave master. My prison guard."

Lily shoots me a sharp look. "Can I just shut him up?"

But I shake my head. Slightly is shorter than I am, but even beneath the hatred in his eyes, I see pain.

I cock my head at Slightly. "What in the blasted stars could have driven you to this?"

His chin tilts up, nostrils flaring, but the anger in his eyes is melting away, leaving behind a raw desperation.

"You *left* us. While you were off flying to hear bedtime stories, we fought just to survive the harsh winters. The ice and frostbite. Finding ways to keep warm and hunt in the winter. We had to deal with you leaving and taking all the sun with you."

No, that's not . . . it wasn't like that . . .

But as much as I fight the utter codswallop coming out of his mouth, each word Slightly says is like the shot of a cannon, knocking the air from my lungs.

I never meant anything of the sort. Thought they just enjoyed the adventure.

A few blokes shove out of the pub, talking loudly and lumbering past the alleyway, but they don't notice us. Instead, the concrete walls on either side begin to close in on me as Slightly keeps going.

"That was just the beginning. It was all about you—what Peter wanted. What games Peter chose to play—not what any of us needed. Not the families that we missed or wanted."

I gulp around the knot in my throat. Slightly used to make up all sorts of stories about the family he imagined he'd had, but I'd never thought he actually meant it. "I didn't—"

"*No.*" He can't even look at me as he says the single, bitter word. "You never bothered to see what we needed. But *he* does, and he offered us freedom. More than that, he offered us enough gold to have a comfortable future on Earth. I'd have been a fool to turn it down, like Tootles did."

I blink. "Tootles didn't join the pirates?"

But that wall is up again and his eyes go dark.

"What about the rest of the island?" Lily asks. "Yes, it was difficult—but it was hard for all of us. My people fought the pirates too, hunted the great crocodile alongside you . . . Yes, Peter was a child. But so were all of you." Her jaw goes tight. "Is that really enough reason to betray everything you believed in? To turn against your home—the people who were your clan? Your family?"

Slightly flinches and his eyes flicker for a moment. But only a moment, and then his lips curl into another snarl.

Lily shakes her head, pressing closer, raising her staff again. "Now, we need some information, and you're going to give it to us."

He's not even looking at her. His glare is fixed on me, lips twisting up into a sizzling sneer.

"No, I'm not. You don't scare me. You'd never hurt me, Peter."

A low gust blows through the alley, and Lily shifts her staff. "I wouldn't be so sure about that."

Slightly only laughs, eyes drilling into me. "No, he doesn't have it in him. He may look older, but deep down he's still just a little boy."

As he talks, I shuffle my shoes against the grimy asphalt, but the regret I felt a moment ago starts to crust over like the hull of the Jolly Roger.

Anger. Desperation.

It's more than just the memories that thunder at my mind like a shot cracking through a mast—this is a torrent of rage that boils from deep inside. Heat flushing through my coiled muscles, *building, building, building,* until I want to whirl and ram my knuckles into the nearest lubber close enough to expel this fury into. Fury I didn't even know I had.

My head twitches, and I sway, trying to fight back the deluge of emotion that roars through my veins—

And then Slightly's voice tears through my shred of control with one sentence:

"You're a coward who couldn't even save Tink."

I lunge at him, slamming Slightly back against the wall so hard it knocks the air out of him. The dusty shadows wrap around us as my hand circles his neck. My eyes are locked on Slightly's wide expression.

"Don't talk about her like that," I growl, every muscle taut. "Tink was stolen from me, and I'm not letting him take Claire too. You have no idea what I'm capable of."

"W-what's wrong with you?" Slightly gulps beneath my grip, the color draining from his face. His lips part, cracked words escaping. "You've changed."

His words tremble, but my vision blurs angrily, and for a blasted second, all I can see is that memory. The glimmer of light, the splash of crimson, and that soft scream of Tink's—like glass shattering.

She falls, dissolving, her light going out.

And I'm holding her tiny body. So cold. Far too cold.

I stare at the shocked expression on the face of the Lost Boy in my grasp. What am I doing? I release my hand from around his neck, stumbling back a step.

"I don't want to hurt you, mate. But I need to know how to find Claire."

He jerks his chin in a quivering nod, his eyes darting between Lily and me. "I'll tell you what I know. But he can't find out you heard this from me."

"Of course," Lily says, watching me out of the corner of her eye as I tuck my arms across my chest.

Slightly might be right—I'm not the same boy I was.

I swore to protect Neverland with my life, and I've already lost Tink. I won't make the same mistake twice. Not with Claire.

But there's something else—something groping for a handhold deep inside me. A side I don't remember. A side of me the island of childlike dreams locked away.

My pulse rages with a desire I've only ever seen reflected in the pirates' cold gazes or behind a tribal warrior's tarnished spear.

A thirst for blood.

A shadowed craving to hunt down the man who killed Tink . . .

And snuff out his light with my bare hands.

3

CLAIRE

Wildomar, California

The outdoor stairs to my apartment seem like a never-ending labyrinth, as winding as my thoughts.

London. Even the word feels distant and blurred. Like a dream.

At least work is finally over, and I can process this. I trudge up one step after another, into a small hallway studded with apartment doors.

London—with its dark skies and curving architecture and rippling Thames that I've only ever seen pictured on TV. I can't seem to wrap my mind around the concept.

Connor. There. Kidnapped away to that place.

Why England, of all places? Why go so far to keep up an illusion? Was it to convince an imaginative boy he was escaping to a fantasy world? To the place where Peter Pan was born and returned to whisk Wendy and the others away?

Besides the fact that the man in the video is a child-stealing psychopath.

Pausing in front of my apartment door, I can't bring myself to step inside. I'm overwhelmed by everything—including that video. But, like my love-hate relationship with Connor's copy of *Peter*

Pan, there's a strange tug dragging me back to that recording taken at the airport.

Like an addict giving in to a craving I pull out my phone and navigate back to the clip from N's text. This time letting my eyes slide gently over Connor's gangly fourteen-year-old form to focus on the man behind him. A stranger with a rigid stance and a sharp tilt to his shoulders.

There has to be some answer, some clue . . .

My thumb hovers over the screen, tracing Connor's small figure. Only fourteen. But from the image, Connor doesn't seem afraid. He doesn't look tense or nervous—instead, his posture is alight with excitement.

N said the man with Connor was practically a ghost as far as finding records of him.

Through the grainy feed, I can just make out the stranger's crimson leather jacket and stiff posture. Dark hair gelled back, face tilted at just the right angle so I can see the faint silhouette of his features. Narrow and sharp. Cruel.

If I find out he has laid a hand on my brother . . . My fingers tighten, a few angry flecks of gold spiraling into the air.

That little voice in the back of my head reminds me to stay calm.

Oh, I'm the epitome of calm.

I'll very calmly tear that man's arms from their sockets if he's hurt Connor.

I don't even bother to shake off the dust that lands on the phone before I stuff it back in my pocket. A strange urgency pulses through my veins, and I enter my apartment, giving one last glance over my shoulder. The sky has begun to die, orange and yellow fingers seeping into the dark shadow of sunset. Like the golden dust from my hands that I used to play with as a child.

Back then, the world was right, and a family had adopted us when we were too young for them to know what I was capable of. Back when Connor and I were actually wanted.

But then my dust became a poison that left the woman I called mother horrendously burned, and we were thrown into the cold revolving door of foster homes.

Right now I need to think through the implications of N's revelation about London.

As if my brother being kidnapped and taken to another country will ever make sense.

I collapse onto my makeshift bed—a mattress pushed against one wall under a small window, piled with blankets and an assortment of pillows scored from the Salvation Army. I wish I could just melt into their soft comfort.

But Connor's in London—or at least he was, last anyone knows—and I need to figure out what I'm going to do about it.

Reaching back, I lean over the comforter covered with worn lace ruffles and plug in my lights. Fairy lights, Connor called them. They cast the small room in warmth and ignite the wall like a field of fireflies.

I kick off my shoes, tuck my legs up under me, and reach for my purse. Pushing through the faded brown leather, I nudge aside my tangled earbuds to grab Connor's copy of *Peter Pan*.

The beginning of this whole mess.

Because Connor claimed he *knew* Peter Pan. He was best friends with this boy named Peter in seventh grade. I'd always assumed it was just a game. He'd even tried to get me to join, but I'd never wanted to play. Life was too harsh for that. But I'd done what I could to shoulder the weight so Connor could escape into a make-believe childhood.

When I flip open the cover of his book, I find the familiar inscription. The nail in the coffin. The reason my brother left with a stranger, his head filled with dreams of adventure.

The front page is faded and dog-eared, and even when my eyes blur with tears, I can still make out the words written in his thick, boyish scrawl. Words forever carved into my soul.

Claire,

I'm going to Neverland with Peter Pan.
Be back soon.

– C

P.S. Don't worry or tell on me to Miss T.

And I'd done what he asked. I'd not worried, not mentioned the incident to Miss Trevor, our foster mother at the time, expecting him to come home that night. Connor always had an especially vivid imagination. But he never returned—and hours became days, and days became years. My brother had been lured away by his favorite bedtime story that I'd read to him.

I should have done *something.*

And now, for the first time in six years, maybe I can.

I slump back onto my bed, the old mattress groaning beneath me. I stare at the popcorn ceiling, wishing it was a rippled white map that could lead me to the answers I need. To London. To Connor.

But it's just a ceiling, and I'm just a poor Circle K cashier who wouldn't know what to do in England, even if I could scrape together enough cash to get there. Although, N probably could help and might know how to pawn something off for more than I would.

I sit up, Connor's fairy tale tucked under my arm, and hop off the bed. I cross the threadbare rug toward my pride and joy—a bookshelf taking up nearly the whole back wall.

Another garage sale find with chipped wood and small Sharpie scribbles on the backboard, it holds my most precious possessions. The small collection of books I've gathered.

As priceless as these tattered copies are to me, they'll only bring in a few bucks, hardly enough to get started on a fund for a flight.

I place *Peter Pan* on the middle row, beside the fundamentals that I rescued from garage sales and library handouts. The worn and dog-eared copies of *Anne of Green Gables*, *Oliver Twist*, and *Treasure Island*.

Anne, Oliver, and Jim had kept me company many a night, but Peter had always been Connor's favorite. My brother had crawled in beside me so many times, head tucked against my shoulder, asking me to read aloud. He could read just as well, but he said there was something about my voice. About the way I made the stories dance to life.

Letting my fingertips skim the faded bindings filling the shelves, I take a deep breath.

I can hardly afford rent and a few packages of ramen, let alone a plane ticket. Still, I look about the room, ticking off the meager belongings that fill the space.

Ten bucks for the worn records and CDs stacked in a corner.

Fifteen for the collection of books and random magazines littering my shelves.

Maybe thirty for the rickety desk and bookshelves I got cheap at Salvation Army.

Fifty—if I'm *really* lucky—for the worn Dell computer with little battery life.

That leaves my phone, clothes, a few dishes . . . and my car. Big Bertha is weather worn, but not in bad condition. It would at least help me get there, and maybe housing for a bit?

Ugh, I'm getting a headache.

Waving a hand through the air to dislodge soft flickers of gold, I turn to the other side of my room. My eyes catch the boxes filled with my clothes, and a carton with old electronics that I haven't had the heart to throw out yet.

I pause beside the hastily stacked boxes and kneel by the one with wires and cracked screens sticking out. Most of them look pretty shot. Still . . .

Only one way to know for sure.

I dump the box upside down and the contents topple all over the threadbare carpet. A broken iPod, a CD Player that's missing pieces, a ton of cords and adapters . . . and two thin slips of paper that make my pulse stutter.

"I thought I'd thrown these away." I reach to scoop up the curling pieces of paper. White, with pristine script detailing a bunch of medical terms I don't understand—but two words are crystal clear on both of them.

"Carthage Institute."

The medical bracelets from our intermittent tests. The ones our foster parents had insisted Connor and I take when we were in seventh grade. A ghostly reminder of the pale white rooms, nurses, doctors, needles, and countless questions. Questions they never could answer, deciding in the end that a foster kid with a skin disorder wasn't worth more than a quick glance and shuffled on.

I turn the bracelets in my palm. My name's imprinted on one— and his on the other.

CONNOR KENTON. Big, blocky, unfeeling letters.

I'd practically cried when Miss Trevor appeared one day and said that she had come to take us away. That she was going to be our new foster mother, and it was time for the tests to stop and for us to adjust back to a full school schedule. That the doctors had done what they could, and she was going to fight for us to have normal lives as the teens we were.

She was the first person who ever fought for us.

We lived with Miss Trevor for a year until Connor met a little boy named Peter and vanished shortly afterward. I now know he was seated on a plane beside a stranger.

No one else cared then.

Not about two orphans trapped in the foster care system with emotional and physical abnormalities that couldn't be explained. No one cared to find him. Not even Miss Trevor, despite the fact that he had even started calling her Mom. And no one cares now.

I crush the scraps of paper, toss them in the trash, and blow out a long breath.

My vision is starting to blur, and my skin grows slick as the room turns hot and stuffy. My thoughts ache from being twisted into so many knots, I don't know if I'll ever untangle them.

Hoping a shower will clear my head, I brush a hand over my eyes and head to the bathroom with a fresh change of clothes.

After tugging off my cardigan, I smooth the wrinkles from my camisole and stare at my reflection in the mirror—a girl I used to be ashamed of. Now, I understand more what I see.

A survivor.

Pale scars peek from beneath the straps of my thin tank top. I massage my fingertips over the deep, rough lines, still a little sore. These more jagged scars are fresher than the ones along my arms from doctors' needles and scalpels.

How long has it been since I jumped from that second-story window? Over a year? The scars are what remain of my silent screams. Painful reminders of the darkest moment of my life. Worse than the time spent in the institution. Worse than the years of bullies and violent foster parents.

I lean my forehead against the mirror for a moment.

I'd given up on Connor. Given up on ever finding him.

Given up on life.

I'd fallen so far I couldn't even feel the light anymore. I'd been so numb, so desperate to stop aching, stop *being*, that I'd decided one day to embrace everything Connor had claimed about Peter Pan. His fantastical idea that my unexplainable dust wasn't some freak disease—but *magic*.

That maybe I was a pixie.

So I threw myself from that window, but my dust hadn't lifted me.

I hadn't flown.

I'd fallen.

Horribly. The split bones had healed, but the broken glass and twisted metal of the dumpster I landed on had cut deep into my back and shoulders, leaving me with the worst of my scars. A message I'd never forget: pixies aren't real.

There is no magic.

But I survived, and that's what's important.

The minute I slip into the shower, the tension in my muscles melts away. The water slides over me, washing the dust and grime from my skin. The pool at my ankles faintly shimmers with gold.

The heat wraps around me, and I can breathe again.

When I finish, I dress and come out of the bathroom. I need some fresh air. I trot down the steps to the ground level. It's dark out.

A soft breeze rustles my damp hair, and my bare feet crunch withered, dry grass. In the dim light cast from the scattered street lights, I make out the road stretching past my faded green apartment building and the cluster of houses opposite us. They're a ragged patchwork, with unkempt yards, walls in need of paint, and car carcasses filling half the driveways. But the homes brim with life and hope and warmth. These people may not have it easy, but they know that family is everything.

Even when your family is halfway across the world.

As I walk past the side of the faded apartment building, I can't help glancing at the starlit sky. Man, am I glad I live in a place where I can see the stars. Without them, the world would feel so dim. So small.

I soon reach the small playground tucked behind the apartment complex. I pause, watching a little group saunter from the slide. A mother and father and two young siblings. A boy and a girl with dark hair and bright eyes.

They spin and laugh and point at the stars overhead.

I can't stop watching them—the way they just fit. So effortless, pieces of each other. Born to have a place together. Even after the little family has gone away and I sink onto one of the plastic swings, the siblings still fill my thoughts.

Their togetherness tears at a place deep in my chest. A place where Connor belongs. Yes, we belong together—but even more than that, he belongs with *me*. I've lost track of how many foster homes we'd been in over the years, Miss Trevor's house being the last place Connor and I had been together.

I push the swing in slow, rocking movements, the tips of my bare toes guiding me forward and back.

Connor always loved the swings best. We'd take turns seeing who could go the highest—and when any other child challenged our swinging prowess, he'd push me so that I could go farthest.

He was always behind me, a steadying hand on my back, reminding me that no matter how hard it got, we could make it. He believed I had the strength to fly higher.

To him, I wasn't a filthy foster kid. I was a fairy princess.

And his opinion was the only one that had ever mattered.

Tears drip down my cheeks, mingling with golden dust and splattering on my white tank top. Small glimmering tracks appear on the fabric.

I can't lock away the grief. The loss.

But I can sure as heck do something about it.

My hands tighten around the chains holding up the swing. If I don't search for Connor now, I'll never be able to live with myself. And as distant as London may seem, I have nothing holding me here.

I lean back in the swing, pumping my legs to gain height as the cool night air folds around me. The wind lifts my hair and fills the air with spiraling glimmers of golden dust. Glowing specks of gold, free from any hint of gray—light and healthy.

Tipping my head back, I stare at the expanse, speckled with twinkling stars. Most of them dim and distant—but two stars stand out against the opaque sky. One shines a bit brighter than the other.

The second star to the right.

And I smile. The first real smile in years.

"I'm coming, Connor. I'm coming."

4

PETER

London, England

"Claire thinks you played a part in kidnapping her brother."

Slightly's words hit me like a slap. I jolt, grinding my heels into the pavement. "She *what?*"

Slightly's voice lowers, his gaze sliding past me to sweep the dark alleyway surrounding us. "She thinks you were somehow involved in forcing Connor to leave, and she's been trying to hunt you down for the past six years. At least, that's what we hear on the streets. Hook doesn't tell us much."

"That's ridiculous. *Girls* are ridiculous!"

Besides, Connor told me he left her a note explaining everything. I can only shake my head. Claire didn't want to come. I had enough trouble saving her brother, with grown-ups butting in where they didn't belong. Still, I'd managed to nab Connor when he got to London and whisk him away to the adventure he'd always wanted. A place where no adult could ever ruin his fun and where magic filled the very air we breathed.

I sigh, rubbing the back of my neck and taking in the figures in the alleyway. Lily has stationed herself between Slightly and me, as if she's expecting me to throw myself at him again. Those rushing currents of unwanted emotions are still there, beneath the surface, thundering in my veins, but they're starting to ebb.

I focus on the blasted mess in front of me. It's just another scrape—and I'm good at getting out of those. Even one as massive as this.

I *will* find Claire and restore Neverland.

There's no other option.

Fists on hips, I stand inches from Slightly and stare down at him. "So, Claire thinks I kidnapped her brother, eh? Once I find her, I'll set her to rights. Now, where is she?"

His shoulders stiffen. "I don't know."

Well, we can't have that.

I glance at Lily, nodding at the knife peeking out of the pocket of her leather jacket, and she tosses it my direction. I catch the blade's handle midair.

Slightly presses back against the damp cement wall of the alley behind us, nostrils flaring. But I don't touch him, only hover a few inches away, spinning the blade over my fingertips.

I picked up the knife tricks after spending long hours lounging on the *Jolly Roger's* mast, making snide remarks at the crew and watching the pirates show off with their weapons.

"As much blinding fun as getting chased over those rooftops was, I didn't go through all that trouble just to see your ugly mug again." The slender, razor-sharp edge spins over my knuckles as I lean close to whisper in Slightly's ear. "Now then, mate. You're a clever lad. I'm sure there's something you've overheard. It'd be a shame to dirty this blade on a bloke like you . . ."

His face pales, his eyes on the knife in my hands. "I swear I have no bloomin' idea, mate! Nibs might—he's in deeper with Hook than I am." Sweat beads his freckled brow. "But even if you do find Claire, what makes you think she'll help you when she discovers what really happened to Connor in Neverland? When she finds out she'll never see her sweet, innocent little brother again?"

I grip the knife tighter.

"*Shut it*! You have no idea what you're talking about." The words come out in a strangled bark as my fist jerks the knife hilt. A strange part of me almost wants to carve that knowing look off his face. "None of that was my fault!"

Slightly eyes me. "It never is. But I doubt Claire will find that so easy to believe."

I growl, spinning the knife across my knuckles and glare at Slightly. "Do you *want* me to stab you?"

A muscle leaps in his jaw. "Claire may be the one thing you can't fight or talk your way out of, Peter."

I narrowly avoid the temptation to clip him with my blade and instead toss the knife in the air. I watch the steel glint in the soft gleam of sunlight filtering from the clouded sky. After all, Claire's just a girl. I snatch the knife before it hits the cement. "I'll get it sorted. I always do."

My eyes flit to Lily for a half second. Worry stains her usual confidence. I try to ignore the low throb starting in my gut.

I never looked back before. Why start now?

Slightly persists. "Everything is always so easy for you, isn't it, Peter? None of it bothers you. Not even what you did to Connor." Then, in a voice barely above a whisper, he adds, "After all, it's not the first time you've lost one of us, is it?"

I flinch from the screams that suddenly echo through my head. Memories slam into me, the crunch of underbrush and a spray of crimson, sprouting into pain that claws across my temples.

I glare at Slightly. I just have to find the girl.

"If Hook knows where Claire is, what's he planning on doing with her?"

"No idea, *mate*." He flings the word at me. "Like I said, they don't tell me much. Too cautious—the dozens of years we spent with you don't just disappear because we pledge our allegiance to someone else. That's all I know. I swear."

Because I've known this boy since he was a toddler—because I'm the one who taught him to lie while also memorizing his tells—I believe him.

I step back, sensing more than seeing Lily arrive at my side. I tuck the knife into my waistband, wishing again that I hadn't lost my own blade when I was forced out of Neverland months ago.

I tip my chin at Slightly. "All right. You can go."

His hard expression melts with relief.

I smirk at the Lost Boy. "And be sure to give the captain a message for me . . ."

The scar on Slightly's chin quivers as he takes cautious steps toward the opening of the alley.

"Tell that codfish that as soon as I find Claire and fix this, I'm coming for him. And this time he'll wish he'd lost a lot more than just an arm to that crocodile."

Slightly's eyes widen, no doubt envisioning having to deliver that little message to the captain of the *Jolly Roger*. Then he races out of the alley, taking off as quickly as his long legs will carry him. He doesn't need to run—I won't follow.

What's the point?

Short of attacking Hook, there's nothing else I can do.

It's a dead end.

Another. Blasted. Dead. End.

I ram a foot into the nearest wall. My trainer bounces off the concrete, and I unleash a few more curses into the misty air.

Lily watches with arms crossed, raising an are-you-finished-with-your-tantrum-yet brow.

I'm not finished in the slightest.

Frustration builds, as does the headache slamming behind my forehead, and I brush a hand over my face, hating the prick of facial hair beneath my palm. It's all so blasted wrong. I wish I could hurl myself into the air and shed this heaviness like a second skin. Wish I could cut out this shadow that has invaded everything I am. Everything I used to be.

The reflection I don't recognize.

I pinch my eyes shut. This situation has to be some kind of bad dream. But when I open my eyes again, nothing's changed. Jagged rooftops and overcast sky. This whole beastly world.

My eyes fog again, turning the cityscape into a shadowed pattern, like a blotch of dripping ink. So grown-up and cold and dismal and average. A place I'd hardly wanted to visit, let alone live in. And my world is slipping through my fingertips. We are still no closer to finding Claire.

And this blithering headache is getting worse.

Lily steps closer, teal-tinted hair falling across her eyes. "Peter, are you okay? I know it's a shame we didn't find out anything new from Slightly."

I shrug roughly. "We could always go hunt down Hook and make him tell us where Claire is and what he's planning to do with her."

Lily grabs my shoulder with more strength than I'd give her credit for. Her coal-dark eyes flash. "*Absolutely not.* If you went after Hook, do you have any idea what kind of all-out war you'd bring on our heads? Especially when you can't fly, don't have your blade, and Hook practically has an army on his side. If we're going to save Claire, we have to play this smart."

A waft of mist fills the narrow alley, and in the distance, I hear the screech of vehicles and the low hum of voices. I step away from Lily. "Play it *safe,* you mean. I've never wanted to be safe, Lily. I want to stop Hook and save Neverland—even if that means a bit of danger." A smirk tugs at my lips. "*Especially* if it means danger."

She heaves a long sigh, then spins her staff in a wide arc, and slams it down into the concrete. The durable spritewood from the strongest timber in Neverland doesn't even creak under the pressure. "Fine. You've always been that way, so I'm not even sure why I try to convince you otherwise. But, before you go throw everything you have into some harebrained escapade, let's at least try hunting down our last option. There's still someone who might have answers."

"Who . . . ?" But the way she looks away, fingering the string of beads at her neck, answers my question. I shake my head furiously, the heavy stench of rain filling my nostrils, like an omen of the oncoming deluge if I encounter the person Tiger Lily wants. "Oh no. He hates me. There's no blasted way I'm going to that chap begging for help."

The Guardian's sharp gaze rises in my memory. The frigid lines of his granite frown that has managed to put a stop to my schemes and ruin my play more than once.

Curses. Couldn't we talk about something cheerful for once? Like . . . cake?

Cake is cheerful. Cake isn't trying to kill me.

I take another step backward into the light spilling from the end of the alley. My thoughts dissolve into images of a mountainous chocolate cake that already has my mouth watering.

I love cake. Didn't get much of it in Neverland. At least London has good cake.

". . . Peter? Are you even listening to me anymore?"

I wave a hand. "Nope, wasn't listening. But I just had a brilliant idea! Let's go buy some cake, eh?"

Spinning on my heel, I'm about to escape toward a bakery and change of conversation, when Lily's iron grip latches on my elbow and yanks me back around.

"Cake? What are you even talking about? Peter, this is serious."

I snatch up the knife from where it's clipped at my side. "Everything is always so serious to you, Tiger Lily. You're quite a wet blanket, really. Might want to work on that." Spinning the knife, I balance the tip of the blade on a finger, and look at her. "But even if the sky was falling, I'd rather lop off an arm and give the croc a second course than go talk to that blasted Guardian."

Lily swipes the knife out of my hands, leveling me with a glare. "Regardless of how you feel about him, the Guardian might be the last ally we have."

Ally—if you can even call him that.

This man who stands between London and Neverland. A peacekeeper who tends to enjoy ruining my schemes more than maintaining harmony. Not to mention that he is so *old* and always jawing on about rules and his responsibility to the people of London and how I need to watch out for them . . . blah, blah, blah.

Rules and responsibility.

Two words that make me want to vomit.

Yeah, like I'd *ever* go anywhere near that bloke—the grown-up is so thick on him, I might catch it by accident.

Still, Tiger Lily is staring at me expectantly, so I scrunch up my nose and bat my tumbling hair out of my eyes. "I'll . . . think it over."

"Well, think it over quickly because every day that passes without finding Claire ourselves, Hook gets closer to his own ends. And once he has Claire, there's nothing standing between them and destroying what's left of Neverland." Lily leans over her staff. "Regardless of how much you hate everything the Guardian represents, you may have no choice, Peter. We're running out of time."

I pass a hand over my face. "And every day Hook is getting closer to Claire and the Lost Boys are falling farther away from me."

"But Slightly wasn't completely wrong." Her voice warns. "You aren't innocent in all of this, Peter. Starting with those Lost Boys you let die all those years ago."

The splintering headache becomes a force of nature. I don't entirely remember the incident with the boys, just flashes of pain, but I do know one thing. "It was an accident, Tiger Lily."

She shakes her head slowly as tendrils of teal-stained dark hair fall across her expression like a shadow. "Even so, your memories, the things you have done—the part you played in the destruction of our homeland—if you can't find a way to set things to right . . ."

Her next words fill the hollow alleyway like the echoing ticktock of a clock, a foreboding omen promising that what is about to come cannot be rewound.

"Then Hook has already won."

5

CLAIRE

Los Angeles International Airport, California

The only thing calming me is the music flowing through my earbuds. The steady crooning of Broadway classics plays from the tiny speakers, and I lean back against one of the off-white pillars, full purse at my feet.

So, this is what it must have been like for Connor.

The wild bustle of LAX at ten o'clock at night is overwhelming. Fluorescent lights drown out deepening shadows outside the windows. People mill every which direction, filling most of the narrow black seats beside the gate I'm waiting to board at. Women in heels, crying children, twenty-somethings in hoodies, men in business suits, and everyone in between.

So. Many. People.

It's enough to make an introvert have a heart attack.

"Just breathe." I try to relax my tight muscles. No surprise that Connor seemed content walking down the terminal with that man. What I wouldn't give for an extrovert to step forward and escort me to the right place.

Instead, I have to fend for myself. Nothing new there.

I scoop up my purse and maneuver around rows of chairs to

an empty seat in the corner and sink into it. There are a good two seats between me and anyone else. Hallelujah.

As long as I can stay calm, everything will be fine. The anxiety will remain in check, as will my dust. No one will get hurt.

Even with headphones in, I can sense the hum of the room around me. Carpet with spiraling red and blue designs matches the artsy pictures hung at intervals on the walls.

Out of habit, my hand goes for the copy of *Peter Pan* in my purse, a token to remind me why I'm braving a bustling airport for the first time in my life. The familiar coarse sensation of the cover immediately begins to push back against that pressure in my chest.

I let out a long sigh. I almost pawned the storybook when N helped me sell nearly everything else I owned, including my car. He was able to get more for all of it than I expected, claimed he had some kind of connection that pulled through. At least I was able to make enough to cover the red-eye ticket, as well as housing and living expenses for a while, and still have a bit left over. I'd just have to make it stretch.

Instead, it will be one of the first things to fill the apartment I rented in London, and a touch of familiarity when I do find Connor.

A little chill trickles down my spine as I realize that I have no real idea what sort of state my brother will be in—especially if he's been kidnapped.

But whatever Connor needs, I will make it happen.

I'll bring him home. And he will be whole. Both of us will.

I flick up the sound of my Pandora station. The phone is another one of the few things I'd kept. But I'm having trouble focusing on the weave of lyrics and notes and harmonies. I'm about to hop on a one-way flight to a foreign country in search of a ghost.

I cross my ankles beneath me, think of pointing my toes from long-lost aspirations of becoming a ballerina. Never happened. Instead, after a year of classes, all I'm left with are a few basic steps.

Connor had always said I could be a professional dancer if I'd had the chance to really learn. He, on the other hand, tried out for sports only once, when we started freshman year at Miss Trevor's. He came home upset, then yelled at me when I asked why and slammed his door. He eventually came out for dinner, bumping my elbow as a silent apology. He never mentioned sports again.

But he'd always told me that I should dance. He would waltz me around the kitchen, singing Disney songs in ridiculous voices. He always knew how to cheer me up, even if he'd had a horrible day he didn't want to talk about.

My brother was a pro at hiding any trouble he'd gotten into at school, anything that could worry me, but I learned to recognize that bittersweet echo reflected in his eyes, even when he hid behind a smile. So I'd hug him, remind him that we had each other, that we were going to be fine, and I'd play "Hakuna Matata" through the muffled speaker on our plastic flip phone.

My throat goes tight, eyes burning. Goodness, I miss him.

I huddle in my chair, wiping at my eyes and press *Peter Pan* against my chest. I refuse to let this fairy tale be the last physical link I have with him. The next time I say his name, he'll be tucked away in my arms. Safe.

Hugging my brother is far better than holding a children's book.

A shudder pricks my arms at the mere thought of the Boeing 747 about to carry me far away from everything I know—with little more than a tear-stained fairy tale to accompany me to a strange new land.

I need something to drink.

As I wring my hands in my lap, specks of dull gold fleck my knuckles. Glancing up at the digital screens hanging at intervals about the terminal, I scan "Departures" and find the nonstop flight leaving for London. I have about two hours until we are due to board. That should be plenty of time to hunt down a Starbucks before I spend all hours of the night on a plane.

I turn down the music a notch and pick up my purse, shoving the book deep inside. Don't need to lose it in this airport, of all places. I cross the room, eyes on the floor, careful not to make eye contact with anyone. I don't want to draw attention. My nerves are already raw.

Hello, social anxiety. What would I do without your aggravating presence?

A few flight attendants wheel small suitcases past the row of seats, their slender figures and red lipstick making my hands clutch even tighter around my purse strap. I am hyperaware of my plain blue sweatshirt and faded Converse and the grimy flakes drifting from my skin.

Just stop thinking about it. No one is even noticing. If I can fade away, no one gets hurt. Except for my heart, growing a bit colder, more calloused. Loss of human interaction can steal the warmth before you've realized the ice of isolation is skimming your skin.

A few rows away, a young mom watches three boys playing with action figures. They speak their own language in garbled whispers, their imaginations carrying them off on adventures. I glance up at the gentle amusement on the mother's face, and my eyes sting.

Did our mother ever care for Connor and me?

My shoulders hunch, and I quickly shuffle past them, around the last row of gatehouse seats and out into the wide hallway that leads to the main area of the airport. Trinkets glimmer from little shops displaying souvenirs, and restaurants charge a day's pay for small pastries.

I wander in the direction of a Starbucks with a mile-long line, but I can't seem to scrub that scene with the little family from my mind's eye. Once people looked at Connor and me the way that mother looked at her children playing in the waiting area. There had even been someone who adopted us—parents that wanted us.

Until I ruined it.

I rub my eyes to clear my head. Gripping the edge of my purse strap to root myself, I shuffle forward in the line and let my gaze wander over the white walls and arching ceiling and people clustering around small shops and dragging luggage. The constant thrum of this airport, the here and now. These things are real.

Connor would have loved all this. The bustling people and the tension of waiting for a massive metal contraption about to shoot into the air. He would have called it an adventure.

An adventure—I can handle that.

The Starbucks line continues to creep ahead, and I pull a few precious bills out of my wallet to splurge on a Frappuccino to help me survive the late flight.

I secure my purse and take another step forward as the line continues to move. My foot taps in time to the music blasting in my earphones, and the motion around me settles into familiarity. I know where my terminal is, I'll be back in plenty of time to board, and I'm getting coffee like a responsible adult.

Everything is going to be fine.

My phone buzzes in my pocket, and I dig it out, glancing at

the unfamiliar number. I almost hit "decline call," but something tells me I should answer. I slide the green button, unhook my plastic earbuds, and press the device to my ear. "Hello?"

"Hi, Claire. It's me."

My pulse jumps. I know that voice. The young man who booked me this flight in the first place, and helped me sell my junker of a car, and find the cheapest rent possible for a flat in London.

"*N?*"

I can practically hear his smile on the other end of the line. "Yep! I just wanted to check in and see how you are feeling. Wish I could be there to send you off in person. You ready for this?"

"As ready as I'll ever be." His familiar voice sets my nerves at ease. "So, why are you calling me from a new number? Did you trash your phone or something?"

"Yeah, yeah that's it. New phone. Look, Claire. Be careful. The answers you're looking for in London . . ." His voice grows thick with a raw intensity. "You may not like what you find."

My mouth goes dry. "Uh . . . what? What do you mean?"

"I know you need to do this. That you need to do whatever you can to find Connor. But, Claire—if he really was kidnapped, then whoever took him . . ." He pauses. "These types of people, they don't play nice. If anything seems off—well, more off—you get the authorities involved, okay?"

I lick my lips. "Y-yeah. I'm going to the police as soon as I get there to file a missing persons report, just as we discussed." My brow knits. "I know what's at stake. Why is this bothering you so much now?"

"Because you're *leaving*, Claire. And I can't be there to jump in if you need me."

I bite back a smile. "It almost sounds like you're worried about me."

The coffee shop line continues to move forward. "You're my friend," he says simply. "Just . . . promise me you'll be careful, all right?"

I nod against the phone, feeling the weight of my purse over one shoulder. "I'll be careful."

For a second I almost wish I could FaceTime him and see his warm, chestnut eyes again before I hop on the plane.

And then I'm shoving the crazy notion away as N speaks again.

"Yeah, just be aware. London is pretty far away . . ." An odd note comes into his voice. "It's practically another world."

Another world . . .

The thought and his hesitant tone should unnerve me, but all I can do is shrug.

"Well, maybe a new world is just what I need."

After all, I've never quite fit into this one.

Two hours later, I'm down the jet bridge and finding my seat in coach at the tail of the plane. I lean my head back and close my eyes.

These types of people, they don't play nice.

N's warning is not the most reassuring thought as I buckle myself into a huge metal object about to hurtle through the sky, flying to a country where I know no one. Where I'll be more alone than I have ever been.

At least, until I find Connor.

My hands grip the seat's armrests as I try to convince myself that I am not getting claustrophobic before the plane has even taken off. I'm thankful to be by the window, even though if I need to make a restroom dash I'll have to crawl over the older couple that slides into the seats beside me.

Still, the chance to press my fingertips against the cool plastic is well worth it. I watch other aircraft and small carts wheeling around on the vast runway, and my heart starts to pound with another emotion. Excitement. The adventurous spirit Connor always found so easily.

Now past midnight, the plane begins to hum with the sound of the engines roaring to life.

The flight attendants give their talk about emergency safety, and the plane very slowly starts to move forward, gains speed, taxiing down the runway. The view outside streams past the window in a collision of night sky and white metal aircraft and fluorescent lights. The nose of the plane begins to arch, and I'm sucked back in my seat, stomach in my throat—

Then we're off the ground.

And I want to cry.

Because I've never felt this before. Body angled toward the sky, fighting against gravity, pulling away from the earth.

Flying.

I close my eyes as a smile breaks out across my face.

It feels so right.

Weightless and free.

After a few minutes I open my eyes. The older couple beside me is talking to one another, and I settle back in my seat. Hours upon hours pass, and the older couple soon falls asleep, leaning against each other, while I switch on the small seat-back television in front of me. With a pillow behind my head and blanket over my lap. The speckled cityscape beneath us eventually gives way to rippling ocean. The moon's pale reflection skips over the ebony sea that stretches farther than the eye can see.

I trade off between reading the books loaded on my phone's Kindle app, or marathoning the in-flight version of *Lord of the Rings*. I take short bouts to sleep or eat or sip drinks. Despite the flight taking ten hours, it's basically a loner's paradise.

Though N's uncertain warnings stay in my head, the calmness of the flight and the dawning knowledge that here at least I'm safe, soon overcomes any unnerving thoughts. I'll have to face a whole world I know next to nothing about in a few hours, so I might as well enjoy the quiet while I can.

Time slips by, as does the view outside, sunlight breaking out over the ocean that has been our only view for hours.

Land and buildings rise in the distance as I catch a glimpse of England. Mottled greens and browns scroll past as we continue to soar through the air—and then the pilot's voice bursts through the intercom, the televisions abruptly turn off, and the seatbelt signs click on. Coming in for a landing, I press against the cool, rounded window for my first sight of London.

The jewel of Great Britain filters into view beneath us, a blend of color and vibrancy and misty streets and brick rooftops.

As the plane angles, my mouth drops open in awe. I lean into the window, straining to catch every detail of the ground rushing up at us.

It looks like a fairy tale.

I can just make out the London rooftops over the arched walls of Heathrow, the screech of landing gear dropping—and then the dark asphalt of the runway fills my view. Soon, a jarring thud

ripples through the cabin when our wheels hit asphalt. We slow
and then taxi down the runway.

I relax back in my chair, force a breath through my tight throat,
try to still my shaking hands, and flick away the specks of dust
sticking to my fingertips.

I've made it—I'm in London.

The birthplace of Peter Pan and my last chance to discover
what really happened to Connor. A new country, practically a new
world, filled with so many question marks that, for a moment, a
lightning spike of panic shoots through me.

I have to be crazy, walking into a new world alone with no real
idea of how to find Connor, other than following a clue that's six
years old. Not to mention hunting down any dangerous strangers
involved in stealing away my brother.

Stepping foot out of this plane may place me in the path of a
danger that could make me vanish too.

But I have no other choice.

That simple truth is enough to still my heart, so I gather up my
courage and my purse as I prepare to step out of this Boeing 747
and into a new world.

As I make my way down the aisle, N's words surface again.
But instead of being the steadying force he usually is, my friend's
warning is only a haunting reminder that deepens the shadow
cast over this new journey—

*"The answers you're looking for in London . . . you may not like
what you find."*

6

PETER

London, England

Knew growing up would be a drag. Blimey, I'd take torture over this any day.

Blowing out a half sigh, I stride across the grassy knoll that hems Kensington Gardens.

I needed to clear my head and so waved off Lily's worries when I left the small flat we rent. Reassured her I'd use the phone in my pocket to contact her if I have another "episode." I guess that's what we're calling them now—the crippling pain when my own body turns against me. Headache pounding and anger taking over, and I feel like I'm coming apart at the seams.

My hands sink into my pockets as I avoid the well-trod path, rounding through the brush and towering trees toward a large, bronze statue sitting in a little alcove all its own. The elaborate sculpture is nestled at the edge of the Long Water lake, surrounded by a hedge of trees and a winding cobblestone walkway.

I hop the fence and go to the edge of the lake and look into the gently rippling water. The wavy reflection staring back is even more unrecognizable than usual.

Instead of my face curving boyishly, my jawline has thinned out even more than when I first arrived in London weeks ago. And there's the faintest hint of light reddish stubble starting to form.

Not okay.

Lily's words about the Guardian come to mind. Just thinking about talking to that bloke makes me want to wretch. But if she's right, and if he's our only chance left . . .

I shake my head and turn away from the water to jog back up to the cobblestone walkway. I pass a group of tourists comprised mostly of giggling girls trying—and failing—to hide that they're staring at me.

Normally, I'd have a look at the newcomers—flash a grin, watch girls' faces turn red, pose for pictures as an *"authentic Londoner"* and the like. Lily's not around to tease me for wielding what she calls my "smile no woman can resist." Except the tribal princess, apparently. Sometimes she can be so bossy, she practically acts like a bloomin' mother.

But today I need space to work things through, so I dodge around the tourists, jaw grinding as I briefly notice the shaded silhouettes spilling across the grass beneath them. *Shadows.* I try not to but end up glancing down anyway. The grass beneath my trainers is clear and bright—no shadow to be seen.

No shadow at all.

The scars on the bottom of my feet twinge at the thought, at the memory of just one more thing carved away from me when I lost Neverland—but I don't let the memory linger. Refuse to let it in and keep moving forward, like I always do.

I take the roundabout way across the grass and shrubbery edging the walkway, fingers skimming the rippling branches and velvet leaves as I walk. This jaunt has always calmed me and helped clear my head. The wide grassy areas and winding trees almost feel like home.

And then, of course, there's the statue of the little boy brandishing panpipes.

My hand goes to the small chunk of a whittled whistle hung on a cord around my neck. It's the only piece of my panpipes left after the skirmish that ended in me being flung out of Neverland. Broken and splintered, like this whole messy business.

Before I can set foot on the round cobblestone pathway circling the statue, something glimmers out of the corner of my eye. My head swings around to catch sight of tiny wings flittering in the sun, followed by the crunch of twigs snapping. Then, I see the edge of a child's boot.

Curiosity kicks up. The decision about the Guardian can wait a peck longer, mates . . .

I head toward the curve of trees hemming in the metal display. I soon find two small, pudgy feet sticking out of the underbrush, and the outline of a little boy's frame wedged deep into the thick foliage. He's completely still, only the slight heave of breath telling me he is still breathing.

Adventurous little bloke.

But before I can wonder what has caused the boy to crawl deep into the undergrowth and stay nearly as still as the statue behind us, I see it again. That flicker of light and the faint whisper of chimes.

He's found one!

They usually only come out at night here, and there are far fewer of the pixies than there used to be in these gardens. They don't shine quite as brightly as they used to, the damage of Neverland weakening the little sprites. But these still manage to shimmer in the trees and whisper in the ears of children when no one is watching.

Although, this time a lad seems to have sighted one of the skittish creatures all on his own.

Bending down, I crouch beside him, gently pushing apart some of the tangled vines to get a better look. The ruddy little boy wears a striped shirt and has dark curls fringing his ears. He doesn't seem to have noticed my presence, his wide-eyed stare riveted on the small creature in front of him.

The pixie dances for the little boy.

The golden light surrounding her flickers and wavers, like a candle's gleam, but through the spark I can just make out her small, lithe form. She's wearing a dress of soft moss with a tiny white flower at her hip, the trail of the gown spinning around her heels as she dances. Her tiny feet perform intricate steps as she spins and leaps, the silvery sound of her laugh like a tiny wind chime.

Or the tinkle of a bell.

My grip on the vines slips, snapping twigs as I scramble for another handhold. When I glance back down, the lad stares up at me, mouth agape.

Well—blast it.

The pixie's wings beat feverishly, her body coiled to flee—and then her eyes flit up to my face and her tiny lips pinch to the side in recognition. She waggles her tiny finger at me, the soft tinkling sound filling the underbrush as she tells me off.

I heave a breath. Bossy little snot.

"I know, I know. I'll try to be more quiet."

But at least she isn't shunning me or some other such rubbish, even with what happened with Tink. Not that it was my fault. If anything, this little pixie and I can bond over our joint hatred of the beastly codfish that I should have tossed entirely to the croc that day. Sure would have saved us a whole lot of trouble.

The tiny sprite flaps her iridescent wings, lifting off the ground, and flies close enough to bat at my nose with a small fist as she chatters away, her glow taking on a pinkish hue in her frustration.

I try to keep from laughing. "All right, all right. I'll be more careful. I don't want the squirrels chasing you any more than you do."

That seems to sate her wild temper for the moment, and with one more finger wag at me, she drops back down to perch on an upturned root. Slowly, she begins to dance again, those tiny bare feet waltzing across the dusty root. Then she throws herself into the air and does a quick spin, glimmers of pixie dust exploding from her body and tangling in her forest-green moss dress.

"Show off," I mutter, which only makes her glare again. She chatters at me once more, using a few choice pixie words I'm glad the little lad still on his stomach can't understand. I shrug.

"Well, if you're going to be like that, I will go. And you can tell the rest of your clan that I won't be bringing any glass baubles or sweet biscuits to you tonight, either."

That catches the fiery little pixie's attention. With a flutter of her wings, she lands on the knuckles of the hand I still have wrapped around a branch. Her tiny feet are a whisper against my skin as she gives me a jaunty little curtsy. Sugary apologies pour from her in a soothing chime.

I smirk and watch her grovel for a moment before finally bobbing my chin in defeat. "You've got me. I'll try to drop by tonight—and I think we might even have some chocolate cake left."

Maybe.

That makes her eyes grow bright, and she flits away from her perch on my hand, doing a few more pirouettes in the air before sending me one last grateful curtsy. Then she darts off through the brush and out of sight.

The temperamental little creature must really be fond of cake. A pixie after my own heart.

Taking a step back from the brush, I flick away a few stubborn leaves that have caught in my green jacket. More twigs snap, and I glance down to see the little chap wriggling his way back out of the underbrush. He dusts himself off and tilts his round face up at me.

"You scared her away!" Dirt streaks his ruddy features.

As he rises to his feet, I crouch down so we're at the same eye level. "Not a chance, chap. She said she was already late to a pixie gathering. They tend to get sidetracked a lot, so their meetings are usually several hours late, anyway."

I give a little chuckle, remembering one of the few pixie conclaves I ever managed to sneak into—and the insurmountable wrath of the few that were actually on time and had to wait half a day for everyone else.

"You can understand them?" The lad's voice draws me from my reverie.

"Aye. Always been able to hear the pixies."

The little boy's eyes go wider, and he cocks his head at me. I can see the wheels turning, and I throw him a cheeky smirk, even as he points a dusty finger over his shoulder at the statue behind him. "Are you . . . ?"

"Yes, but don't tell anyone." I duck down a little more, one finger to my lips as I whisper, "It'll be our secret, all right?"

His face lights up, and he nods quickly. "I knew it was all real!"

"Real as rain," I quip.

The young lad can't be more than eight or nine, but he grins at me with glee. "Mum said that it was just a story, but when I started finding the pixies here, I knew she was wrong!"

"'Course you did." I wink at him. "Grown-ups can't see the pixies anymore, but you—you can see everything." I smile at him, feeling that familiar tug to take this little one's hand and show him just how magical the world can be.

To show him a place where pixies and Lost Boys fly free, the sky is always blue, and the crystal-clear waters teem with enticing creatures with faces like women and tails like fish. Where anything is possible.

Perhaps even getting Neverland back.

Straightening, I put my hands on my hips and grin down at the boy. "If you come at first light, you can see even more pixies. Especially if you bring some piece of dessert—they love sweets."

The little boy smiles up at me, eyes round and filled with that dancing glow of a young heart shining with imagination. The same look in each of the Lost Boy's eyes when I first brought them to Neverland, first rescued them from the neglected, unhappy homes that hadn't wanted them.

When I ushered them into my world. When *I* wanted them.

The tiny lad's awestruck expression shatters when a woman's voice breaks through the glade. He looks over at a couple standing at the edge of the small fence surrounding the statue. They motion for him to come to them, and with one last wistful glance in my direction and a quick wave, he darts off.

I watch them smile at the boy, the man scooping him up into his arms. I watch the way he somehow fits—a rubbish bond that's never made much sense to me.

I turn back to the hedge of trees circling the bronze statue. Snapping off a long strand of grass shooting up beneath the roots,

I stick the green sprout between my lips, chewing on its edge. I amble toward the statue, watching as the crowd disperses and tourists move down the path that leads away from the sculpture and winds around the Long Water. Soon, the grove is empty, save for the large bronze statue sitting in the middle of a round platform of cobblestone.

Hands in pockets, I make my way to the base and gaze up at the little metal silhouette of a boy perched at the top of the statue—barefoot and holding a long panpipe to his lips.

I tilt my head at the jaunty figure. "Just you and me again, eh?"

He doesn't respond, only stands there. Eyes straight ahead, knees slightly bent, as if he sees something I don't—an adventure in the distance just waiting to be had. That rush of excitement, that elation as you dance at the edge of danger, that cheeky laughter that drove Hook mad. Everything that made me—*me*.

"It wasn't supposed to be like this. I just wanted a place to call mine. My Never Never Land." The quiet words are little more than a hush filling the air, even as I lift a hand to touch the foot of that little boy. "But now Lily says the only way to get back there is for me to ask that Guardian for help, and it's all just so . . . *wrong*." The cocky bronze boy towers over me at the top of his platform. Other smaller figures are carved out of the bronze hill he's perched on, reaching for that Pan as if he has all the answers.

He doesn't.

But I find myself asking him all the same.

I scratch at the back of my head. "It was supposed to be somewhere safe, where anything could be possible. Someplace I could be . . . alive."

And I want to get back there. Now. The frustration of how

long this is all taking makes me want to crawl out of my skin.

I take another glance up at that little Peter Pan, the lad without a care in the world. The one who only worried about himself and how to escape the next trap the pirates made for him. Never about anything else, anyone else. If anything did happen, the memories would simply disappear. The pain would disappear and only the happy thoughts remained. It was all so simple, until it wasn't.

"Oh, blasted stars!" I kick at the cobblestones beneath my feet.

How I despise this. All these memories, all this loss, all this guilt. If I could, I'd shed it like a second skin. I'd take the forgetting and having my island back over all this weight any day.

I groan and grasp onto the nearest prong of the statue. Feel the metal bite into the underside of my hand. But it doesn't alleviate any of the burden pulling me down.

I can't escape this nightmare, no matter how hard I try.

Maybe there's only one way out. Maybe Lily's right. Still doesn't mean I have to like it.

As I look at the statue, my eye catches one of the smaller sculptures. It's so very familiar—the determined story girl who would sit in her dormer window and tell tales of my adventures in Neverland.

Wendy.

The girl I'd almost forgotten. The girl who chose to grow up rather than stay with me.

Why can't you just grow up!

The words burn into my thoughts, sudden and unbidden. The angry tone echoes through my mind, dashing away the bittersweet memory of the Darling children and sending ripples of anguish through me.

Hang it all! I groan again and tighten my grip to steady myself against the cool bronze of the statue. On second thought, the Guardian is looking more pleasant than *this*.

The new memory is as distant as they come, a sharp pulse at the back of my head, pointing to *him*. The tall figure with my green eyes and thick, reddish hair. Lips that pull into an angry snarl. Bitter eyes never content, never happy.

My father.

The words alone cripple me, spiking through my limbs, driving me to my knees. *Blast . . . blast . . . blast . . .* I cling to the edge of a bronze pixie's wing as the pain crashes over me. I don't want to see this. But I can't seem to pull myself through it or push it away. The dogged and vague memory floods my senses. A memory so painful, I'd buried it as deeply as I could.

"S-stop . . . *no!*" The word comes out in a mangled gasp. I curl against the statue, hands over my head. Desperate for him to go away—but beneath the pain, curled like a fist, is the anger. The sharp reminder of why I refused to grow up in the first place. Because if aging meant becoming like him . . .

Then I'd rather die.

So instead I escaped on the day I turned ten. I fled to find my Never Never Land—where voices never screamed when you forgot to make your bed, where you never cried yourself to sleep, where you were never told you weren't good enough, where you never had to hide in your closet against drunken rages. Where a birthday wasn't a sick reminder of the mother he blamed you for losing. A place where you never had to grow old. A Neverland where magic was real.

Holding the statue, I drag myself to my feet and glare up at the solid figure of a boy who never thought he would grow up. Who never thought he would hurt his island or the people who were his makeshift family. Who could leap into the air and escape the weight, the pain.

"I will find a way back!" The words explode from my throat. I won't let him win. I won't die here, becoming a concrete shell of the person I once was, watching my life waste away before my eyes. I won't let Hook steal from me the only thing I have left.

No matter what I have to do. No matter what I have to tell the Guardian, or what I have to risk to face Hook, or how far I have to go to convince Claire to trust me.

I will fly again. I will get home.

And not even the stars can stop me.

7

CLAIRE

London, England

I spent my first two days in London hiding in my tiny flat.

I slept for twelve hours straight the first day, fighting nausea and jet lag. When I finally had my wits about me, I managed a quick walk to a nearby store. After struggling to convert the price tags to American currency, I was reminded of what I already knew: London is expensive.

Also, doing math for everything you buy is way less fun than it sounds.

The high prices mean that, starting today, I need to make as much headway as possible before I have to find a job.

Tick. Tock. Tick. Tock. You've already wasted two days.

I'm beginning to see how Hook could go mad.

Guzzling down a cup of water from the metallic-tasting tap, I shoot off a text to N, letting him know I'm going to put the first step of our plan into action. He's texted me a bit since getting here, and I have a feeling he was relieved that I've been taking it slow.

But not today. No more waiting.

And despite his worries, there's a bubble of hope forming in my chest. I'm closer to finding my brother than I've ever been.

I stuff any necessities into my purse and head for the door. Locking it securely behind me, I step out into the crisp London morning. I descend down the rickety steps and survey the empty street. No creepers—check. Even though I can only afford a small hovel of a room, the area seems safe enough.

I toss my thick, wiry curls back and look up at the cool sky. I don't mind the misty chill. There's something alluring about it.

My chest already feels lighter as I go down the street, past a row of flats, and find a busier cross street where I can flag down a cab. The black vehicle has a small lighted sign attached to its roof flashing the word TAXI.

The cab pulls over, the driver glancing up at me above his partially rolled-down window. "Where to?"

My voice seems steady. "The nearest police station."

The cabbie's brows arch, but he just inclines his head. "Hop in."

I clamber inside and find there's a lot more space than I expected. The vehicle is almost the size of a small station wagon, with one long string of black leather seats against the back and two opposite that are tucked behind the driver and passenger seats. You could easily fit five passengers in here.

The cabbie pulls onto the road, and I watch as he navigates the winding London streets and thoroughfares. The vehicles inch by on what should be the wrong side of the street, stuck in gridlock that would rival L.A.

The cabbie speaks in quick, eager sentences as we drive— mentioning sights as we pass, places to visit, and streets we are turning onto. I try to soak it all in—but I only get impressions.

Towering buildings with molded siding and metal knockers . . . rows upon rows of flats filling a side street . . . small, circular gardens with a tree or two . . . and people walking briskly down sidewalks. The sky remains shadowed while raincoats and umbrellas hang from nearly every arm. It's all sharp angles and mottled, dusky colors and throngs of people better dressed than I'd expected.

We drive through side streets and pull up in front of the Bishopsgate Police Department. I pay the cabbie, grateful that I swapped my American funds for British pounds, and take a deep breath, throw open the door, and step onto the sidewalk.

The large police building, several stories tall with dozens of windows, seems solid as a rock and just as formidable. The words *City of London Police Department* are inscribed over large double doors. A chilly breeze rustles my sweatshirt, loosening a few flecks of gold and launching them upward.

I take another deep breath then grasp the heavy double door, pull it open, and step in. I walk over to the imposing front desk where a man in a black vest sporting a police badge stands typing at a computer. He glances up as I cautiously step forward.

"Can I help you, miss?" the officer asks. My thoughts scramble for a way to explain why I'm here, chasing after a fairy tale.

I hope it doesn't sound as insane as it seems.

I dig in my pocket and pull out my phone, hands shaking as I scroll over the smudged screen.

"Officer, sir . . . my name is Claire Kenton, and I'm wondering if you have any information on a missing person's case." My voice sounds strangled, but I keep my eyes on the phone, searching for the saved picture. *Please, please believe me.* "My brother disappeared six years ago, and the last lead I have is that he was taken to London."

The man gives a surprised cough then leans across the counter. His name plate says *Officer Norton*.

DUST   6 7

"You could fill out a report, miss, and we will do what we can."

My thumb slips across the touch screen but finds the correct image. A zoomed-in picture of Connor and the strange man in the LAX terminal.

I turn the phone around and slide it across the counter toward the officer. "This is the most recent picture of my brother. I'm happy to fill out anything you need, but I guess I was hoping . . ." I lick my dry lips. "I guess I was hoping maybe someone already had news of him?" Something. Anything.

"What's his name?" The officer scoops up my phone, staring at Connor, and then his lips tighten. He uses his thumb and forefinger to zoom in on the image, but not on my brother—on the blurry profile of the man in the suit.

I catch the flicker of recognition that flashes in his eyes. "Do you know who that man is?"

The officer examines my face, and then he sets the phone down. He calls over his shoulder. "Jeremy? Can you come here for a second?"

Another officer approaches from the hallway. It's not his broad shoulders or considerable height that captures my attention—but something about the way he commands the room. As if it were built for him. Officer Norton nods to this new man with a sheen of respect in his gaze as he steps back a pace.

Who *is* this guy?

Jeremy's brown hair shadows green-gray eyes that look into mine. For a moment, I'm uncertain what to do—and then he gives me a quick, reassuring smile and turns to the other officer.

"What do you need, mate?"

Officer Norton picks up my phone again, shows it to Jeremy, and they have a quick, whispered conversation. I catch my name and Connor's along with someone called James Hocken, and then both men are nodding.

I stand completely still, breath frozen.

When they turn back to me, Jeremy gives me a hesitant smile, fingertips drumming on the edge of the counter. I catch a glint of gold on his ring finger.

"Miss Claire Kenton, is it? We will do our best to look for your brother, ma'am. If you wouldn't mind filling out the correct paperwork? However, six years is a long time, and I can't promise we will have results. We will still do everything we can. In the meantime . . ."

He glances back at his friend, and they seem to have a silent discussion in that short space of time before Jeremy finally nods and steps around the desk. His eyes deepen with sincerity as he leans down to me.

"I may have a lead on the bloke in the picture." He pauses, cupping the back of his neck with a hand. "I'd need to get the paperwork in order, but sometime in the next week or so I can open a formal investigation and start asking questions. It's not something I can involve a civilian in, however. I will be sure to keep you abreast of the investigation when the time comes."

The thunder of my blood rushing in my ears drowns out his voice.

He might *know* him.

I can feel the dust beginning to speckle my knuckles as I fight to draw in a breath. The numb shock thaws, and I force myself to focus on that one thought—

They might know who took Connor. And now, so do I. I heard the name as clear as day.

James Hocken.

After six long years, I'm not sure whether to cry or laugh. So instead, I wipe my gritty palms on my sweatshirt, and lean forward to grab the officer's hand.

"Thank you!"

His clasp is warm, the band of gold on his ring finger worn and steady beneath my touch. Though the officer seems caught off guard by my sudden impulse, his eyes smile at me.

"Of course. I have to go, but Officer Norton can supply you with the paperwork." He gently releases my hand and pats my shoulder reassuringly. "We will help you, Claire."

Something about the way he says it carries a depth beyond just his duty as a police officer. There's a thread of knowledge, of understanding, as if he knows that there is more to Connor's case than meets the eye.

And then I notice his name plate. My mouth drops open. "Officer *Darling*? Like Wendy Darling?"

The informal expression drains from Jeremy Darling's face as his whole body goes stiff. I become very aware of his police badge. It stands like a wall between us.

"Darling is a common surname here, miss. I assure you it has nothing to do with the fairy tale."

His words are formal but not unkind. I glance at Officer Norton and find a smirk crinkling the edges of his mouth. *Ah—I see.* I would bet my favorite copy of *Inkheart* that Jeremy was teased mercilessly through the police academy for his last name.

Touchy subject, I guess.

"Of course. I didn't mean any disrespect, sir." I practically curtsy to Officer Darling, and the muscle in his jaw relaxes just a bit.

"Take care, Miss Kenton." With a nod, he crosses back around the desk to the hallway behind it, disappearing around the corner before I even say goodbye.

The room feels a little more hollow.

Officer Norton gets the forms, and I spend the next hour explaining the Connor situation and filling out endless paperwork for a missing person's report and other legal necessities. He gives me an estimate of when I'll likely hear from Jeremy, and then with one more document, I'm done.

"We'll get started as soon as we can, Miss Kenton. Have a good day."

I flash him a wave, hurry out of the double doors and back into the dim sunshine.

Yes, we will start an investigation soon.

But if they think I'm waiting a whole week, they've sorely underestimated me.

I walk a block down the street, and then flag another black cab. Hopping in, I settle against a leather seat and lean forward, making eye contact with the driver. It's a long shot, but I might as well ask.

"You don't by chance know who James Hocken is, do you?"

"The rich recluse? 'Course. Everyone knows who that bloke is."

Well, that was surprisingly easy.

I rake my fingers through my hair and sit straight up. "All right. Take me to him."

I rattle off the address I'd found online. He nods and pulls the cab back onto the road. I buckle in as the little vehicle skims along the busy thoroughfare, carrying me toward the man who helped kidnap my brother.

8

CLAIRE

London, England

The cabbie tells me there's a rumor that James Hocken made his fortune on pirate gold.

Pirate. Gold.

That's reassuring.

Hocken's estate sits against a carved-out cliffside miles from London. The several-story building is constructed of faded brick and weathered wood accents. Timber shutters are pulled closed, and massive pillars hold up a front porch that looks a little creaky, even from this distance.

The cab halts, and I try not to wince at the amount I pay the driver. I step out into the cool late afternoon, tasting the strange scent of salt in the air.

The cab peels away. I block out the alarm bells clanging in my head, hand straying to where my phone is tucked in my pocket. It's just a house, Claire.

Taking careful steps, I reach the tall fence that surrounds the entire area. The fence tapers into two massive gates, the only way in or out of the reclusive estate. At one point, the gates must have been the pride of a gifted craftsman—iron curled and welded into the image of two massive waves crashing into each other—but they've been neglected long enough for the metal to rust, and the bottom of the right gate is missing a few rungs.

If Hocken is going for the creepy abandoned mansion look, he's nailing it.

A sprawling lawn hems the manor, the grass a pallid color, filled with cracked statues of ships and strange, malignant creatures.

I reach for the towering gate, tracing the curling pieces, and peer through it at the shadowed mansion that's even more foreboding up close.

A dry wind rustles my sweatshirt, but I shake it off, flecks of gold leaking from my skin. Expectancy pulses through my veins. The same hint of wildness that gave me the courage to hop a plane to London in the first place. I'm so close—I'm convinced the man on the other side of this fence has actually *seen* Connor since he disappeared.

I bend down, feel around the missing metal pieces at the bottom of the gate, making sure there's nothing sharp—and then duck under it.

I suck in my stomach as I scramble under the gate and slowly emerge on the other side.

I'm in.

Somehow that isn't comforting.

The sky is overcast, although it is only midafternoon. Fog has rolled in over the estate, thick and heavy, like a pale ghost suffocating the world. The quiet is chilling as I take small steps across the lawn, glancing back and forth, searching for any sign of another living creature. Only the strange statues stare back at me. I warily avoid a creepy mermaid-like sculpture—a half-fish creature with a gaping maw filled with rows of jagged teeth and a spiked tail that looks sharp enough to sever a limb.

What charming taste in art.

Shoving my cold hands in my jeans pockets, I remind myself to breathe and hurry the rest of the way across the lawn. A front deck of weathered wood tapers to a door that looks like it was pieced together from the hull of some ancient ship.

Every step feels weighted, and when my heel catches a twig, the snap jolts my raw nerves and I nearly jump backward. Get a grip, Claire.

I cross the worn porch in a few quick paces and stop in front of the door. I'm close enough to touch the smooth wooden planks and the large curling handle. My eyes catch deep crimson stains that splatter the door.

I really, really hope that's paint.

I nearly lose my nerve, but I shake my head to try to clear out the cobwebs. This may feel like the opening scene from a scary movie, but unlike the generic blonde who usually dies in the first ten minutes of a horror flick, I'll get out of here and call the police the minute anything seems off. Well, *more* off.

I'm *so* close. If I back out now, the what-ifs will tear me apart. For all I know, Connor could be trapped inside, just within my reach. Or maybe he's not. Maybe this is too easy. Maybe it's another dead end—or I'll find an answer I don't want.

But either way, I have to at least try . . .

The longer I stand frozen in front of the towering door, the harder it becomes. Then I realize it's unlocked and open just a crack.

Maybe I can take a quick glimpse inside. Get an idea of what I'm dealing with. This place may actually be as abandoned as it looks.

I tug the massive door open a crack. It takes my eyes a second to adjust to the dark. Or rather, the flickering light lapping at the walls. A massive chandelier hangs in the center of the foyer, dangling from a thick chain that snakes up one wall into the darkness until it reaches an arched ceiling.

But there's no one in sight.

Squeezing in through the door, I fight a shiver and take a few steps, grateful the floor doesn't creak. I take in the strange decorations hanging from walls—canvases with images that are too bathed in shadow to identify, ancient-looking weapons, and wooden sconces that match the chandelier. Straight ahead, a massive spiral staircase sprouts from the floor.

Still, no people.

I lick my lips, wondering if I should say something—or just keep wandering around this creepy house. Then it would really feel like a scene in a horror movie.

Dang it! Stop thinking about horror movies, would you?

On second thought, maybe it would be better to have Officer Darling come with me later. Plus, I'm kind of trespassing, now that I think about it.

Yup. Officially talked myself out of it.

I turn back around and head for the door.

"Going already?"

I freeze.

I'm alone in a house with the reclusive millionaire who kidnapped my brother, and not even the police are aware I'm here. Hocken could kill me and dump my body and no one would—

No! *Don't* think like that.

I pull in a ragged breath. Connor. He was only fourteen when he had to face this man—and now he is depending on me to have the courage to get him back.

My heartbeat is a ticking bomb in my ears as I turn away from the door and face the source of the voice.

A tall figure detaches from the shadows, stepping through a doorway I hadn't realized was set into the wall to the right. The light from the massive chandelier casts strange, dancing flickers that illuminate a familiar profile.

Tall and broad-shouldered, with a sharp jawline and eyes as blue and untamed as a restless sea. His dark hair and trimmed beard are laced with gray, but he carries himself like an army general.

One hip dips a bit lower in a subtle limp as he crosses the room. His tailored crimson overcoat swishes about him as his cane tap-tap-taps across the floor.

James Hocken's right hand is tucked into his jacket pocket, and his eyes never leave my face as he takes measured steps toward me. The uneven tempo of fear in my chest cracks open, exposing something more. Something full of fire and anger and pain.

This is the man who ruined my life.

This man with a limp and a cane who stole my one spot of light.

Pale, translucent dust begins to rise from my trembling hands, but instead of gleaming—it darkens the air, turning an ashen color, graying and shriveling and sinking. It sizzles when it hits the hardwood floor, leaving tiny burn marks.

Part of me should be unnerved. Part of me should desperately want to stop it. Part of me should be afraid. But I'm so far past fear now, all that's left is a broken kind of anger.

"How could you kidnap my brother?" My full attention is rooted on James Hocken, his tall shadow falling across me.

Curiosity and coolness bead his expression—but not a speck of remorse.

My feet are moving before I even realize it. I barrel toward him and his grip tightens on his cane, right hand starting to slip from his coat pocket.

A desperate sob rips from my throat. *"Where is he?"*

I make contact with the recluse, batting at him with my fists, but he merely takes a few uneven steps out of my reach. My shoulders tremble, eyes burning as I watch him flick ashen specks of dust from his sleeve. His eyes narrow. "Interesting . . ."

My whole body is somewhere between dissolving into a puddle of tears and burning up in a torrent of flame. "He was just a child! How *could* you?"

I try to hit him again, but he easily dodges my sloppy punch. His dark brows tug together.

"How could I—what? I'm afraid I have no idea what you mean, love." His voice has a silky edge.

"How could you steal my brother?"

Angry tears fill my eyes and my strength fades as grief replaces my fury. I glare up at Hocken through the blur.

"Why did you take Connor to London?"

The man pauses, head slightly toward the side. His forehead creases, and for several seconds I watch the gears turn behind his cool, calculating expression. "Connor . . . ?"

I practically scream at him. "My fourteen-year-old brother you forced on a plane at LAX, never to be heard from again."

His brows knit tight, and then something like recognition dawns. "Oh! You mean the little chap who needed someone to escort him on the flight from Los Angeles to London?"

"Escort? Is that what you call kidnapping?"

"Kidnapping?" He breaks into a disbelieving laugh. "I didn't kidnap the lad, love."

"Don't call me that," I snap. My dust has begun to dissolve from the cool air around me.

James Hocken straightens his coat, right fist still buried in his scarlet pocket, and then lets the fingers of his left hand tap along the cane's engraved silver handle as he speaks.

"I was asked to help a Connor Kenton because he was traveling alone. He told me he was going to his new family in this fair city, and the woman—his advocate with the adoption agency, I assumed—asked if I would be willing to help the little mate with the lengthy flight."

His cool gaze continues to regard me with tantalizing calmness, and as much as I hate to admit it, I can't find a trace of dishonesty in his tone.

This *can't* be right. He has to know what happened to my brother.

"Liar! There never was any adoption. You stole him from me!"

Miss Trevor pretty much disappeared after Connor did and a case worker moved me to another foster home. There was at least a *possibility* that our foster mother had tricked the reclusive millionaire into escorting Connor to London and into the arms of whatever purpose she might have had for my brother here.

Could Hocken be telling the truth?

"Prove it." My arms are crossed over my chest.

"There was no adoption?" I'm surprised again by the look of utter shock marring James's expression.

He shakes his head, crossing over to the far wall and leaning his cane up against it. "I'm so very sorry for any part I had to play in your brother's disappearance."

He flicks a switch, and the dangling chandelier lights brighten.

With the room no longer bathed in shadow, I realize that the odd shapes on the walls are actually paintings and wooden sconces. His features aren't quite as sharp as I'd first thought. His face bears the weathered lines of someone who has seen a lot of life, but his eyes are almost kind.

"I am truly sorry. I offer my greatest apologies. I can show you the record of my flight, if you'd like. And possibly a better introduction?" Hocken steps closer, boots clipping across the hardwood floor with that odd gait from his limp. He stops a few inches away and reaches out his left black-gloved hand for me to shake.

I hesitate, eyeing his hand, and then flash back to his expression. His hesitant smile is almost hidden by his dark beard, but even though his eyes drip authenticity, I don't miss the darker glint in them.

I've dealt with enough darkness to recognize when someone isn't entirely honest.

"Can you prove your story?"

He pauses and then draws his hand back. His bearded jaw ticks and he nods.

"That I can, love. Just one moment."

I cringe at his use of *love* again but can only scuff a toe at the floor as he turns and disappears through one of the doorways behind him. I'm once again left in this massive entryway alone. But it seems a little less foreboding with the lights up. The paint is peeling, and the decorations could use some dusting, but mostly the building is just old.

My pulse begins to slow, and within a few moments, Mr. Hocken returns. He's carrying an iPad that seems out of place, but he holds it out to me nonetheless.

I take the device from him and find a blurred picture of a plane's seat back and a little triangle indicating it's a video.

"What's this?" I glance up at Hocken.

"To pass the time on the flight, your brother and I recorded a little video. I hope it might confirm my story. I knew I had it stored in the cloud somewhere."

At the mention of Connor, my eyes blur again. With another look at the broad-shouldered man towering over me, I tap the *play* icon. The image on the screen begins to move, flashing up from the dizzying angle of the seat back, and sweeping around to reveal two faces trying to both be caught in the same shot.

One of them looks a little younger and less gray but is clearly the man in front of me. The other person is Connor.

"Hi there!" He waves at the camera, his tan face lighting up with a wide smile. "We're on our way to London. Can you believe that? Oh, and this is Mr. Hocken . . ." He points toward James. "I told Miss Trevor I don't need a babysitter, but she still didn't think I could make this trip on my own." He rolls his eyes, and at a half cough from Hocken, Connor grins. "It's okay because he says he'll show me around once we get there. We're going to go see Big Ben!"

"Only if your new family says it's all right, of course." James smiles at the camera and fondly pats my brother's shoulder, but Connor is off on another tangent, talking a hundred miles a minute, as he always did.

"I'm sure they will. At this rate, anything is better than a group home. Especially if they give us an allowance." He winks at the camera. "Claire, I can't wait until you come too. Miss T said it should be soon, there was just paperwork or something? Weird, but you know how it is. Everything takes paperwork. Flying is fun so far. There's just a lot of people, which Claire probably won't like . . ." He snorts. "But then again, you didn't like *Peter*, so maybe you're just kind of weird anyway. Although . . ." He leans forward, voice dropping to a conspiratorial whisper. "Peter said he'd meet me in London, so you'll have to get used to him, Claire, because we—oh wait!" His eyes focus on something out of frame. "Looks like they're handing out snacks. Got to go!"

The camera flashes toward the rows ahead and attendants pushing a cart laden with cookies, and then Connor's ruddy face fills the screen for a half moment—before his finger reaches out and the video ends.

I'm left jaw-dropped, staring at the iPad in my hands.

James Hocken lets the silence stretch for a long moment before clearing his throat. He takes the iPad and sets it on one of the mounted shelves behind him. His voice is smooth as his satin coat.

"I don't know if that will convince you, but I didn't take your brother, love. I was simply guiding him from one place to another."

It's hard to dispute him or the video. But if it's true, if James had nothing to do with Connor's disappearance . . .

"Then what did happen? Where did he go? What happened when you arrived in London?"

He rubs an uncertain hand over his beard. But when he speaks there's a catch in the calmness of his tone. "Well, he . . ."

"He what?" I step forward. "What happened to my brother, Mr. Hocken?"

He blows out a long breath, eyeing me. "You won't believe me if I tell you, love."

I grit my teeth, feeling the grainy sensation of dust coating my palms. "Try me."

He shakes his head. "I really don't know—"

I grab his arm and stare up into his eyes with all the desperation that has been building for years. *"Please*, I need to know."

For a moment, Hocken's eyes fill with a dark, victorious spark— and an almost cruel smirk etches across his face. Then, just as quickly, it's gone. Replaced with that silky, warm expression.

His eyes fix on my face, voice low and carrying as much weight as the crashing waves in the paintings surrounding us. "The minute we landed in London, your brother was taken by Peter Pan."

9

PETER

London, England

I hate this place.

I glare at the sign dangling above the small pub tucked on the outskirts of London. It features a dangerous winding creature: half-woman, half-fish—and all attitude. A fact I know far too well after my years of tangling with the barmy sirens.

This pub is a secret haven for the outcast underbelly of Neverland. The filth who plummeted to Earth, mostly pirates and rebellious Lost Boys. Not really my crowd.

Not to mention they're all so blooming *old*.

But there's no way around it. If I want to save my island and stop these painful memories, I need to find Claire. And no matter how much time I've spent the past several weeks chasing down every thread of a clue, no matter how much I've tried to ignore the darker possibilities, no matter how many times I tell myself it'll all just magically come together . . .

I've reached a dead end. A massive, crushing dead end.

Short of hunting down Hook and holding my blade to his neck, there's only one option left: the Guardian. No way I'm blowing this.

Cor, I just wish he didn't have to be such an old chap.

I glare again at the hardwood door leading into the pub. Nothing for it. Squaring my shoulders, I scoop back my jacket's hood, then run a hand through my tangles as my other hand grazes Lily's knife handle strapped to my waist.

Time to take back what's mine.

I step through the peeling doorway, and the raucous sounds crash over me like a wave. I'm soaked in garish discussions, uproarious laughter, and the clink of tankards. Above the heads bent in conversation, a familiar grease-smudged mural stretches across one wall, and while the pub brims with all manner of filth, I don't sight a certain pirate with a hook for a hand.

Ah, this'll be cake.

Letting the door fall closed, I bounce on my heels and have a look at the overflowing tables filled with stocky, tattooed men and women in slinky dresses. I spot a small crowd of Lost Boys hunched over a table at the back of the dimly lit pub.

None of them have noticed me yet. I know what it's like, dealing with these scallywags—if they're going to let me stick around long enough to have a chat with the Guardian, they need to know I mean business. And that they can't touch me.

I settle my hands on my hips and throw my head back to let out a loud crowing sound that echoes through the room, shaking loose the cobwebs and throwing the entire pub into silence.

Shocked stares swivel around to glare at me, but I only cock my chin and grin.

"Miss me, fellas?"

They look too stunned to move. Then a particularly bulky pirate slams a fist into his scuffed table and growls. "You must have a death wish coming here, boy!"

I chuckle, taking a step forward, hands dropping to my pockets. "A death wish would be quite the adventure, but you can stop quaking in your seats. I'm not here for any of you blokes."

Several angry conversations erupt around the room as another pirate jumps to his feet, looking quite brassed off and pointing a dirt-streaked finger my way. "What do you say we get ourselves a Peter-bird, eh mates?"

Several hearty consents of "aye" fill the air.

"Peter-bird?" I roll my eyes. "Couldn't you at least be original with your threats?"

Trotting away from the door and around the edge of the clustered tables, I glance about the room and to the bar across the far wall to my right. The bartender watches me with an amused look.

Still no sign of the Guardian.

"Listen to me, boy!" The rambling pirate shoves a stool, knocking a few tankards loose. They topple and clatter on the floor. Several of his mates also get to their feet, about to come at me.

I cross my arms. "Oh, heave off, will you? I'm looking for someone more important than your ugly mug."

The pirate spews several curses and kicks aside a chair to round his table. "You've toyed with us long enough! Now you have no pixies, no magic, no way to hide."

His lips form a razor-like grin, but I've lost my patience with the bloke.

I lean against the wall and smirk, watching the pirate's face blanch with more anger, but then my elbow bumps into something hung along the wall behind me. I turn slightly to find a lantern swinging on its hook. It creaks as it rocks, but there's something else, a muted, high-pitched tinkling like tiny bells.

What the . . . ?

A quick glance reveals a familiar flickering glow. Three tiny bodies clamber around inside, wings crinkled and tiny fists banging against the glass.

At first my mind goes white with shock—and then my thoughts turn a boiling, angry red. Oh, you bet they're going to regret this.

I spin on my heel, gaze darting past the pirate who is on his feet, only two tables away. I scan the rest of the lanterns hung at intervals throughout the room. They're all casting the same flickering, otherworldly glow. The blasted scoundrels have enslaved nearly a hundred pixies!

Fury hums through my body. I grab the lantern from its hook, fling it open, and speak quietly to the terrified creatures inside. "Don't worry. I won't let them hurt you. Go—you're free."

There's that soft sound of chimes as they murmur quick thank-yous and flutter out of the lantern. Leaving tiny kisses on my cheek, the pixies dart away, heading for a cracked window.

The animosity in the room churns and ripples, and suddenly chairs are overturned and drinks spilled as indignant pirates leap to their feet. Between curses that would have made Wendy faint, I catch snippets of them snarling about me "freeing the glowies" and all the ways they're going to carve my limbs from my body.

My fist tightens over the lantern handle.

In the dim light, I can make out the glint of knives, but it's the flash of a pistol in some gaffer's unsteady hand that makes my jaw tick.

This may be getting a tad out of control. *Where* is that Guardian?

Still gripping the lantern, I angle toward the counter. The massive bartender sends me a sympathetic shrug but doesn't move to intervene.

The pirates advance, and I quickly discard any hope of finding an ally in the volatile crowd. A few I recognize—pirates who've captured me, aging Lost Boys.

I've faced off against groups this large before, but never without my magic. Without pixie dust.

I leap on the nearest table, lantern still in hand. Blimey, now I can see why Slightly always bragged about being the tallest.

The pirates swarm. But I'm ready.

I raise the lantern high above my head, their crazed gazes following the motion, and then toss the lantern on the stained tile at the feet of the nearest pirate. It shatters in a crunch of splintering glass and contorting metal.

That gets their attention. The voices ebb as I level my gaze on the seething crowd. Time to do the only thing I can think of in a situation like this—

Talk my way out of it.

Throwing my shoulders back, I smirk at the angry mob. "I'm warning you, chaps. This is not the time or place to start something."

My words are met with angry guffaws and even some booing that I suspect comes from the antisocial Lost Boys in the back corner.

Oh, blow off.

But I also catch sight of small golden bodies darting along the back wall, and then watch the tiny door on one of the lanterns swing open, a few more glowing forms flittering out. The pixies are freeing their mates while I have the room occupied.

Knew it would work out somehow.

My attention turns from the pixies when the angry horde starts for me, but before their grubby hands can reach the table

I'm perched on, a sound bursts from my chest, stilling their steps.

I crow—louder than before. It's the same throaty, earnest signal I would give the Lost Boys whenever we were about to fall into an adventure, or when we escaped one of the pirate's intricately laid traps.

"Do you have any idea who I am?" I widen my stance, fists planted at my sides as I face them. Sure, the question is rhetorical, but that's the whole point. "Do you know who has won over a horde of sirens and escaped? Who was made a chief by the tribal leaders?" Well, I only got to wear the ceremonial headdress for a few minutes—but details, details. "Do you know who rules an island that floats in the sky? Who has more magic in his little finger than most of you have in your thick heads?" At least, I used to. "Do you know who lopped off the captain's hand and fed it to a beast?" My voice rises through the room, each phrase filling my chest like air, reminding me even as I remind them.

"*I* did. I am the Pan."

Behind the gaping mob, the small group of pixies continue to dash from lantern to lantern, releasing their fellow sprites.

I eye the blokes clustered around me. "So, before you think you can challenge me, you'd better remember who it is that created Neverland in the first place."

The spiderwebbed fluorescent lights above my head squeal and flicker, clicking on to bathe me in lackluster light. I watch the angry expressions on the faces of the mob flicker along with the lights and slowly dim into cautious doubt.

They're starting to actually believe my load of codswallop.

I glance up just in time to see the pixies free the last few of their mates from the final lantern. The small procession escapes through a cracked window, and I heave a relieved sigh.

I take in the riotous crowd in front of me. Fierce glares still barrage me, pirates and tribal men alike terse with anger.

I reach for the knife strapped to my side, slipping it from its scabbard. Fist circling the grip, I point the blade at the crowd. Just lifting the slender piece of iron causes several in the room to sink back to their seats.

"I am not here for any of you. I'm only here to talk to the Guardian. But if you want to settle your scores . . ." I flick the blade toward the irate pirates at the front of the crowd. My eyes narrow. "I would never run from a fight or the chance to remind you why not even that old codfish has captured me."

A shocked gasp fills the room, drawing another smirk from me. I keep the knife extended, but my heart presses against my ribs, almost weightless—like my feet aren't touching the ground.

I've found it.

The thing that thunders in my chest like a roaring Neverbeast. The courage that turns my eyes to the sky even as my feet are clamped to the earth. Even without Tink or Neverland, I'm still plucky enough to escape to a place of dreams and daring.

I am still Peter Pan, even without the stars to guide me.

I tip my head back again to crow once more. Letting it out— that sense of rightness, of wholeness. Of being who I was created to be. The person that's been slipping away the past few months. The person I'll still be, even if I have to ask a grown-up for help.

As the sound vibrates through my lanky frame, nervous conversation courses through the room, followed by the creak of men sinking back into their chairs.

And then a voice cuts through the throng—

"He's flying!"

I quickly look down to see that my feet hover a few inches

above the table, my head nearly brushing the roof. A shiver sweeps through my muscles, lungs frozen. *How . . . ?*

And then I see them. The tiny golden silhouettes darting around me, leaving thin streams of pixie dust.

My eyes burn, as every inch of me hums with the thrill of weightlessness. I can breathe again.

My throat closes up as I meet the pixies' bright expressions. They hover just in front of my face for a moment, and understanding flashes between us. They get it. They've had their homeland stripped away too. But this moment is a promise, a spark of magic, a hint of the impossible. A reminder of those two bright stars that beckoned me onward, unlocking the window that had kept a scared little boy trapped. Freeing a weightless soul.

These seconds of flight soar into a desperate inner war cry that someday, somehow . . .

I will be free again.

10

CLAIRE

London, England

James Hocken is totally bonkers.

I back away from this deranged lunatic.

I've heard the whole Peter Pan spin before. It's haunted my footsteps with that inscription in Connor's book. While I may have no idea what truly happened to my brother, I know the difference between fact and fiction.

A fairy tale is nothing more than a poisonous lie.

"Uh—well—okay, then . . ."

I glance over my shoulder at the door to spot my quickest way out. The walls of the mansion feel like they're closing in on me. My skin goes cold.

Hocken reaches forward. "Wait, no—"

I bat away his hand. "I've been down this road before, and it never ends anywhere good."

His eyes narrow and he straightens, taking one limping step ahead. "Claire, just let me explain."

I suck down a breath. "Look, I've heard it all before. I used to wonder if my brother had been stolen by a myth—but then I realized the truth." I hold my hands out, trying to keep him calm and stall long enough for me to get the heck out of here. "It's just a story. A cover-up for a kidnapping."

And if you'll excuse me, I'll make my way back to reality.

"It *is* real."

My legs turn to jelly as dust speckles my fingertips again. I dart another glance over my shoulder at the door. I'm close enough to make a dash for it . . .

It's now or never.

I spin around, feet blurring into motion—when I hear a whoosh of metal against fabric, and something loops around my arm, yanking me backward.

"Sorry, love, but you need to hear me out."

I whirl back, and my jaw drops. James Hocken is holding both arms out in front of him—but he doesn't have two *hands*. His left hand is raised, palm out—but where his right hand should be, there is a massive curving prong of metal sticking out of his crimson cuff.

A hook.

Oh *heck* no.

"This had better be a sick joke." My thin voice sounds volatile to my own ears.

He shakes his head, gray-laced dark hair shadowing those piercing blue eyes. "It's no joke, Claire. None of this is a joke."

Crazy *and* delusional.

His voice is steady, carrying that disarming tone that makes my ribs tighten. "Please, love," he says again, "just hear me out."

"I told you to stop calling me that." I inch backward again, but keep my wary gaze glued on that *thing* sticking out of his right arm. *Run—run—run.*

"If you let me say my piece, I'd be happy to escort you out

myself. I can even call you a cab. Please, just listen for a moment."
His tone seems sincere, but since there's a giant metal hook
sticking out of his arm, I'm far from inclined to trust him.

But at the same time, I don't want to make him angry and
end up with that hook at my throat. I bite my lip and then lift my
chin in a nod.

"All right. Speak fast."

"Peter Pan is real—and far darker than the fairy tale you people
from Earth know." James Hocken speaks slowly, carefully.

Sticking my shaking hands in my pockets, I try to steady
my voice as I face the man in front of me. My fingers bump the
familiar rectangular shape of my phone and I cling to it like a
lifeline. If I can buy myself enough time, I can move away from
this creep and dial the police.

I gulp. "And let me guess—you're Captain Hook?"

His lips twitch into half a smile, and he tugs on his meticulously
groomed beard. "A nickname." He lifts the chunk of metal
protruding from his right arm in a shrug. "My full name is James
Hocken—or James Hook. I was once a Lost Boy. Before Peter
took someone from me too. Before he stole her and sliced off my
hand as a warning to any other boy who dared to fall in love."

My hands still. Well, that's not what I expected.

I turn his words over and over in my mind. A Lost Boy
turned pirate?

It sounds insane, but then again I'm the girl who bleeds
unexplainable dust.

"Yes, Peter took someone from me too." Hocken takes a
halting step forward. The tilt of scarlet-covered shoulders as the
so-called pirate leans down toward me. "My first love. I lost her to
Peter's selfish whims, just as you have lost your brother to Peter."

I want to call his bluff. I want to grab onto that thread of fear coiled around my heart and cling to it like a lifeline to pull me from these illusions. I want to call the police and step back into the sunlight and search for my brother like a sane person.

But I'm not a sane person.

The thought snaps like a whip, dislodging a memory I've buried as deeply as I can.

A scream of agony. The sizzle of gray, shriveled dust hitting skin. The look of utter fear on the face of the woman I called mother as my dust burned and charred and pried the skin from her bones. As she writhed, screaming at me to stop.

Screaming for her tiny adoptive daughter to stop killing her.

No one could ever explain how I'd done it. But this man may have an answer. And I owe it to myself and Connor to search every possible explanation.

I try to corral my thoughts as I twist the ends of my hair. James waits, still as a statue but with a presence that somehow fills the whole room.

I clear my throat. "So, what . . . he took Connor as soon as you guys landed in London? And how did you just happen to be the one who escorted Connor? That doesn't make sense."

Hocken runs a finger over the ridge of his hook. "I don't know anything about your . . . Miss Trevor, was it? Maybe she truly did have an adoptive family lined up for you and your brother. Or perhaps not. But, whatever the case, she asked me to guide the little chap to London. As soon as we arrived, Peter was there. This is *his* city, after all."

Hocken snarls that last sentence. "I tried to stop the cursed fairy spawn, but I couldn't keep Pan from taking your brother. I'm not as young as I used to be—and even then, I was rarely a match for the little demon who could fly."

Acid might as well drip from his words for all the bitterness behind them. James must catch my nervous expression. He tucks both hands behind his back, and gives me an apologetic smile.

"Sorry, love. Didn't mean to scare you—but it's the truth. Whether or not you want to believe it."

That's the question, isn't it?

But the more he talks, the more I realize just how capricious this man is. There is no proof to his claims. And Pan—flying?

I need to get out of here.

"Is that it? I can leave now?"

The pirate's restless cerulean eyes bore into me for a moment before he gives a slight shrug. "Yes, you are free to go."

I race for the door. Even as I near the massive hardwood exit, his voice echoes at my back.

"But if you leave, you will be walking away from the only person on this whole planet who knows what it's like."

I try to fight against his voice. But his words are a siren's song, touching a part of my heart I thought no one could see—the broken, forsaken part. The hopeless part.

The words wrap around me, slowing my steps like a coil of rope reeling me in. "Ah, yes, to know what it's like to lose a loved one at his hands. To have that little demon masquerading as a boy snatch away the only thing that ever brought beauty and light to my life."

No! He can't be telling the truth. This can't be real.

But it *feels* real. As if he's crawled inside my head and is laying out the thoughts and fears I could never tell anyone.

"I know that feeling when your heart is fracturing, shriveling in your chest. When every laugh or smile makes you sick . . ."

My fist closes around the doorknob, my breath coming in short spurts.

"The rest of the world laughs at your pain—calls you insane. They all give up on what is important. Everyone but you."

Tears sting.

This scarlet-coated captain has done more than just describe my fractured pieces. He has described his own.

It's like he's taken that hook and sliced open my calloused heart, exposing it. But rather than causing pain, it acts like a balm, a connection, drawing me back toward him.

Shoulders slumping, I release my grip on the door. I hear Hocken take another lumbering step.

"I understand you, Claire Kenton." His voice is low. "And more than that, I want to help you."

He—he wants to *help* me?

I glance over my shoulder. Hocken stands a few feet behind and has pulled a handkerchief out of his breast pocket, a crimson thing trimmed in lace, and is nonchalantly rubbing it over the curving metal prong jutting out of his right cuff.

When our gazes connect, his lips form a soft smile. "I couldn't save the girl I loved, but maybe we can rescue your brother."

I turn to face him. "And how do you intend to do that?"

"By giving you every resource at my disposal." He spreads his arms, the light glinting off his hook. "This place may not be Buckingham, but I am definitely not in want of finances."

He gestures up the massive stairway. "There's plenty of room, and I will take care of all your material needs so that you can focus entirely on finding your brother."

He moves toward me, dark boots thudding on the wooden floor. "I'm happy to finance your search. I can give you more pounds than you'd make in a year at the *Siren's Song* pub." His eyes drift over my face, darkening with intensity. "Let me help you, Claire . . ."

This pirate is reaching out a hand of generosity—but I've seen how quickly that offer can contort into the curved prong of a hook.

As much as I hate the story of Peter Pan, there was still a villain in the fairy tale. The treacherous sea captain with a hook for a hand. The very image of the man standing before me. He is offering me everything I could want.

But I'm not making any deals with the devil today.

I'll find Connor my own way.

I gather up my nerve. "I'm sorry, but that's not an agreement I'm willing to make. Thank you, and have a good day."

His jaw tightens, eyes flashing, and a tremor ripples through the hook clenched at Hocken's side—but the pirate doesn't try to stop me. Instead he watches me turn away, posture stiff as if he's trying to hold himself back.

"My offer will always be open, Claire. And whatever you decide, remember this . . . I didn't lie to you. I am not your enemy."

I don't answer, instead I rush out the door and scramble across the lawn. Past the creepy-looking creatures that are even more shadowed in the overcast late afternoon, and back under the gate. I call a cab and am soon heading for my flat.

Although I try to push James Hocken's words away or tuck them into the recesses of my mind, they still claw at my subconscious.

Because if there is a sliver of a chance that he is right, if this man truly is Hook . . . then my last hope may lie in a pirate.

11

PETER

London, England

I just managed to escape getting keelhauled by a pub of angry pirates by defying gravity. I can find the backbone to talk to one blasted grown-up.

"If yer lookin' fer the Guardian, 'e be there." The bartender standing behind the counter I'm lounging at thumbs over his shoulder. I follow his thumb to a figure in a navy coat, sitting quietly at the very end of the bar.

I nod to the bartender. "Thanks, mate."

I start for the figure sitting at the last barstool. The voices filling the pub have reached their usual volume again, eyes glancing my way but now holding a begrudging awe.

But it's not the pirates that make my pulse throb.

Don't be so daft—he's just one man.

One man who represents everything about manhood that I despise.

Just smashing.

Maybe having Lily here wouldn't have been so bad.

I reach the end of the bar and find three empty seats beside the bloke. I refuse to acknowledge the way the hilt of a knife peeking out from beneath his coat makes my throat go dry. I grip the edge of the counter and slide onto the chair beside the man.

He stays absolutely still for an achingly long moment, and I stare down at my toes, taking in the lack of shadow that is becoming more and more commonplace. When I'm about to blow my top and say something brash, the Guardian finally turns his head toward me. Most of his face is hidden behind his upturned collar. His gray-green eyes cut through me with a silent warning:

No more games.

This is the Guardian, standing between two worlds—one of magic, one of man.

The distant grandson of John Darling himself, bearing the weight of an inherited responsibility to guard humans against magical threats, which often include Hook and yours truly.

The Guardian props an elbow on the counter with a wry smile. "Nice speech. You're fond of those dramatic declarations, aren't you?"

I sit up straight. "It worked, didn't it?"

"That it did." His eyes narrow, an odd edge to his expression. "I have to say you're looking a little taller since the last time I saw you. And in need of a shave, are—"

"Don't be a wazzock!" I snap, unleashing a slew of colorful curses that only make the man chuckle. He shakes his head as if amused by a child throwing a tantrum.

Already he's managed to unnerve me. He's so much like John, the long-dead relative to blame for this delightful line of Guardians. I should have had the Lost Boys shoot him down when they had the chance.

The Guardian clears his throat, interrupting that delightful mental image of his grandpappy shot from the sky like a top-hat-clad pigeon. "So, you wanted to talk to me?"

I fidget, looking sideways at this bloke who spends his days guarding London, the center point of most of the magical mayhem. Time to just get this whole business over with.

I lean forward, fingers drumming on the counter, and say the last thing I ever expected to tell a grown-up:

"I think Hook is hunting down another way to further devastate Neverland."

The Guardian's lips quirk in a knowing smirk. "Really?"

"Aye. But I don't see what's the least bit funny about that."

His smile fades. "I get it, Peter. I really do. But if I go and investigate every one of Hook's schemes, I'd never have time for anything else. Especially if I was to add looking into every mess *you* cause as well. Besides, you know the code."

Curse that blasted code! The ridiculous set of rules that this man lives by, the things he claims allow him to remain unbiased, like a set of justice scales balancing precariously between our two worlds.

I wanted to shoot a cannon ball through those blasted rules years ago.

My foot jogs against the bottom rung of the barstool. "There has to be *something* you can do. You're the bloomin' Guardian, after all."

His shoulders shift beneath his navy coat. "I've had a feeling that there's something else amiss, beyond Hook's usual shenanigans. Still, I'll need more proof to warrant kicking that hornet's nest."

I slam down a frustrated fist. "A Lost Boy told me there's something dodgy happening with Hook—that's not enough proof for you?"

This Guardian is flamin' useless.

Before he can answer, the bartender wanders over and slides a plate across the bar to him. It's layered with massive chunks of red meat that look anything but appetizing. The Guardian thanks the stocky bartender, who gives a slight nod and saunters off to fill another empty tankard.

"You hungry, Nar?" My eyes widen as the man tosses the meat to something at his feet. I hear the loud shuffle of paws, and the snapping and scuffing of some creature downing the chunk.

What in the name of the lagoon?

I lean down and catch a glimpse of a small, mangy dog sitting at the foot of the man's stool. It looks like a stray, with one ear flopped over, a tongue hanging out so far, it nearly touches the tile floor and a tail that waggles in a quick blur. Its muzzle drops open in a sloppy almost-grin as it stares up at its owner.

But the Guardian doesn't miss a beat. He keeps talking to me as he tosses massive slabs of meat to the small dog.

"I know losing your island has thrown off the balance of everything else. This dangerous game you have been playing for so long is starting to escalate—but, there's only so much I can do, Peter. I'm just one man trying to protect an entire planet of humans."

"Then why not go to the source of the problem!" I shove back from my stool, bouncing on the balls of my feet to manage the nervous energy. "Hook is sitting posh and free in a mansion on the outskirts of this city while you're here feeding your mutt."

The pooch growls. Its owner takes on a gravelly edge. "I'm a Guardian, Peter—not judge, jury, and executioner. I have to be so careful with the moves I make. I have to be absolutely certain that I'm sticking my blade into the right crack in their armor, or

I may end up with a dagger in my back."

I look at him sharply. My hand strays to the knife strapped to my side.

"But you *are* going to draw a weapon? You won't just stand on the sidelines and let them do whatever they bloomin' want?"

His eyes glint. "I've always taken a stand when the need arose." He rubs a thumb along the gold band circling his ring finger, an expression I can't identify crossing his features. A sense of care as weighty and vast as the Neversea.

Ah! Right! The one time he ever broke his own rules. Since John started this whole flaming tradition decades ago, this man is the first Guardian to ever break the code—and he did it for love.

The very idea makes me queasy, but at least it's a chink in his armor.

Because if this bloke was able to defy his own code to rescue a young tribal healer who'd been caught by pirates one day while out gathering herbs—and then even had the gall to marry the lass and bring her back to London with him—maybe he'd be willing to break the rules again for another girl in need. Not to mention that marrying Tansy had nearly turned Neverland inside out.

I lean back on my stool and briefly take in the rest of the room. Several of the pub's occupants still eye me distrustfully, but none are within earshot.

I desperately hope that this mad gamble with the last piece of information I have to help me return to Neverland won't come back to nip me in the rear.

"I have another question for you. Sort of about the same thing, but different . . ."

Smooth. Real smooth.

He must catch the tremor in my tone, because the Guardian

takes a swig from the tankard sitting beside the plate and swivels on the stool toward me.

"Yes?"

I lean over so I am close enough that no one else will hear our conversation. "It's about a girl."

A grin stretches across his face. "Well, Peter! I never thought the day would come—"

My face is in flames. "No! Not like that," I hiss.

Pulling my hood up, I try to avoid the heat spiraling up my neck.

"I need to find someone I left behind." Before Hook does.

"Is she human?" His tone is a bit more somber.

Would that change things? He said he can't step in between a fight that Hook has with another magical being, but maybe if he was threatening a human . . .

A lump forms in my gut, but I keep my gaze steady, holding back the tells that might alert him my next word is a lie. "Yes."

The Guardian rubs at his clean-shaven face, which only makes me painfully aware of the faint stubble marring my own chin. And how to the usual passerby, we probably look nearly the same age. Cor, I'm so done with this whole aging rubbish.

"What's her name?"

I still a breath. Guess there's no use in keeping it under wraps.

"Claire Kenton." As soon as the name passes my lips, his eyes widen. The Guardian tries to keep his features neutral, but I still catch the look of recognition before he can mask it. You'll have to be quicker than that, mate.

I push up my sleeves, continuing to talk and watching his expression closely for anything more.

"She'd be in her late teens by now, Lily thinks. We were trying to find schools where she might have gone, but my memory's not as keen as it used to be."

The man beside me shifts. "Why are you looking for this girl?"

And why won't you admit you know her?

"I need her for something,"

When Darling's expression shuts down, I realize how odd the response sounded. Cripes, now he thinks I'm some kind of kidnapper or something.

Well. I am. Kind of.

"Look, what I mean is that I need her help to get back to Neverland. I just need to find her and explain . . . things."

Blast, blast, blast! My brain screams at me for sounding like a bumbling idiot.

The Guardian crosses his arms over his chest, eyeing me closely. "You need to hunt down a normal, human girl so she can help you get back to Neverland?"

It sounds like complete tosh, even to me.

I blow out an elaborate sigh. "She's . . ." I pause. Well, he's bound to find out eventually. "She's Connor's sister."

His reaction is immediate. "Are you sure that's wise? Especially if she's human too?"

"At this point, we've got nothing else to go on."

He regards me for a moment. "What aren't you telling me, Peter?"

The same thing I'm not telling the Lost Boys or Lily. The secrets that are so twisted around my soul, I will take them to my grave.

The little boy that cost me a whole world.

I work up a charming smile. "Can't you just trust me, mate? I'm trying to save Neverland."

He snorts a laugh, shaking his head. "Peter, if you think that

I'm enough of an idiot to trust you any more than I do the rest of the pirates in this pub, then you really are the ignorant child Hook makes you out to be."

I stiffen. "What's that supposed to mean?"

"You're not the good guy, Peter Pan. You're just the other one vying for control of Neverland."

I shoot up from the stool, fists tight. "I'm the one trying to *protect* Neverland. They're the ones tearing it apart, you lout!"

London's Guardian rises, the dog at his heels in a second. He towers over me like a dark shadow, his voice deceptively calm.

"You have caused plenty of havoc yourself, Pan. You protect the island and the people in it as long as it serves you. But as soon as you grow tired of people or purposes, you cast them away."

My gut twists.

He leans closer, eyes boring into mine.

"You are a child who only cares about his own happiness. A child who, for decades upon decades, has been able to do whatever he fancied. And thankfully, up to this point, you have never really had the same sense of greed and bloodshed Hook has." His eyes darken.

"But your own whims could change like that—" He snaps his fingers in my face. "And if you chose to turn your back on the creatures of Neverland, or even on this city, you could cause more damage than Hook could ever dream."

Rubbing my damp palms on my trousers, I lean away from him as he continues. "So, no. I don't trust you, Peter. But I agree— at this point, you are the better option for Neverland."

Well, we're hot and cold, aren't we? Spearing me as a conniving twit one moment and then praising me the next.

"You mean . . . ?"

He gives a slight nod. "Yes, if I find out anything about this Claire girl, I will let you know."

The sigh that vibrates through my chest is thick with relief. "Thanks, mate."

He adjusts his jacket and sinks back onto his stool. After downing another gulp of whatever is in his tankard, he grabs the last slab of meat from the plate and tosses it to the dog once again seated at his feet. Then, finally, he looks back at me.

"I'm not the villain, Peter. I just want this world to be a safer place. For everyone, including my wife and our child on the way."

Child?

My head jerks up, and I stare at him.

Nothing about the man sitting near me, able to still a room with a glance, and single-handedly keep peace in the middle of a magic-riddled battlefield, seems like what a father would be. At least not the ones I've seen.

Not the angry, controlling, manipulative men who have done nothing but drain the color out of their children's worlds.

Then again, I have to begrudgingly admit that this man is nothing like them—like those men who shuffle their days in dull monotony or angry bitterness.

No, the Guardian of Neverland and London is something else.

I spend the next several minutes trying to wheedle any information out of the bloke, but he refuses to play along. So I storm away from the bar in a flurry of frustration. Still, I can't seem to summon the same anger I've had before at the man who stands guard between this world and Neverland.

Much as the bloke so often makes me want to slug him in the face, he's still one of the good ones. And as I stride quickly through the pub, heading for the door. I can't escape a single, dangerous thought.

Because if this man can believe in magic and stand for justice in a way I've never understood, if he can take care of a wife and have that much pride and care in his eyes for a future child . . .

Then maybe growing up doesn't always mean carving out the magic from your soul. Maybe—just maybe—growing up can be a way of letting your dreams expand, like a falling star becoming a magical island resting in the middle of a galaxy.

Maybe growing up isn't letting your soul die but entering another adventure.

Or maybe I'm daft.

Still, I can't help but feel like I'm closer to finding Claire than I've ever been. And whatever comes next, it's going to be one heck of a journey.

And I can never turn down an adventure.

CLAIRE

London, England

As soon as I return to my flat, I call N. His voice sounds groggy when he picks up.

"H-hello? What's up, Claire?"

I wrestle off my shoes with one hand, sitting on the edge of my little bed, phone tucked against my ear with my shoulder. "I wanted to tell you about the day I've had. You won't believe it."

He moans. "Just give me a second to find coffee. It's too early to think."

I look at the clock. Two in the afternoon. "Oh! The time difference. I totally spaced. I have something crazy to tell you. What time is it there?"

"Six o'clock," N mumbles, and I hear a clatter as he stumbles out of his room in search of coffee.

Oops. "Oh, I'm so sorry! Want me to call back later?"

I get my shoes off and scoot back on the stiff cot to lean against the wall, crossing my legs under me as I take in my small flat. Fluorescent lights bathe off-white walls in a sepia color and filter over the stiff chairs and tiny kitchenette. N's voice sounds clearer when he speaks again.

"No, it's fine. I want to hear, and I've found the Keurig, so we're good."

"I think my coffee addiction is rubbing off on you."

"Or maybe it's *my* addiction affecting you."

"Touché."

There's the hum of the coffee maker starting up, and then N yawns. "Okay, go ahead. I can listen as I throw together a cup."

Massaging my forehead, I stare at the stained ceiling. "Well, I went to see the police this morning. It feels like an eternity ago now. And I found out who the man in the video with Connor was."

There is a long pause, and N's voice is strained when he finally reacts. "Who?"

"His name is James Hocken." I wrestle my thick hair into a knot at the nape of my neck. "I went to his house this afternoon."

"You *what*?" N's voice explodes through the phone.

"H-hey! Calm down! I don't need anyone else yelling at me today."

"Claire, that was dangerous. Who knows what he could have done to you!"

The room feels stifling, and I unzip my teal sweatshirt, tugging. "I'm fine, N. That's what's important. And I found some answers—or at least, James Hocken's wild theory."

I hear the clank of a ceramic mug as N retrieves his coffee. He lets out a sigh. "All right. Tell me everything."

So I do.

My hacker friend listens in complete silence as I talk, and my palms go sweaty with every passing moment that his end of the line remains quiet. I keep plowing through despite his lack of response, just wanting to get it all out there. And to have N tell me that I'm crazy for even giving a second thought to the eccentric man's claims.

But N doesn't tell me I'm crazy. "You should go to the pub."

"I-I should what? What are you even talking about?"

"James Hocken's story is crazy but no less insane than some of the things Connor said in his note. And there tends to be a bit of truth in every far-fetched tale."

"You can't seriously think–"

"No, I'm not saying I think Peter Pan is real." I hear a tap-tap-tap and picture him drumming his fingers across his mug. "I'm just thinking that maybe there is some thread of truth in what James Hocken told you. Maybe Miss Trevor did send Connor to London to be adopted, but he was kidnapped there? Who really knows?"

He pauses. "But the best way to figure out how stable and trustworthy the man's words are is to go talk to someone who knows him. Go someplace he frequents. You said he mentioned some pub?"

I slip off the bed, and cross speckled linoleum to the small kitchenette, where I fill a glass of water from the tap.

"Yes, he mentioned some place called the *Siren's Song.*"

"I would go there and just listen. See if anyone mentions him, find out what kind of rep that guy has. If you can believe anything he says. Besides, you will need a job eventually."

I nearly drop my cup. "And you think a barmaid is a good fit?"

N chuckles. "You don't know what kind of place the pub is. I'd at least go check it out. If it feels off, you can leave."

Tucking the phone against my shoulder, I take a sip of tap water and lean back against the sink. Wasn't he just berating me for going to James Hocken's estate? Now he wants me to sit in some pub and apply for a job?

"N, are you sure? You're usually the one steering me away from dangerous situations."

Unease threads his deep voice. "Honestly, Claire . . . I don't know what else we can do at this point. James Hocken was the last clue we had, and unless you know whether or not his wild story is even somewhat viable, we're back where we started."

Leaving the cup on the kitchenette counter, I glance at the locked front door. "I can always have the cabbie wait outside the pub for me . . ."

And call the police if things go south.

N takes another gulp of his coffee, voice even more alert now. "Yes, exactly. There are ways to be sure you're safe. And you know I wouldn't suggest it unless I didn't see any other way."

"I know." Going back across the small room, I pick up my discarded shoes and a yellow cardigan as well. "It's the best chance we've got."

The cabbies in London seem to know every nook and cranny of the city, including the small, hole-in-the-wall pub called the *Siren's Song*. It is buried deep in one of the older boroughs, set on the corner of a row of ancient brick buildings sporting everything from a tattoo parlor to a greasy restaurant with standing room only.

My throat goes dry as the black cab pulls up to the curb. I rub my damp palms over my jacket and quickly pay the cabbie extra, asking him to wait for me—and call the police if he hears me scream.

His eyes fly open. "Yes, ma'am, Are you sure you're all right?"

I bite my lip as I reach for the door handle. "I sure hope so."

I've already survived a run-in with a delusional eccentric with a hook for a hand—what's a little pub? *Ha. Maybe I'm the one who's delusional.*

I force myself out of the cab and onto the sidewalk. It's late afternoon, and this part of the street isn't well lit. With the graying sky overhead and the mist rolling in, the faded brick buildings are like specters watching my every move.

My footsteps echo hollowly as I walk past the tattoo parlor and another smaller building I can't—and probably don't want—to identify. And then it's in front of me—the *Siren's Song.*

Pressing my purse to my hip, I tiptoe across the sidewalk toward the little pub. It looks like something straight out of the movies, with a carved wooden sign hanging over the door. The words *Siren's Song* are etched in swirling font, and beneath them, in smaller script, *Brew Pub and Eatery.* The S's on the beginning of the words *Siren* and *Song* are shaped into two sirens.

Like the statues littering James Hocken's lawn, these mermaid-like creatures' mouths are open, displaying rows of sharp teeth.

Checking over my shoulder again to be sure the cab is still there, I pull my cardigan tight and step up to the pub's front door. It's made out of the same carved wood as the sign and does little to hold in the noisy din erupting from inside the pub.

On second thought, I think I'd rather face Hocken's creepy mansion again.

I hear a loud crash from somewhere inside, and a woman shrieks.

Yeah, I'll have to tell N we're finding another way.

I'm about to turn and hightail it back to the cab when the heavy wooden door to the little pub swings wide open.

And smacks me hard in the shoulder, nicking my forehead.

My legs feel like putty, knees buckling. The shadowed surroundings churn around me in a dizzying arc.

A masculine voice pierces through my haze, but the words are distant.

Before I can smack into the concrete, I'm grabbed roughly around the shoulders. I'm eventually aware of two strong hands and a smooth voice.

"Whoa! Sorry, mate! Didn't mean to hit you. Are you okay?"

I blink, trying to clear my vision.

"I-I think so." The words are thick on my tongue.

He continues to hold me steady and with a few more hard blinks, the world comes into focus. I'm looking into the most vivid green eyes I've ever seen. Vibrant emeralds with specks of gold that tease me like flickers of my own dust. Reddish-blonde curls frame the striking face those eyes belong to. His teasing dimples wink at me, a splash of freckles cover his cheeks. From the slight auburn stubble grazing his strong jaw, I'd guess he's around eighteen or nineteen.

I'm tongue-tied, and my loss of speech has nothing to do with the door he apparently whacked me with.

Wow, I've never seen anyone so . . . beautiful.

It's like he's made of stardust.

His eyes study me, and then his lips curve into a smile that makes me forget my name. "All right, can you stand?"

My head bobbles in a dumb nod, and he lets me go, backing up a pace. He's wearing a forest-green hoodie that doesn't hide his athletic build. I sway on my feet, dumbstruck.

Claire—brain! Watch it! Don't stare!

Not even my internal scolding can come out in complete

sentences. What has this boy done to me?

"Are you sure . . . ?" His eyes flicker, brow creasing. "You seem . . . have we ever met?"

"Uh—don't think so."

I'm pretty sure I'd remember that face.

He looks at me for another long second, then shrugs, his entire countenance lightening. He pushes his hands in his pockets. "Ah, whatever. Probably just saw you about Kensington or some such. Are you sure you're all right, mate? You going inside? Be sure to sit down."

Yes. That sounds like a good idea.

"Thank you." I manage to get out the words as he gives me one last reassuring look and then continues on his way down the sidewalk, leaving me standing like an idiot in front of the door to the pub. Suddenly, though, my nervousness isn't as suffocating.

I pinch my eyes closed as a flush creeps up my neck. I quickly check my face to be sure it's only bruised, not bleeding, and then try to pull hair over my temple to hide any swelling.

The inside of the building is even louder than I expected, an uproar of chattering voices, gruff arguments, and the thud of some kind of rock music playing through the speakers hanging above my head.

I scan the room for the bar and make a beeline for it. The curving bar is set against the back of the right wall, and I sink into a seat at the far end, holding my purse close against my chest.

Just—breathe—take a breath . . .

I cross my arms over the bar, palms against the cool wooden surface, trying to root myself in the realness, the steadiness of the counter. The grainy sensation of dust is coating my sweaty palms, so I tug my long cardigan sleeves down farther.

This was a bad idea.

Several dozen tables are wedged in between a colorful array of patrons. I try not to stare at the huge men with biceps larger than my head bearing scars on every inch of exposed skin, or the women in brightly colored corsets and bustles that seem like some kind of lewd Halloween costumes.

A few young men huddle around a table at the very far corner of the room, hoods pulled up on their dark jackets. Their whispering, intense presence seems oddly out of place, but at the same time, they seem faded into the background. *Probably their intention.*

A massive mural of some fantasy landscape covers one wall of the pub—swirling teal waters crashing against a pebbled beach studded with sloping palm trees and beautiful tropical flowers. Droplets of gold glimmer throughout the painting, resting on the edge of a flower or beneath a palm frond, like beads of living sunlight.

I shift in my seat, strangely drawn to the mural, when I catch sight of the creatures rising out of the waves on the opposite end of the image. Dark, writhing creatures—half-fish, half-man or woman. Sirens, the same mythical beings that give this pub its name.

The sirens look like they could crawl right out of the painting.

Psycho decorations: check!

No wonder Hocken likes it here.

What even is this place?

It has a different atmosphere than any bar I've ever been to— not that I have much experience, other than sneaking into a bar once with the other underage girls in my group home. That did not end well.

"What'll ye 'ave, miss?"

The thick accent brings my attention around to the man standing on the other side of the counter. The bartender is massive, with a greasy apron thrown over his broad shoulders and a bandana around his buzzed head. His coffee-colored eyes are unmistakably kind, however, and my unease lowers a fraction.

"U-um, do you have root beer?"

Because I'm adventurous like that.

He gives me an odd look, then shrugs. "Aye. One root beer comin' up."

I turn my attention back to the rest of the pub. The hum of voices begins to settle around me, no longer a knife filleting my raw nerves, but rather a familiar sensation that provides a safe cushion between me and the electric nightlife.

Should I ask someone about James Hocken? One can only eavesdrop for so long.

I scan the excited crowd filling the pub, ears perked for anything interesting, but instead I find my gaze snagged by several people staring straight at me.

A shiver ripples up my spine, and I immediately look away, but their sour expressions are branded across my mind's eye. There are five greasy and large men sitting at a table toward the back of the pub, sending me unadulterated glares.

My fingertips are sticky with dust. When I check again, the men are still staring at me.

They scowl, and my skin crawls.

Just ignore them.

Then they stand, their bulk rocking the table as they rise to their feet. Blood drains from my face.

These men are massive, several covered in tattoos, while dirt and scars stain their faces. Their unsettling stares remain on me, and I'm suddenly very aware of the weapons beneath their coats—weapons I'm sure aren't legal.

I clutch my purse, one foot already off the stool. Could I make it to the exit in time?

I search desperately around the room, praying for someone else to sideline these men. But everyone else ignores me.

I jolt in my seat as heavy footsteps pound behind me. The bartender standing at my shoulder, leaning over the counter. "'Ey there! She ain't worth it, mates. Leave 'er be."

The five Terminator wannabes don't even blink.

I try to corral my thoughts into an escape plan, wondering why I haven't run yet. Maybe I can duck around them? Or I could dive behind the bar and find something to defend myself with? Maybe there's a back door?

The thoughts tangle and dissolve. I can't breathe, can't think.

My skin is slick with dust, and my legs are shaking. I jump off the stool to make a mad dash for the exit. The men close in, and the room starts spinning—when someone rises from a stool at the opposite end of the bar.

"Don't touch her."

The room goes dead silent. The five Goliaths freeze, and every head in the room turns to the man who's spoken. He takes slow strides around the bar, his very presence commanding respect. He's wearing a navy jacket, with the collar up to mask his features. But as he nears me, the flicker of the lanterns exposes his terse expression, his dark hair and gray-green eyes. My mouth falls open.

It's Officer Jeremy Darling.

13

CLAIRE

London, England

Every eye is glued on the police officer, but I have a nagging suspicion it's not his title as a lawman that garners respect. There's something *knowing* about the look in his cool gray-green eyes, an understanding that pierces.

"You'll have to find some other victim tonight, boys."

His voice is low, but Jeremy's attention locks on the burly men standing a few feet away. I watch the muscles in their jaws clench, the way their meaty hands curl into fists.

A mangy dog darts out from under a table and dashes to Jeremy's heels, all big ears and floppy tongue. The men's gazes slide from Jeremy to the mutt and back. Finally, with a throaty growl, their vehement expressions give way to something more resigned.

All five take a few steps back, nodding in Jeremy's direction before dissolving into the crowd.

My lungs learn how to draw air again, and I slowly ease back onto the barstool. Wow. I've never seen someone turn a fight around like that.

The tension begins to subside, and the officer moves over to me. Hesitant conversations begin to blossom throughout the room until it's filled with nearly the same energy as when I first came in.

Jeremy Darling stands before me. "You went after Hocken, didn't you?"

I bite my lip, fingers tightening around my purse strap. "Maybe?"

He shakes his head, then reaches for my arm. His touch is light.

"Let's step outside. There are too many ears in here."

I let him lead me from the pub into the chilly night air. I notice that my cab is still waiting, but the sight of the small, puttering black vehicle disappears as Jeremy escorts me around a corner. We pull into a shadowed alley wedged between the *Siren's Song* and the building back-to-back with it.

Gasping down a lungful of cool night air, I slump against the pub's wall. My legs tremble. My arms itch from the dust coating my skin, hidden by the cardigan.

Keep it together, Claire.

Jeremy Darling stands a few feet away. Far enough to give me space to breathe, but not far enough to impede his ability to protect me. His broad shoulders twitch as he scans the alley. Clearly on alert for someone. He turns sharply, checking every angle. The dog yaps at his heels, a wheezy bark echoing like a growl.

"Nar, stop!" Jeremy glares at the mutt and it quiets.

The mist rolling in around us brushes the hem of his jacket.

"I think we're safe to talk. But if I say run, you have to get to your cab and out of here, okay?"

I force a quick nod, tightening my arms around my chest.

"You have no idea what you've stumbled into, do you?"

I rub the knitted sleeves of my cardigan together, trying to coax out some warmth from the tight weave, but only managing to get them soaked in the thin specks of dust that are getting harder and harder to hold back.

"No, but I'm trying to figure it out. Somehow this all plays into Connor."

Jeremy shakes his head again. "Claire, whatever happened to your brother, I highly doubt it would help to draw attention from the underworld. That bar"—he gestures over his shoulder—"it's filled with some of the most cutthroat scum you've ever seen. Any one of them would slit your throat in a second if you rubbed them wrong. Why are you even here, anyway?"

I press into the wall, hoping the solid surface at my back will remind me of the fact that I'm out of danger.

"James Hocken mentioned it when he was telling me his crazy story about what happened to my brother. I wanted to know if anything he was saying was true."

Officer Darling stands in a defensive posture—aware of everything around us. But at this, he looks at me. "James mentioned this place by name?"

"Yes."

Jeremy's mutt rubs its thick muzzle against my shin, sending a strange jolt of electricity through my jeans. The dog stares up at me with big eyes, lolling tongue rolling out the side of its maw.

"Nar, leave her alone." Jeremy pulls a thick piece of jerky out of his coat pocket. He throws the meat down the deserted alley, and the mangy dog's paws turn up a massive amount of dust as it howls and darts after the jerky.

"Wow. He really likes that."

Jeremy gives a half smile. "Yeah, he's got quite the appetite." Then his smile disappears. "If James told you this place by name, that explains a lot. Maybe he was hoping his men would rough you up a bit. I'm glad I stepped in."

Me too. You have no idea.

Jeremy must take in my frightened gaze and pale face, because his expression softens. He puts a gentle hand on my shoulder.

"Claire, you've had a long day. We will help you search for your brother, but not like this. Go home, be safe. Come back to the department tomorrow, and I'll see what we can do."

His hand tightens slightly as he leans closer to make eye contact, the silver in his irises swirling like a crashing wave. "But you need to stop searching on your own. There is danger in the shadows, Claire."

He means it as a simple warning, but the solemn reminder severs my last thread of control. Something inside snaps. Despite how tightly my arms clamp over my chest, despite how I pull my sleeves down even further—the dust still escapes.

I feel it race through my veins, breaking out over my arms in a heavy flood and layering my palms. I try to turn away, try to hide it.

"Claire, what's wrong?"

I squeeze my arms around my torso, feeling those tremors skimming through my bones. *Keep it in—keep it in—keep it in.*

The chanting isn't working.

The dust lifts from my skin, thin and silky and unwanted. I rock on my heels, arms wound tight like a straitjacket, eyes pinched shut. Try to force the dust to recede back to that place deep inside.

But I've been holding the dust captive for days.

"Claire, what's—"

"*Get back!*" I shout at the officer.

I try to pull myself away from him, but I only make it a few steps across the concrete. My closed arms are thrown open, and the dust bursts from my pores. It shoots through the knitted fabric, pours from my fingertips, and ignites the dim alleyway. This time, in this strange world filled with myths and magic, I let the dust pour from my skin.

The gold flecks spiral into the air, piercing through the mist and dangling in the shadows like a thousand tiny specks of sunlight. I marvel at how *golden* it is. No longer that pale color I'd seen back at the Circle K in California. No longer disgusting flakes that could pass for a skin disease.

This dust is like shattered stardust—gold and iridescent.

I stare at the dust, pulse thundering, waiting for it to turn gray, to start burning. But it doesn't. It holds its shape and color, glimmering in the narrow alley and wrapping around us like teasing fireflies.

Thank God. It's not going to hurt anyone.

Not today, at least.

A strange sense of awe settles into my veins. Because here— hidden away where it can't hurt anyone and glistening in contrast to the thick, ashen fog—my dust is almost beautiful.

There is an unintelligible exclamation.

I swivel to find Jeremy staring at me.

My pulse quickens. "I'm sorry! I can explain—"

He shakes his head and mutters something about a *lying little wretch*. "No, I think I owe you an apology."

Jeremy's wide-eyed expression takes in the spiraling dust. He raises a hand, the gold band on his ring finger standing out against the graying mist, just like my dust. His fingertips gently nudge one of the glimmering specks. It dissolves the minute his skin touches it.

I've never seen anyone look at it that way before. Entranced and in awe and with a hint of a knowing smile on his lips.

"It doesn't scare you?"

"Scare me?" His sparkling eyes meet mine, and he shakes his

head. "No, I've seen far stranger things, Claire. But I was wrong earlier—it looks like you belong in this world after all."

Did I hear that right? "What do you mean? Are you going to help me get the answers I need?"

Jeremy's thoughtful posture is interrupted when his mutt comes galloping back from across the alleyway, flecks of gold tangling in its scruffy fur. The officer pets the dog behind its ears, and then glances back at me.

"I'm in an odd position, Claire. Standing at the middle point between two very precarious worlds and just trying to keep them from destroying each other." He gives the mutt one last pet and then straightens. "I'm not supposed to interfere with the dealings between them. I have to be an impartial judge."

He thoughtfully rubs his thumb over the golden band on his ring finger. "However, I've never really been able to turn down a young woman searching for answers in a world that hasn't treated her kindly."

Jeremy continues to finger his wedding ring, a distant look in his eyes. Finally, he looks at me with determination.

"Do you want to find out what that dust really is? And what it means for you and Connor?"

The glimmering specks of gold begin to sink through the mist, dissolving the minute they hit the concrete.

I stare in disbelief at Jeremy. "My dust? You know what it is? No one has ever been able to diagnose it."

Jeremy's voice is kind when he speaks. "It's not an illness, Claire. It's the most natural thing in the world. Just not in *this* world. But I know someone who could explain it and even teach you how to control it."

He brushes a few flecks off his sleeve and looks around again.

He steps closer and whispers, "You'll find him at Kensington Gardens tomorrow morning. Early, just as the sun begins to rise, standing in front of the Peter Pan statue. It's where he goes to think."

I rub my trembling fists on my cardigan. "Who is he? What's his name?"

But Officer Darling only shakes his head. "I've already told you more than I should. I shouldn't even be stepping in like this. Just go to Kensington tomorrow, and you'll find everything you need to know. Tell him I sent you."

Jeremy draws back, slips his dog another piece of jerky, and then motions for me to follow him back to my cab. As my hesitant steps carry me around the back of the pub, I glance behind at the alley one last time. A faint glimmer of gold highlights the roiling mist, but other than that, all traces of my dust are gone.

But the warmth, the light, has settled deep in my chest. It lifts my chin and draws my shoulders back. I'm filled with an airy sensation I was afraid I'd never feel again.

Hope.

14

PETER

London, England

I need to clear my head. Again.

Kensington is empty this early in the morning, but after a restless night, that only makes me more impatient to discover what the Guardian knows. I can't stand to stay corralled inside any longer.

And these gardens have always been the place in London I feel most at home.

As I tread over the crisp grassy lawns of the gardens, the still morning broken only by the shuttering sound of sprinklers and the whistle of distant birds, shimmering pixies dart around me and whisper in their lilting, bell-like voices. They weave thin streams of glimmering dust to light my way. You almost wouldn't know their glow was softer than usual, thanks to the desolation of their homeland.

The pixie dust falls to the grass, lifting a stray flower from its place here and there. The morning chill raises the hair on my arms, as plumes of fog fold into the quiet gardens. My trainers thud along the cobblestone path that leads to my statue, the bushes and trees glinting with dew in the moonlight.

Already it's getting easier to breathe.

A few pixies land on my shoulder, quieting as if they sense my somber mood. They're just as lost as I am about how to solve this whole beastly mess.

I turn another corner, watching the gleam of the sun creeping over the horizon. What I wouldn't give for the pixies to let me fly again, just for a moment.

Instead, I'm painfully aware of the weariness in their faces, the way their wings even seem heavier. The cost they are paying behind the glamour, as Hook continues to twist the magical island where they replenish their magic.

I've been so daft, not seeing that it affects them too.

Such cheery thoughts. Maybe I should have taken a stroll through a cemetery instead. I round the bend along the Long Water that leads to the elaborate bronze statue depicting my adventures in Neverland.

But as I draw near to my statue, I realize I'm not alone. *By the stars...*

The pixies dart off my shoulder and disappear into the brush. My footsteps slow, curious as to who would have snuck in at five thirty in the morning to consult Peter for answers.

As I draw near, the hesitant golden shades of the sunrise fall across a slender figure standing in front of the statue. I take another step, careful to be as silent as possible.

Cor, she is beautiful.

A little nose and big blue eyes that gaze up at the statue, a blue as vibrant as the Neversea and equally capable of swallowing me up. Not that I would mind the drowning.

Drowning? Where'd that come from?

Blowing a long breath, I slow the heat rising up in me, but cor, there's *something* about this girl.

Her hair is the color of pale stardust, curling and wispy around her features. But it's the flicker of color that flushes her skin—a golden glow speckling the fingertips clasped over her heart—that halts my step. This girl fits here. In this garden where the pixies peek out of the bushes and her stray curls get caught in the soft breeze blowing in from the river.

She belongs in Kensington, this small alcove that's as close to Neverland as anywhere in this world. There's a magic about this girl—something soft and airy and hopeful.

And then it connects. *Blast!* It's the girl I ran into on my way out of the pub yesterday!

Here she is again. And here I am.

Great, she's going to think I followed her.

I don't even realize I've reached for the whistle dangling around my neck until my damp fingers are rolling it back and forth.

I wonder if I should flee into the underbrush with the pixies. But one look at this otherworldly girl tells me I can't do that.

What if it's *her*?

She seemed nice enough in the alley, if a bit flustered. Not to mention that she's come to consult my statue, which means she can't be all bad.

I stow the whistle away and try to work up the right words to break the silence. What's wrong with me? I'm never this nervous.

With most girls, all I have to do is flash a smile and they faint at my feet. But this one seems different.

I smooth out my green jacket and sink my hands into my pockets, trying to look nonchalant. "You're a fan of Peter Pan too?"

It's a good thing Lily isn't here or she'd be giving me a massive eye roll.

The girl lifts her head, startled.

She looks like she's about to give me a tongue-lashing, but then her eyes flicker with recognition. "Wait—you're the boy from the pub."

"The one and only." My lips curl into a smirk, but that only seems to make her more flustered, so I plow ahead, trying to explain myself. "I like to take morning walks through Kensington before the rest of London is awake. I've just never run into anyone else here."

I watch a pinkish tint creep up from the neckline of her pale blue jacket. Even her voice has an otherworldly lilt. "This is the first time I've come. How long have you been standing there? I guess I got lost in my own thoughts. I can give you your space—"

I wave a hand. "Oh, you're not a bother. And there's plenty of space for both of us in this garden."

I hope the smile I give her is reassuring. Her eyes dart about like a frightened animal's, gauging the best way to run. Yet the determined set to her shoulders tells me she might just stick around for a bit longer.

I hope she does. There's something special about her.

Stars, this isn't puberty, is it?

I almost collapse at the thought. The girl sends me a sympathetic glance. "Are you okay?"

I manage a smile that makes her face heat again. "Just fine, thanks."

She shies away a bit, turning her attention back to my bronze counterfeit. She moves around the side of the statue, glancing up at my metal likeness. I walk around the other side, trying to collect my thoughts.

I run a hand over the curve of the sculpted pixie's wings and then focus on the real-life pixies hiding in the grove behind us, their flickering pale forms like tiny spots of golden light peeking through the foliage.

"I don't like him."

I take a step back, peering around the statue at her. "Eh—what was that?"

"I don't like Peter Pan. And actually, the longer I stand here, waiting for answers to questions that he can never give . . ." She bites her lip. "The more I find out about him, the more I realize I don't just dislike Peter Pan . . ."

I'm half-inclined to shove my hands over my ears, but I can't move.

"I *hate* Peter Pan."

Her words thunder into me, and I grit my jaw to keep from rocking backward. I don't know how to make sense of her words. I blink at her expression, filled with pain and laced with bitterness, and let her declaration seep in.

She's the first to say something like that.

Sure, the pirates hate me. And at times the tribesmen may want to aim an arrow at my heart. I can't even count all the times the Lost Boys have brassed me off and I let one of my moods throw the island into chaos.

But I've never had anyone stand before me and curse Peter Pan—the fairy tale, no less—with such intensity.

What did I do to this girl?

I gulp down a lungful of cool air, desperate to ease the thick tension that has clammed up between us. I stare down at my trainers, trying to think of some way I can excuse myself without showing my soul on my sleeve. I just want to hide from this girl with her gaze that cuts through me. To shove my hands over my ears and sing inappropriate pirate shanties until the whispers and angry accusations rattling around in my head go away.

Instead, I cock my head at her. "Are you always this intense about fairy tales?"

That draws a near smile out of her, and she shakes her head. "No, and I'm sorry—I'm not even sure why I'm telling you this. It's been a long week. A long year." She gives a sad little laugh.

"It's just something about this story," she continues. "Ever since I was young, I couldn't stand it. The idea of a little boy who never wanted to face responsibility or answer to anyone for his actions, who stole away children from their families. I know what it's like to lose someone in my family, and if I ever find out who took him . . ."

She glares at the statue with such a look of anger that I am shaken.

Wow. She's not just spun from starlight but has the writhing, fiery heart of a star inside her. I would not want to be the person on the other side of that.

The Peter Pan statue stares down at me. *In case you forgot, you are the one she hates, you duffer.*

"Ach." I wipe a hand over my eyes.

The girl turns her back to the statue, blinking away misty tears swelling in her eyes, and finally gives me a genuine smile.

"I'm sorry to unload all that on you. I don't usually yell at perfect strangers."

I lift a shoulder in a half shrug, trying to regain my composure. She lifts a hand for me to shake.

"Let's start over. What's your name?"

Before I can drudge up an answer, her small smile transforms into a friendly grin that lights up her whole face. I am speechless.

A few specks of golden dust drip from her open hand, catching the dusky wind and spiraling through the air. "I'm Claire Kenton."

The wind is beaten from my lungs. I can only stare at her—at *Claire*. My Claire. Connor's Claire. The girl I've been searching for, the one who can help me save Neverland.

Of course!

It all makes perfect, wonderful, horrible sense. No wonder she carries herself like a pixie, light and golden, with wisps of blond hair framing her features and with a fire that reminds me of Tink. No wonder she fits—this girl *is* Neverland.

Magic drips from her fingertips and fills her veins.

And yet as she stands before me, hand still extended, the horrible realization settles over me: she's waiting for my name. This girl who just told me how vehemently she hates Peter Pan.

I feel the blood draining from my face, my skin going cold again.

The girl who is my only hope of returning to Neverland despises everything I am.

So I do the only blasted thing I can think of. I jut out my hand and tell one of the biggest whoppers of my entire life: "I'm—Ben."

Claire's hand slides into mine. Warm and strong and right. She gives me another hesitant smile. A *surname*! Right!

Raking a glance at the gardens spreading out around me, I spout out the first word that comes to mind.

"Kensington." She raises her brows, and I huff a nervous chuckle. "Ben Kensington."

I try to think of a good way to soften the lie and not make it seem even more ridiculous, but nothing comes to me.

She shakes my hand, and while there's a hint of hesitancy in her smile, it stays in place. "No wonder you like coming here to visit, then. It's nice to meet you, Ben Kensington."

On her lips, the name sounds strangely welcoming.

But I can't ignore the sinking feeling in my gut. Or the suspicion that this twist of the truth could not only risk Neverland, but Earth as well. Claire Kenton doesn't know it, but she is filled with starlight. This girl can change everything.

Or destroy it.

15

CLAIRE

London, England

I don't usually make it a habit to spout off at hot guys with British accents, but something about Ben affects me more than I'd ever care to admit.

"Hey, I really am sorry about all this," I tell him. "I'm only here because the police told me to come."

His mouth drops open in a way that is dangerously cute. He rubs at his shaggy reddish-blonde hair, and his look of surprise settles into a smirk. "Don't tell me—Officer Darling sent you?"

Now I'm the one looking shocked. "Wait—you know Jeremy Darling?"

He leans back against the statue with a look in his eyes as if he's waiting for me to catch an inside joke.

"You're the one Jeremy sent me to find!"

His green eyes dance in the dusky light. "Right-o, mate. Any idea why exactly he'd send you my way?"

Something about his tone tells me he already knows, but I humor him. "He said you could help me find my brother and with my . . ."

I squeeze my eyes shut, hands shoved in my pockets beginning to quiver. Already flecking with dust.

"He said you might be able to explain . . . *this*." I slowly lift my fists from my pockets. Instead of shrinking away, Ben's entire face lights up. His round, green eyes soak in the golden flecks dripping from my skin.

I brace myself, waiting for his shock–his disgust.

Instead, he reaches out and takes my hands. His warm skin covers mine, the grainy sensation of my dust filling in between our touch. Our fingers tangle together, and heat spikes up my arms, but I force myself not to pull away.

Ben takes a sharp breath, but not in a shocked, disgusted way. There's a contentment, a happiness. His eyes are closed, face lifted toward the sky.

I wish I could see what he sees.

Then his eyes open, and a gigantic, boyish grin spreads across his lightly stubbled features. He pulls me across the cobblestone walkway and onto the grassy knoll behind the statue.

"Ben, what are–?"

"Don't you want to know what it is? How it works?"

He's still holding my hand, which is making me flush, but his beaming smile prompts me to nod. "Y-yes."

He throws his head back and laughs–a deep, echoing sound that sends a shiver across my skin. When was the last time I heard someone laugh like that? When was the last time *I* laughed like that?

He lets his touch slide away from mine, but his palms are now coated in the dull golden flecks.

Ben rubs his hands together, sending the dust spiraling in a small cloud around him. "What do you think it is?"

As I watch the flecks glimmer in the early-morning light, I shrug and blow a wayward strand of dust-speckled hair out of my eyes. "I don't know. Some kind of skin disease, or something?"

His laugh is so incredulous that I stumble back a step, grass crunching beneath my heel.

Ben waves a hand, letting the dust whip around his fingertips, and then tosses me a lopsided grin. "No, Claire. There is nothing wrong with you." He cups his hands, lifting them toward his lips. His eyes dance as he catches my gaze. "There is magic in your veins, Claire Kenton."

Then he blows on the golden flecks coating his hands, and the dust explodes toward me, swirling and catching in my hair. Dramatic, much? But . . . it's kind of cute.

"Magic? How is that even possible?"

The dust grows thicker, blurring my vision. This can't be real. A curse, I could see. But *magic*?

"How is anything possible?" Ben's voice echoes through the gardens, but when I've managed to swat the dust away, he's nowhere to be seen. The grove is filled with glimmering flecks of gold.

"All it takes is a little bit of faith . . ."

At his breathless whisper, I swivel and gasp as I catch him a few feet behind me, covered in a cloud of shimmering dust. His arms are firmly planted on his hips, and he grins. "And trust . . ."

He lifts his hands and swirls them through glimmering golden specks that ignite the air around him. I almost don't recognize my own dust, the way it glows and flickers against the forest-green of his jacket.

Ben gives a delighted, slow-burn smile that makes my breath catch.

"And pixie dust."

Then he glances down, and I do too.

My head goes light, vision whirling. Ben Kensington isn't standing on the grass. He's hovering above the ground, no shadow visible in the dim light.

"No. Way."

My stomach does a somersault. Fear and nausea kick through my veins, knees going weak. How could my dust possibly . . . ?

"Wait, Claire, don't—"

Ben thuds to the ground, landing in a half crouch. The dust around him begins to sink to the ground as well.

"I-I'm sorry. I don't even know what that was—"

My gut lurches. I'm going to throw up. He was practically covered in that cloud of dust. If I had freaked out, if it had started burning . . .

I turn and make it a short distance away before I'm bending over, retching. Eyes wet and stomach twisting and knees shaking. Unable to fathom what is even happening. *Magic?* How on earth could grimy flecks that can burn skin from bone ever be considered magic?

He's got the wrong girl. I'm no pixie.

I feel a gentle hand on my back when I finish losing the contents of my stomach. Ben hands me a leaf filled with water from the lake. It's not a bathroom sink, but it'll do.

I splash the water on my face, clean myself up the best I can, and dig a stray mint out of my pocket and quickly pop it into my mouth. I chew it down and lift my eyes to meet Ben's gaze again.

"S-Sorry . . ."

We take a few steps toward the cobblestone walkway, and my hollow bones grow stronger.

Ben glances down at me, brow arching. "Why do you keep doing that?"

"Doing what?"

"Apologizing for things that aren't your fault."

I look away. He doesn't move. I bounce on my heels a bit in the soft grass.

"I'm not sure. I just seem to . . . make things worse."

I bat at a stray fleck of dust that drifts by my nose, but Ben reaches out and gently catches it. Balances it on the pad of his thumb. Then he lifts those startlingly green eyes and studies me. Like a child who can't understand why their mother is crying.

"You have no idea how special you are, do you?"

I cough a bitter laugh. "If by special you mean freakish? Then, yeah. I have a pretty good idea."

He shakes his head. He reaches out for my hands again and presses his fingertips against my palms, coating them in dust. Then he reaches for a stray leaf at his feet and skims his fingers along its edge, leaving behind a thin trail of dust. He gently tosses it into the air.

The leaf starts to rise toward the brightening sky, spinning and glowing a faint golden hue.

My jaw drops.

Ben winks at my shocked expression. "You can make things fly. And you don't think you're special?"

"I-I didn't realize it could do that." Once or twice when I was a child, I might have made a toy float longer than usual. But then my dust turned to acid, and suddenly all I could do was try to hold it in. Hold it back.

It was a threat, a curse. I couldn't risk anything else.

But Ben just chuckles, scooping up a few more leaves and sending them spinning into the air. "What did you think it could do?"

Burn. Scar. Hurt people.

I reach for a dainty flower. Rub my thumb over the delicate petals, leaving behind tiny glimmers of golden dust. My hand trembles as I slowly lift it into the air—and let it go.

I fully expect the flower to pull apart and collapse, spiraling back to the ground.

Instead it floats and rises faster than Ben's leaves, spinning as it reaches for the stars.

It's beautiful.

Tears come to my eyes. "What am I?"

I feel the warmth of his breath as Ben whispers in my ear.

"You are the daughter of one of Neverland's most magical creatures. That's why you can create pixie dust."

Pixie dust?

Neverland?

My world starts to spin again, and I grab on to Ben's steady shoulder, trying to control my anxiety. Doubts kick in, threatening to turn my dust to ash. I won't let myself unravel. I want to understand this. I *need* to know this.

All my life, I've believed the pale flecks were a disease or a curse. A dark side of myself to keep hidden.

But for the first time, I see something . . . different. A side that isn't toxic and broken. Even now the flecks that trickle from my fingertips gleam a healthier color than before.

I could almost believe that it's pixie dust. A magic too whimsical to explain.

"You think I'm part pixie?" I feel dizzy.

"Are you going to lose your supper again?"

I straighten my cardigan and lift my shoulders. "It's just a lot to absorb."

Insane, actually. This is all insane. But, if I follow his wild story . . .

"Does that mean Peter Pan is real too?"

Ben nods, shifting weight from one foot to another. "Aye."

I narrow my eyes at him. At this boy who can fly and knows more about pixie dust than seems natural. This boy from Neverland. "How do you know so much? How do I know *you* aren't Peter Pan? Why should I trust you?"

His face blanches. He gives a hacking cough, then slowly shakes his head. "I know so much because . . . I was there. I was one of Pan's Lost Boys. That's how I know about your dust. And I saw him . . ." His expression is carved with pain and furrows of anger. "I saw him destroy everything."

I stare at this boy for a long moment, weighing his words. But the gravity in his eyes, the haunting echo—you can't fake that. I know that look too well. And his explanation holds up as much as claiming to be a fairy tale character can. Besides, a *police officer* sent me here. That has to count for something.

"Did Pan really take my brother?"

Ben's hands fidget with the drawstrings of his hoodie as his gaze traces the distant horizon. The moment stretches out, an eternity of waiting and hoping and disbelief in those few seconds.

Then he finally lifts his head and meets my eyes. His gaze sparks and sizzles with intensity. "I know what happened to Connor, but you aren't going to believe it."

I close the space between us in an instant and grab him. "I *need* to know, Ben. No matter how crazy it is, I need to know."

I practically met Captain Hook. I've already got one foot in crazyville. What's another step?

His lips twitch with a teasing hint. "Once I tell you, there's no going back."

I've flown halfway across the world for these answers. "So be it."

"Okay, I know what happened to Connor and how to find him." Ben's hands land on his hips again as he tilts his head at me. "But first you have to tell me . . ."

I'm hanging on every word.

He smiles and says in an alluring whisper, "Do you trust me, Claire?"

And for some reason, I, Claire Kenton, the girl who doesn't trust anyone but Connor . . . who doesn't believe in fairy tales . . . who threw herself from a second-story window desperate to shed the weighted numbness . . . the girl who spent everything she had on a wild search for a brother the rest of the world has forgotten . . .

The girl no one wants. The girl who doesn't want anyone.

The girl who is a closed book.

That girl. She looks up at Ben Kensington, a boy she has known all of two hours, and says four words she never thought would leave her lips:

"Yes. I trust you."

16

PETER

London, England

Claire Kenton has just agreed to trust me and my wild plan to save Neverland.

Then why do I feel so—*guilty?*

Oh, it might have to do with the fact that I just sold her more lies than would fit in the *Jolly Roger*'s hull. Cor, what am I doing?

Saving my own skin and all of Neverland, that's what.

I finally realize I've been having a conversation with myself for the past minute when I glance up to see Claire watching me. Blast—she's waiting for me to dish on her brother.

I clear my throat, balling my hands in the material of my forest-green jacket. "Well, it's a bit of a long story. Let's find a place to sit."

While I find a way to spin a yarn that will convince her not to hate me, Ben Kensington, but to hate Peter Pan.

This should be a jolly good time.

I lead Claire away from my statue—ignoring the sense that its beady bronze eyes bore into me judgingly—and toward a little wooden bench beside the Long Water hemming the grove. I perch on the edge of the bench, one leg slung over the arm of the seat, and turn to watch as Claire settles onto the opposite end of the bench. She perches on the seat lightly, with all the gentle grace of a sprite.

Good gad, if she's not part pixie, then a pox on me.

Claire folds her hands in her lap, angling her head at me. "So, how do you know so much about all of this?"

I shift a little away from her, placing my elbow on the back of the bench and leaning my chin into my palm. I let my eyes scan the path that winds around us, taking in the sunlight peeking out over the glistening water.

I used to love to fly at this time of the day.

I take a deep breath and start telling her as much of the truth as I can. "I was a Lost Boy in Neverland for years and years, until recently when I was forced to escape and fall to Earth. I've been grounded here for months, trying to find a way to get back and save Neverland."

"Neverland, really?"

I nod. Her lips purse, but her eyes round into an inquisitive stare. "Save it from what?"

"Not what—*who*."

A little tremor ripples over her shoulders. I'm about to continue when I catch sight of a shadowed silhouette out of the corner of my eye. My instincts snap to attention, and I vault off the bench, eyes darting over the dim gardens winding around the lake.

A lone figure is treading soundlessly down the cobblestone path toward us. I relax, recognizing the lithe form. I've been the cause of the stubborn set of those shoulders more often than I'd care to admit.

Tiger Lily.

I heave a breath of relief—and then that breath turns frigid and strangling. *Lily!* The minute she gets close, she'll call me by my name or do something to spoil the ruse.

No, no, no, no!

"I—uh—wait just a tick." I sprint across the grass toward Lily.

Cor, slow down! You look like some kind of guilty blaggard. I force myself to slow as I reach Lily, a confused frown across her smooth, ebony features.

"What's going on, Pe—"

"*Ben*! It's Ben."

She stops abruptly, and her dark hands tighten around the woven grip at the center of her staff. My nervous feet can't stand still for one blooming moment.

Calm down. It's just Lily.

Yes, Lily—who can spot a lie from a mile away. Who chose to fall to Earth with me instead of fulfilling her birthright as the ruling chief of her people because she believes I'm the key to saving Neverland.

I doubt she ever thought I'd do it this way.

"All right, *Ben*, what's going on?"

Lily leans around me, eyeing the blonde girl I pray to the stars is still sitting on that park bench. Lily wears a thick navy blouse that hangs to her knees and brushes against her leather trousers. Her teal-tinted dark hair fringes her cool expression.

I forgot how unnerving it is to be on the other end of that granite stare. "Well, I—uh—I found her! Claire. Good news, right?"

Tiger Lily's eyes go large, and she takes a quick step around me, staff thudding against the cobblestones as she stares at Claire.

I quickly offer assurance. "Yes, Jeremy sent her to the gardens hoping she'd run into me."

"Great! We can explain everything now. Let's go—" Lily starts to head for the girl, but I grab her wrist. I can feel the quick, surprised jolt of her pulse beneath my fingertips.

Tiger Lily wrenches her arm away and spins to glare at me. Her eyes spark, and the thick staff begins to spin in a slow circle around her.

Not a good sign.

"Peter . . ." Her voice sizzles. "What did you do?"

I try to pour some honey into my tone and take a slow step toward her. "You see, it's a long story . . ."

She swings the staff to slam it against my chest.

"Cut the rubbish. What did you tell her?"

I heave a sigh, wrench my hands through my tangled hair, still slick with a few specks of Claire's dust, and tell Lily the whole story. My gaze darts back to Claire a few times, but she stays on the bench, watching us and fidgeting slightly.

She'll have her answers soon enough. One way or another.

As I finish my explanation, Lily lets the staff drop away. She's deathly silent, hiding any reactions behind a calm, commanding expression that only makes me more nervous.

When done, I pull the hood of my jacket over my head and take a step back. Preparing myself for the volley of disapproval and reminders of how much of an idiot I was to think I should lie to the girl we've been searching for.

If there's ever a time I wish I could fly and put a few more inches—or miles—between Lily and me, it would be now.

But instead of giving me a royal tongue-lashing, Lily remains silent, and I can see the thoughts churning behind her calculating brown eyes.

"She really hates Peter Pan?"

I give a stiff nod, wrinkling my nose at the twisting in my chest.

"But she seems to trust you? As Ben?"

Another nod. The breeze starts to warm as the sunlight rolls across the cobblestones.

Lily shakes her head and sighs. "Well then, let's go tell her what happened to her brother."

My eyes snap wide. "Really? You'll go along with it?"

Her dark fingers tick against her staff. "I don't have much choice."

Together, we go back to the park bench. Claire is seated at the very edge, looking like a nervous rabbit. Lily slows down, letting the staff hang loosely, and gives Claire a smile.

"Claire Kenton?" She extends her hand.

Claire rises from her seat, a slight quiver skimming over her pale hand, but she reaches out and takes Lily's.

They stand like that for a lingering moment—one pale, gold-flecked hand interlinked with a dark one. Glimmering silver tattoos peek out from beneath Lily's long sleeve. The heir of a tribal chief and the daughter of a pixie.

Hook has no bloomin' idea what he's up against.

Lily's expression slips into a bright grin that lights up her whole face. "I'm Tiger Lily. You have no idea how good it is to finally meet you."

Claire's mouth falls open, and I fight back a smirk as those glimmering blue eyes dart from me to Lily and back. "Tiger Lily—like, from the story?"

Lily gently releases Claire's hand and gestures for her to sit again. Leaning her spritewood staff against the edge of the bench, Lily positions herself on the opposite end of Claire.

"It's no story, but yes. The same tribal princess."

She gapes at Lily. "You're . . . not what I expected."

The warrior princess winks. "Let's just say Barrie got a few of his details wrong. My people are Neverland natives, we've lived there for generations, but that's about where the cultural similarities end."

I hold back a little chuckle, once again reminded of how different the warrior princess in front of me is from the depictions of her in the storybooks. This Tiger Lily has a sense of bold, untamed power and freedom that Barrie could never capture, born on the island with Neverland in her bones.

Claire's face pales. "So, you're from Neverland? You both are?"

"Yes, and we can tell you what happened to Connor. If you'll let us."

Claire rubs a hand over her eyes, her lips pinching together for a second. Then she offers a shaky nod. "After everything I've seen, everything Officer Darling said, I think I have to believe it. Connor always did believe in fairy tales. Maybe he was right."

More right than she can imagine.

But Connor once believed in a lot more than fairy tales. More than just the whimsical stories—he was also entranced with the darker myths. The sides of Neverland that I'd never cared to dabble in.

Focus, Peter!

As Lily asks Claire how she is feeling about all of these developments, they have a moment of girl bonding that completely eludes me, and I settle down on the grass in front of them, sitting cross-legged. I watch them for a whole minute before I let out a long groan. Followed by a cough.

Followed by a rather loud, "Are you two going to jaw on all morning?"

The girls stop mid-word and swivel to stare at me.

Lily seems vaguely amused. Claire looks a little shocked.

Better get used to it, sweetheart.

"Shall we get started? Or do you want to keep admiring my good looks?" I wink at Claire, and her face turns bright pink. I fight back a ridiculous grin.

Lily coughs, rolling her eyes at me. "Yes, we're ready."

I pluck a strand of grass, rub it between my fingers as I meet Claire's dazed expression. "Are you ready? Because this is going to be a doozy."

Lily snorts, blowing a strand of hair out of her eyes. "Oh, stop being dramatic."

I stick my tongue out at her. "Look who's lost her sense of a good tale! I remember there was a time when your whole tribe would gather around to hear—"

She shoots me a glare, and I realize Claire's eyes are starting to glaze over. I can practically see her sinking back into her shell. I'm not so good with shy people. Or anyone mildly grown-up. Much better at slaying pirates and commanding escapades.

Well, you'd better learn pretty blasted fast.

"When I was a lad, I was taken to Neverland."

At my words, Claire's expression clears as her eyes fix on me. Lily coaxes me forward, even as a warning hovers in the way her brow ripples. Tread carefully here . . .

"I was kidnapped by Peter Pan, just like your brother and so many other boys." There's a sharp stabbing between my ribs. A hesitant suspicion that this story may not be as fabricated as I'm trying to convince myself.

"At first, things were great fun. Peter let the boys run free and have all sorts of fantastic adventures. Neverland was a beautiful place."

I cross my arms over my chest, wishing my jacket was a little thicker.

Claire scoots to the edge of the bench. "Then what happened?"

She reaches out a hand to catch a bead of sunlight that dances across her skin.

That's the question, isn't it? What happened? When did we go wrong?

Lily's steady voice fills the eerie silence. "Something changed. Shifted."

I can't bear to look at her eyes, and she can't seem to meet Claire's.

"Peter became selfish and proud. He decided he didn't want to answer to anyone. That he didn't want to share what was his—and as his soul cracked, as the shadows seeped in, so did Neverland. The island broke."

I think I see tears glisten in Claire's eyes. As if she grieves for the island too. If only she knew how deeply connected she is.

Lily continues. "Neverland shattered. It began to fall apart, to break, and as it did so, Peter continued to spiral. He couldn't pull himself out of it, couldn't control it. He only became angrier and more twisted. And as the island was desolated, even the pixies that fled here to Earth were weakened. But it wasn't just Neverland that he began to tear apart—it was the people too." Lily's voice breaks.

Claire gasps. "Wait—your people? He hurt them?"

"And the Lost Boys. Everyone. They stopped being his friends, his brothers. They became something else to him, and he grew so fearful of losing them that he held them with an iron grip." Her eyes go to me. "Ben and I tried to fight back, and he cast us out of Neverland. We barely escaped with our lives."

Claire falls back against the bench like she'd hardly been breathing.

"I had a feeling it was something horrible, but that is just . . ." She shakes her head as if to clear it. "So, Connor is still there? In Neverland? With Peter?"

"Yes."

But Connor really isn't waiting for her. Not in the way she thinks.

I lean back, planting my hands in the grass and muster a smile that would convince even a pirate. Because this is the important part. This is what could save Neverland.

"Yes, Connor is in Neverland, along with so many others. And the only way to get back to him and save the island is to fly there."

Claire brings her knees up to her chest and looks at us over them. "Fly?"

"Yes, using pixie dust." Lily gestures with her hands, her tone coaxing. "We would have gone back weeks ago, but the pixies have become so weak. Not to mention that most of the ones on Earth have been threatened with extinction if they help us."

"Good grief! Peter really is a psychopath, isn't he?" The hint of fierceness bubbles beneath Claire's words. "What about Hook? How does he play into any of this?"

My mouth goes sour. "That blaggard is still as wretched as ever. But when Pan lost control, not even Hook dared cross him . . ."

Lily nods, her eyes growing darker, haggard. "It's all turned upside down. Hook now manages the Lost Boys—some of them have practically joined his crew. The pirate captain is pretty much allowed to run rampant however he likes. Thus the mansion and pirate gold he's hoarded on the outskirts of London."

Claire's eyes round and she murmurs, "So it was him . . ." She leans forward. "So, how do we stop him? How do we get my brother back if everything is pretty much in Pan's control?"

She really seems to be buying this convoluted version of the truth.

Cor, this lying bit is going better than I thought it would.

"That's where you come in. Your pixie dust is the key to everything. If you can learn to master it, you could help us all get back to Neverland."

Claire looks at us with a doubtful expression on her face. "My dust could help me get to Connor?"

Lily and I nod simultaneously. "Yes."

Claire rubs at her forehead and a few flecks of gold fall from her fingertips. "But I can hardly make a leaf float, let alone three people. To fly to another *world*?"

I wish I could tell her just how powerful she is. She could lift an entire ship and crew into the air if she so chose.

But she's not ready for that. Not yet.

Instead, I leap to my feet. "I know how to navigate the stars and can guide you there. As for the flying bit, we'll teach you. You're capable of more than you can ever imagine, if you'll just let us show you."

Slowly, she straightens in her seat and searches my eyes. As if she's desperately trying to believe my words. The rising sun's rays dance across Claire's uncertain expression, and Tiger Lily smiles at her.

"Claire, I'm guessing you've probably always felt a bit like an outcast in this world? Am I right?"

Lily reaches for her staff. She lets her hands roll over the woven grip—a patchwork of vibrant colors that are the closest thing she has here to the neon war paint of her people.

She tilts her head toward the blonde girl. "I know that you're different because we all are. We don't belong here. You don't belong here, Claire."

More glimmers of dust seep from Claire's skin and catch the breeze. Lily watches them rise. "But where we come from, you more than belong. You can thrive in Neverland. But only if you let yourself believe that."

I cross my arms over my chest. "She's right, you know. You can be so much more than this, but only if you want to. If you stay here, you can grow old and spend your days in a cubicle and continue to never feel like enough. To never belong. Or . . ."

I reach out toward Claire with an impish grin.

"Or you can come with us where dreams are set free. You can be Claire, the girl who saved her brother—and all of Neverland. You can be *extraordinary*."

She just sits there, staring, staring, staring. My gut twists tighter than a salt-riddled piece of rigging as her mouth thins into a frown.

No, no, *no*!

"I—this is just a lot to process, Ben."

I rub a hand over the back of my neck and let out a low whistle. "Ah, right. Well, maybe I can show you a bit more of the flying stuff?"

I bounce on my heels, pulse already spiking in excitement, but Claire's eyes half close. "I think . . . I just need some time to process what all of this even means."

Rejection stings the back of my throat. "Are you sure? I could—"

But before I can get another word out, Lily's elbow slams into my ribs. Hard.

She shoots me an iron-sharp glare and then gently pats Claire's arm.

"Don't worry, Claire. We'll give you some space." She wields that glare in my direction again. "Time to think without *some* of us talking your ear off."

'Ey! Low blow, that.

"But just remember that the longer you wait, the more danger you and your brother could both be in. If we've found you and know what you're capable of, who knows who else could too. Hook, the Lost Boys . . . any of them. The more time you spend deciding is more time they have to come after you."

Claire's breathing staggers. "Oh! Okay. Thanks for warning me. I'll be careful—and try to sort things out quickly."

With a nod at the younger girl, Lily sidles toward me, her gait ridiculously silent as I jog in place on the spongy grass. "Do you ever stop moving?"

I make a face. "Do you ever stop asking barmy questions?"

She quirks a brow at me and leans forward to whisper, "You'd better watch this lying habit of yours. You may have convinced Claire for now, but if she finds out what's really happening—you could lose her for good."

And if we lose Claire, we lose it all.

17

CLAIRE

London, England

Listening to Ben and Lily banter is like watching a dizzying fencing match. My thoughts blur.

Everything I've heard sounds insane. Utterly insane. But somehow, it may be the most logical explanation of all.

Okay, so—Connor really was lured away by Peter Pan.

It's more of an answer than anything else I've found in the past six years. And it's backed up by James Hocken and Officer Darling, as strange as those sources are.

And then there's Peter Pan himself. The boy who never grew up has apparently hit an emo phase that is not only tearing Neverland apart, but also ruining everyone's lives.

Sounds about right.

I glance down at the dim flecks of gold caught on my jacket. And then there's my dust making that flower fly—making a Lost Boy fly.

Not that I know much about Lost Boys to begin with. And with everything he's said, it makes sense. And he seems to despise Peter Pan as much as I do.

That means he's somewhat trustworthy, right?

Ah, this is going to give me a headache. I mean, an even bigger headache.

I gaze down at the cobblestones as my thoughts churn and collide, but my attention is sidetracked by Ben's scuffed shoes. They're constantly moving, as if he can't stay in one place.

I follow the shoes up from his jeans to Ben's green sweatshirt, pulled tight over strong shoulders, and find his eyes on me again.

He and Lily are both watching me with obvious curiosity. Tiger Lily has pushed up the sleeves of her leather jacket, and I can just make out the hint of silver patterns across her wrists. Tattoos. Glimmering and striking and almost wild.

There's a story there. Just like the staff she's balancing beside her.

"All right, mate . . ."

I find myself following the lilting curve of Ben's mouth as he speaks. Something about his very mannerisms make it hard to look away. Mesmerizing. Charismatic. As if this boy could talk his way out of anything.

I'll have to really watch this one's silver tongue. Flying may not be the only thing he learned from Peter Pan.

"I know we've dumped an awful lot on you," he says. "But I'm just wondering . . ." For a moment that cheeky confidence is replaced by something uncertain. But just as quickly, Ben grins again. "So, are you keen on our story? You ready for us to help you find your brother? Do you want to learn how to fly, Claire Kenton?"

And there it is. The agenda.

There is always an agenda.

With the foster parents who wanted the extra income. With the girls who wanted attention from being around the mysterious new kid. With the boys who wanted your kiss but not your heart.

But when I examine Ben and slide my gaze to Lily, I'm surprised to find a different expression on their faces. There's nothing greedy there. I am no mere commodity to them.

They seem sincere. Desperate, maybe, but sincere.

Maybe they don't want to *use* me. Maybe they just *need* me.

Ben runs a hand through that thatch of reddish-blond hair, and I catch a glimpse of something in his eyes that I haven't seen in a very, very long time. It's the way Connor used to look at me when he tried to convince me to go on an adventure with him.

It's childlike hope.

And it stirs up the smallest grain of hope in my chest. I look away. "I . . . need a bit more time to think about it."

Ben's shoulders slump with disappointment. His feet still, and he slowly turns his back to me. He's facing out toward the restless lake.

"*More* time? Okay, we'll give you a few more minutes to think it over."

I can't help a laugh. "It's going to take me a bit more than that."

If I say yes—if I commit to this—then I'm all in. It's like finding Alice's rabbit hole and deciding to plunge down headfirst. Not the kind of choice I want to make in an instant.

Because if I'm wrong, then I could be blowing my last chance at getting Connor back.

"It's been a very long morning," I finally say. "I'm going to head back to my flat, and I need at least a day."

Ben spins back toward me, eyes wild. "A whole *day*? That's going to be forever—"

Lily unwinds from the bench, and in two quick steps slaps a palm over Ben's mouth. Her grip tightens on the staff in her other hand as she shoots me an apologetic glance.

"Sorry. What Ben means to say is that it's understandable you'd need time to think over such a big decision."

Lily's gaze bores into the young man towering beside her. He glares back but finally dips his head in agreement, and she releases her hold over his mouth.

"We are happy to give you all the time you need."

Ben backs away from the fiery tribal princess, rubbing at his stubbled jawline. "Cor, Lil, you could have just nudged me, y'know?"

"Just be glad I didn't have you put a cork in it."

His responding chuckle slides into a wry grin. "All right, we'll give you your time. But when you realize I'm your best chance at finding your brother, just give us a buzz."

Wow. Conceited, much?

But I can't stay mad at him for long, not with the dimples he flashes me as Lily enters her number into my phone. It seems out of place that this storybook princess has a phone, but then again, she's also clad in leather pants with hints of teal streaked through her braid. I thank her and slide my iPhone back into my pocket.

I turn to Ben. "Thanks for showing me what my dust could do, and for—well, everything."

Ben sweeps his arms out in an elaborate bow and, ignoring Lily's snort, winks at me. "I have a feeling life's always going to be a wild adventure with you, Claire Kenton."

I feel a little smile of my own rising to meet his. "My brother always said those are the best kind."

Ben gives a surprised laugh that skims across the gardens like a burst of sunlight. "That they are."

With a wave at the young man with boyish eyes and the princess with skin as dark as an enchanting night sky, I follow the pathway out of Kensington Gardens.

I walk briskly through the gardens, the sky stifled with clouds and the trees bending toward me in the slight wind. People have begun to arrive, tourists wanting to see the famed gardens and the silvery Peter Pan statue. I can't get out of here fast enough.

This place makes my head spin. The impossible merging with the tangible.

It can't be real. It can't be.

And something about Ben feels . . . oddly familiar. Too perfect.

There's still something otherworldly about him. But if I let that thought unravel, I don't like where it could take me. The darker, twisted doubts tug at the back of my mind.

And, as much as I don't want to admit it, I've started to kind of root for this Ben. Started to kind of like him.

I couldn't bear undercutting the one full chance I've been given yet at finding Connor.

Maybe these doubts are *me*.

Perhaps my own hatred and distrust of anything Peter Pan is overshadowing the elements of this story that are worth trusting. I need to keep my eyes open, but maybe I need to have a bit of faith too.

The cab drops me a short walk from my flat, and after paying with the last few bills in my pocket, I head down the alleys toward my new home. A roof over my head that I won't be able to afford much longer if I don't get a job soon.

If Ben and Lily are right, that would certainly make my search a lot clearer.

I dig out my key and push into my flat.

There's an odd chill, but I find the light switch and flick it on, bathing the room in a familiar glow that chases away some of the shadows. Still, something seems—*off*.

I'm probably just jumpy. It's been a weird day, after all.

Going into the small kitchenette, I pour a glass of metallic-tasting tap water and guzzle it down. Droplets of water land on my chin as I take a long gulp, eyes darting around the kitchenette and catching on the window to my right. A window that is cracked open.

What? I take a few hesitant steps toward the window and peer out. It's a good twenty feet off the ground—no one could have even reached it from outside. Goosebumps rise on my arms.

Maybe I just forgot to close it? Am I overreacting?

I turn to scan the room once more. Nothing is missing that I can see, and there's not so much as a new print on the rug. It's got to just be a coincidence . . .

I set the cup down on the edge of the kitchenette's counter and shove the window downward. Then the pane thuds into place, closed, and the chill begins to fade.

I let out a long breath, collapsing back against the window. It was all in my head.

"It had to be," I mutter, letting my head fall back against the cool glass, eyes closed. "No one could have climbed through that window."

"Not unless they used a rope."

My eyes fly open and the room comes into view.

I'm surrounded.

The flat is filled with a dozen young men in black jackets with hoods pulled up to shield their faces. They stand in a semicircle around me—all carrying weapons. Knives, pistols, one even carries a staff.

Fear crashes over me. I open my mouth, but nothing comes out.

One of the dark figures steps forward, hefting a coil of rope with a multipronged hook latched to the end. I can just make out a lanky frame and freckled nose beneath his jacket's hood. "You need to come with us, Miss Kenton."

"How do you know my name? How did you even get in here?" My voice cracks, and I brace against the window frame behind me. "What do you want?"

The one with the rope takes another step forward, and I stiffen, but instead of reaching for me, he speaks again. "My name is Slightly, and we're here to take you to your brother."

My throat goes dry. "How do you know about my brother?"

A broader silhouette standing toward the back of the gang speaks up. "He was one of us. Before Pan—"

"Curly—shut it!" Another voice, sharp and quick, cuts off the first speaker.

And then the eyes revert back to me. Flickering and hungry beneath their hoods.

My gaze darts over them, mind racing to piece together what is happening. Something niggles on the edge of my subconscious, something I should know, something about this that makes sense.

Slightly . . .

Curly . . .

Pan . . .

They said Connor was one of them.

And then it clicks. The fear that had paralyzed me moments ago begins to thaw, as the mystery of my intruders fades into iron understanding.

My fists close. "You're Lost Boys, aren't you? Here to drag me to Pan like you did with Connor?"

A ripple of unintelligible whispers filters through their dark ranks. The one who spoke first, Slightly, pushes back his hood, revealing a freckled face not much older than mine.

I catch sight of the phone lying only a few inches away from me on the counter. If I can just reach it . . .

Slightly takes a step closer, and I can see the thin scar marring his cheek. His fist tightens on the rope. "Claire, you have no idea—"

I dart out a hand. A metallic glint flies through the air, whipping the phone away from my reach and spearing it through.

I stare at the jagged metal blade protruding from the flickering screen. I could have lost a finger.

Instead, I've lost something worse. My last source of contact with the outside world. I have no way of contacting N again. I don't have his phone number memorized. I don't even know his last name.

No one knows I'm here.

I'm utterly alone and at the mercy of this gang.

Slightly's expression has grown cold. "You are coming with us. The captain has some questions . . ."

The *captain*? If that's who I think it is . . . then I'm really glad I didn't decide to take up his offer back at James Hocken's estate.

I slowly inch away from the window and around the kitchenette counter, hands scrambling behind me for something—anything—I can use to protect myself.

"And if I don't want to go?"

The ranks of Lost Boys stiffen. Knives glint, shoulders lower. Slightly reaches up to brush a hand over the sharp, pronged hook at the end of his rope.

His eyes narrow. "You *are* coming with us."

No space for discussion, huh?

Ben's whole most-of-the-Lost-Boys-turned-evil story is starting to feel likelier by the second. And they all seem about his age and have that same wildness. Not to mention they've practically admitted they're working with Hook.

My fingertips continue to rove behind me, and finally my hand closes around a thick metal handle. The frying pan I'd used for eggs that morning. I pull it a quarter inch closer, grip tightening, though my hands are shaking. I'm about to take on an angry, armed gang with a single frying pan. Well, it worked in *Tangled*.

I really don't have any other option. And if this is how I go out, it'll be how I've lived most of my life—fighting for Connor. Fighting for a chance to prove that I'm not a freak.

That I deserve to be here.

I whip the frying pan around, holding it out in front of me with both hands. "Stay back!"

A few of the Lost Boys laugh, others raise their three-foot machetes higher, but they don't slow their aggressive advancement. My hands continue to shake as dust begins to spiral from my skin, falling on the cast iron pan. "Stay back!" I shriek again, but they still don't stop.

Slightly releases the rope, letting it fall to the ground. "Claire, we just want to take you to Connor—"

"What? Are you insane?"

This mob really thinks that breaking into my flat, raising weapons at me, and practically threatening kidnapping is going to convince me to go anywhere with them? And then using my *brother's* name?

My dust comes out in a dizzying flurry now. The thin, dull gold flecks whip around me, sticking to my cheeks and getting caught in my hair. They coat the frying pan. The Lost Boys seem to have finally caught on, and Slightly's face pales. They stop moving, a few of their hoods slipping back far enough for me to see their stunned expressions.

"I didn't know she could do that," one of them whispers.

"I doubt even Pan knows," another mutters.

Pan? If I wasn't certain about how valid Ben's story was, I'm beginning to have a sense now. Everything about this fairy tale has gotten so twisted.

The fear that has been blurring my thoughts fades to the back of my mind. I square my shoulders and meet the glare of the Lost Boys.

"There's a lot you don't know about me." My angry words echo through the small flat.

This is for Connor.

I throw the frying pan.

It catapults through the air, straight for Slightly's face. He tries to duck, but it clips his jaw. He's thrown off balance, a nasty redness swelling on his jawline as a gasp rises from the other boys.

My heartbeat races in my ears when I turn to follow the frying pan's trajectory—

And I freeze.

The pan is sticking out of the wall beside the front door, sunk nearly halfway in.

Did I do that?

The Lost Boys are gaping at me like I just grew wings.

I can hardly throw a softball, let alone heft an iron frying pan.

But it didn't feel like throwing a chunk of metal. It felt light as a feather.

I stare down at the dust coating my hands and then at the specks covering the pan's handle. Is it possible . . . ?

"Well, well. And here we thought you were just a helpless little girl." Another Lost Boy pushes back his hood, revealing a busted lip and sharp buzz cut. This bedraggled group must be no strangers to scrapes. His eyes narrow at me. "Turns out, you're not so helpless after all."

He moves forward, and the rest of the Lost Boys surge around him.

Slightly cocks his head at me. He reaches for the rope again and swings the pronged metal end in small circles.

"You're just full of surprises, aren't you, lass?"

I reach for a butter knife and fork I noticed sitting in the sink behind me.

"Oh, I wouldn't do that." Slightly thuds across the scratched floor toward me.

The utensils quiver in my hands. The wave of shadowed bodies, rancid breath, and sharp weapons presses in on every side. I have nowhere to run.

Slightly lets a length of rope slip through his hands, ready to tie me up and cart me off.

"We've been given orders not to hurt you . . ." Slightly raises a brow at the rest of the Lost Boys clustered around him and gives them a quick nod. "But that doesn't mean we have to play nice."

The Lost Boys let out loud, echoing hollers that turn my blood cold. Then they surge in, weapons raised. A fairy tale has not only become a nightmare but invaded my real life.

And there's no waking up from reality.

18

PETER

London, England

I stand in the same nook of Kensington Gardens for ten agonizing minutes after Claire has disappeared before my last shred of patience snaps. I spin toward Tiger Lily.

"We can't just let her walk away."

I kick at a stray twig.

"Not to mention, once Hook realizes we've found her—*talked* to her, even!—the codfish's going to do everything he can to get to her."

To ruin my last shred of hope.

Lily just keeps sitting there, brown eyes cool, spinning her staff across her lap, not saying a blasted word. I stomp across the worn cobblestones over to her.

"C'mon, Lil. She could be in trouble. We need to go make sure—"

"I agree."

"—that Hook doesn't hurt her or—wait?" I blink. "Did you say you *agree*?"

Lily's expression sombers. "Yes, I did. I agree that by meeting Claire and telling her everything we did, we've no doubt made her even more of a target for Hook."

I shake off my stunned stupor. "Right. So we should keep a close eye on Claire and do what we can to protect her."

"Wow, Peter. That almost sounded like a halfway responsible plan."

"Now, don't get ahead of yourself." I head for the small fence rimming the walkway. I quickly hop it, aiming for the small outcropping of trees across from us. "If we cut through the brush, we can trail Claire so we can find our way back to her house."

"Ah, so now we're stalkers?" I don't see the eye roll, but it's undoubtedly there. I do catch a soft thud as she follows my lead, jumping the fence and going on into the hedge of trees. Her staff makes a soft swish as she bats low-hanging branches out of the way.

She stays just inside my peripheral vision with an eerie stealth, despite carrying the staff. Her grace makes me look like a lumbering fool. My feet seem to keep finding every stray twig and unsteady rock in this grove.

Never had this problem before. When I could fly.

When a girl's blooming smile couldn't unhinge me like this.

"What if something does happen to Claire? How are you planning on protecting her?" Lily's voice is so soft it almost blends into the morning birdsong.

I shrug. "I have my ways."

I duck through the hedge and out into polished grass bathed in dappled sunlight.

Lily moves to my side. "Of course you do. And undoubtedly it will be entertaining."

That's half the fun, isn't it?

I've prowled these gardens more times than I can count—or

even remember—and so I lead Lily quickly around back corners, cutting across lawns. We reach the nearly empty exit just in time to see Claire duck into a cab.

Well, now it's getting interesting.

Lily flags down a cab of our own, and we tear down the road, following Claire at a distance. We pass dark streets, alleys, and towering buildings, but I am fixated on the distant glint of Claire's cab weaving through traffic ahead of us. Focused on this girl I've lied to, who I've asked to trust me when she has no idea who I really am. Though she seems to have an understanding of the damage I've caused. *Cripes.* I'm mussing this up again, aren't I?

No. The word is like steel.

I won't let this play out like the last time. I won't let Hook win—he can't have Claire too. Can't take her from me like he's taken everyone else.

The thought settles over me like the drizzle of rain that fills the city just outside this window.

"Maybe there is a way we could tell her the truth. Once she gets to know you, we can change her mind about what she thinks of Peter."

I look at Lily in astonishment. She's trying to help, but she's even more delusional than I am. "Maybe someday."

When the Guardian sent Claire to me, I'm sure this wasn't how he thought things would go. It's definitely not how I always envisioned finding the Pixie-Girl.

The knot in my stomach reminds me why the stories are there. The ones that make her hate Peter Pan. And the darkest truth of all, the one that crashes over me with every memory, every headache.

Maybe I really am a monster.

I jerk out of my seat, unhooking my seat belt and gasping for air. When did this cab suddenly get so blooming stifling?

Lily leans toward me. "Peter, are you okay?"

The cabbie glances at me in the rearview mirror, but I just shake my head.

Grappling with the side of the door, my thumb jams down the button that releases the window, rolling down the glass.

I stick my head out the window and close my eyes as the wind whips through my hair. It's as familiar as an old friend, this sensation of cool air rising and rushing past me. Lifting.

"Yeah, I'm all right, Lily."

I stay like that, chin out the window despite the honks from other drivers, until we pull off the road to stop at the same curb we saw Claire turn down.

Let's get to it, then.

I'm out of the cab before Lily can finish paying, staring at the sky. Soaking in its bigness. Then I take off down the alleyway I saw Claire disappear through a short time ago.

Lily runs to catch up with me, her staff *thud-thudding* across the asphalt. "Aren't we trying to be inconspicuous?"

As I tread through a shadowed back street, my skin starts to crawl. Something's off . . .

I turn another corner and see a row of dilapidated flats in the distance. One of them has a door that is standing partially open.

"Peter . . ." Lily's voice is a taut whisper. We slow our steps. She raises her rod, fist wrapped around the grip. She senses it too.

We walk silently toward the flats, scanning the area for any sign of big, burly, and ugly pirates with bad taste in tattoos—but all that greets us is the ghostly stillness of the morning chill.

We take a few more steps, Lily as coiled as a predator.

Then a loud crash and a scream break the silence.

We take off, and I race past Lily. I can hear the sounds of a fight coming from the flat. It must be Claire's. I take the stairs in two leaping steps.

If Hook thinks I'm letting her go this easily . . .

I enter the room, curbing my footsteps to silence my entrance. Tension ripples through every muscle as I take in the fray.

A dozen Lost Boys in dark coats fill the small flat. A blonde figure stands on top of the kitchen counter and flings anything she can get her hands on into the threatening crowd.

Have to give her points for creativity.

Claire's hair is as wild as the look in her eyes, pixie dust spiraling around her as she raises a butter knife. Dust skims from her hands and coats the blade. With a screech, she chucks it. The blade zips through the air, clips one boy and plunges into another's arm.

Ooh. That's gotta hurt.

Behind me, I hear Lily take a quick breath. "Wow. Imagine if this girl actually knew how to fight."

Yeah. She'd not only be the magical creature Hook is looking for but also his weapon.

With another quick look around the room, I take a quiet step toward the Lost Boys, who look about ready to sweep Claire's feet out from under her and stuff her in a bag. Lily is beside me, swinging her staff in a slow, fierce circle. Our eyes meet and she gives me a knowing nod.

I shove past the nearest Lost Boy and push my way into the center of their group before they can react. "'Ey there, blokes! What? No one invited me to the party?"

The swell of animosity grows as every eye shifts from Claire to me.

Curly is a few feet to my left, stocky and—from the confusion painted across his round features—still not the brightest of the pack. Slightly is at the front glaring at me—and if looks could kill, well, I'd be dead ten times over.

The twins are here too, both carrying blades and wearing identical buzz cuts. They whisper to each other as if scheming the best way to divide my demise between them. One has a new scar that makes my throat go tight.

There is so much I don't know. So much they've survived without me.

I recognize nearly all of the boys raising weapons at me. Some are blokes I've spent decades with, racing through jungles and trapping pirates. Others I only added to the crew shortly before all of Neverland fell apart.

All thoughts of lost comradery fall away when Curly comes at me, raising a massive staff. It's like a cheap imitation of Lily's spritewood one.

"Still playing with sticks are we, mate?"

I cock a brow at him, feigning a yawn as he brings the weapon down—only to dart out of the way at the last minute, swing around, and swipe at his knees with a swift kick.

He goes down in a thundering slump.

My fists land on my hips, and I smirk at the seething gang circling me. "Who's next? I could do this all day. Oh, wait—I have. Teaching the lot of you how to cover your rears."

One of the Lost Boys growls, and the group swarms in on me.

Lily prowls around the outside of the mob, movements fast and lithe and soundless. She rounds the group and catches Claire's eye. The princess places a finger to her lips and raises her staff, ready to take out any boys who happen to notice.

I bring my attention back to the Lost Boys just as a knife comes at me. I dodge around it, spinning to the side as another boy tries to pound a fist into my ribs. Not once do they glance up at Claire.

Tsk, tsk. After all the times I've taught you how to do a snatch and grab, I would have thought you lads would be a little more savvy.

One Lost Boy tries to ram me, while another swings a rusted hatchet. I wink at the hatchet wielder. "Better watch your aim there, chap."

I duck to the side at the last minute and slam my knee into his elbow. The hatchet keeps moving, and the twit slices his own mate standing beside him.

They both fall away, one clutching his bleeding arm, while the other drops his bloodstained hatchet in confusion.

I square my stance and face the rest of the lot. Their expressions pulse with a mixture of anger and fear. I unzip my jacket and shrug it off.

"You know . . ."

I duck around another fist, heat spiraling through my muscles.

"I tried to warn you."

I kick one dark-cloaked chest, sending the boy stumbling back into two of his blokes.

"Really, I did."

I grip the sleeves of my jacket tightly in each fist.

"But did you listen?"

The twins come at me together, both brandishing daggers. My gut twists. I found these two abandoned in an alleyway and gave them a chance to really live—and now they're trying to end my life.

"Did you mind your own blasted business?"

I start at the twins, watching their eyes snap wide when I fling my jacket around both their fists clenching the knives and pull the loop tight.

"No."

Material knotted around the twins' wrists, I leap backward in a spin that wrenches their arms at unnatural angles. There's a snap. Two guttural gasps. The clang of knives falling to the floor.

"No, instead you joined the *enemy*."

The twins scramble backward, nursing their sprained wrists. I pick up my jacket, surveying the room to find that all the Lost Boys except Slightly have fallen back.

I put on my green coat and cross my arms. "Is that the best you've got? Pity, I thought I'd taught you more."

Slightly shoves aside a Lost Boy in front of him as his furious gaze bores into me. "Will you just *shut up*?"

"Will you stop taking what's mine?"

Slightly hefts a coil of rope over one shoulder and begins to spin an end of the weave that sports an ugly looking pronged hook. Then he turns toward the front door and stops.

The two girls reach the door just as the load of Lost Boys notice. Lily throws them a victorious smirk, while Claire manages a pale, hesitant wave at me—and then Lily pulls Claire through the door and out of sight. Out of earshot.

Slightly looks like he's about to combust. "What have you done, Pe—?"

"What you should have known I would do." I interrupt him, hoping Claire didn't catch Slightly's near-use of my real name.

Slightly kicks aside the remnants of a few broken plates, and he comes toward me, spinning that metal on the end of his rope again. "This is just going to make him want to kill you even more."

"Brassing off Hook is my favorite pastime. Nothing new there."

I take a step back onto a discarded blade. Sliding it to the side, I nudge the toe of my trainer under the handle.

"Now, you can either let me walk out of here right now"—I take in the haggard Lost Boys looking at us from where they slump against the shadowed walls—"or you can see what I'm really capable of."

I drag the knife a little closer and then flick the toe of my shoe, launching the blade upward. I pluck it out of the air and twirl it between my fingers, smirking as Slightly's face grows pale.

"Do you really want to challenge me to a knife fight, mate?"

He runs his tongue over a sharp incisor, watching me for a moment. Then he lowers his head, drops his rope, and takes a step back.

"Good choice."

With knife in hand, my foot skids on a spot slick with blood, and I realize what bad shape this whole place is in. Claire's flat has been torn apart. The Lost Boys don't look much better.

Curly hangs his head, but the brown eyes that glance at me are filled with despair.

I take a breath and catch hold of the doorframe. I pause on the top step and then sigh.

"I—I didn't want it to be like this, mates. I'm sorry."

Some of them nod, some of them spit, but none of them say a word. I throw one last glance in their direction before I turn away. I leap down past the steps and race toward Lily and Claire, who are walking briskly down the end of the alleyway.

Lily still grips her staff tightly, ready to take out any threat who might follow. I reach them in a few seconds, but I'm unable to get that look on Curly's face out of my head until I meet Claire's eyes and see the numbing fear in them.

I reach for her hand, and she doesn't pull away. Her skin is sallow and chilled. Not a good sign.

"Claire, are you okay? Did they hurt you?"

She shakes her head and Lily's brief nod confirms Claire's assessment.

"Okay, then we are going to get you out of here. Can you run?"

We turn a corner and Lily scouts ahead, leading the way down another side street.

Claire's quivering hand tightens around mine. "Yes, I can run." She pauses for a moment. "How did you learn to fight like that?"

My footsteps clip across the pavement. "The same way the rest of the lads did—from Pan. I just happen to be one of the best."

"Well, thank you for rescuing me. As crazy as all this is . . ." She bites her lip. "I think I believe you. About Hook and Peter and how dangerous they are. This whole magical world."

Her eyes that were dazed a second ago are now clear and determined. "Let's get out of here—and then I want you to teach me everything you know about this dust."

As we start off down the street again, I can't keep my eyes off the golden-haired figure beside me. This girl is a survivor. More than that, she's a spark.

I squeeze Claire's hand as footsteps thud in quick rhythm along the pavement, then lean down to whisper in her ear.

"Time to fly, Claire."

19

PETER

London, England

There's flying . . .

Then there's teaching someone else to fly.

I lean against a wall in our flat, watching Claire and Lily at the kitchen table. Claire's shoulders hunch under her soft blue jacket, a stark contrast to Lily's confident posture as the tribal princess lounges in wild, brightly colored dress.

"So, flying is just half of the equation? Ben also will need to guide us to . . ." Claire hesitates for a moment. "To Neverland?"

Lily smiles lightly. "Exactly. Navigating the stars is far harder than you'd expect. I don't even know how to retrace our steps back, not that I've been to Earth very often anyway. And certainly never this long."

Claire's head dips in understanding. "So I'll need to figure out how to fly, and then Ben leads the way."

"Aye, pretty much." I quip.

It's been a day since the Lost Boys attacked Claire in her flat, and yet I'm still no closer to puzzling this flying thing out.

I can vaguely remember teaching Wendy. Faint images lurk in my mind's eye of watching her faltering and falling and tiptoeing across her ceiling. Of her brothers breaking a bed trying to jump high enough to soar. Of the dog—what was that mutt's name again?—straining against its tether to join us off the ground.

There's just one thing I can't quite put my finger on.

The flying bit.

Good gad, it's like a horrible joke. Peter Pan forgetting how to fly.

Lily is never hearing about this.

I glare at the flat's high, arched ceilings. It's like the building is mocking me. With a sigh, I go back to observing the girls seated at the table with mugs in their hands. Claire takes a little sip, her brows rising.

"Mmm. This is different than anything I've tasted before. But it's probably a staple in U.K. cupboards, right?"

I muffle a snort. Try, otherworldly.

Lily stretches back in her seat, hands wrapped around her cup. "They're actually herbs from Neverland. I get batches now and then from Tansy, Jeremy's wife. She was our tribe's healer in Neverland, and we've kept up a bit since I arrived here."

I blow out a long breath. How she can be almost chummy with the Guardian's wife is beyond me.

Ignoring my sour look, Lily finishes her explanation. "Tansy brought a collection of herbs when she moved to London with the Guardian. Though it broke his own rules to do so."

Claire's cup stops in midair. "Ah, that's right. I knew he was married, but didn't expect . . ." She pauses. "He must have loved her a lot to defy his own code like that. It's got to be quite the story."

"You have no idea." Lily says. She puts her own cup down. "Anyway, how are you feeling?"

Claire pushes back one of her blue jacket sleeves, showing a hint of purple swelling on her wrist. "A little bruised, but fine."

Lily smiles, then glances at me, then back to Claire. "Are you ready to learn how to fly?"

Blast! I've taught scores of people to fly—Lost Boys, Darling children, a few rambunctious tribal boys. I even helped an uncertain pixie figure out how to use her wrinkled wings.

But watching Claire as she rises to her feet, eyes bright and golden hair an untamed halo, my mind goes blank.

This is it. This is the blasted moment I've waited months for.

I can't botch this.

I must stare blankly at Claire for several aching minutes, because she awkwardly clears her throat. Lily elbows me.

"Hey!" I shoot her a glare, but then I catch Claire's smile.

Oh, hang it all.

Pasting on a careless grin, I wave a hand at the girls. "Right. Let's do it, then!"

Funneling a mask of lucid confidence into my steps, I lead the girls through the flat and toward a small door facing the side of the building. Pushing it open, I step out onto the rickety metal porch attached to the rusted fire escape. Claire's big eyes get a little wider as she takes in the unsteady staircase.

"We're going up there?"

"Yup." Grabbing onto the nearest rung, I swing up onto the cold steel ladder, then turn to reach a hand down to her. "Up you go!"

She bites her lip, looking up at me for a long moment, and just as my pulse goes heavy as a tribal drumbeat, her hand grasps on to my outstretched one.

"You'd better not let me fall."

I grip her hand a little tighter. "Never."

Together, we scale the metal rungs toward the platform at the top of the fire escape, just a short leap from the rooftop. Claire is nimble and quick. I try not to be too aware of her smooth skin beneath my fingers, but her warmth and the grains of dust beneath my palm make every sense come alive.

We finally reach the top and I help her up onto the roof. My chest aches when I let her hand drop away. Claire pauses in the middle of the flat, rectangular rooftop, surveying the view.

"Wow . . ."

Lily follows soon after, her sleeveless dress patterned in bright, wild colors dangling about her knees. We take in the sight around us. Rooftops and chimneys and brickwork and metal gutters pierce the cloudy midmorning sun all around us. With the eerie mist seeping in, the whole city appears to be dozing.

The Lost Boys used to sleep in extra long on cloudy mornings, since there was no drizzle of sunlight to wake them. I would sit in my chair at the head of our makeshift table and listen to the rise and fall of their breaths. The peacefulness. The all-rightness of the moment.

Before I'd kick them all out of their beds and lead them into some grand rainy-day adventure.

Claire's head is tipped back, soaking in the sunlight drip-dropping through the thick cloud layer. At first, it seems she has somehow captured the shimmer of the sun itself in her thick curls. Then I realize it's just flecks of pixie dust caught in her hair.

A smile pulls at my lips, and I catch Lily smiling too. This is it—this girl is the answer. All I have to do is teach her how to do what she was born to do.

"All right, let's do this." I take a few quick steps across the rooftop toward her and reach for Claire's shoulders.

"What are you doing?" She shrugs off my hands and shoots me an uncertain look.

"Well, flight requires three things: faith, trust, and pixie dust."

Claire nods slowly. "Okay. How does it work, exactly?"

That's the real trick, isn't it?

Out of the corner of my eye, I see Lily standing back a few paces with her arms crossed, those thin silver tattoos skimming down her bare shoulders.

Don't even think about asking her for tips—you'll never hear the end of it.

I turn back to Claire. "Well, first off, there's trust. You said you trusted me and this whole crazy story—so that should be enough."

She looks a little less sure about what she believes as she eyes the distant ground.

"And then there's the pixie dust. Which you have in abundance." It seems to be multiplying by the minute as flecks swirl around Claire.

"And the last one?"

I gently guide her with me to the rooftop's edge.

"Right, the last one—faith."

I take a deep breath and bounce on my heels, eyes focused on the open air past the edge of the rooftop. It's so close. The freedom of flight. Just a few inches from Claire's feet.

This'll work. I think.

I ruffle my hair, sending Claire what I hope is a reassuring smile. "Faith is learning to trust in things that aren't there. Like trusting that your pixie dust has the capability of helping you fly. And there's only one way to do that."

My pulse starts to pound. Claire gasps, and tries to spin toward me, but I take hold of her shoulders firmly . . .

And shove.

It worked with the Lost Boys.

"*No!*" Tiger Lily's voice explodes behind me as Claire starts to topple over the edge of the building, face white, mouth open in a silent scream.

Lily springs toward her, and grasps the hem of Claire's shirt. She wrenches Claire away from the edge just before she fully loses her footing.

Together, they stumble back across the roof, sinking to the middle of the flat surface. Claire doubles over, heaving, shaking, gasping for air.

"I—I can't feel my hands . . ."

"Ah, well, this is how Pan taught—"

"*Help* her!" Lily's voice is frantic. "She's in shock! Quick, go get her some water and a blanket."

Oh.

Oh.

Maybe that wasn't the best idea.

"*Go!*" Lily's fierce shout sends me to the ladder and back down to our flat. I quickly grab a cup of water and a blanket and scale back up to the rooftop as fast as I can.

My own hands tremble as I hand the water to Lily. Claire is bent over, arms wrapped around her knees, as if trying to collapse into herself.

I did this to her.

A wall of remorse slams into me with such force, it knocks the air from my lungs.

I try to spread the blanket out around Claire's shoulders as Lily offers her the water. Claire takes it slowly, tipping back the smallest sip.

Lily drags her hands through her hair, looking ready to sock me in the face.

"What were you *thinking*?"

I shrug helplessly. "It's worked before. I thought if I could just make her believe in herself, in her dust, then it would all click together."

Lily's sharp glare spikes at me. "And you seriously thought throwing her off a rooftop was the best way to do that?"

I rub a hand over my eyes. "Now that you put it that way . . ."

Lily wraps a protective arm around Claire. "We'll find a better way without scaring the poor girl to death."

"No, we won't." Claire's voice is faint and fragile.

"What?" My heart drops. "Why?"

Claire reaches for the cup, takes another drink, and raises her head. The eyes that look up are glazed and desolate, bringing to mind another expression, a reflection of her with that same emptiness in his gaze.

My chest clenches.

"I should never have agreed to this." Claire's voice cracks as her thin fingers dig into her jean-covered knees. "It brings back too much."

I hesitantly reach out to brush away a strand of hair from her slick temple as I crouch beside her. "It was a dodgy plan, sorry. We'll find a better way."

She shakes her head, setting a few flecks of dust adrift. "That's not what I meant."

Lily tucks the blanket tighter around Claire. "What is it, then?"

"It's . . . *me*."

Claire seems to shrivel deeper into herself with these words. Fighting off Lost Boys or convincing someone of the impossible—

those I could do in my sleep. And with flair, at that. But knowing what to say to this girl right now on this rooftop? That leaves me tongue-tied.

"What do you mean?" Lily gently prods Claire, and I thank the stars again that I'm not here alone.

Claire's sea-colored eyes are barely visible over the top of her knees. "If you knew what my dust could do, you'd see that this is a bad idea."

I don't have any blasted idea how to fix this, how to repair whatever's been broken inside her. Blimey, I'm not even sure how to teach her to fly. But I do know one thing.

"You can't scare us away, Claire Kenton."

Her face tenses. "You have no idea what I've done."

I shrug as a cool breeze trails across the rooftop. "We're not going away. Not again."

I can't. I swore to the maker of the stars that I was going to get Neverland back—and that starts here.

Lily's voice is assuring. "Yes, Ben and I aren't going anywhere. We're here as long as you need."

Claire gives a little sniffle, her nose reddening, and that splash of freckles above it taunts me. Her eyes glisten with something between fear and gratitude.

Leaning back on my haunches, I grin at her. "I guess you're stuck with us, Claire Kenton."

Claire sniffles again, but her trembling lips part in a small smile. "I guess I am."

She pulls the blanket a little tighter around her, but sits straighter, and I catch the way her hands still shake. The tribal princess reaches out and gently takes one of Claire's hands, rubbing it between her own to generate some warmth.

"Claire, do you feel that? That concrete beneath your feet?" Lily's steady, earthy voice seems to pull Claire in and she turns to face the princess.

"Yes."

"Are you falling?"

Claire's looks puzzled. "No, of course not."

I watch the girls intently. Curious, but not daring to speak and break the spell.

Lily cranes her head at Claire. "Why? Why aren't you falling?"

"Because the rooftop is holding me up."

"Exactly." Lily smiles. "That's what it's like. The magic. It's there, under your feet, holding you up. You can't feel it . . ." She knocks her ebony knuckles against the dusty rooftop. "Can't quite touch it—you just have to believe it's there. Because it's so much bigger than you or me. You were born for this, Claire."

For the first time since I've met her, I see something new in Claire Kenton's expression: awe.

Lily's eyes gleam like the constellations imprinted in her skin. "By the stars, this is who you are. You have to believe that, have faith in that."

Claire looks at Lily for a long moment, as if drawing strength. Then she lets the blanket fall away and slowly rises to her feet.

"Okay."

One word, but it makes me want to throw my head back and crow.

Instead, I settle for leaping to my feet.

Lily comes and stands beside me. Neither of us say a word. Claire's eyes are squeezed closed, and the dust starts to spiral from her body, swirling and covering her in a cloud of glimmering gold. Then she lifts her chin and spreads her hands.

C'mon, c'mon . . .

I hop from foot to foot, willing her to get it. To rise off the ground.

Her toes rise a hairsbreadth off the rooftop before Claire's expression darkens. Her face pales and her eyes open with a gasp. She starts to stumble, tilting, as if she's gotten vertigo.

"Whoa there, mate." I jump forward, catching her as she tips backward. With an arm around her waist, I steady her. "You all right?"

It takes a moment before she seems to get strength back in her legs, bracing herself with a hand on my shoulder. "I think I need a moment. The height is getting to me."

You're part pixie and the height is bothering you?

But one glance at the tortured shadows in her eyes, and I know it's not just the height. It's the memories. And like a complete idiot, I've just set her fears off again by nearly shoving her off the rooftop.

Good one, Peter. You almost killed your only shot at getting to Neverland.

"We can go back inside, if you like."

She nods, and I help her back down the fire escape. Lily is on our heels with the blanket and the cup. We get Claire situated on the cot wheeled into Lily's room and then retreat to the kitchen to give her a chance to later unpack and recoup from—well, everything.

I sag against the nearest counter, glaring at my trainers speckled with dirt and a few droplets of blood from the row with the Lost Boys yesterday.

"Well, today was a load of rubbish."

Lily sits across from me, tucking her feet beneath her. "Why was it so bad?"

I drift toward the refrigerator and rustle through in search of cake or some kind of sweet. "Really? I nearly tossed her off the side of a building."

I poke my head in farther, reaching for a slab of lemon loaf in the very back.

Lily sighs. "You'll figure it out."

I tug the half-eaten piece of lemony sweetness out of the fridge and bump the door closed. "You really think this will work? All of it?"

She shrugs. "You've done it before."

I break off a corner of the loaf. "Yeah, but it's been a long time. And I've never taught anyone how to harness pixie dust, let alone create it. That's like teaching a fairy how to fly or a siren how to swim."

I shove the bite in and shake my head at Lily. "I'm just not so sure."

Lily rises from her chair and steps right up to me.

"If anyone can do it, you can. Claire may not realize who you really are, but that doesn't lessen the truth of it. Of everything you've done. Everything that your name means. You've done the impossible time and time again. So, figure it out."

Her dark eyes flash with certainty, and she points her finger at my chest.

"You are Peter Pan. You'll find a way. Doubt that again and it'll be my turn to shove *someone else* off the roof."

20

CLAIRE

London, England

In the room I share with Lily, I sit on the edge of a cot they got from who knows where, peering out the window. Shadows dart about outside, and through the wall, I can hear Ben and Lily's dim, distant voices.

Ben is clearly apologetic for the almost-getting-shoved-off-the-roof situation, and considering that's apparently how Peter taught the Lost Boys to fly, there's part of me that can't be too angry with him. It's just more proof of how much of a sociopath Peter Pan is.

No wonder Ben seems a tad off in the head himself.

Which only spirals more doubts through my fraying thoughts. What if this is just the beginning? What if next time Ben does something even worse? What if there's something they're not telling me?

Something seems . . . not quite right. Even though I can't put my finger on it.

But what's the alternative? Turn to Captain Hook and the horde of Lost Boys that tried to abduct me in my own flat? No thank you.

At least Lily seems to be fairly stable. And she and Ben have been generous enough to cover my room and board, saying that me helping them to Neverland is more than enough payment in return.

I'm stepping into their world, a place of magic and shadow that I know nothing about.

I want to call N and talk to someone from my old life—someone who isn't involved in this tangled, wild story. Someone solid and normal to just *be* there as a steady haven in this breathless storm that my life has become.

A tinge of guilt chides me. Connor hasn't even been found yet, and I'm already wishing for a way out.

But I can't call N even if I want to. My phone is history.

A frustrated sob bubbles out, and I rock forward, white-knuckling the windowsill and glaring at the world spreading out past the glass. That world is starting to click into place, but it only reminds me again that this is no fairy tale. I am unaware of how long I've sat here.

Because I'm not seeing London anymore. Not seeing this flat, this room, this place.

Instead, I'm back in California. Back in that apartment building, two stories up, jumping out of the window, glass exploding around my plummeting body.

Falling. Lost.

So, so lost.

I scrunch my eyes shut, but I'm still falling. As overwhelmed by the dizzying vertigo as I was on the rooftop when Ben pushed me toward the edge—as shaken by the memories that sickened me far more than the height ever could.

Memories of all the times my dust failed me.

When I'd leapt from that window, I was desperate for a taste of magic, desperate to feel *something*. But my dust didn't help me.

I slammed into the dumpster, shattering bones in my shoulders, scarring my back, and narrowly avoiding snapping my spine.

The scars itch beneath my shirt's sleeves, and I wrap my arms around my head.

The scars are nothing compared to the damage I've seen my dust do.

She was only trying to help when I nearly burned her to death.

Connor and I were barely five years old, playing together with the specks of my dust floating through the air. All she did was take the plastic Pegasus toy out of my hand, saying it was time to clean up.

But I wasn't ready to be done.

I started to cry—started to shriek—and my dust began to pour out. Exploding from my little form, crinkling to dark, ashen colors. Burning, singeing.

My foster mother's screams seemed to last for an eternity, even when my dust had stopped and the paramedics arrived. Even once they'd rushed her away in an ambulance, wondering at what strange chemicals must have burned her.

Her screams echoed in my mind for years.

And still echo.

I clutch my head, trying to push away the memories. I fight back the stinging tears. If Ben and Lily truly knew what I could do, they wouldn't want to help me.

I'm not a pixie.

I'm a curse.

And yet Ben and Lily have embraced what I'd always locked away. They said my dust could be beautiful. Something whimsical and magical.

Maybe I really can fly.

And that scares me in a totally new way. Because if that's true . . .

My fingertips slide down the cool glass of the window, leaving behind a trail of gold-streaked smudges.

If that's true, then my dust isn't really a curse. It's a part of me. A part I can control.

And, if so, it's not just my dust that hurts people—it's *me*.

Suddenly, the room seems to tighten like a noose pulling taut. Shrinking, boxing me in, stealing my breath.

I need some air.

I let the blanket drop away and watch as glimmering dust dribbles from my balled hands filling the room with a soft glow. It's the same otherworldly look that my dust took on that day in Kensington Gardens when it lifted Ben off the ground.

In the dim glow, I notice Lily's phone wrapped in earbuds sitting beside her bed. She did say I was welcome to use it whenever I needed to . . .

I scoop the device up, shove it in my pocket, and start for the door.

Every breath feels labored as the carefully erected wall around my heart starts to crumble, brick by brick. But if I stay like this, if I continue to lock it all inside, I'll suffocate.

I push open the door, creep quietly down the hall, and head up for the fire escape.

The minute the earbuds are in, the rest of the world fades away, music drowning out everything. It's just me and this rectangular slab of rooftop, enveloped in London mist, the stars fighting for view overhead.

The haunting rise and fall of notes whisk me far from here, a piano soon joined by a soft voice. Earnest, raw vocals skim over my nerves, settling my awkward steps.

The song swirls around me, coaxing my feet to move. And so my bare feet dance over the cool rooftop, each step becoming an extension of the lilting music.

Lifting, drawing, guiding.

The wind catches me and stops my steps. My clothes wrap around me as I continue to dance, not caring anymore what I'm doing, or where I am. I lose myself in the music. Swirling, spinning, pirouetting.

And my heart breaks open.

Clenched fists loosen.

Because as much as it scares me—here, I am *complete*. Here, I belong. The only person in the middle of an endless sky, with no one to hurt, no one to let down. Simply alive.

The dust lifts from my skin. Not cutting or burning, but rising. Whirling around me. I let my eyes flutter open, making sure I'm not near the edge, and find that my pixie dust is lighting up the whole rooftop. It shines in the mist like a reflection of the stars overhead. Pouring out. Unbridled.

I close my eyes and keep dancing, moving, whirling. Daring to hope that somehow this will work. That the two in the flat below truly can help me find Connor, and one day his laughter will once again light up the darkness as brightly as my pixie dust.

Safe and whole and home.

The music crescendos.

It almost feels like my feet aren't touching the ground.

21

PETER

London, England

Claire's been in her room *forever*.

My patience is running out faster than the plank Hook likes to dangle over the side of the *Jolly Roger*. I drop the knife I'd been practicing tricks with and go to Claire's door.

It's open. No one is inside, but I hear a slight shuffling sound and creaking on the fire escape.

What in blazes could she be up to?

Leaving Lily to her nightly meditations, I creep toward the fire escape and scale the metal contraption. As I near the top, I can hear the tap-tap-tap of bare feet skimming the concrete roof.

When my head pops above the last rung and I get a good view of the rooftop, I halt. By the stars . . .

Claire is dancing.

Her eyes are closed as she leaps and spins. Her dust twirls around her, glinting and glowing like specks of sunlight swirling from her skin.

The girl doesn't even notice that her feet have lifted off the rooftop.

She's *flying*.

I'm unable to take my eyes off her.

Cor, she's the most beautiful thing I've ever seen.

The way she spins through the air, hair framing her delicate features in airy curls, with all the gracefulness of a pixie. The dust glimmers and gleams but hardly touches her as it keeps Claire suspended in the air.

My chest thunders, the world blurring a bit as I watch her. Am I getting sick?

But I've never felt so alive in my life. I can hardly contain myself as I leap silently up onto the roof. I stand well out of her way at its edge. Even at this distance, a few specks of glowing pixie dust land on me. My jacket lifts away from my body, and my trainers lose contact with the concrete.

I grin. That pulse of magic in my veins rises with Claire. Reaching out to her.

Cor, do I miss it.

That sense of wonder painted all over her face, that belonging.

That rush of weightlessness charging each breath like electricity. That lightning storm in your chest that declares: *You. Are. Limitless.*

I inch forward for a closer look. She's now easily three feet off the rooftop, spinning in the air, her eyes still squeezed closed, contented smile on her face.

This strange girl is flying without my help and creating more pixie dust than Tinkerbell could in a week. A thin sheen of gold glosses over nearly every inch of concrete.

The rooftop is coated in it.

I tip to the side, try to catch my balance again, as pixie dust floats down like starlight falling from the sky.

"*Wow.*"

The word pops out of my mouth before I can stop it.

Claire's eyes open, and she sinks through the air.

She falls the last two feet and lands in a little heap. I run over to her, kicking dust out of the way.

"Claire! Are you all right, mate?"

She slowly raises her head, nodding dully as she takes in the rooftop around her, then squints. "Ben?"

I rub at my jawline and smile sheepishly at her. Feeling a bit like I just got caught listening in through a closed door. "Ah— yep. It's me."

"I—what happened?" Claire rises to her feet, limping faintly. Bewilderment creases her brow, then understanding dawns. "Wait, was I actually . . . ?"

I can't hold back the grin now, perching my hands on my hips. "Right-o! And all by yourself, at that."

She reaches up to tug an earphone out, slowly swiveling to take in a full view of the rooftop, as if she still can't believe it. "I was just dancing. Music always helps me process. I didn't realize . . ."

"You did it, Claire. You *flew*."

The word soars through the air like a shooting star.

Claire still looks dazed with disbelief. "Are you sure? I didn't feel like I was doing anything."

I chuckle, kicking at a few specks of remaining dust littering the rooftop. "No doubt about it. And you did it like a champ. You were made to fly, Claire."

Her eyes glisten, and I'm overcome with the strangest urge to reach out and trace my thumb along those Neversea-blue eyes. Wipe away the tears before they even have the chance to fall.

Oh, blast it all! Don't go soft now, Peter.

I cross my hands over my chest to keep them from misbehaving.

Claire blinks. "That's it? I just have to dance?"

"Who knows? Not sure if Hook would agree to a dance-off, though."

I burst into a fit of laughter, but Claire's expression darkens.

She puts out a hand. "Ben, I'm being serious. I'm not even sure what just happened."

"You found your happy thought." I say simply, holding her gaze. I don't miss the slight blush that colors her cheeks as I lean in a bit closer. "You found what you need to think about in order to fly. Now we just need to determine what exactly that was and how to repeat it. Then, you can help others fly too."

She bites her lip—blasted heck, why is that *so* distracting?—and slowly nods.

"Okay, then. So I just need to figure out how I even flew in the first place, and then drench a bunch of other people in my dust and hope desperately that it doesn't—" She abruptly cuts herself off. "Never mind. This is just amazing to have done once. I guess this magic stuff really is real."

"Amazing, huh?" I wink at her, and she colors again. Girls do that a lot.

Clearing her throat, Claire's eyes soak up the rooftop around her, as if trying to convince herself that it really did happen.

"You flew, Claire. And if you can fly"—I lift a hand to reach for the stars twinkling over our heads—"then nothing will ever hold you down again."

Claire stares at the galaxy spread overhead, a few specks of dust caught in her lashes like stardust.

"The sky is yours, Pixie-Girl."

My finger traces toward the second star to the right, winking a little brighter than the others. "Neverland is only a breath away."

For all of us.

22

CLAIRE

London, England

"Maybe it was just a fluke."

"C'mon, try again."

"I've been trying all week."

"Just think of something—"

I groan, as I sit cross-legged on the living room carpet. "I know, I know. Think of something *happy*. Like wiping that smug look off your face."

Ben shrugs, smug grin widening. "Sorry, can't help that it all comes easily to me. I'm just brilliant like that."

My frustration builds, bordering on hysterics, because I am *so* close. A few days ago, I was hovering several feet off the ground, but today . . .

Today I'm failing.

"I can't seem to do anything other than make this stupid flower fly!" I snatch the rose out of the air, crumbling the petals in my palm, and then toss the whole mess across the room at Ben.

They pelt his face, and he scrunches up his nose, laughing as he wipes them away. Specks of the pixie dust from the rose catch in his hair, lifting a curl off his forehead and making it stand on end.

I titter, the ridiculousness a thankful break from the stress of trying to do what I was apparently born to do but, for whatever reason, can't.

Ben's face goes beet red as he tries to pat the loose strand of hair back into place. I can't help but laugh.

He's just so flustered and adorable.

And for once, he doesn't realize it. Which only makes it better.

"Okay, maybe we try something on the roof?" Ben taps a thoughtful knuckle against his chin.

For a Lost Boy . . . he's kind of terrible at this stuff. Peter Pan must have not taught him very well.

"Why don't we take a break?" Lily comes out of her room to join us. "You've been practicing all day. Let's give Claire some time to rest."

I stand and look at the clock on the wall. It's well past six o'clock, which might explain why I'm feeling a little dizzy. I could use some dinner.

"Yes, I think my head hurts from concentrating for so long."

I feel like I've run out of happy thoughts—even my memories of Connor are soured from the long hours trying to squeeze joy from that tense situation. I'm locked in my own head again.

I wordlessly down the toasted sandwiches Lily offers, and even Ben seems less chatty than usual. Lily scoops his jacket up from where he slung it haphazardly over the arm of the couch and tosses it at him.

"What's this for?" He catches the coat.

"It's a little nippy outside, and since you both need to get some fresh air, I'd take it."

"You both? Us?" He looks taken aback as he gestures to himself and me. "I'm not sure I—"

Lily smirks at him. "And while you are out for a stroll, maybe you'll figure out what Claire's happy thought is."

If I didn't know better, I'd say there's a glint in her eye.

Ben huffs, tries to argue, nearly throwing his jacket at Lily—and finally sighs in defeat.

"Fine. We'll go." His eyes narrow at her. "But you'd better stop acting like such a blasted mother, Lily, or you're going to be too grown-up for Neverland."

The cold edge to his tone catches me off guard. To my surprise, Lily nods, taking a step back, shoulders curved beneath her red leather jacket.

A chill creeps up my spine. For all their banter, I didn't expect that. Whatever *that* was. The sudden show of respect. Who is Ben that a tribal princess would surrender to him without a word?

Well, at least he's doing his best to help me, if clumsily. He and Lily have given me a place to stay and are showing me how to get to Connor. I can focus on that.

I shrug on my coat as Ben finishes zipping up his hoodie and heads for the door. He doesn't bother to hold it open for me as he dodges outside, flipping his hood up over his ears.

Well, someone's in a mood.

I race to keep up as he goes down a small side alley. It's overcast, as usual, and some of the shops we pass are preparing to close for the night.

I'm usually pretty comfortable with quiet and significantly less comfortable starting a conversation, but this silence is so awkward, I finally clear my throat.

"So—uh—where are we going?"

Ben doesn't look back. "Kensington."

"Again?"

His shoulders stiffen. "It helps me think."

"Oh."

I scuttle to keep up with his long strides and throw glances at his brooding expression. He almost looks like he's pouting.

At the thought, a giggle escapes me.

Ben quirks a brow at me. My cheeks heat and I look away, but his voice is lightly teasing. "Don't try to hide it."

I roll my eyes. "I'm not hiding anything."

He grins, those dimples winking at me. "Good, because it'd be a shame to hide that smile." His voice turns sugary smooth and he leans in toward me. "You have the prettiest smile of any girl I've ever seen, Claire."

I splutter a laugh. "Oh, goodness. Really? Cheap compliments?" I mean, seriously.

Ben's expression drains, and I bump his shoulder with mine. "Does this kind of flattery ever really work for you?"

He utters a short laugh. "Generally."

And just like that, the dark cloud has evaporated and the comfortable sensation has returned.

He pauses his loping gait to scan the road for a cabbie to hail, when another thought occurs to me. I giggle again.

Ben shoots me a long look. "Cor, what is it now?

"Well, I just realized—you like to go to Kensington to think?"

"Aye. What's so rubbish about that?"

"Well, it means that you like to go to the garden named after you in order to think. Ben Kensington in Kensington. It's practically like talking to yourself."

His face blanches and he glances away. "I told you it's an old family name."

"Whatever you need to tell yourself."

"Blast, you really are—" Ben steps and swivels slowly, taking in the buildings and shops rimming the sidewalk, and the mildly busy road to our right.

"What is it?"

He shushes me, gaze continuing to dart about. Then he pauses, head tilting toward the rooftops. The city smells of must and rain and aged stone.

I crane my head back just in time to see several shadows dart across sloping shingles, backlit by the dripping orange of a sun beginning to slide downward.

My blood goes cold. Could it be . . . ?

Ben grabs me, his skin like ice, sparking green eyes boring into mine.

"*Run!*"

We take off down the sidewalk like there's a horde of demons on our tail.

Maybe there are.

Ben's hand is clamped around my wrist as he pulls me forward, leading me down one alley and through a small side door into a shop. We burst out the other side, change directions again, and keep running.

It sure would be nice to fly right about now.

My legs burn, and I see dark shapes surging around the building just before Ben leads us around another side street.

"Who are they?"

But I know the answer even before he says it.

"Lost Boys."

I try to pick up my pace. "What happens if they catch us?" I pause for breath. "Will they kill us?"

"Mate, if they catch us, death'd be a happy dream." He grins. "But they won't catch us."

He pulls me down another alley and quickly switches back to skirt around a tall brick building with ivy skimming its walls.

"How can you be so sure?"

He shrugs.

"I certainly hope you're right."

"I am."

Cocky, much?

But I almost believe him.

At least, for the next ten minutes, until my steps grow heavy.

"I think they're gaining on us," I huff, falling behind.

He glances upward at the buildings towering over us, and then back at the dark-coated silhouettes cramming the alleyway at our backs. "How keen are you on scaling rooftops?"

"What? No—you've got to be kidding."

We duck around another corner, and he heads toward the fire escapes. This is not going to end well.

But before Ben can drag me up any steps, another shadow fills the side street.

It is much, much bigger than the crowd of Lost Boys on our heels.

The air goes icy as the shadow falls across me. Even the dying sun seems to shrink. A loud howl splits through the alleyway, the sound rumbling so deep it burrows under my skin.

Fear spikes through me as I try to get a look at the hulking creature, but Ben pulls me roughly into another alley filled with low-income flats.

We duck into a doorway, my back pressing against the musty frame. Ben crams himself in after me. Rough wood pierces my jacket, and my heart is drumming so loud, I'm certain the creature can hear it.

Before I can speak a word, Ben puts a dusty hand over my mouth, raising his other finger to his lips.

"Shhh. Be quiet now," he whispers, the warmth from our bodies pressed together seeping into me.

I want to push him away, but then I realize he's trying to squeeze into this narrow doorway, too, as he tries to hide.

We stay silent for several long minutes. I shudder at the howls and growls and the thunder of retreating footsteps. But all I can see is Ben, hovering barely an inch away from me, reddish-blond hair falling over his ears and freckles splashing his cheeks. His dark eyes hold mine, imploring me not to make a sound.

His hand remains clasped over my mouth, so he doesn't need to worry about that anyway.

Even after the sounds dissipate, we stay crammed in the doorway, Ben unmoving, but his head craned, listening. Waiting.

Finally, he lets out a deep sigh. "Right, I think they're gone. Blimey, that was dodgy for a minute there."

He gives a breathless laugh. My response comes out muffled against his calloused palm.

"What was it you were—*oh*!" He pulls back his hand and gives me a lopsided smile. "Sorry 'bout that."

He steps back out into the alley, and I follow, suddenly cold without him. I pull my jacket a bit closer and trail Ben as we slink onto the small street where the Lost Boys had been only minutes ago.

The street is eerily empty save for a few massive paw prints marring the dusty gravel.

"What *is* that?" I take a hesitant step toward prints that are easily large enough to fit both our feet inside them. The imprints are ragged and scarred with deep grooves at the front of three curling toes. Whatever the creature was, it had claws.

Hands shoved in his jeans pockets, Ben stares down at the prints. His round eyes fill with recognition—and something else. He's unnerved.

"It's a Neverbeast."

"Neverbeast?" I take a quick step back. "Do I even want to know?"

But Ben just keeps staring at the massive impression.

"Ben? What's wrong?"

"I'm not sure, that's just the problem." He presses a palm to his forehead. "Blasted heck—"

He winces and his knees buckle. Worried, I reach for him. "Ben? Ben, talk to me. What is it?"

His hand is still at his temple, his eyes squeezed shut. "I'm fine."

He doesn't sound fine.

He stumbles away from the tracks, reaching out to brace a hand against one of the dingy houses lining the abandoned street. Dull beams of waning sunlight glint over his tousled hair. He groans, doubling over.

"Ben? Please, tell me what's happening." I grab his hand.

"Blast it, I said I'm all right." But he can't even get the words out without grimacing. "If I can just push through, it'll all be all right. It'll leave me alone."

"Push through what?" His skin looks sallow, his hand in mine far too cold. "Did the Lost Boys manage to do something to you? Was it the Neverbeast?"

"It's not what they did to me, it's what I did to them . . ." The words come out cracked and hollow.

I'm standing beside him. "Does this happen often?"

"Unfortunately."

I'm beginning to understand why Ben disappeared at random throughout the past week, and why Lily always shot him a cautious look when he complained of a headache.

Ben makes a strangled sound. "It's the island. The more Peter pulls it apart—the worse it affects us. Me. Anyone who was connected to it."

Droplets of sweat bead his brow, but it's his eyes that worry me. The spark of mischief that always gleams in those brilliant green irises is tarnished, distant.

Ben's features are strained, and he groans again. I grab his shoulder, trying to keep him on his feet.

"Ben?" I plead. "Ben, how can I help you?"

"Just give me a minute."

He stumbles back against the building, eyes clenched shut. His jaw is tight, a white-knuckled fist pressed against the wall "Not this time. Not this time. Not this time . . ." he mutters with every shuddering breath.

Slowly, I begin to see the lines across his forehead smooth out. His eyes drift open again, and his body sags.

I don't realize how tense I've been, unable to breathe, until suddenly we're both inhaling deeply.

Watching him like this is crushing me. Because I *care*. More than I'd ever dare to admit. And the caring can be dangerous. It starts to dim the doubts, overlaps with the acute need to have him be okay. Despite the pieces that don't quite fit, in this moment, it is all that matters. Ben being all right.

Gingerly, I draw closer. "You okay?"

"Getting there."

His hands shake as he shoves them into his pockets.

"Is this all because of Pan? The more he tears Neverland

apart, the more he hurts everyone who was connected to it? Lost Boys. Lily's people, even you?"

He flicks sweat-tangled hair out of his eyes, giving a half shrug as he lopes down the alleyway again. "Let's get out of here. Before that Neverbeast decides to double back."

"You sure you feel up to it?" I hurry to keep up.

"Absolutely. Off we go."

I follow him out onto the street, but now I'm the one trembling. If Peter can hurt people like this without laying a finger on them, what could he be doing to Connor? What would happen to someone who is literally on the island as it's being torn apart?

"I *despise* him," I say aloud. Ben stiffens but keeps walking. "When I get to Neverland, I'm going to make sure he can't hurt anyone ever again. Ever."

"And how do you plan on doin' that?"

I have no idea. "I'm not sure yet. But there's one thing I do know."

Ben is watching me out of the corner of his eye

My fists curl as I feel the dust spark. "I'm going to make Peter Pan regret ever threatening those I love."

CLAIRE

London, England

We always seem to end up in Kensington when it's dark.

I stand beside Ben, staring up at the massive iron gate circling the gardens—firmly locked shut. The air is thick with moisture, chilled enough to nip at my nose and make me pull my cardigan a little closer. The sky has already started to fade into shadow. I hadn't realized how late it was when we left the flat an hour ago.

"Well, I guess that answers that," I say to Ben, who continues gazing up at the swirling metal fence. "We'll just have to go back. You could probably use some extra rest after what happened in the alley."

Ben cocks his head at me, and gives a slow, secretive smirk. Oh, brother. What's he up to now?

"We can't go now, Claire. We've arrived just in time."

"Just in time for what?"

Ben grins again. "Well, you'll just have to follow me and see, now won't you?"

"Follow you?"

Before I can further puzzle out his words, he strides across the cobblestone walkway, reaches for one of the rungs on the swirling gate, and climbs up.

I gasp. *"Ben*! What are you doing?"

I'm thankful that the entrance to the park is empty for the moment, dreary twilight mist creeping out over the cobblestone.

At the top of the gate, Ben pauses. "What are you waiting for, mate?"

I just stare at him.

"It's trespassing!" I hiss.

I may have crept into James Hocken's estate, but that was different. Kinda.

Ben raises a brow at me, eyes twinkling with that taunting mystery. "Get a move on, Claire. You won't want to miss this."

"Miss what?"

My hands grasp the cool metal of the fence, and I tilt my head back to watch him. He perches precariously and winks at me.

"I thought we were going for a walk."

"Blimey, you overthink everything, don't you?" He leans backward enough to make me gasp before catching himself and grinning again. "There's something here I wanted to show you. Something few others have ever seen."

His voice is hushed, as if revealing a special secret, and I'm the only girl in the universe he's deigned to tell.

My face heats, and I curse myself for not steeling my reactions better. It just feeds his dramatic side. "What if we get caught?"

"Well, that's half the fun, isn't it? Come on, Claire. It's an adventure!"

His whole face lights up with delight, like a little child inviting a grown-up to see a new creation they've made. He's inviting me into his world.

Taking a deep breath, I reach for the fence and begin to climb.

"Thatta girl!"

I climb, hand over hand, reaching for the next curl of metal and pulling myself up.

I cautiously scale the gate, ignoring the way my palms are slick with sweat and dust. Trusting Ben Kensington is a bit like trusting the magic that lifts my dust.

Ben extends a hand toward me. "Up you go, lass."

I grab hold. His warmth filters into my skin, and I'm surprised by his strength as he lifts me the rest of the way up. I settle on the top of the gate beside him, knees brushing, and catch my breath.

"See? That wasn't so hard, was it?"

I look around at the craggy charcoal outlines of the buildings surrounding us, masked by the fog.

"I guess not. Let's just get down to the other side before someone sees us."

Ben swings himself over the other side of the gate and helps me down.

I take a deep breath of the thick London air. "All right, what is it that you wanted to show me?"

He shakes the messy tangles of red hair out of his eyes and cocks his head at me. "It's brilliant, I promise. Just stick close to me, and they shouldn't attack you."

"They won't *what*?"

Instead of answering, Ben grabs my hand and pulls me across Kensington Gardens, around colorful beds of flowers and beautiful fountains and through quiet groves.

The moon casts silver reflections across the gardens as we trek through, my hand tucked securely in his. We turn down a slender path, and he guides me toward a little pond on the outskirts of the gardens.

The moment I step onto the grassy knoll surrounding the

pond, I can sense a shift in the air. A sweet scent fills the earthy glade, and a soft gleam glints across the water, a golden flicker twinkles in the grass and the shrubbery.

"What is . . . ?"

Ben puts a finger to his lips and coaxes me across the little bridge arching over the pond.

At the middle, Ben releases my hand and leans against the railing, propping his elbows on the edge and peering out over the pond.

"What's going on?" I whisper.

His forest-green eyes gleam like the moon above us as he looks to the shimmering pond and the grove behind it.

"*Watch . . .*"

I lean out over the edge of the bridge, trying to make out the gleam.

The spark grows, winking to life. For a moment it looks as if the cluster of trees and hedges and wavering grass are alight with flame.

Then the gleam filling the grove begins to move.

It lifts from the foliage and fills the air before breaking into a thousand tiny pinpricks of light. Small, gleaming balls of gold that are caught on an invisible breath as they rise off the ground and begin to dart about. They fill the garden, skimming across the lake and swirling in delicate, graceful movements.

I can hardly breathe as I watch them, drifting nearer and nearer. A part of me wants to ask what they are, but an even deeper part of me already knows. Especially as the fluttering balls of golden light float near enough for me to make out the soft trail of glimmering flecks.

The thin streams of dust swirl and intersect and ignite the air like a golden crown woven through the darkness.

I don't know when I took Ben's hand again, but I'm clutching it now. My heart thunders in my chest as the glowing creatures draw closer, and I can see tiny forms inside the balls of light.

Little faces with big eyes and pointed ears. Dainty hands and little clothes made out of leaves and moss and flower petals. Tiny feet that perch on the very edge of the bridge as they peer up at us. At me.

But it's their wings that really make my legs weaken. *Wings!* Translucent, fluttering things that sprout from their backs in iridescent colors.

I can hear them now, too. The high, tinkling sound of their voices. Like soft chimes drifting on the wind, wrapping around me as their dust speckles my face and lifts tendrils of my hair.

I stand there motionless for what feels like hours, just watching the little creatures as they come to rest in inquisitive rows on the bridge and hover in the air around us. Afraid that if I move a muscle, they'll dissolve like a whimsical dream.

I'm also afraid that if I move, the tears pricking my eyelids will escape. I *know* these magical little creatures. I've never met them before, never seen them, never heard the soft chime of their voices or watched their glowing dust light up a night sky. But I know them. As clearly as I know that warm hum of magic in my veins. As surely as I know my own dust, the specks lifting from my hands, mingling with theirs in the air. Mine doesn't gleam as vibrantly, but somehow, someway . . .

We're the same.

A little cry breaks through my lips, and at the outburst, several of the little creatures skirt away.

All save one, who darts close to my face, hovering in front

of my nose and speaking in a gentle, twinkling voice that I can't understand. But the sound is lovely. Caring.

A tear slides down my cheek.

How—how is any of this possible?

As if on cue, Ben gives my hand a little squeeze and leans forward. Instead of addressing me, he speaks to the little sprite.

"Aye, she is quite beautiful. And a bit sad. But she can't understand you. At least not yet."

Startled, I look from the little creature to Ben and back again. "You can understand them?"

He nods, and I realize that he has several sitting on his shoulders, a few peeking out of his pockets, and two very determined little creatures attempting to braid a strand of his unruly hair.

He waves a hand. "Claire Kenton, meet the pixie kingdom." One of them pinches his cheek and waggles a finger, and Ben winces. "Ah, right. Meet my *family*. Many of these pixies raised me."

"Pixies?" I blink back the sheen blurring my eyes. "I mean . . . I'm not sure what else they'd be. But, real-life *pixies*. Wow."

"Aye, quite the sight, aren't they?"

The pixie that had been talking to me alights on my shoulder and begins to stroke my hair with her tiny, pallid hands.

"And they raised you?"

Ben nods again, almost shaking loose the pixies in his hair. "Right-o. When I was brought to Neverland, they did a better job than my own mum would have. Or Peter, for that matter."

The way the pixies are flocking over him, it's not hard to believe they raised him. He has a way with these little creatures.

There are still questions stuttering through my mind, but they suddenly don't seem important.

I just want to enjoy this. The golden gleam lighting up his wide eyes, and the creatures dancing around him. I'm happy for him to just be Ben, no other wonders or doubts.

"And . . . you said I can create pixie dust?"

His white teeth flash. "Aye."

As Ben leaps up onto the railing of the bridge, several pixies dart out of his way to avoid being crushed and chatter noisily at him. But once he settles on the railing, the pixies fill back in around him.

I take a slow step, so as to not uproot the pixie still nestled on my shoulder. "So, if I can create pixie dust, does that mean . . . ?"

He bobs his head, lifting a few of the little sprites out of his pocket and holding them in his palm. Two grab hands and begin to dance, swinging in a jaunty little circle. Ben's green eyes flicker in the pixies' glow as he gazes at me over them. "Again, yes. You are part pixie, somehow."

He's said it before, but it still seems unbelievable. Even more surreal. "How is that even possible?"

Ben's jaw tightens then he shrugs, sending one pixie flying and another grabbing desperately for his earlobe. "Ah—well, I'm not so sure. But we'll figure it out when we get to Neverland."

I look at the pixies. "Do you think they know?"

Ben flicks at one of the pixies, sending it spinning through the air a few times before it rights itself, apparently unhurt. "I already asked. If they do, they're not saying a word, the lot of 'em." He glares at the pixies dancing on his hand. "Blast it all, the lady wants to know."

A few of the pixies dart out of the air over our heads and chortle at him, and Ben rolls his eyes. "No, I didn't bring you any cake. I brought you a big person who can create bloomin' pixie dust! Isn't that enough for you?"

The pixies swirl around Ben, leaving dizzying arcs of their own dust as their singsong voices echoing through the air. I step closer to the edge of the little bridge and notice a cluster of pixies huddled on the wooden railing. But something's not quite right—the pixie in the middle lies on its side, one wing limp and at an odd angle.

"Aww, what happened to this little one?" I reach out to gently touch its petite hand. The tiny fist curls around my finger, and the pixie's color fluctuates to a sickly green.

Ben sidles up beside me. "Looks like the little bloke has a broken wing. Why don't you try holding it? Maybe you can help?"

My brows rise. "Help? How?"

"There's a lot we don't know about your dust. No harm in trying."

I peer down at the pixie to find the tiny winged sprite reaching for me.

Well, only one way to know . . .

I lean down and gently scoop up the pixie. Cradling it gingerly in my palm, I carefully navigate its broken wing into the right position and stroke it's tiny face. "How'd this even happen?"

The pixies hovering around us start chattering again, and Ben translates. "Something about a run-in with an angry house cat."

Poor thing.

The pixie looks so uncomfortable, pallid and green against my palm. Hoping to cushion it, I let more dust flow from my skin, pooling around the little creature. The soft, golden flakes dust the sprite's body, smoothing over its broken wing, and I find myself wishing it could feel some relief.

My dust continues to pour out, shining a little brighter.

Wishing . . .

It could fly again.

A little ripple skims through the pixie. It says something soft in that light, wind-chime voice. And then the sickly green begins to fade as the natural golden glow starts to fill in over the tiny creature.

I stay completely still. "Wh-what's happening?"

Ben's eyes have widened. "I have no bloomin' idea! But—look!"

I gasp. The pixie rustles against my palm and sits up. Then it begins to flutter its wings, lightly at first and then faster. Both of them beating together. *Healed.*

With a squeal of delight, the pixie rises into the air and does a dainty spin.

"That's impossible!"

Ben winks. "I would think by now you've seen enough impossible things to stop saying that."

I blink at the little pixie as it spins again and then sweeps forward to pelt my face with tiny kisses. "Did *I* do that?"

Did I somehow heal a pixie?

Ben beams, eyeing the pixies dancing in joyous circles around us. "I knew you were special, Pixie-Girl."

I murmur a thank-you to the pixie who has finally stopped showering me in kisses and is darting off with some of her friends. "But how did I even do that?"

"I wish I knew." Ben's expression dims, and he slides his gaze to the pixies again. "They either don't know or don't want to tell us. Both, most likely. They've been threatened by Hook, and it's got them all in a mood. It's taken weeks for me to gain their trust enough for them to come out like this."

"Well, what do they want? Right now?"

He smirks at the pixies twirling across his palm. "What pixies always want. Sweets and parties. And since I didn't bring any cake, they want to dance."

That seems to please them, as the cool air fills with the sound of dozens of lilting chimes. Ben laughs.

"Okay, okay. It's not my pipes, but I will do my best, mates."

He gently shuffles the pixies off of his palm and reaches for the cord around his neck. I like this side of Ben—playful and yet caring. Understanding their world, but also taking care of it.

It's almost what I thought Neverland should be, when Connor and I would read the fairy tale. Before I became disillusioned with the story.

This was what I thought Peter Pan should have been—light and clever and playful, but also caring for the world around him in a way no one else could.

And I like this version of me. The Pixie-Girl who, through his eyes, can make things float and heal broken creatures.

I want to cling to this image as long as I can.

Ben lifts an oddly shaped little bamboo whistle strung from the cord. There are a few holes across the top of it.

I lean against the railing to watch him. All thoughts of Peter Pan and Neverland fade away the minute Ben sets the whistle to his lips. His long, tanned fingers prance across the holes, and the tune that he draws from the thin tube is as airy as the pixies themselves.

A cheerful melody floats from the flute. Perched on the edge of the bridge, he is like an elfin pied piper.

The pixies' voices join in glee, and then they shoot up from the bridge to dance around us. They grab each other's hands, spinning and gliding and leaping above my head.

Trails of pixie dust streak across the sky, the air alive with electricity. A little male pixie bends his tiny frame in a regal bow to the pixie in a sunflower dress sitting on my shoulder. I watch her cheeks redden, and then she nods and reaches for his hand.

Together, they begin to waltz across an invisible dance floor.

The pixies spin around us, brushing my shoulders and lifting strands of my hair and the hem of my shirt with their dust.

As they dance, my own body begins to respond. Toes tapping, hands lifting, glints of dust dripping from my fingertips.

I trace small circles as my feet tap across the worn boards of the bridge. Some of the pixies skirt around me, grabbing for my fingers and the sleeves of my jacket and pockets of my jeans.

Before I know what's happening, they're guiding me into a little pirouette. Their tinkling voices lift me as they rotate my body in a light spin. My heart sings. They're dancing with me.

Why do I feel like crying again?

I begin to move my feet, but the pixies' chime-like voices only rise, and a flicker of red tinges one of the pixies as she tugs my arm hard to the side.

"Ouch. What are you doing?"

Ben's music stops abruptly. His eyes glare at the pixies tugging at me. "Take it easy on her, mates."

Their little heads snap toward him, and they chatter again. His brow creases a bit, and he nods slowly.

"What did they say?"

He leaps off the banister, glancing down at a few pixies that have landed on his flute and are attempting to blow into a hole. "'Ey—you'd better not break it," he says to them. "And wash it out once you're finished."

They give him a tiny salute and go back to their attempts to make the whistle sing. After a few tries, they get the hang of it, each pixie blowing or blocking a different hole in order to draw out a melody. It's not nearly as alluring as Ben's playing, but it's something.

Ben nears me, his expression something I can't quite make out. He cocks his head at the pixies still attempting to pull and prod me into mimicking their movements.

Several of them prattle at Ben again.

"They say that you're too stiff." He shoos the pixies away.

I self-consciously smooth out wrinkles in my jacket. "I'm trying. I really am. It's just . . ."

I pinch my lips to the side, glancing up at the pixies gliding above our heads. They dance beautifully, spinning and swirling with delicate grace.

"I don't think I could ever do it like that," I say wistfully.

Ben shoves a hand through his hair, tugging apart the half-finished braid. "You're part pixie. You were born to be weightless."

Maybe that's the problem. Since I was born, I've felt nothing but weight. Heavy, crushing weight.

I can't look at him, at the earnest, childlike belief in his eyes.

I feel Ben's hands take mine. My head tips up and I stare at him. He's holding my hands out, his own legs bent, the same stance as the pixies dancing above our heads.

His eyes spark with determination. "You need to let go if you're going to fly. Here, let me show you."

"You know how to dance?"

He grins. "You saw how determined the pixies were. Imagine living with them for years. I could dance a fairy jig practically before I could walk."

And then we're dancing, my hands in his, our bodies swaying and sweeping together. It's the kind of closeness that's horrifyingly uncomfortable for an introvert, and yet—while my face is on fire and my body feels taut as a spring—there's something almost peaceful about being wrapped in his arms.

Something that keeps me moving along with him. Ben's hands, strong and calloused against mine, press and guide and draw me in and out. He's surprisingly graceful, with perfect balance.

As we dance, the pixies drop a little lower to spin their own unique steps in the air around us. We're soon encircled in thin, gleaming strands of pixie dust, catching in our hair and sticking to our clothes.

Left, right, double step, right, left . . .

Just when I think I've got the hang of the steps, Ben pulls me in, one hand dropping to hold my waist. We are so close, I can see the splash of freckles on his cheeks in the dim light. His face is flushed, a hesitant gleam hidden behind the playfulness in his eyes.

Ben's body goes taut when I brush against him for a minute, as if this has caught him off guard. As if he's not sure if he should run for it.

Please don't run . . .

I meet his eyes again and realize just how close we are. Our noses almost touching, breathing the same air. Running is the very last thing I want this boy to do. I want him to *stay*. Us to stay. Like this.

Whole.

That spark of hope and lightness that I see in his gaze? I want to be wrapped in it, be surrounded by it. Because if he can see me like this, if he can somehow see beauty and light in this shattered girl, maybe I can see it too?

The moment snaps. Ben takes a deep breath and twirls me out again.

My stomach is filled with beating wings, and my heart pounds.

Then the doubts set in.

What if I'm reading into this? What if I'm making a total fool of myself?

Heat spirals up my neck, all of the awkward repercussions of developing not-so-little feelings for Ben dive-bombing through my thoughts.

Before I can collapse into a puddle of red-faced horror or spin back toward Ben—

I trip.

My foot hits a loose nail and I tumble toward the banister and slam into the side of the bridge. I'm so dizzy that I lose my balance, and tip forward . . .

Right over the edge.

I throw my arms out and close my eyes tight. Ben's face is the first thing to pop into my mind. A distant hope that somehow he'd catch me.

I await the icy water, my mind's eye locked on Ben.

But—no water.

Instead I hear soft chimes.

I pry open one eye to find a pixie hovering in front of me, waving her arms wildly with an impish grin on her face.

I let the other eye pop open and dare to peek down.

I'm hovering a foot above the glassy surface of the pond.

Hovering.

Ever so carefully, I turn my head to the side and can just make out Ben's shocked face peeking out over the bridge several feet above me. And then his face fills with a slow, triumphant smile.

"Look, Ben! I'm—"

But as I call up to him, a wave of embarrassment hits me.

With a scream, I splash into the icy water below.

24

PETER

London, England

I race down the bridge and around the side of the small pond, crouching at the edge of a little embankment over the water. My eyes dart across the glassy pond, searching, searching.

Where is she? She should have come up for air by now.

Even the pixies have noticed something is wrong. They flit forward, tiny feet pitter-pattering across the hauntingly still pool of water. I kick off my shoes and chuck my jacket, about to dive in after her.

This whole beastly mess is because of me.

But how was I supposed to know that dancing with Claire would be *nothing* like dancing with the pixies? Not with the way her hands in mine sent flashes of heat throughout my body, or how when I spun her close, she just *fit*. Nestled against me, like a piece of myself I hadn't realized belonged there.

I shake my head, trying to dislodge the thoughts. But I can't ignore the way Claire's face had flushed when I drew her close— or the look in her eyes.

Blimey, the look in her eyes.

And then she flew.

And now she's probably drowning.

Stop just standing here, you idiot!

I scan for Claire. The pixies speak in uncertain, hushed tones, the soft chime of their voices skittering across the pond.

Just before I launch myself into the water, a golden head breaks the surface just in front of me, dust and water spraying into the dark night air.

My heart staggers. "Claire? Are you all right?"

I search for her face through the spray and dizzying haze of gold that's hiding her like morning fog.

The pond is ghostly quiet, as if the pixies hold their breath too—and then an airy and melodic sound breaks the stillness, echoing through the garden.

Laughter.

Claire is laughing.

I blink, certain my eyes are playing tricks on me, but then she's coming into focus. Stroking through the water toward me, her laughter carrying across the distance between us. When she pulls up a foot from the shore, she treads water and looks at me.

I hardly recognize this Claire.

Her hair is loose, rippling around her as the water catches it. Her eyes are bright and flickering. Her face is filled with delight and she tilts her head at me, wild and untamed and glowing as a fairy queen.

"You're okay?" I ask foolishly.

"I'm very okay." She laughs again. "I've always been able to swim pretty well. And the water is fairly warm actually."

Claire's dust skims out across the water, the golden specks igniting the pond like a sea of gold. Warming it too, I'd guess. The pixies titter with joy, their lilting voices rising like bells. They flood around Claire, spinning and dipping. They kiss her cheeks, burrow into her hair, and dance around her.

You almost wouldn't know they've been weakened by the damage done to Neverland, not with the way they've been carrying on all night. Maybe Claire's presence gives them all strength, like it healed that one pixie's wing.

The sound of my makeshift flute fills the air again, several pixies making it sing once more, and soon the entire small kingdom dances across the water. They swirl and leap, leaving behind streams of pixie dust, kicking up small sprays of water.

Claire has turned to watch them, and she laughs again, the sound almost like a tinkle of bells. There's something so . . . *untamed* about her. This is the girl she's so afraid to let out—the one who bleeds magic and can capture the night sky with a laugh.

I can't take my eyes off her.

My chest tangles in a mess of stampeding emotions. I've never . . . felt this way before.

Like I have the flu and a jolt of adrenaline at the same time. With Wendy there was something, but never like this . . .

"Ben? Did you hear what I said?"

My throat closes up. Face heating, I look at her floating a few feet away.

"Are you going to toss me your jacket? Or do you just intend to stare at me all night?"

She strikes out, bringing herself to the edge of the pond, and rests her arms on the bank.

I lean back on my haunches and wince.

Claire's eyes flicker with concern. "What is it?"

I shrug, settling into the grass and rubbing at the underside of one foot. "Ah, nothing. Just some scars that are still a bother from time to time. Nothing to worry your pretty 'ead about."

But that glint of curiosity has already started. "How did you get scars on the bottom of your feet?"

"Uh—well . . ." *It wasn't pretty.*

I hesitantly lift a foot so she can see the dirt-streaked, calloused underside of my heel—and the jagged, not-quite-healed scars crisscrossing the worn skin.

"What *happened*?"

I brush a hand over my face. "Well, it was my shadow. Pan cut it off when I was trying to escape."

She gasps. "Your shadow? You mean you don't have a shadow at all?"

I shake my head and gesture to the dim light from the pixies falling across the glade, and the lack of any type of dark silhouette mimicking my movements. "Not anymore."

"So, it hurts?"

"Sometimes." I rub at my nose and reach for my trainers. "Sorry, probably not something you fancied seeing. Girls don't like scars and things, do they?"

She regards me for a long second. "No, I don't like them . . . but I do understand them. I have quite a few scars of my own." Her hand absently drifts toward her back. "But you know, when I'm here with you and the pixies, I don't think about it."

I grin. "Only happy thoughts, y'know."

Claire smiles back at me. "Maybe the pixies were right—I am a bit stiff. I forgot how fun it was to swim."

Her eyes glimmer as she rests with her arms on the edge of the bank, and for a moment, she almost looks like one of the sirens, flirting and batting eyelashes and attempting to drag me to a watery death.

But Claire's smile is all sweetness and pixie dust, and any resemblance to the sirens fades. She reaches out a hand.

"Would you give me a hand up?"

Her blonde curls swirl around her, as her bare feet kick through the gold-tinted water beneath her.

It's certainly not a bad sight, and I'm almost regretful when I reach to grab her hand.

Once out, she slips into my jacket and pulls it around her. Her eyelashes glisten with pixie dust and water droplets.

"You good?" I ask.

Claire nods, water flicking from her hair. "Easy fix."

She shows me a small tear in the jacket with a laugh. "I'll just need to borrow a needle, some thread from Lily—and maybe a thimble."

I can't breathe.

"A-a thimble?"

She bites her lip, all innocence and curiosity that only makes my neck warmer. "Yes. Why?"

A *thimble.* That's when I notice the tiny kiss perched precariously in the right corner of her mouth.

How did I never see that before?

It's like I forgot to breathe—like the world forgot to breathe in that moment. She drifts closer, Claire's Neversea eyes peering up at me through gold-streaked lashes like she wants me to steal that kiss.

I want to. Stars, do I want to.

And that knowledge shakes me to the core of my being.

I launch away from Claire. Blast it! What am I doing? It all comes back. Like gravity crushing in on me, the fears pile in one after another.

Never fall in love.

Falling in love meant growing up—and there was nothing worse than that.

I'd seen it wreck everything over and over. Like in the Lost Boys who'd fallen for a tribal girl or a Londoner, and then started to grow *old*. Their imaginations shrunk, their bodies aged, and then they lost sight of everything. Left Neverland, forgot how to fly, forgot who they were.

I refuse to forget the magic.

I will *never* grow up, never be like him.

I take off barefoot down the cobblestones, flicking away any pixies who try to slow me.

But as I flee through Kensington Gardens, I can't run away from the blasted thought that has crowded past the others: I'm manipulating Claire for my own means.

What I'm doing to Claire makes me no better than that man whose angry shouts fill every headache-induced memory. The man who said he loved my mother—but who only brought bruises and tears and locked doors.

If that's what love is, what growing up is . . .

I want nothing to do with it.

I wipe a hand at my face, as the exit to Kensington comes into view. Yet once I'm out of this place, once I'm back in my flat, it won't change the dark suspicion.

No matter how much I try to deny it, or how many crazy schemes I create to get back to Neverland, it might not be enough—I might already be like my father.

Perhaps the magic is already slipping away.

25

CLAIRE

London, England

What—what just happened?

I stare dumbfounded at his retreating figure.

Did Ben really just run away because we almost had a moment?

Granted, I've only known him for about two weeks, but I'm not a girl who kisses a cute boy the minute she meets him.

At least, not usually.

Pixies' voices fill the air, saying words I can't understand—but when they wrap around me, kissing my cheeks and hugging my arms and patting at my head, I get it.

I nuzzle one of the little sprites kissing my cheek. "I'll miss you all too. But I'll be back—I promise!"

With that, I force myself to pull away from them and all the warmth and belonging I felt when I was with them. Like I'd come home.

I think I'm going to like Neverland.

If I can get there.

Right now, I just need to make sure Ben Kensington hasn't decided to walk out on me completely.

I swallow my hurt and manage to catch sight of him just as he leaves the gardens and flags down a cab. Thankfully, a second cab is nearby and I jump in.

The city lights scroll past, dull and pulsating. Thick, dark clouds layer the sky like a waiting predator.

I don't understand what happened. Whatever it was he must regret it. All of it. The closeness we felt, how close we came to . . .

I pinch my eyes shut.

Maybe I was crazy to think he could care about me that way.

He's so strong and capable and playful and courageous. He deserves someone like Lily.

As his cabbie pulls to a stop, Ben ducks out quickly, and I soon follow.

Why is he so determined to get away from me?

Ben takes the stairs two at a time and rushes inside.

I enter as Lily comes out of the kitchen. "Ben, what's—?"

He pushes past her and disappears inside his room, slamming the door shut. We can hear the sliding bolt.

The room falls into eerie quiet, and I stand, breathless from running, feeling so alone. It was as if I'd burned him with my pixie dust. Lily's lithe body shifts beneath her long, orange tank top and she looks toward Ben's room, then at me.

"What was that?"

Before I can fumble through some kind of explanation, the tribal princess shakes her head.

"You know what's wrong?" I ask. "Why is he acting like this?"

She regards me thoughtfully. "I have an idea. Trust me," she says kindly. "It's not your fault." She glances at a clock hanging on the wall. "It's almost two in the morning, We'll figure all of this out tomorrow after Ben has some time to sleep it off."

Somehow, I'm not sure that will help. But warm clothes and a warm bed do sound nice.

I settle into the dry, soft cot, and an ache builds as my brain replays the scene a dozen times before I finally drift off into the relief of nothingness.

The next morning, Ben looks like he hasn't slept a wink. Dark circles rim his eyes, and his wild, copper hair is even more unruly than usual. He stalks around the flat like a caged animal. He hardly responds to any questions Lily asks him, a distant look in his tired eyes.

Finally, Lily heaves a long sigh and pulls me aside. "He gets like this sometimes. Thank the stars we're not in Neverland, or the whole island would be thrown into a monsoon and a torrent of hail."

"What?"

Lily's face pales for a split second and she blinks. "I need to go shopping for more supplies—do you want to come? I think it would be good to get out of the house."

I glance at Ben sitting on the arm of one of the living room couches, sharpening a point out of a broken chair leg. My heart catches. "Yeah, that might be a good idea."

Ten minutes later, Lily's thrown a thick brown coat over an off-the-shoulder tank and neon-patterned leggings.

We flag down a cabbie, and Lily tells him to take us to the nearest shopping area.

When we climb out of the black cab in the Camden borough on a street that's studded with a wide variety of shops, Lily heads toward a little grocery store.

I toy with the hem of my wool top, which seems bleached of

color compared to the attire of the tribal princess. Lily smiles at me. "I'm glad you came. Ben is horrible to shop with—he gets distracted by everything and then loses attention almost immediately. Plus, he never knows what to do at the register and gets frustrated."

I don't know if she's trying to set me at ease, but it's working. A little smile surfaces despite my own frustration with him. "I can picture that."

Lily glances at me as we tread across the cobblestones.

"You know, Claire, regardless of what happened with you and Ben, it's probably better this way."

My heart falls.

"Wait, no, I don't mean it like that." Lily's tone is distraught. She shakes her head. "I'm just trying to tell you to be wary of Ben."

I search her eyes for a hint of jealousy or malice—but don't find it. There's only sincerity in her voice.

Even though she's crushing my innermost hopes about a young man, I can't help but respect this tribal princess.

Lily reaches a store and pulls the door open, letting me through after her. She lowers her voice as we start down the first aisle.

"Listen, Claire, I know Ben can seem alluring and intriguing. But he's really just a little boy inside, still learning to grow up."

I halt. Something about this feels a bit too familiar. "Ben's not a child . . ."

Far from it, especially considering the tangible sparks I felt between us.

Lily pulls her jacket tighter, glancing around as if afraid someone will overhear. There's a bittersweet note in her voice.

"No, but he's not a man yet. You may be the newest shiny thing, but it doesn't last. It never does." Her earth-brown eyes flicker. "I just don't want you to get hurt. There's a lot you don't know about him."

And a lot I'm beginning to suspect about the dynamic between the two of them.

As I stand there, in the middle of the biscuits aisle, surrounded by all kinds of British sweets, my stomach begins to churn, palms becoming wet and gritty.

"Did you—were Ben and you ever . . . ?"

Lily's expression dims. "Once, a long time ago. I thought we had something. But . . . he moved on and I grew up. I began to really see what kind of person he was. I was soon going to be a tribal queen. He was still just a boy. He didn't really care about me the way you mean."

A Lost Boy . . . or a boy who lost himself? With Ben, I'm beginning to wonder if maybe he's both. Or neither. A boy who'd rather lose himself in a carefree daydream than face the changing world around him.

No, it's more than that.

The distant look is replaced by a determined smile. "But that was all right. I could never feel for him like I did back then, and I don't think I could ever be what he needs. But I'll always be there for him, always on his side."

Lily's vulnerability makes me realize just how honest her words are.

I touch her arm. "Thank you."

She gives me a slight smile. "Someday you two will be a force to be reckoned with. But for now, I just want you to know that whatever Ben is wrestling with, it's not your fault. You don't need to carry that weight for him."

Clearing her throat, she looks around. "I've got to go get some bread, milk, and cheese. Why don't you see if there's anything you'd like?"

At first, I'm tempted to say I'll just stay with her, but then I realize she's giving me a moment to myself intentionally.

So Lily.

"All right, I'll meet you over by dairy in a bit."

She gives me a reassuring smile and takes off. Since I'm already at the entrance to the biscuit aisle, I take a stroll down it, admiring shelves upon shelves filled with boxed goodies—and contemplating why British people call a cookie a biscuit.

What do they call a biscuit, then?

Ben would know.

And just like that, I'm back around to him.

I wish I could shake him off and move on. To be okay with the fact that all morning he's avoided me like the plague. To ignore that little stutter in my chest every time I hear his name. Or the way my heart lifts just being in the same room.

When you've tasted a hint of magic, it's hard to root yourself to the ground again.

I pick up a package of shortbread rounds when a ghostly familiar voice breaks the silence.

"You'd better keep a closer eye on your surroundings, love. You never know who could sneak up on you."

The hair on my arms stands on end as I spin around. The sloping posture, hardwood cane, crimson coat, and the glint of steel protruding from one arm—*Captain Hook.*

I step back, glaring at him. "What are you doing here?"

He grips the engraved handle of his cane in one hand, while the sharp gleam of the metal hook juts from his other cuff. "Wanted to catch you alone for a moment, love. I have a proposal for you, Claire Kenton."

His eyes glint like pools of ink beneath silver-streaked brows, and the cool look in them does nothing to calm my nerves. This is the man who sent a horde of dangerous Lost Boys to kidnap me in my flat and has done who knows what else.

No way am I going anywhere with him.

"What makes you think I want to hear anything you have to say?" I hold fast to the box of biscuits, dust flecking my palms. Wonder if chucking this box at him might give me a few minutes to take off.

James Hocken's lips pull to the side in a sharp smirk. "You want to get to your brother, don't you?"

My heart stills.

"Talk fast."

He chuckles, but the sound has a disconcerting note to it. Nothing like Ben's boyish laughter. "There's that fire I've heard so much about."

If he's trying to be creepy as heck, it's working.

Hook's smile fades, and his brows draw together. He takes a limping step closer. "There is so much you don't know about Peter, Claire. He's not your ally—no storybook account could ever prepare you for how despicable he truly is. What he's done to his own Lost Boys, to me—and even to your precious Connor." His voice almost carries genuine concern.

Setting his cane in the crook of an elbow, he sinks his hook into a satin pocket and reaches out his other hand toward me, palm open. Inviting.

"I have a ship, Claire. And I know the way to Neverland. We could leave within the hour. You could be in Neverland by nightfall." His eyes darken. "You could be with Connor *tonight*."

I can't breathe as I stare at him. At that extended hand. I could be with Connor? Tonight?

"Really?"

He nods, his wrinkled features smoothing into an imploring expression. Offering me everything I've so desperately wanted for years.

"All you have to do is come with me and help lift our ship with your pixie dust."

The spell shatters, and I lurch away from him. "You need me too, don't you?"

He straightens, pulling his hand back. "I have never lied to you, Claire. I told you that Peter Pan kidnapped your brother, and now I am telling you that I can get you back to him. I only want one of his many, many atrocities made right."

He taps the rounded edge of his hook against his lips. "I can fix things for you and Connor in a way that I never had the chance to do with the woman I lost."

If I can even believe that story.

There's a soft patter of footsteps, and my thoughts immediately fly to Lily. I spin around—but it's not her. I can hardly believe my eyes when I see the dark-skinned young man standing on the other end of the aisle. The uncertain tilt of his broad shoulders, the hair wisping over his ears, the eyes that always seem to glisten with worry whenever he looks at me. That same look he gave when he arrived at the hospital two years ago after I threw myself from a window.

My fingertips go numb.

My mouth opens, but no sound comes out.

The newcomer takes a step toward me. "The captain is telling the truth, Claire. He's going to take you to Connor."

"*N?*" I take a stumble backward, staring in disbelief at the computer hacker who was one of my few friends.

A nod. "Yes. But"—he clears his throat—"my name isn't N, Claire."

The floor reverberates as Hook lopes past me to stand beside N.

"I–I don't understand." The numbness in my fingertips is spreading up through my hands.

James beams a toothy smile and bumps his curving hook against N's shoulder. "Claire, meet Nibs. One of the best of my growing crew."

Nibs . . .

One of Hook's . . .

Everything I ever thought I knew about N collapses. My breathing comes in ragged spikes as I gape at them, trying desperately to place his name.

Nibs, Nibs, Nibs . . .

And then it clicks.

I'm such a fool.

Such. A. Fool.

"You're a Lost Boy."

Nibs gives a half nod. "I was one of the original boys Peter brought to Neverland. It's . . . a long story."

"So all this time? You've just been pretending to be my friend? Secretly—what?" My pulse is rising. "Keeping tabs on me?"

"Watching out for you, love," Hook says. "We knew that if we just came out and said it, you'd never believe it. So, Nibs here was tasked with getting you on the trail of what really happened to Connor—and also making sure Peter wouldn't do the same thing to you."

N looks at me pleadingly. "I was just trying to help you get to Connor. I still am."

James Hocken brushes the edge of his hook along his scarlet coat, and then offers his other hand to me again. "Let us take you to your brother. Peter doesn't—"

"I know Peter Pan is a psychopath," I snap, cutting him off. The numb shock I'd felt seconds ago at Nibs's betrayal coils into hard, cold fury in my gut. "I know Peter's untrustworthy, and that's why I've *never* wanted his help. But I don't need you. I've got Ben and Lily—and they're actually my friends." My words come out in a quick, angry burst, and I turn my sharp glare on N. "I don't even know who you are anymore."

Not that I ever knew.

N looks like he's about to argue, but Hook gives a long whistle. The pirate captain takes uneven steps, stormy eyes locked on me.

"*Ben*? Who is Ben?" Suspicion tints every word. "Wait, you think . . . ?" Hook gives a bitter laugh. "Oh love, Ben isn't—"

"Back away from her, Hook!"

In a blur of vibrant colors and obsidian fury, Tiger Lily whips around the corner of the aisle and is at my side in an instant, blade in hand. Her body trembles with rage as she lifts the knife and levels it at the pirate captain

Hook leans on his cane and flicks his hook at her. "Stow the weapon, Princess. We couldn't lay a finger on the lass even if we wanted. However, we were in the middle of a very interesting conversation—"

Lily grabs me. "We're leaving. And if I catch you lurking around her again, I will slice both of your throats."

Her voice is stone cold. Hook's smile lessens, but Nibs doesn't flinch, and I think I catch a ghost of a smile on his lips. Lily glances at him, scowling, and I'm struck by the realization that these two know each other.

But before Nibs or Hook can say any more, Lily practically drags me toward the store's exit.

"We need to get out of here before he can rally any more men. Walk fast, and if I say run, take off as quickly as you can." Her hand clamps like a vise around my arm. "Understand?"

"Yes."

We hurry out of the store, across the street, and down a couple back alleys. I notice that she moves along the same quick switchbacks as Ben—but with a little less certainty.

After several long, breathless minutes, Lily looks halfway certain we're not being followed. We collapse against the side of a little villa.

"Are you okay?" she asks.

I nod, gasping for breath. "Does this happen often?"

She sighs. "More than I'd like to admit. I'm just glad we got you out of there."

I look anywhere but at Lily. "Yeah."

Probably not a good time to tell her that I've spent quite some time around the pirate captain.

"Claire, Hook is more dangerous than you can imagine. You cannot trust him."

I'd figured that out myself. Although the danger part is a little harder to comprehend—other than that prong of metal sticking out of his arm, Hook himself never posed much of a threat to me.

And then there's N. *Nibs.*

The sharp fissure that opens up inside is only made more painful by the realization that, no matter how betrayed I might feel by Nibs, it's nothing compared to what Ben must have felt watching the entire gang of Lost Boys turn against him. Watching Peter turn against him.

I've lost a friend—but Ben lost his family.

And I can relate to that far more than I wish I did.

Lily and I start off again, walking briskly this time instead of running.

"When you warned me earlier about being cautious with Ben and that he always leaves, what exactly did that mean?"

"It's a little hard to explain." Lily unzips her jacket to tie it around her waist as we walk, letting the breeze brush her bare shoulders and toy with the end of her braid. "I've known Ben for a long time. He's gotten used to running. To escaping anything that might threaten the carefully crafted story he's made for himself. He might enjoy something for a time, but if someone gets too close, too serious, too weighty . . ." She snaps her fingers. "He's gone."

I wince. "Gone?"

She nods and waves down a cab. "He thinks it's safer that way. It's not, but that's not a lesson either of us can learn for him." As the cab slows, Tiger Lily adds, "But that's not to say it's something he'll never learn. It just might take some time. Don't give up on him, Claire. He needs you, even if he can't see it yet."

Her words are like a blanket settling over me, softening the impact of some of the colder implications of her words. "I don't intend to give up on him."

Lily grins. "I know you don't."

Lily and I climb into the cab, but I hardly notice what streets we take.

It wasn't just that Hook was in that store. But N was too—the hacker who helped me search for Connor and talked me down off more than one ledge—trusts Hook. Maybe there's more to him than Lily knows?

And if that is true, then it brings up an even more dangerous option.

"Oh love, Ben isn't—"

Hook's words ricochet through my mind as the cab crawls through traffic-laden roads. His warning swirls through my thoughts.

I glance at Lily seated beside me. Hook couldn't have been telling the truth. He *couldn't*.

But why would he say that? Some massive ploy to manipulate me and play off my weaknesses?

They've lurked there all along.

And I can't even fathom the repercussions. Because if Ben isn't who he says he is . . .

The chance that my dust might be worth more than pain—that *I* might be worth more—it all unravels. I lose my last chance at finding Connor, and this beautiful world of pixies and magic becomes tainted and shadowed.

If Ben is a lie . . .

Then I truly am broken.

26

PETER

London, England

Something is wrong.

Well, *more* wrong.

True, Claire already pretty much hates me after the almost-snogging-a-pretty-girl-and-ruining-everything disaster. The worst of it isn't that I almost kissed her—a decidedly grown-up thing—it's how badly I wanted to. *Still* want to. And that is driving me insane. Even being in the same room with her is like being on fire—everything raw and heated like I'm going to explode.

So I've taken to running. Jogging. Was even followed by the Lost Boys a few times, which made for a jolly good chase that got my mind off the whole tangled-up situation for a bit.

But I always have to return to the flat, and there she is. Furious and hurt and utterly captivating.

Every taunting twitch of those lips spinning my thoughts.

And then Lily tells me Hook has made a blasted appearance. Stopped them in a supermarket. The princess assured me that she'd arrived before he could say anything much.

But all I know is that something isn't right. Since they arrived home two days ago after that run-in with Hook, Claire has been—different. Sullen, cautious, isolated.

Untrusting.

And that is far more unnerving than the almost-snogging.

I heave a sigh and swing out the window and onto the fire escape. I prowl silently up it as I hear Lily's encouraging tones coming from the rooftop above me. A few seconds later, my head crests the top of the roof, and I can see them. Lily sits cross-legged on the rooftop as she watches Claire who is hovering a few feet in the air.

Blimey, she's getting better.

I watch as Claire rises a few more inches, bathed in a cloud of glowing pixie dust. Her hair is tied back, but loose strands float about her. Concentration pinches her eyes closed and cheap new earbuds are pressed in her ears.

"That's it, Claire! Focus on that thought—let it lift you."

Claire gives a small nod.

My heart twists as I watch them. That should be me helping Claire. But a wedge has been shoved between us, and I'm not even sure where to begin to dislodge it.

I'm silent as a cat, but the minute I set foot on the rooftop edge, Claire's eyes fly open. And then abruptly slam shut again.

Blasted stars—how does she do that?

I watch her sink a few inches as I make my way over to Lily. The coolness echoes out from Claire in waves, and I cross my arms over my jacket. Sinking down beside Lily, I turn from the seething girl suspended in the air to the tribal princess beside me.

"Think she'll ever warm up?" I whisper to Lily.

Claire drops a few more inches.

Lily shrugs. "There's only one way for you to settle whatever's off between you two."

She rises to her feet and heads toward the fire escape, long purple jacket snapping about her knees.

"What? Hey—what are you doing? You can't leave me here with her . . ."

"You need to get it together, or this whole thing will fall apart." She winks. "C'mon—I thought you lived for the danger."

"Conniving girl," I mutter under my breath, watching Lily disappear.

Now it's just Claire and me.

I lean back and look at her. Her face screws up, lips pinched to the side like she tastes something sour. Even her dust seems to be dimming.

Now where have I seen someone's mood change like that . . .

A memory hits. *Tink!* Of course.

Claire is half pixie, so it would follow that she'd inherit some of their personality traits. Like flicking from one all-consuming emotion to another. No wonder she can go from being reserved and quiet to wild and whimsical in the blink of an eye. Or why she has to work so hard to hold her dust in. It wouldn't take much for her emotions to take over.

Especially the angry ones.

At least she can have more than one emotion in her head at a time. Pixies cannot—and it always makes for an interesting time. Like when Tink grew jealous of Wendy and tried to kill her.

Twice.

I shake my head at the memory, but then the guilt sets in.

Just like it always does when I think of her. Especially when I realize how long it has been since Tink has crossed my mind. Blimey—I've been so caught up in everything with Claire that it's been days. Weeks, even. And as much as it twists me up, there's also a part that doesn't entirely mind. The forgetting is so much less painful than the remembering.

That's what got you into this blasted mess in the first place, idiot.

Forgetting. Losing sight of the things that I shouldn't have. The mistakes that have come back to bite me in the rear.

"How long are you planning on sitting there?"

At Claire's voice, my head comes up. I'm surprised to find her glaring down at me, now only about a foot and a half off the ground. The London skyline stretching out behind her seems as snappish as the girl hovering in it. I shrug, scratching at the back of my head.

"As long as it takes for you to talk to me?"

She snorts. "I have nothing to say to you right now."

Right. That's likely.

"Is this about"—I try to keep my tone careless—"what happened at the lake?"

She wavers in the air. "*No.*"

But her eyes practically scream the opposite. "I—uh—I think that for now it's probably better if we're just—"

"Oh, shut up!" Her feet thud to the rooftop. Taking a deep breath, Claire shakes her head. "It's not about that. Well, I mean, it is . . ."

She bites her lip and then pulls her new phone out of her pocket, a courtesy Lily felt warranted digging into our pirate gold. She cranks up the music.

"Never mind."

Scrunching her eyes again, she manages to rise a few inches off the rooftop, but the dust leaking out around her is dull and unsteady. The way her body shudders against a torrent of locked-away emotions, eyes clamped shut and lips drawn in a thin line, brings to mind another angry young Kenton.

With the same golden hair and stubborn streak—but a far worse temper.

Connor.

She looks just like her brother did when he'd get brassed off.

My stomach takes a nosedive, a headache slamming into my temples.

Oh, blast.

I drop to my knees, hunched over, hacking my guts up. I manage to lean over the side of the roof just in time for the projectile to miss the rooftop. My trembling hands grasp the flat edge, struggling to keep my balance and not tip over.

When there's nothing left to dislodge, I wipe at my mouth and lean back, stomach still twisting into more knots than Curly's hair.

I thud back on my haunches, arms wrapped around my gut, rocking back and forth. *Claire*, focus on Claire. I pry my eyes open to see her still hovering behind me, but the sharp lines of her face have changed to concern—to compassion. The pain begins to subside.

Thank the stars.

I'm not certain how much longer I can last like this. The longer I'm away from Neverland, the worse it becomes. Shrugging out of my jacket, I wipe my lips again on a sleeve, finally able to draw a full breath.

I let out a long exhale.

Claire's voice is quiet. "Does that happen because Neverland is falling apart?"

"We just need to get to Neverland," I manage to say.

She drifts a few inches higher, toes just off the ground. "So, how does it work? Whatever it is that makes Neverland's destruction hurt you?"

A lot of details I can't tell you without blowing everything. "I— uh—it's all rather painful."

I pull myself to my feet and stand near to Claire, who's hovering.

"If you lean into your dust rather than trying to force yourself off the ground, you'll rise easier."

But she isn't listening, instead she is studying me through the haze of glittering gold around her.

"That's all you're going to say about nearly puking your guts out? You shouldn't keep things trapped inside. It just ends up cutting its way out. Trust me, I know."

"I won't. But right now I've gotta work on your flying, mate. I'll figure the rest out eventually—I always do." I toss her a lopsided grin.

Instead of smiling back, the nervous, pulsing swell of her dust fluctuates again, and she plummets to the rooftop. She lands awkwardly on her right foot, twisting her ankle beneath her.

"Claire!" I start toward her. But she lifts her head, and the ice in her gaze slices through me.

"That's just the thing. I'm not so certain you will figure it out. In fact, I'm not sure I even know you, Ben. Not really."

Hook, what did you *do*?

Claire winces as she takes a limping step backward, eyes dropping to the concrete, voice barely above a whisper.

"I've only known you and Lily for a few weeks. I have no idea who you really are, other than what you've told me."

I gape at her, at the trembling words tumbling out of her mouth. I fight against the rising panic. She's doubting me, doubting everything.

I've lost her trust. And with it, my chance at ever getting off this rock.

Blithering stars.

"I've spent so much of my life trying to find Connor and a

place where we're safe. Where I can finally let my guard down. I-I don't think I can handle it if the ground is swept out from under me again. But these past few days . . ."

Claire glances around the rooftop. "I'm not so sure anymore."

I run my tongue over my teeth, watching her sway. Tipping precariously toward panicked. Did she sleep at all last night? Dark, round circles rim her eyes.

I lift my hands, speaking in a gentle voice as if I'm trying to talk down a skittish Neverbeast.

"Just take a deep breath, Claire. We're going to figure this out."

She gives a frustrated half sob.

"I'll tell you what you want to know, but first, let's go get you some grub and fix up that ankle."

She rubs her hands together and eventually nods. She tries to take a step toward me—and then everything turns into a blasted nightmare. With a little shriek, her feet spin out from under her, and she skids across the cement rooftop and collapses in a little heap.

I race toward her, pulse stuttering. Why isn't she moving?

Gleaming dust drips from her skin, flaking off her palms and spilling down her cheeks. Her whole body shakes, the dust swelling faster and faster around her—gold at first, then darkening.

That can't be good.

I reach out to touch her. A dark, graying fleck of dust lands on my hand, and a scorching sensation spikes across my knuckles. I jerk my hand away, biting back a curse, and glare down at the tiny red mark, beginning to swell.

This dust burns.

I stare at her, trying to make sense of this as the flakes continue to pulse out from her body. Gut-wrenching sobs echo with each pulse.

Slowly, Claire pulls herself upright. Bloodied scrapes run across her jawline and right cheek, the crimson droplets mixing with the graying flecks seeping from her skin.

Her lips are dry and cracked, words thudding into each other as she speaks in a half-hysterical voice. "I need to find Connor. I need to get him back. It's been so long—I can't handle it if this is all a sham . . ."

Claire seems to be spiraling out of control. So not the way I saw this going. "We will find Connor. But first, can you make this stop?"

"Wh-what?" She blinks numbly at me and then looks down at her scraped and bleeding hands and the ashen flecks spiraling out from them. The darkening dust fills the rooftop, creating a smoky haze around her.

Claire's eyes tear to me, and her face fills with one all-consuming emotion: fear.

"Claire, we can figure—"

I start forward, but Claire's raised voice cuts me off. "No! Don't come any closer, Ben!"

Her hands snap closed, tightening into fists. Tears leak down her cheeks, and she mumbles, "Not again. Please, not again."

Words that sound familiar to me.

She draws her knees up to her chest, locking herself in. I watch her, realization slowly starting to fill in. No wonder she was so uncertain about her dust. So afraid to let it out.

Claire Kenton is deathly afraid of her own magic.

I take another step toward her, but she scoots back. "No, Ben, you have to get away." Her voice trembles, rising higher and higher as she speaks. "It'll—I'll—you'll get hurt."

I've fought pirates, stitched up my own wounds, battled out

of the jaws of a crocodile—yet I've never seen anything like Claire Kenton.

Slivers of darkness pour from her skin, singeing anything they touch.

You can't fight a shadow.

She starts to shake again, and dust crumbles from her skin. It spirals around her in a massive, gray wave. I try to cover my face, but burning flecks pelt my cheeks and singe my knuckles.

How is this even possible?

My feet are glued to the rooftop, watching her from between splayed fingers.

The ashen flecks rip through the air. She's not just a pixie . . .

She's a weapon.

"Ben, what are you doing? Why are you standing there? You need to leave. Now!"

Claire's wavering is hardly more than a rasped whisper, but it cuts through my numb surprise. Her blue eyes are blurred with tears. Swelling red welts speckle my arms. A burning, scorching sensation rips across my whole body, seeping into my skin.

"Ben!" Claire chokes as she folds into herself more, eyes filling with chilling terror. *"Run!"*

27

CLAIRE

London, England

Blood leaks from the scrapes on my hands, mingling with the ashen dust that cascades from my skin and swirls into a small tornado of singeing, burning magic.

My blackest parts laid bare.

Fear seeps through my bones, contorting my already wracked chest, as I try to force down a breath but only manage to heave another fractured sob. I tighten my fists until my nails cut into my skin, releasing more blood, more dust.

My vision, my world, is consumed by it.

No!

"B-Ben!" His name is a hiccupped sob. I can't hurt him—won't hurt him. "Get out of here!"

But even as the words leave my lips, I can't find the strength to lift my eyes to him. Just desperately hope that he isn't writhing in pain somewhere on this rooftop. That I'm not killing him. Not prying the skin from his bones.

I should look up. Try to stop it. Try to help him.

But I can barely hold my weight, and bile rises in my throat. I can't bring myself to stare my fears in the face. It's not just this darkness that scares me.

It's the look I'll see in Ben's eyes. Beyond the fear and the pain . . . Utter repulsion.

Then he'll do what everyone has always done. What he should do. Not just get away from this rooftop—

Get away from *me*.

I pull my knees tighter against my chest, feeling the wind gaining speed. Whipping around me, plastering my crimson-streaked cardigan against my torso. I try to breathe in through my nose and finally acknowledge what has set off this tornado of burning ash.

It was never just about losing trust in Ben.

It's the fear that, not only do I not know who Ben is, but that I've placed a part of my heart and hopes into the hands of a boy who could walk away in an instant.

Just like Peter Pan.

All the shadowed, twisted *what-ifs*.

What if they've just been using me this whole time? Or what if I am never able to figure out how to fly? It's been weeks, and I've hardly been able to get off the ground. Wendy learned how to fly in an evening.

What happens if I'm useless?

What happens now that he's seen how toxic I truly am?

I'll be cast aside like the end of the storybook, when the Lost Boys decided they wanted a chance at families—and Peter just turned his back on them.

That's what he does. That's what they all do.

I slowly lift my head, cracking an eye, struck only by the veil of dust that is practically a sandstorm now.

And then I catch sight of Ben.

He huddles against one of the far corners, somehow managing to evade the torrent of dust. I've never seen his usually confident, cheeky expression completely wiped clean. Pallid and uncertain and—fearful?

He should be.

And if I don't do something, I'm going to kill him. Burn the skin from his bones.

I squeeze my eyes closed and try to reach for that shadow. Try to reach for that shattered, aching place deep inside that is churning up the dust. Try to picture the ashen flakes softening, slowing, crumbling back into me. Banished to the darkest parts of my heart where I don't even dare look.

But it doesn't work.

The shadow just keeps expanding, farther and farther, my fears and shame feeding into the whipping wind. My mind is whimpering for the dust to submit, to hide, to back away—but my heart is screaming that it's no use.

I can't control this.

I'm not strong enough to defeat my own monsters.

All I can do is fall.

I force my eyes open again and see Ben, who is still frozen but watching me.

"Get out of here, you idiot!" My voice sounds hoarse and broken to my own ears, but I keep screaming. "I can't stop it!"

A few flecks spin toward Ben and he grimaces when they singe his forehead.

"You need to leave! This is who I am. All of this. I'm not a pixie, Ben. This isn't magic—it's a curse."

Ben's shirt is singed, his back bent to brace against the burning haze of dust.

"*Please*," I gasp, pleading with every fiber of my being. "I don't want to hurt you too."

He throws a hand over his eyes, bare feet clambering around the edge of the roof. My heart sinks as I watch him pick up his jacket from beside the fire escape.

Leaving.

My breath breaks in my lungs at the realization, but at least Ben and Lily will be safe. And I'm so exhausted. So tired of fighting. So tired of trying to lock my fears away. Too tired to open my eyes again.

Maybe I'll just dissolve into ash and save the world from my shadows.

Another sound cuts through the swirling dust. The slap of bare feet against the roof and masculine groans growing louder, closer.

What?

My eyes snap open to find the blurred silhouette of a certain young man forcing his way through the dust—toward me.

He's wearing his green hoodie again. I am aghast as Ben trudges doggedly through the maelstrom, shoulders set determinedly.

All I can see are the angry red welts covering his skin.

"It's burning you. Go back!"

He doesn't even flinch, but closes the distance until he's only a few feet away. His face is inflamed, one eye even purpling and swollen—but his expression is filled with such fierce determination, it takes my breath away.

He moans again and tries to angle his hands to shield his face.

I can't watch him do this to himself.

"Ben—please . . ."

Ben's body crashes into mine before I can even process what's happening, and his arms wrap around me. Strong and secure.

"Claire . . ." He drags down a deep breath. Our faces are inches away. The welts on his nose and cheeks make my stomach lurch.

Cloth-wrapped hands clasp the sides of my face. His gaze holds mine captive. "You're falling. You need to stop falling."

His body presses hot against mine, his skin feverish.

"F-falling?"

"Yes, falling. Letting the bad thoughts drag you down." His green eyes pierce through the shadowy haze. "You need to think of something else, Claire! Happy things."

"I-I can't."

Ben's hold tightens.

"Yes, you can. Trust me, I know what it's like. Having your fears drag you down, slam you into the ground. But you *can* fly— you can rise past this."

I can't tell if he's the one trembling or me, but the tears start again.

"But what if this *is* me? What if this is all I am?"

"We all fight the shadows. Even the ones we can't remember."

His hands drop from my face as he puts his arms around me again, drawing me close. Despite the burning dust, despite how many times I've told him to walk away, he just holds me.

"What's your happiest memory of your brother?"

"I'm not sure."

My limbs are heavy as concrete, mind fractured and numb.

"I feel so heavy, Ben. So, so heavy."

Stalking my past, every heartbeat. The deeper I try to look to find that flicker of hope, all I see are shadows.

Ben tenses and looks at me, eyes glazed.

"No happy thoughts at all?"

I give my head a half shake. His brows knit, as if he's never even considered that. Then he speaks.

"The stars shine in the darkness . . ."

"What?"

A smile crosses his cracked lips, and he leans in, mouth brushing my ear, voice steady.

"The stars shine brightest in the darkness, Claire. Pixie dust chases back the shadows. Maybe that's it—maybe that's what the shadows are all about. Finding the light through them, and . . ." He tilts his head back. "We all have our shadows to fight, but maybe that's so we can grow stronger."

"How am I supposed to do that?"

"You just need someone to remind you of the light. The happy thoughts." Something distant taints his voice. "Just like she reminded me when I was falling."

A tremor ripples through him and he jerks straight. I can't even imagine how much pain he's in. But Ben smiles—a full-on grin. Filled with so much childlike optimism, I can't breathe.

"You're the girl who sprinkles pixie dust—Cor, you can create light and fly. That's pretty incredible. You took care of your brother better than most mothers." He quirks a brow. "And watching out for rowdy chaps is no easy feat. I should know."

The deluge is beginning to slow. I lean my head against Ben's chest, the pulse of his heart in my ear.

"I want to. But I'm tired, *so* tired . . ."

"I know." He squeezes me a bit tighter, one hand lifting my chin and cradling the side of my face. "Just keep fighting for me, Pixie-Girl. Okay?"

Something about the way he says "Pixie-Girl" builds a little spark of warmth inside.

I muster a nod. "Okay."

The word is a fractured breath, but a promise.

"You're the girl who sold every bloomin' thing she had to

chase down a fairy tale. A bit bonkers—but plucky."

I hiccup a laugh against his chest. I focus on slowing my breathing to match his. His eyes glint.

"You're as stubborn as a pixie, clever as a siren, as brave as the tribal warriors . . ."

I take even breaths and a half smile quirks the corner of my lips. "Really? Clever as a siren?"

He grins. "Aye. And almost as brilliant as me." He winks.

I blink away the last specks of dust clinging to my eyelashes. The dust has simmered down to a slow breeze around us, but it is still ashen.

I reach out a hesitant hand to trace a finger along the edge of his jaw where a particularly nasty burn fillets his skin. "I'm so sorry."

Ben gives a half shrug. "You're just full of surprises, aren't you? Gotta say, that burning dust wasn't on the top of my list. But if anyone can figure out how to master that bit o' darkness, it'll be you. I have no doubt."

His head is a little closer. "The light is far brighter than the darkness. Don't forget that."

"Wow. That was really mature and inspiring."

Ben's face pales and he leans away. "Blast, you're right. I must be losing it."

That brings a chuckle out of me. My eyes look past Ben, taking in the rooftop, and I'm shocked to see the dust bleeding with color, lightening to a healthy gold, like sunlight flooding the rooftop.

I blink, tears pricking at my eyes. "Thank God . . ." I breathe.

The light in you, is far brighter than the darkness. Don't forget that.

Ben is unwrapping his hands, shoving the strips of cloth in his pocket and blowing on the blisters scattered across his knuckles. My eyes widen when I see that the glaring burns that had bubbled his skin moments ago have already begun to soften into a pinkish hue.

Taking a slow breath, I reach out to touch the side of his face. Ben flinches, but otherwise he doesn't move.

"Your burns—they're already starting to heal. How is that possible?"

"Not sure. Maybe you're not the only one with a bit of magic in them?" His typical wink is followed by a grimace. "These things hurt like the dickens, but they're already starting to cool off. Plus, you weren't really trying to hurt me. That has to count for something."

"No, I would never—"

"I know." He reaches out a hand. "What do you say we go inside and finish that chocolate cake I snuck in to Lily's shopping cart a few days ago?"

He flashes that lopsided, carefree smile, and I can almost imagine that the past hour was nothing more than a bad dream.

But when I slip my hand into his and let Ben pull me to my feet, my knees quiver. "I'm so sorry."

"You need to stop talking like that." Ben nudges me across the rooftop toward the fire escape. "I'm going to have to explain this to Lily in a second, and you feeling bad isn't going to do anything but make me look like I'm going soft."

He strides toward the edge of the rooftop, as if that ended it, but my eyes blur for what feels like the thousandth time in the past hour. Watching him lumber over the edge of the roof and down the fire escape, pausing to make sure I can get down safely, a flash of realization dawns like the sun climbing over the Thames.

Suddenly, I know. And that knowledge blots out the doubts. Paints over them with the acute knowledge that Ben is who I choose to believe he is:

The boy who saw light in a shattered girl. Who fights dauntlessly to return to his fractured home, despite being just one against hordes of pirates and Lost Boys.

And if that is who my Ben is, then I refuse to believe he's anything like Peter Pan.

Ben Kensington is the boy who stays.

28

CLAIRE

London, England

Ben would never admit it, but he must be in a world of pain from the bubbling burns that redden his skin. He goes to bed right after sipping some warm broth, and I can't ignore an acute sense of dread as I stare at the empty place at the table where he should be.

"Do you think he secretly hates me?"

I don't know where the question comes from, but it bubbles out before I can stop it.

Lily, sitting beside me, pauses in taking sips of her broth. "Of course not."

I stare down at my nearly untouched bowl. "I know he said it doesn't matter, but after what happened . . ."

Lily leans back in her chair, crossing her arms over her gray leather jacket.

"We've all done things, Claire. Ben, of all people, understands that. What's important is learning how to mend what we've broken and doing our best to move forward."

I sigh. "I would never have purposefully hurt him. I just keep . . . ruining things."

Lily strums her silver-painted nails along the edge of the table.

"As I said, Ben is a boy in a lot of ways. There is so much he still needs to figure out for himself. But, with you . . ." She pauses. "With you, it's different. When he looks at you, I see something new in him. He doesn't hate you, Claire. I doubt he ever truly could."

Before I can fully mull over the meaning of those words, Lily pushes back her chair and gestures toward the door.

"C'mon, let's go sit outside."

I heave out a long breath, set my dishes in the sink, and blow off a few paper-thin specks of dust from my knuckles. I follow Lily out the front door.

She sits on the top step of the short wooden stairway leading to the sidewalk below. Resting her staff behind her like an old friend guarding her back, Lily smooths out her colorful knee-length dress and motions for me to join her.

A row of well-kept houses with dainty lawns sit across from us, their dim lights flickering through the drawn drapes and casting odd shadows along the sidewalk. I can only imagine how many pounds Ben and Lily must have had to dish out in order to live here. Their pirate gold explanation is sounding less strange by the day. Especially if they fled Neverland, where Peter was notorious for hiding Hook's treasure around the island. It made sense a Lost Boy would have access to at least a bit.

A breeze ripples through the little street, kicking up some of the crinkled leaves littering the pavement and tossing them toward the darkening sky. Stars wink through the clouds overhead, far above the arching rooftops. They glitter like morning dew. Everything smells of old brick and rain and a hint of fireplace smoke.

It's so peaceful here. As if the fate of a whole world doesn't hang in the balance.

"I love this time of the night," Lily says. "The coolness and starlight almost feel like home. Although in Neverland, our night skies are in constant motion—and tell stories."

That would explain the tattoos.

"They tell stories?"

She laughs. "Yes. My tribesmen tell of the Ever One, the deity who hung the stars in the sky and spins stories through them. The prophets and the tribal leaders are taught a sacred gift of reading the skies, the constellations above us."

I glance up at the stars again, and I'm struck by the reminder that somewhere out there is Lily's home. A place I've never been, one that almost seems like a myth—and as whimsical as the spiritual beliefs of Lily's culture.

"What kinds of stories do the stars tell?"

"Oh, histories and prophecies and destinies. And, while not everyone has the gift of reading the stars, most of our tribesmen have tattoos that serve as reminders and messages. A way of showing everyone who they are and what they think of themselves. Writing their own destinies . . ."

I try to picture this distant, glorious world. It's like a fairy tale all its own.

"Here, let me show you . . ."

Lily removes her jacket and lifts her hands in the faint starlight. The night's soft glow falls across her arms, and images begin to appear, flowing over her shoulders and cascading down her back. The darkness coaxing them out like awakening stars.

The night sky comes alive across her skin.

The silver tattoos now become a masterpiece written in swirling images across her skin. It's a pattern of interconnecting dots and spirals—a map of the night sky. The tattoos spiral up her arms, dance across her shoulders and drape down her back.

I am unable to think of a single word to say—until I get a closer glimpse of her arms and find other patterns beneath the glimmering tattoos. Thin, ragged scars that feel too familiar.

Why would Lily . . . ?

I swallow, specks of gold flecking my fingertips—but the dust is dull compared to the shining night sky that flows across Lily's skin. Everything about this girl has always emanated confidence. A rightness in who she is, in her own skin, and not giving a thought to what the world thinks. From her tattoos to the wild, bright colors in her hair and the way she carries herself, not letting anyone—even Ben—hold her down.

But the thin scars beneath the tattoos are far too . . . raw. Hopeless.

I've seen scars like these—created some of my own.

Leaning a little closer, I rub the sleeve of my thick red wool sweater between my palms and then hesitantly reach out to skim a finger across a particularly deep scar on her wrist.

"Who did this to you?"

Lily's eyes glimmer like wet river stones. "I did."

My brows rise, and I'm hyperaware of my own scars. The ones from leaping out that window and the times my dust cut into my own skin. The jagged marks covering my arms, my back.

"Why?"

She's silent for a moment.

"There was a time, not so long ago, when I lost sight of who I was. I knew I wasn't like Peter—I had outgrown him—and I also wasn't like the rest of my people. I didn't crave the prestige of my royal heritage like my siblings. And I wasn't ready for the arranged marriage my mother had planned—didn't know if I'd ever be ready for that."

I lean back, resting against the step behind me as I listen to her, slowly realizing something that had never quite hit home before: there are other adults in Neverland. A whole tribal culture functioning on its own. Living, loving, full of families and legacies. Experiencing a depth of life that Peter and his Lost Boys never could, frozen for decades as children.

Lily's voice fills the cool air again. "I had another path to walk, one no one else could walk for me. So I got these tattoos as a reminder of the heritage of my people and who the stars say that I am. A reminder that I can simply *be*, even when I may be walking my path alone . . ."

The tribal princess's head dips down as she stares at her bare feet. But it's not sadness or loneliness I see in Lily's eyes. Only a sense of stillness. Of wholeness.

And that wholeness bleeds into every part of Tiger Lily. No wonder she seems unperturbed by the way she doesn't quite fall into step with the rest of London. Shoulders back, vibrant teal woven in her hair and through her clothing like war paint. She walks her own path.

I can't imagine living like that. With nothing to lock away, nothing to hide.

Content in who you are, but strong enough to fight your demons.

"You definitely have never struck me as someone who needed a man to rule a tribe."

That brings a laugh. "I certainly hope not. But I forfeited the role as chief when I left Neverland, so I guess we'll never know."

My hands go cold. "*What?*"

"You didn't know?" Lily reaches for the staff settled behind her, letting her hands filter over the aged wood. "I guess you wouldn't. Yes, in order to leave Neverland and help Ben save it,

I had to give up my tribe. I was defying the tribal elders who all believed we should fight. But I knew—I *know*—that this is the only way to save Neverland. So, I took the risk."

I shake my head. "How are you so certain of everything?"

"Oh, I wasn't always." Lily lets her hands drift from the weighty staff to run a thumb over the scars on her wrists. "I wasn't ready to be a wife, wasn't ready to play the political games as tribal leader, and wasn't just one of Peter's gang anymore. I didn't know who I was becoming." She takes a deep breath. "I just knew I didn't like her. And that trying to be something for everyone was tearing me apart."

Tears fill my eyes. "I—I know exactly how that feels."

Lily puts an arm around my shoulder but doesn't say anything. Doesn't have to.

"For so much of my life, I hated myself." My eyes blur again, but I blink hard. "The things I'd done, the way I'd damaged people—sometimes it felt like I deserved to hurt like they did. The only times I ever felt I was worth having around was with Connor. . ." I rub at my eyes. "When it's just me, I can't see it. It's like I'm this bottomless black abyss, and I can only stuff it for so long before it swallows me up."

Lily's arm tightens around my shoulders. "You are so much more than that, Claire. Even if you can't see it right now, someday you will."

"I really hope so."

"You will." She gives me another reassuring squeeze, and when she moves her arm away, her hand is speckled with a few flakes of my pale dust. The gold slivers bring to life the rich tones of her beautiful skin like shimmers of starlight intermingled in a gorgeous night sky.

Tiger Lily smiles at the dust patterning her fingers. "You are a creature of magic, Claire—born for Neverland—and nothing can undo that. You have value simply because you exist. Because you are here."

I gulp around the lump in my throat. "I wish that were true."

That I'm not just a mistake. A fluke. An outcast.

"I know it's hard, feeling like you're missing a part of yourself." Lily's eyes glisten. "But if you keep letting the whispers around you tell you who you are, pretty soon they will suck you dry. I lost myself in the shadows. In the doubts." She glances down at her scars again. "That magic in your veins means you have a choice, Claire. You were created for more than to bear the weight of your shadows—but you have to choose to no longer let them define you. You have to choose to let the light shine through the shattered pieces."

I don't even know what that really means. But there's a small, childlike voice whispering deep inside. A younger Claire. The little girl who would play with her dust and spin and laugh. The little girl who didn't know she could hurt anyone. That little girl is still tucked away somewhere, and she's whispering impossibilities— *maybe Lily is right.*

My eyes blur again as I stare at Lily's hands, and I can't see the scars anymore—only the brilliant silver of the tattoos that are a map, a reminder, across her gorgeous skin.

I follow her gaze as she tips her head back to the sky. What I wouldn't give to see a Neverland night—where the galaxies are in constant motion, and the stars tell stories.

"And who do the stars say you are, Lily?"

A smile spreads across her face, and I have a feeling Tiger Lily isn't seeing the blurred speckles nearly drowned out by the

London city lights—but a brilliant reminder stretched across an ebony sky, swirling and silver and clear as day. The message written in the stars for her.

"They say I am a queen."

A shiver skims over me, and I close my eyes for a second, trying to picture what she sees. The message left across Neverland's night sky by the one who hung the stars.

I may not believe in everything Lily does, but I can't help the curiosity that bubbles up inside.

I wonder who the stars say I am.

29

CLAIRE

London, England

Lily and I stay like that for a while, soaking in the stillness as I churn her words over and over in my head. A new aching pulse beats in my chest when I think of Neverland now. An expectancy.

Exhaustion soon takes over, and we head in for the night. I crawl into bed, ready for some rest after the emotional roller coaster of today. But as I drift off to sleep, it's not Ben groaning in pain or my own poisonous dust that fills my dreams—but stars. Beautiful and airy and hopeful.

And a particular one, second to the right, calling to me.

But when I awaken abruptly a few hours later, it's not to the stars calling my name but Ben's harsh whisper, his calloused hand clasped over my mouth.

"Someone's in the flat. Stay quiet."

My groggy mind processes what he's saying. Danger.

I bolt upright, and he removes his hand.

Who is it? I mouth, and his green eyes dart about in the stifling darkness, the swelling all but gone from his right eye.

An ominous creak echoes through the flat, followed by the shuffle-scuff of faint footsteps. Even before Ben raises a hand, one finger curled in a silent answer, I know.

Hook.

I take a shattering breath and push aside the covers—glad I'm wearing a thick, baggy T-shirt over a pair of leggings that would be relatively easy to run in, if need be. Ben's jaw is set firmly, but his shoulders slump with fatigue. Who knows how many intruders are out there, and if Ben's not up to full strength . . .

This isn't going to end well.

Ben presses a blade into my hand, then whispers, "Let me go out first and then once I've distracted them, run."

My fist curls around the knife handle. "That's a horrible idea."

"Got a better one?"

"Yes, how about we both sneak out together."

"And all get caught? Brilliant plan." He twirls his knife. "Don't worry, mate. I'll handle this."

Before I can argue, he moves silently toward the door, pausing only long enough to gesture for me to stay put, his expression pleading. Then his lips crack into a wide smile, and with a smooth half bow, he slips out.

That vise grip crushing my chest is back, and I can feel panic fraying the edges of my vision. I can hardly throw on my jeans and yellow cardigan, but somehow I manage.

A quick glance at my phone tells me that it's only four in the morning.

Good grief. Couldn't the fight have a least waited for a less horrendous hour?

When the sounds of a scuffle erupt from outside my room, I fly toward the door, knife trembling in my grip.

I murmur a prayer and reach for the knob. I creak open the door, and it takes my eyes a moment to adjust to what I'm seeing. A blur of seething bodies and screams and groans.

At least fifteen strangers flood our flat.

Several are distracted by a tribal princess wielding a hardwood staff, her braid whipping about her fierce expression as she spins and stabs at any intruder close enough. But she's outmatched—seven to one isn't great odds, even for the fury of Tiger Lily.

A handful of the dark silhouettes closing in on Lily are the vaguely familiar shapes of Lost Boys, but many are broader and bigger.

Hook's crew?

I hear another groan and a shuffling sound that sidelines my attention as three men leap on a slight figure with tousled reddish-blond hair. They've stuffed some kind of gag into Ben's mouth and he kicks and fights to break free, but the men grasp him roughly, throwing a rope around his wrists and cinching it tight. He keeps struggling, but I can see the exhaustion streaking his forehead and the heavy look in his eyes.

There's too many of them. And no magic to save him.

No! This can't be happening.

I look back toward Lily, but she's surrounded by so many of the dark intruders that I can't even make her out anymore in the dim moonlight stealing through the kitchen window. And then her sharp, agonized gasp of pain pierces through the scuffle. They must have struck her.

No!

Clenching the knife tighter in my free hand, I burst into the mayhem.

"Leave them alone!" I scream, drawing the attention of every eye in the room. I lift my knife, trying to stop it from quaking. A chill fills the room, and as I scan the dozens of men crouching in the flat, I feel really, really small.

Before I can come up with something more fearsome to say, the heavy thud-step of a limping gait reverberates across the wooden flooring.

"Well, there you are, love. We were beginning to think you wouldn't be joining us tonight."

I turn to face the pirate captain.

Hook stands like an eerie shadow, his coat the color of dripping blood, even in the dim light. He reaches up to scratch at his gray-speckled beard with that curving prong of metal.

This is it. The part of the fairy tale where the villain stops pretending to play nice, and the girl realizes she's no hero.

And then all get their throats torn out by a hook.

Turns out this is not a fairy tale—it's a tragedy. A horror story.

I grit my teeth until they hurt. *Happy* thoughts, remember?

Hook's eyes flash. "There's much to discuss, love."

At his words, Ben goes wild, and he begins to lash against his restraints. Throwing his weight forward, he kicks and writhes out of the grip of several of the pirates holding him. Ben's eyes hunt down Hook, as he shoves himself a few more feet and spits out a few words past his gag.

"She's not yours, Hook! You coward, don't you dare—"

The pirate captain spins toward Ben, then slams the blunt end of his curving hook into the side of his face.

Ben's head snaps to the side, blood trickling from his temple.

"Not so easy fighting without flight, is it, boy?"

Flight? Does Hook know what Ben and I have been trying to do?

A bruise forms on Ben's temple, and a thin line of blood trickles down his cheek. What if Hook decides to slash Ben again—this time with the razor-sharp end of his hook? He could kill him.

I lift the knife in my quivering hands, and dull dust sweeps out from my touch, speckling the blade. My eyes burn, but I grab hold of the iron-hot anger rising inside and channel it into a throw.

It's a solid throw—but Hook merely leans to the side and the knife misses him, clipping a pirate behind him.

That's it—I've lost my last weapon. My last chance at escape. Numbing panic washes over me. I scan the room for something else I can use, but the intruders are blocking any chance of reaching even an umbrella to throw.

We weren't prepared.

I wasn't prepared.

With an amused smirk, the pirate captain twists his hook so that the light glints off the edge. "It took us a good deal longer than I'd expected to find where you were hiding. Even then, I chose to bide my time and not rush in. I wasn't about to let the little devil escape again." He shoots a narrow glare at Ben and then shifts his attention back to me. "Let's get this started, shall we?"

Ben roars through his gag, kicking and fighting like a mad person—but the pirates holding him refuse to give an inch.

Hook's cane thuds against the wooden floor as he takes a dogged step closer, then another, his sharp gaze never leaving me. When we're only a few inches apart, he pauses.

"There's something you need to know."

I force myself to stand tall. *Don't let him see that you're afraid.*

"You have something to tell me? You could have just knocked."

His lips twitch. "Brave. Good, you'll need that."

I wince at his words, which only amuses Hook.

"I told you, Claire. I've only ever wanted to help you get to Connor. I've always told you the truth about my identity. I do have a ship, and we can leave the minute you give the word."

One of the Lost Boys yelps. "The blasted princess bit me!"

There's a momentary shuffle as they kick Lily's feet out from under her and shove a gag in her mouth.

I glare daggers at Hook. "You call that helping?"

His eyes narrow. "They'll survive. Not that it really matters to you."

"What? Of course, it matters! They're my friends."

"You see, that's just it, love . . ." He smooths out a wrinkle in his coat, and then gestures toward the horde of lackeys. Someone strikes a match, and a lantern throws the room into flickering light. The wavering gleam casts strange shadows across Hook's face as he leans closer, just enough that I can smell his foul breath.

"These two are not your friends."

I take a step back, pulse thundering. The uneven light leaves parts of the hallway and kitchen in shadow while igniting others and giving the whole room a skeletal appearance.

Wrapping my arms around myself to stave off the sudden chill, I meet Hook's steely gaze.

"They're more of an ally than you've ever been."

"Now, that's where you're wrong." He slowly swivels away from me and gestures to the group to bring Ben forward.

They shove him toward us, gripping fistfuls of his green hoodie and forcing him to his knees. A shudder ripples through him, brow beaded with sweat.

"This *boy* isn't your friend." Hook's voice is an ominous snarl. He bends just enough to press his hook beneath the young man's chin and lift his head.

Ben's narrowed green eyes bore into Hook with such disgust that even my stomach turns. But Hook merely smirks. The tension between them is palpable.

"This boy has been lying to you, Claire. He's manipulating you.

He's using you so that he can get back to his precious Neverland."
He slides the hook lower, pressing against Ben's throat until he
gasps for air.

"Stop! You're suffocating him!"

At my shout, the pirate captain flashes me a look but pulls his
hook back.

"Even now, you're protecting him. But he doesn't care for
you. The longer he's away from his precious island, the more his
body ages. He'll shrivel without the magic of Neverland—and he's
willing to do anything to get back."

Hook's eyes are on mine, with a rawness that traps the breath
in my lungs.

"Even lie to the sister of the boy he kidnapped."

The air feels thin. "Lie?" I say faintly.

"Yes, you're starting to see it, aren't you?" He takes a lumbering
step and then lifts his hook to point at the boy still kneeling on
the ground, shoulders slumped, face drawn. Hook's lips curl into
a triumphant snarl.

"It's time someone used his real name. No more tricks . . .
Peter Pan."

30

CLAIRE

London, England

Peter Pan.

Ben is *Peter Pan* . . . ?

Bits of dust lift off my palms and sprinkle the air. As much as it cuts through me to hear those words uttered aloud, there's a deeper knowing. One that drums through my veins with every heartbeat.

With this boy who has become as familiar as my own breath. Who taught me to fly. And no matter what Hook says—

I know this boy.

I drop to my knees beside Ben and pluck that stupid gag out of his mouth, despite the mutters from pirates and Lost Boys.

I wipe the blood from his temple and smooth back strands of auburn hair out of his eyes. Eyes that look into mine with hope.

Behind me, Hook continues to spew words. "Do you see? He has lied to you, stolen from you, destroyed what you cared about— just as he destroys everything."

I touch a swelling burn along Ben's jawline. "You're wrong."

I rise to my feet and glance upward. Vaulted ceilings that had seemed excessive for a flat—but are now perfect.

Hook's voice cuts through the room. "What?"

"I said *you are wrong*. I know exactly who he is." A light, airy feeling fills me, like when music whisks away my fears. The same feeling when Ben held me close, believing in me.

Now, it's my turn to believe in him.

"He's the boy who saved me. He's Ben Kensington."

I refuse to believe Ben is anything like the boy who wouldn't grow up.

He's light. Hope. He's everything Peter isn't.

Pixie dust pours out of my body. It slips from my fingertips and floods through the weave of my cardigan. Light and glowing and breathless. My feet ease off the ground. I look down at Ben, and his smile meets mine.

I cup my hands, lifting them to my mouth—and blow.

Pixie dust explodes from my palms, raining all over him, catching in his tangled hair and clinging to his green hoodie, and he rises off the ground.

A grin spreads across his face.

The Lost Boys leap at him, but Ben throws himself into the air and knocks them backward. A knife clatters to the ground, and Ben grabs, slices through his binds, and shoots upward.

Dust carries as I soar toward the ceiling. I look for Lily, still surrounded by several burly pirates.

Hook bellows for someone to grab me. Hands shoot out, but I'm already out of reach.

I put my hands out to cushion my contact with the rafters and then laugh. This is incredible. I'm literally floating in the air. And it feels as right as breathing.

"Don't let them get away!" Hook bellows. In a smooth motion, he clips the end of his hook beneath the metal crown of the cane's handle and pulls upward. A sword slides free of the body of the cane, the curling metal grip of the cane forming the blade's handle.

Of course he has a magical cane-turned-sword.

I sink a little, but Ben's laughter reverberates toward me. He floats effortlessly on his back.

"Fetch Lily," he says, eyes shining. "Hook is mine."

His excitement is contagious. My heart gives a little stuttering leap, and I flash him a sharp salute.

"Aye, aye, captain!"

Ben flips right side up, darting quickly through the air toward Hook, who raises his sword. My dust continues to pour out, bathing the room in a glimmering, golden glow. The pirates curse and bat at it. Some of the Lost Boys seem to be trying to rise with the dust, only to fail miserably. Apparently they're fresh out of childlike faith, trust and belief. Can't say I'm surprised.

But for *me*, the pixie dust is like oxygen, filling in and around my body, holding me up.

I maneuver toward Lily. Ben has already created a break in the wall of dark-cloaked bodies trying to hold her down as he targets Hook. Ben kicks and spins, knocking one Lost Boy out and landing a foot in another pirate's face.

He's wielding the knife he stole from a pirate, and a curved hook darts out, meeting Ben's blade.

At the sound of metal clashing with metal, every Lost Boy and pirate turns to Hook and Ben.

The pirate captain and the boy move with quick, familiar accuracy—Hook striking at intervals and Ben always staying just out of reach. Frustration rolls off Hook in waves, but Ben seems to be soaking it in, that reckless grin painted on his face. Their dangerous stalemate has the attention of everyone in the room.

I see the opening and take it.

Darting down, I grab Lily's hands, which are bound in front of her, and lift.

Her weight almost pulls me from the air. I fight to stay balanced, forcing myself to keep rising. I hold on to Lily until my arms feel like they're about to pop out of my sockets, but I refuse to let go, and slowly float upward. I barely get her out of the Lost Boys' reach.

More dust pours out around me, helping to lighten the load, and Lily loops her arm around my shoulders. I pull the gag from her mouth as we hover above the heads of the writhing intruders.

Lily takes a deep breath and spits unceremoniously. She gives me a small smile. "Sorry—wish I could fly as well as Ben. I knew you could do it."

"It's okay, I—"

But with my concentration split between conversation and flying, we drop a few inches. *Oof!* I scramble to pull us upward again.

"I'm not sure how long I can keep this up."

Tiger Lily is watching Ben, still locked in combat with Hook. He hangs in the air, nearly upside down, knife jabbing in and out at the captain, almost playfully. Teasingly.

I dearly hope none of this group has a firearm. Ben can't outfly a bullet.

Lily rolls her eyes. "Stop being such a diva, Ben! Get over here and help!"

No response.

"*Ben!*" Lily snaps, and his head pops up, auburn tangles batting his cheeks. He takes in the sight of us, then glances back at Hook.

"It's been a pleasure, but we'll have to continue this lovely dance some other time. Ta!"

Hook growls and jabs with his hook and a blade, but only

catches air. Ben is already at the other side of Lily taking most of her weight.

I sigh with relief.

Lily, ever the practical one, is pointing. "Aim for that window?"

There is an open window just behind Hook.

I feel like I'm treading air as I glance at Ben. "Think we can make it?"

"Easy." His eyes gleam. "On my count we go as fast as we can. Okay?"

I gulp. "Okay."

This is insane.

Below us, the room is alight with pixie dust. The pirates and Lost Boys continue to curse and raise their weapons, their scowls bathed in cobwebbed shadow. But no one can reach us, since they can't even manage to rise an inch off the ground.

One of the pirates draws a firearm.

"Don't hurt her!" Hook barks and reaches for the pirate, but the man doesn't seem to be listening. He cocks the weapon, and I tense.

Ben catches my eye. "*Go!*"

We surge forward. I let go of Lily as Ben pulls her close. We dart over Hook's head and aim for the small window. Ben and Lily narrowly burst through, and my body careens toward the small space of freedom. A hand grabs at my shoe, but I shake it off, dust exploding around my body.

I blast through the window and into the cool night air.

Body swirling in a glowing haze of pixie dust, I shoot upward, higher and higher, unhindered by the air rushing past me or the pirates left far behind or the gravity trying to hold me down.

It's like the world is depthless. Like my body has become a

cloud. I can feel every whisper of air, the magic in my veins.

I belong here, with the stars.

Lily was right. Hope is a little like pixie dust—it shines brightest in the darkness and makes the soul soar.

"Uh—Claire? A little help?"

I find Ben and Lily dropping several feet through the air below me, the pixie dust surrounding them fading the farther away I am.

"Oh! Hang on." I dart toward them. The pixie dust that continues to coat my skin and fill the air around my body, glowing and shimmering, showers down on Ben and Lily.

Immediately, they begin to rise, Ben's secure arm helps to keep her in the air.

I dip down beside them to help. "Can you believe we just did that?"

Lily's eyes glint in the starlight. "*You* did it, Claire."

I glance down at the city so far below, a mottled patchwork of misty streets and towering buildings and cobblestone walkways. My feet dangle in the air as glistening dust surrounds us like mist of its own. Even the wind up here feels fresh and nippy.

I smile.

Ben's shoulder brushes mine. "'Knew you could do it."

He adjusts his hold on the tribal princess. "Now, don't take this the wrong way, but you're getting quite heavy, mate. Mind if we find somewhere to land?"

She grips our shoulders tighter. "Not at all. Just don't drop me."

"Right then. I know just the place."

Ben guides us out over the streets of London, as if he has flown this way a million times. The Palace of Westminster is just ahead, and beyond it—

My breath catches. "Is that . . . ? Are we . . . ?"

Ben grins. "Aye, that we are."

A thrill flashes through me as we fly through the cloud layer above the palace, and I gaze down in wonder at the intricate towers and craftsmanship. And then we're past it. The massive, golden clock tower appears below us.

Big Ben arches toward the sky, and the three of us slow, dipping downward. I can hardly breathe as Ben guides us to one of the clock's massive iron hands.

His bare feet skid over the thick metal, and Lily lands right behind him, dark braid floating about her.

She's still holding on to me like a lifeline, and my feet suspend just above the clock's hand. I let them brush the metal, then plant down soundly.

"Wow . . ."

The metal arm is surprisingly steady. The face of the clock is like a giant moon, with numerals inscribed across its peaked features. The top of the tower tapers up, the golden filigree speckled with flecks of my dust.

"This is so much better than the movie."

I am awestruck by the city spreading out around us. The Thames on one side, with vehicles moseying their way over the bridges spanning the waterway. A maze of buildings stretch out as far as the eye can see. Pale blue siding and arching spires and sloping rooftops and brick siding and red arched cranes.

Connor, how I wish you could see this.

Lily beams. "Thank you, Claire. I've always wanted to know what this was like."

Ben steps off the clock arm, still wrapped in my dust, and floats to hover in front of us, one hand out in case Lily needs it. He gives a little flourish.

"Best view in the city, if I do say so myself."

"It really is."

Ben's smile widens. "How do you feel?"

"Me?" I brush hair strands out of my eyes. "I feel *great*. Which is crazy, considering I've just really, truly flown for the first time and we got attacked by Hook."

"Aye, and we were lucky."

"Lucky?"

"Hook's never hesitated to shoot at me before. He's aimed a bloomin' *cannon ball* at my head. But for some reason, he's pulling punches with you. We got out with just a few bruises."

"Maybe he knows I won't help him get to Neverland if I'm dead."

"Maybe . . ." Ben shares a knowing look with Lily.

The tribal princess scoots a little closer across the clock's hand. "Claire, do you know what this means? Being here?"

I blink at her.

"Claire, you can not only fly but have more than enough dust to be able to fly far."

Then Ben's mouth is beside my ear, warm breath heating my skin. "Let's fly to Neverland."

It's nearly six in the morning and Lily makes a good point when she reminds us that sailing off for the stars in broad daylight is a little obvious. Plus, exhaustion will kick in eventually, especially if we don't get some food soon.

So when she insists that we get something to eat before we

take off for the stars, and maybe find a hotel to stay in until it's dark, Ben and I don't disagree.

Ben helps Lily to the ground, and I watch her quick, determined strides head down Victoria Embankment, the streetlights glinting off the dark asphalt. Meanwhile, Ben and I return to our perch on Big Ben to figure out what this whole flying-through-the-universe-toward-Neverland will look like.

The sky seems so big.

The questions tumble out of me. "Do you really think I can do this? What if I get tired halfway there? What if we get burned up on the way out of our atmosphere?"

Ben reclines on the minute hand, one leg hanging lazily off, toying with the drawstring on his green hoodie.

"Have you seen the amount of pixie dust you've been covered in, mate? That's more than enough to get us to Neverland. Once you get the hang of it, the dust will come easily. I've made this trip loads of times. Trust me—I'll get us there safely. And don't worry a piece about Earth's atmosphere—it doesn't work like that."

This is sounding more and more like an episode of *The Twilight Zone*. At least Ben knows the way—I have no idea how to even find Neverland, save aiming for a certain star.

I rub my hands together, watching dust spiraling from my skin as it joins the haze filling the air around me.

"You've always been capable of flying to Neverland, Claire. You just needed to tap into your own magic." Ben throws his hands out. "Now that you have, the sky's the limit."

I snort. "Very punny."

"I try."

His forest-green eyes grow a bit softer, and he pushes himself up off the metal hand, floating closer to me. He flicks away a clump of pixie dust caught in his hair and then reaches out to graze my shoulder with his hand.

"I'm quite proud of you. I knew you could do it, Pixie-Girl."

Only a day ago he was pushing through a haze of burning dust to settle my panicked fears—now he's defying gravity suspended hundreds of feet above the ground.

I've never seen Ben so completely himself as he is right now. Even the freckles dancing across his nose look healthier and happier, his whole face almost healed from the burns.

As I notice the way his emerald eyes churn like mischievous pools, I realize how very near we are. Our noses nearly touching. Again.

He's in the air, legs out behind him, hovering at eye level with me.

My pulse goes wild when he ever so gently tucks a dust-flecked strand of wayward hair behind my ear, floating a breath closer. Heat crashes over me in a wave, and I scramble to my feet, turning and walking a few steps down the rim of the large clock hand. I wrap my arms around myself, feeling chilled.

Ben doesn't follow.

As I stand there, so far above London, I feel alone. A flash of heat crawls down my arms. *I'm doing it again.*

Putting up walls.

I rise to my tiptoes. My pulse begins to pound as an idea lifts me up.

I gather up my courage and race back across Big Ben. My feet rise off the thick metal hand, and Ben's brows arch as I fly toward him.

I reach him—my hands grip his collar, watching those forest-green eyes go wide. And then I kiss him. It's warm, explosive and quick.

Like a falling star.

31

PETER

London, England

It's so sudden and unexpected that I'm hardly able to register her lips on mine before Claire flits back.

I gape at her, a whirl of dust surrounding her slight form as she peers at me with hesitant hope in her eyes. Heat swells like pixie dust inside my chest, lifting and igniting every sense.

She has no idea what she's just done.

A hand goes to my mouth, and I continue to stare at her. "Y-you took it . . ."

Claire's face goes beet red, as her feet hover above Big Ben's minute hand. The wide gleam of the clockface behind us highlights Claire's blush and the way she twists her hands.

"I'm so sorry!" I can't seem to drag my stupid gaze away from her lips. "I should have asked, shouldn't I? I didn't think."

I chuckle. "Oh no, your eyes asked more than enough."

Claire's blush deepens, and she looks confused.

I drift through the air toward her, pixie dust tangling in my hair and sticking to my jacket. "I mean that you took *it*. My hidden kiss."

"Your—what?"

We're only inches apart. I trail a finger down the side of her face, my thumb brushing the corner of her mouth.

"Everyone has a hidden kiss. It's tucked in the corner of their mouth, and only one person in the whole bloomin' galaxy can have it." I let my hand drop away from her. "Of course, girls have been trying to steal mine for decades. But none of them could, not even Wendy . . ."

Claire's expression sharpens. But she is still breathless and riveting.

"But you . . ." I give a little, disbelieving laugh. "You just waltzed right in and took it."

A spark of a hope blossoms like a sunrise in her eyes. Thoughts ricochet through my head as I hover beside her. The lies I've told her. The times that she's cursed Peter Pan.

And everything that *this* represents.

"Ben?" Claire's voice is soft as a feather as she floats a breath away.

Suddenly it's all pouring out.

"I never wanted to fall for someone, you know. That rubbish was for grown-ups—and I refused to ever be like that. I never wanted to care for someone, to *need* someone like air. I never wanted to fall for you, Claire Kenton . . . But somehow, I did."

And all of a sudden, it's just Claire.

No fears, no expectations, no loss, no father, no danger. I can't even blooming remember why I was so against girls in the first place.

Just Claire, with her fierce loyalty and light, and those Neversea eyes that see farther into me than I see into myself.

I haven't felt this weightless in far, far too long. Claire has taken to the air like the pixie she is—and she seems every bit as comfortable high above the city as I am. She *gets* it.

She was born for Neverland.

We are the same, she and I. Stronger, better, more whole together.

I close my eyes for a moment, but once they are shut, Claire disappears, and the world goes cold. Dark. I can't imagine a world like this—one without her light.

Without her.

Something breaks inside me. And before I even know what I'm doing, my mouth collides with Claire's, my hands tangling in her hair. Her arms wrap around my neck, and I pull her closer, her small body nestling so perfectly against mine.

Our kiss is magic—soft and glimmering, then growing into a force that sweeps through us like a blast of light. Claire's dust wraps around us, and our bodies begin to rise higher and higher. Even as we ascend, I have not the smallest inclination to look at the world below. Only to hold this stardust-girl tight in my arms, deepening the kiss.

If only I could stay like this, stay with her forever in our Never Never Land.

Because this caring for someone is not what I thought it would be. It's not losing who I am. It's finding my soul interwoven with another—and chasing the stars together.

And that might just be the greatest adventure of them all.

32

CLAIRE

London, England

The world drops away, and I'm lost in Ben's arms as we rise together through the air. His hand gently cups the back of my head, and his kiss makes a thrill ripple down to my toes.

Ben is warmth and color and passion and strength and magic. His strong arms encircle me like he never intends to let go.

I dangle in the middle of an ocean of stars, enveloped in the arms of this boy who has shown me what it means to be weightless, and in this instant everything feels . . . perfect.

For one single, glorious moment the world is perfect.

Ben's other hand gently releases its hold on my back, and he pulls away just enough to peer into my eyes.

I'm unable to hold back a shy smile.

He's breathing hard, face flushed, reddish-blond hair even more unkempt than usual. I don't miss the flush creeping up Ben's neck, but he tosses me a grin that is far more distracting than it used to be.

"That was . . . wow."

I give an embarrassed laugh and rest my forehead against his. Eyes closed. Breathing in unison.

"I've never . . . felt more at home," I whisper.

"A kiss is a powerful thing, huh?"

You could say that again.

"I mean it, though. I don't want this to ever end."

I know how insane it all is, how impossible these dreams may seem, but he's come to mean so much. And he's given me all . . . *this*. For the first time since my brother, I'm wanted.

I touch his face. "I want to be like this, together. Always. No matter how old we grow."

Color drains from his face. His arms stiffen. "G-grow old?"

He releases me, and the sudden space between us feels like miles.

"I mean . . ." My dust dims. I sink slowly through the air as embarrassment spikes through me. "That's moving too fast—I'm sorry. I was just"—my eyes sting—"just talking."

Just revealing a fraction of my heart. Too fast and too far.

Ben shoves hair out of his eyes. "No, it's not—" He glances around us as we slowly descend through the sky. "The sun has already started to rise. Better get to that hotel Lily mentioned before any chaps see us, and all."

Stupid, stupid Claire! You pushed him away again!

Why am I so needy?

Why couldn't I have just left it alone?

Because a kiss is a powerful thing. And it's rarely ever just a kiss.

I straighten my cardigan as we continue to drift downward, and the world spreads out around us. London is a textured, mottled canvas. Brilliant golden streaks of sunlight reach up like they want to capture the pixie dust that suspends us. But their warmth feels shallow.

My body still hums as we drop onto a small cobblestone path hidden behind a collection of variety shops. I set my feet squarely on the ground, smoothing my wrinkled cardigan and note that my dust has ebbed to little more than hints of floating gold specks. We've landed about a mile from the clocktower, on a side street that Ben says leads toward a district with hotels where we can reserve a room and lay low until the evening.

He still hardly meets my eyes.

I'm not sure what to say. What to do. "Um, all right . . . I guess I can text Lily and let her know we'll go look for a hotel?"

"Sure." Ben leans against a nearby building, but his shoulders are angled away, body language as shut down as his expression.

My stomach is tangled up in confused, harsh knots.

I want to be angry, frustrated, anything other than this overwhelming sense of . . . guilt.

I still can't find words to say, so instead I quickly text Lily, but when I turn back to Ben, he's already several feet away, reaching for a back door to one of the small shops.

"What are you doing? Where are you going?"

He has the door halfway open when he stills, then turns toward me. His brows rise. "Oh, you're still here?"

"*What*?" My voice is shocked. "Of course I'm still here. We were in the middle of a conversation."

Ben's lips twist to the side. "Ah, yeah. Eh, you can go ahead and find the hotel. I'll just be a minute."

Ben pulls at the door again, eyes shining with excitement.

"What's in there that's so important? We need to talk about . . . what happened." I take a few steps across the cobblestones toward him. "We have to, Ben. I don't understand what's going on."

His shoulders stiffen, but otherwise he seems to completely

ignore me. He pulls the door to the shop open wider, and takes a step over the threshold.

"A sweets shop? That's what this is about?"

I rush forward and wrench him away from the store. Willing him to come back to me. "Can you stop thinking about your stomach for five minutes and tell me what–?"

"I said I don't want to talk about it!" His voice is so sharp I recoil. Ben's eyes are wild and . . . afraid?

His words spill out in a rushed, angry flood. "I don't know what happened, don't know what that was, and I don't want to talk about it. Stop being such a blithering nag!"

I cross my arms over my chest to steady their trembling and take another step backward.

This isn't the Ben I know.

"You're being ridiculous!" My voice is rising. "But you know what–*fine*. You stay and get your stupid candy."

He sticks his tongue out at me. "Fine!"

"Lily is right–you are such a child!"

His eyes flare. "Yeah, well at least I'm not a blasted grown-up like you."

"You didn't seem to mind it fifteen minutes ago when you were kissing me!"

I spin on my heel and storm away. Before I know it, I'm racing down the street. I'm not sure where I'm going; I just want to get away from Ben.

From this boy who is so . . . selfish and wild.

So much like everything I've heard of Peter Pan.

I whip around a corner and step into a thick river of Londoners clustering the sidewalk. They move along in quick, fluid lines, some wearing coats and others wheeling bikes. I hunch my shoulders and shove upstream, my heart pounding.

Someone grabs my arm.

Someone with a chilled loop of metal for a right hand.

Hook pulls me off the sidewalk, crimson coat swirling around us. His left hand, clammy but very human, clamps over my mouth to muffle my screams. The blunt curve of his hook presses into my spine as he practically shoves me into a nearby alleyway.

What is it with this city and getting pulled into alleys?

I twist against Hook's steely grip and open my mouth to bite him, to scream, but before I can do anything, a familiar voice cuts through.

"Claire—wait! We just wanted to talk."

I freeze. Even though I now know where his allegiances lie, I doubt this will ever get easier.

Hook releases me, and I look past him. N is here. No, not N. *Nibs.* The Lost Boy that I hardly know, after all. He stands stiffly a few feet behind Hook, nearly motionless. In his dark leather jacket, he practically fades into the shadows.

Nibs takes measured steps toward me. "I'm not going to try and stop you from leaving. Just please give me a chance to explain."

I shrink back, glancing over my shoulder toward my escape, but even the pirate captain is giving me space. He smooths out his coattails and strokes the shaft of his cane that I now know sheathes a sword.

Hook's windblown grey eyes connect with mine like a stroke of crackling energy. "You may not believe me, love, but at least hear the lad out."

"Yes, please, Claire." Nibs's imploring expression reels me in. "I know you. I know how hard and long you worked to find Connor, and I tried to help you as much as I could . . ."

My eyes narrow. "Help me? You knew that Connor had been taken all along, and yet you never said anything. You took *years* to even point me toward London. You were stringing me along!"

A flash of pain crosses Nibs's face. "You would never have believed me or had the determination to go all the way to London and hunt down Peter Pan if I had just sprung it all on you at once. I was supposed to keep an eye on you, make sure you were coping alright. Plus, we didn't even know when you'd be emotionally ready for . . . all this." He sweeps a hand through the air, gesturing at the hook jutting out of the scarlet-suited pirate captain's cuff, the water-stained wall of the building beside us, and the rest of London beyond view. "To hear that your brother was trapped in Neverland and that the only way to get to him was to fly there."

"Why can't you just bring Connor here? How did you all even get to Earth in the first place? Can't you just fly back? How do I know you haven't hurt my brother somehow?"

Nibs looks at Hook, who gives an almost imperceptible nod. "We fled Neverland when it started falling apart, but Peter wouldn't let us take your brother. We couldn't take him from Neverland. And the pixie dust we used to get to Earth . . . Well, let's just say the pixies have been less than helpful. As it is, it would take a small army of pixies to be able to lift the *Jolly Roger* into the air. And as Neverland weakens, so do its magical creatures."

I glare at Captain Hook, whose expression is as aloof and unreadable as always. I shift my attention back to Nibs. "So, the only way for everyone to get back to Neverland is through me. You all need my pixie dust to fly home."

The Lost Boy thumbs at the brass buttons studding his jacket. "Yeah, that's about it."

"Why didn't you just tell me all this years ago? Why all

the secrecy?"

Nibs shuffles his tennis shoes on the asphalt. He rubs at his nose, then lifts his chestnut eyes. "Like I said, we had to be sure you were ready. I wanted to be sure it wasn't going to send you over the edge . . . again."

Again?

Oh.

Again, like the time he flew to a hospital to visit a girl he'd only known for a few weeks. A girl who'd nearly gone mad from grief and uncertainty and threw herself out a window. A girl who couldn't believe in her own pixie dust.

No, don't trust him! He's just trying to manipulate you.

But Nibs's eyes are earnest, and even Hook's coolness seems thawed by his words.

"Okay . . . what is it that you wanted to tell me? It had better be pretty dang convincing since you just snuck into our flat a few hours ago, and *someone* raised a sword at me." I shoot a scathing glare at Hook, who only seems mildly amused.

"Claire, you can't go to Neverland with Ben." Nibs clears his throat, his eyes darkening. "He isn't who you think he is. He's lying to you—and he's *dangerous.*"

I cross my arms. "I've heard this story before, and still don't believe it."

Won't believe it.

Nibs grabs my shoulders. "Claire, don't do that. Don't shut down. You have to *listen* to us."

I lift my chin. "I'm listening, I just think you're lying."

Hook gives a scoffing cough, but Nibs grips my shoulders. "I'm trying to help you. You have to stop doing this!"

"Stop doing what?"

"You get so attached to people that you live in denial of who they really are."

My jaw tightens. "I do not—"

"Yes, you do!" He shoves me backward a step; and the shadows curling out from the mottled cement walls almost seem to lick at him. "You're so desperate for someone to make you feel special that you become blinded to who they really are."

Hook's uneven gait clips across the pavement, but Nibs doesn't even glance at the captain. "That boy you call Ben is Peter Pan. But you refuse to acknowledge it. To see how he's using you . . ." Nibs's voice breaks. "We're just trying to help you. But you'd rather live in denial than see who he really is. You've done it with Peter—just like you did with Connor."

Before I can even find words to react to that, Hook moves with astonishing speed. He slams the blunt curve of his hook into Nibs's temple and his head snaps to the side.

Nibs gasps, knees nearly giving out, but he manages to stay unsteadily on his feet. He presses a hand to his head, and it comes away with blood glistening wet against his fingertips.

Nibs turns to look at the pirate captain who is wiping the blood from his hook with a handkerchief. Instead of anger, Nibs bows his head and mumbles an apology.

But I'm only focused on one thing.

"What did you mean about Connor?"

Nibs's voice is halting. "He wasn't everything you thought. He left you behind."

"And there we come to the reason for this delightful little chat." Hook steps in front of Nibs, continuing to polish his hook with his bloodstained handkerchief. "Come to Neverland with us instead of with that beastly little runt. We can help you get to your brother and can reveal all the details about Peter that you don't know." His voice drops low, lips pulling into a slithering smile. "And there is so very much you don't know, love."

I want to back away from him, but his commanding presence has cemented my feet to the ground. "I'm not going anywhere with you."

Nibs may have poked holes and started pulling out pieces of the foundation of everything I thought I understood, but that doesn't mean I'm anywhere near taking Hook up on his offer.

I just need to talk to Ben.

Hook cocks his head. "Is that a no, then?"

I glare up at him. "It's no—and never."

His eyes narrow. He carefully folds the crimson-stained handkerchief and slips it into his pocket. "I had a feeling you'd say that." He reaches into his other tailored jacket pocket and retrieves a second handkerchief, along with a small blue vial. "Pity."

"Captain, wait—"

Before Nibs can finish, Hook pops the cork off the small vial and dumps its contents onto the cloth.

I bolt for the exit of the alleyway, screaming, but the sound is quickly muffled by the handkerchief shoved over my mouth. Hook's metal hook wraps around my arm, the sharp point digging into my flesh and stopping me.

I try not to inhale, but the bitter chemicals snake through my nose and mouth. My knees quiver, and I look up at Hook.

I should never have let my guard down. Hook's the villain of the story.

And I'm about to become another casualty.

The captain's gray-speckled beard shifts as he smiles at me. "Don't worry, love. This will only smart for a moment. You'll thank us later."

I glare at the pirate even as my vision starts to go dark.

The world spins and closes in, the shadowed edges fraying and crackling and blacking out my vision. For a moment, my dazed eyes catch on the victorious, crocodile smile of a madman—and then the chemical I inhaled reaches its course.

Like a candle being snuffed out, I sink into dark oblivion.

33

PETER

London, England

Claire has vanished, and I think . . .

I think it's my fault.

I'm dumbstruck at the thought.

Cor, I don't know if I've ever actually said that before.

My fault.

If I'd just realized it and looked for her sooner, maybe we'd be halfway to Neverland by now. Instead of searching through Hook's mansion for any sign of Claire's whereabouts.

I take stock of the room around me: shelves and drawers empty as gaping tombs, chair slid in behind a mahogany desk. The floor here is missing the hasty, muddied footprints that tracked through the other rooms as Hook's crew must have quickly gone through the rest of the mansion.

This empty chamber must be Hook's study, as it's the only room in this whole blasted mansion that looks like it was neatly packed up.

If she was ever here, she's not now.

Lily's prowling through the north wing, but I know she won't find another living soul. Hook and his men have cleaned out, taking Claire with them, if the tracks of glimmering pixie dust and the strand of blonde hair I found mean anything.

But there are no footprints small enough to be Claire's.

Which means she either flew in—or was carried. Knocked out, taken, kidnapped.

Blast it all!

As if Lily's scathing glances throughout this whole beastly search haven't been enough. She nearly knocked me over the head when I told her Claire had gone missing.

I drum my fingers on the edge of the desk and let my gaze roam across the area one last time—and land on the only thing left in this study. A small, wooden container, padded with black velvet. A few glass vials lie atop the lush material—but they are empty. Half of the case is bare, missing at least a dozen more vials.

"Blast it all!" I spew several curses into the air and then lean a little closer to the case, sniffing the spicy scent of the vials' residue. I notice a few round dribbles staining a corner of the velvet. I reach out, but a dark hand slaps mine away.

"Peter! It's *poison*—don't touch it!"

I stifle a sigh and roll my eyes at Lily. "I was just trying to guess what he might have used. Don't go getting your trousers in a twist."

"They're called *leggings*. And touching something that might be toxic is a great way to get yourself poisoned. Whatever happened to Claire could happen to you."

I perch on the edge of the desk, not a shred of shadow anywhere to be seen, as usual. "Are we even certain anything happened to Claire? Couldn't he have just packed up the rest of the blasted bottles?"

Tiger Lily slowly shakes her head. "I doubt we're that lucky. If Hook kidnapped Claire, there's no telling what he'll do."

"Well, let's go find the codfish and get her back!" I'm getting impatient.

Lily slides her hands down the length of her staff. "We will, but if Hook used some kind of poison on Claire, we'll need someone who can put together an antidote. Jeremy's wife, Tansy, saved many of our people when she was still a healer in Neverland. Besides, if Hook has kidnapped Claire, the Guardian will need to know. Either way, this is getting out of hand and we need backup. I'll go find Jeremy and you—"

"I'll go to the docks." Usually I'd rather lose an eye than rely on a grown-up for anything. Especially Jeremy, with his uncanny habit of sticking his nose right in the middle of my schemes.

But today is different.

As Lily and I duck out of the study and quickly make our way out of the mansion, her staff thudding through the empty hallways, the whole estate starts to close in. Swallowing me up with its bare walls and shuttered windows and arching ceiling. The scent of salt and sweat and the metallic twang of blood rises from the floorboards.

While I was running through the dismal alleyways of London just to stay one step ahead of an angry horde of Lost Boys, Hook was living like *this?* Like a king off the gold he stole throughout the years?

I despise that codfish.

Storming across Hook's dingy lawn, I ignore the statues sprouting from the graying grass and the look Lily gives me. Shoving past the large gate, I start off down the faded asphalt road and prepare to call for a cab. But as I stalk in the opposite direction Lily needs to go, she races up to grab my arm.

"Peter—wait!"

I jolt to a halt. "What?"

The sunlight warms the top of my head, which seems inconsiderately cheerful considering that the girl I might sort of maybe be falling for may have been kidnapped by a pirate.

Lily stands right in front of me, momentarily prying my thoughts away from Claire.

"Peter, I wanted to say that whatever happens with Hook"—she pauses—"you need to find a way to face it. To face all of this. And to tell Claire the truth. Not just about you—but about Connor."

My tongue feels thick. "She'll hate me if she—"

"Do you regret it? What happened with him?" Her eyes spark.

"Cor, Lily. Of course, I do!"

"And you care about Claire?"

My chest burns with a deeper ache than if some bloke had shoved a knife between my ribs. I jerk a nod at Lily. "More than I'd like to admit."

Lily points her staff at me. "Then *tell* her. You're human, just like the rest of us. And, even though it's taken you an eternity, you are growing, Peter. I see it every day. Little by little. But you can't keep hiding from everything you've done." Her expression goes sharp and intense, like a crack of thunder. "You have to face the truth, Peter, or it will devour you."

Tiger Lily turns away and heads back down the road in the opposite direction.

I pull on the cord around my neck, freeing the panpipe whistle to roll it between my fingers. "Lily?"

She glances over her shoulder, flecks of teal standing out in her dark hair. "Yes?"

"You're a proper queen, and once we get back to Neverland, the whole bloomin' universe is going to know it."

She grins broadly as she throws a careless wave my way. "Go get your girl."

I start hunting for a cab.

I want to believe Lily is right, that there is a way to show I am doing all of this to try to save Neverland. But I can't help thinking that if she knew everything, Claire would leave. Like they all do. Walk away, forget about me, slam their windows shut and lock them.

Like the window I once dared to return to, hoping my father would have left my bedroom open—but found that it'd been barred and locked. There was no one there anymore. No one waiting for me.

Or when I went back to the story girl, hoping to hear her voice just once more—but found her gable window fastened. Peering through the gap in the drapes, I saw someone else inside.

A husband and a daughter.

Wendy had grown up.

So I'd left. I'd *run*.

And I've been running ever since. I ran when I kissed Claire, ran when she needed to talk. I ran when she needed me.

But the running doesn't work. I've spent my whole life trying to escape shadows by hiding in the stars . . .

Only to find the darkness was inside me all along.

34

PETER

London, England

By the time I reach the port where the *Jolly Roger* is anchored, secluded and hidden away from any humans who might pass, dusk has begun to fall. The coming night catapults toward the ground, sky turning pallid as the evening fog spills in, sending chills down my spine. Or maybe the shiver is from seeing this familiar ship bobbing on the edge of the Thames.

Or from the way a familiar golden gleam speckles the deck.

If those beastly pirates have done anything to her . . .

I race down to the weather-beaten dock, across the planks of salt-stained wood as I draw closer and closer to the *Jolly Roger*.

How many times have I run toward that ship to take on Hook or rescue a friend?

And I've always won. Always outsmarted the codfish—this time won't be any different.

But it's already different. Because of Claire.

I try not to picture her tied up. Beaten. Bruised.

The ship is anchored a few feet off the end of the dock. The arched bow is well above my head, but they haven't cast off yet. A ramp bridges the gap between the dock and the ship, and several pirates and Lost Boys are loading the vessel for its voyage. Salty spray churns against the hull as I catch the flash of a scarlet coat at the stern of the ship—and that wretched skull-and-crossbones flag waving at the mast. I can still make out the glimmer of gold dust, but no Claire.

She has to be there somewhere!

The crew catches sight of me and an angry uproar breaks out. Blades glint in the fading sunlight as weapons are drawn and men cluster to the *Jolly Roger's* edge.

I reach for my own weapon, the blade I borrowed from Lily.

I give a crowing cry, as I lift my knife and run onto the ramp.

Oh, just try to hold me back, chaps!

I barrel into the first pirate, ramming my shoulder into his chest and launching him into the water.

The next three pirates come at me together, and I dart under one's arm, block the next one's saber with my knife, and twist around the final pirate. I avoid being skewered by the three brutes, but one rusty knife still nicks my arm. I bite my cheek as pain spikes through my bicep.

Blast, that stings.

I flex my knees, facing the next several blokes filling the creaking ramp, and barely manage to duck as a sharp stone careens past my ear.

'Ey! What was that?

My gaze sweeps over the blokes in front of me—Lost Boys. Curly towers over the twins, gripping a hefty slingshot and aiming another sharpened rock at my head.

Curses! Why did I teach them how to fight?

The twins grip throwing knives painted in the bright colors of Lily's tribe. What poor warrior did they pinch those off of?

Two massive pirates stand in front of the Lost Boys; one of them sporting an open grin that shows off his gold tooth—cliché, even to me—and the other holds a large spiked club in meaty hands that look like they're on backward.

Footsteps approach behind me, boxing me in.

Not my favorite odds.

It'd be really nice to fly right about now.

A muffled shriek reaches me, and every eye turns to the deck directly above us. I stare past the pirates pressed against the edge the ship—past the curls of rope and dangling rigging and crates of supplies—to the small figure tied to the mast.

Claire.

Thick coils of salt-encrusted rope lash across her body, tangles of matted blonde hair hanging around her wide, terrified eyes. A handkerchief is shoved in her mouth, but she's doing her best to scream around the gag.

Her eyes meet mine, relief filtering through those Neversea-blue eyes.

Rage, sudden and burning, floods through me. Claire's wrists are chafed and her skin so, so pale.

Those blaggards! I'm going to tear the lot of 'em apart.

But I can't get near enough to her. Not like this.

The pirates and Lost Boys have begun to close in again. The sky around us seems foreboding, littered with dark clouds heavy with rain as the ashen evening sets in.

Time to change the rules of the game.

Taking a deep lungful of salty air, I level my eyes at Claire and mouth two words: *pixie dust.*

She gives the faintest nod. Her eyes fall closed and flickers of golden dust ripple out from her. Slipping from her skin, tangling in her cardigan and falling to sweep across the deck.

Claire's dust drifts over the *Jolly Roger* in slow waves, the thin, filmy specks of gold out of place on the splintered and windblown ship.

But before the dust can reach me, a loping gait thuds across the deck, churning up the gleaming flecks. Like a scarlet-coated devil rising from the cool evening mist, Hook has left the stern and strides across the ship, dark beard shadowing his face in the thickening night. He comes to a halt at the edge of the bulwark, peering coolly down at me, lips tilted in a snarl.

"Well, look who finally decided to show up. I thought we'd have to stall for a few more hours, boy." He flicks a nod to his crew.

I blink, startled by this odd reaction, but before I can puzzle it out, I'm set upon by a dozen pirates and Lost Boys. Weapons swing at me, and another razor-edged rock shoots past my head, but I duck and spin to avoid their blows.

Then one connects with my ribs and my knees buckle. I manage to avoid a swift kick from the pirate with the gold tooth and then glance up.

I can just see the edge of Hook's polished boots. Specks of gold waft over the heels and drip down the side of the ship.

I may be outnumbered, but I have an advantage not even the Lost Boys can replicate. I'm still a bloomin' child who believes in pixies and magic and can turn a happy thought into wings.

So, I do what I do best.

The impossible.

I spin around one of the twins as the lad tries to chuck a knife at my face and throw myself at the edge of the ship. My hands grasp the rough wood and the pixie dust covers my fingers. It only takes a moment for the dust to spread down my arms and over my shoulders.

I think of Claire and an island in the stars and skies that belong to me alone . . .

And kicking Hook's rear.

I begin to rise through the air.

Oh. Yes.

With a laugh, I throw myself higher, reaching for the sky and climbing above the Lost Boys and pirates. I'm floating on my belly, suspended above eye level with the Captain, just out of reach of his hook.

"Miss me, Cap'n?"

"Oh, you have no idea." Hook's eyes narrow. "Although, nowhere near as much as you must miss that little pixie. Pity she had to meet such a gruesome end. What was her name again? Ah, right . . ." He lifts his hook to gesture sharply through the air. *"Tinkerbell."*

Another ball of anger—but this one is fiercer, more painful. It crashes over me in a tsunami that swells into a raging headache. I can see her. Blood spraying through the air and a look of horror and pain etched across her tiny features.

Tink. My pixie, my family. The one who showed me how to chase the stars.

"How dare you speak of her!" I roar and thrash my knife, blasting toward Hook in a spinning corkscrew.

The blade collides with his hook, but he just turns a knowing glance to Claire, who stares at us with a new expression. A slow, bitter kind of understanding.

No! Ah—I'm not sure I'm ready for our playing pretend to end yet.

Our weapons clash again. The other pirates and most of the Lost Boys have clustered in a semicircle around him, but they're not making a move to help their captain.

What in the stars is happening?

The pirate captain's hook slides along my knife blade with a metallic clash, but he just smirks up at me as I dangle over him.

"Oh, come now, *Peter.*" Hook's voice is like the deceptive lure of poison drip-dripping. "We've played this game enough times; surely you can drop the theatrics?"

He pauses to gesture toward Claire with a far too friendly wave.

"How many times is this now? That I've kidnapped your shiny little doll and tied her to my mast, that is." He scratches at his beard with the blunt end of his hook and then starts to tick them off the fingers of his good hand.

"First, it was Wendy . . . and then when you'd tired of her, it was her daughter Jane. Last time it was some lass from Yorkshire, I believe? Hard to remember, they all bleed together, don't they?"

I want to carve out his throat, but I can't move. I sink through the air, the scent of salt and the tang of blood thick as I drift lower and lower. I can hardly breathe as I look at Claire.

She looks like she's on the verge of crying. She's shaking her head, again and again and again.

My heart drops, and a second later my trainers hit the deck.

No, no! This is not—I'm not ready!

"He's lying, Claire! I can explain."

I move across the deck, and though the tension that swells out from the crew and Lost Boys is palpable, none of them move.

When I'm only paces from Claire, one of the Lost Boys steps forward. A tall lad with dark skin and sharp, revealing eyes.

Nibs.

Lily had warned me he'd joined Hook, but it didn't really hit me until this moment.

This lad was once my best mate of all the Lost Boys, one of

the few who'd dared to challenge my schemes and suggest ways to make them better. And though it made me want to drop the chap and his blasted big brain off on some deserted island, he was usually right.

Nibs doesn't say a word. He just steps around the mast, glares at me, then kneels to remove the gag from Claire's mouth with surprising gentleness. He murmurs something to her that's too low for me to hear.

Nibs has a soft spot for Claire?

Why does that make me want to feed him to a crocodile?

"Claire! Hang on. I've got you!" I race over the traces of her dust skimming the deck, my heels starting to rise again, but Claire won't look at me.

Nibs straightens. "You can take on this whole crew, Peter. You can even free Claire and whisk her away . . ." He shakes his head. "But you know she won't really be free. You've done something far worse than anything Hook has ever done. You've caged her soul."

He lifts a hand toward Claire.

"And no amount of well-spun lies can justify clipping a creature's wings when it's meant to fly."

I'm frozen midair, made of stone and ice and confusion. I stare at Nibs, then glance at Claire, and back at Nibs.

He's a Lost Boy who betrayed me—I should hate him. I shouldn't give a blasted thought to anything that duffer says.

But when I look at Claire, at the pixie dust lingering in the air around her, at the tears that leaked down her cheeks to leave a trail of golden flecks in their wake, at the way she's bound . . .

All I see is another person caught in the middle of the game I've been playing.

Another person with scars and wounds from the adventure I've had.

Another creature trapped by the dark things I've tried so hard to forget.

Nibs looks to Hook and then, at a gesture from the pirate, he pulls a knife from a sheath at his side—

"No, wait!"

But instead of plunging the knife into Claire's chest, Nibs severs the coils. They loosen from Claire's body and fall to the grimy deck, leaving Claire free.

Free?

What are they doing?

"Sorry, love." Stepping around me, Hook smiles apologetically at Claire as she stands in shock, her back still pressed against the mast. "We had to find a way to keep you in place long enough for Pan to come get you and finally reveal the truth."

This was all a ploy?

I should have known.

No wonder the pirates clustered around us are holding back—this was Hook's plan all along.

Nibs looks at Claire with such pleading intensity my insides twist. "We didn't know how else to convince you."

Claire finally steps away from the mast and turns to me. Her irises glistening like glass, she says the first words she's uttered since I arrived.

"Who are you? Really?"

And this time, as I stare at her, I can't lie. I know what it's like to be grounded, caged, and although I never meant to do it, maybe I have been chaining her down. Maybe the things I've been shoving down have been burying Claire, too.

The whole ship seems to hold its breath, the eyes of pirates and Lost Boys alike trained on me. Even Hook doesn't speak, simply watches with that perpetual expression of triumph.

I step toward Claire, past Nibs, past the pirates and the games and the make-believe tale I've spun so effortlessly. I reach out to gently touch her face and say . . .

"I'm Peter Pan."

Her whole body starts to tremble, but she doesn't look away. Just stares at me and says in a voice so hollow I almost don't recognize it, *"Why did you lie?"*

The evening air goes very, very thin.

Hook's icy voice echoes across the deck. "Yes, Peter. Tell her why you lied. Why you have been lying to her, manipulating her, since she first met you?"

There's a soft thud as Hook moves to stand beside Claire. The Captain traces a finger over the curve of his hook, his eyes on Claire's splotched features.

"In fact, why don't you tell her why she was left orphaned on Earth in the first place?" Each word that slithers from the pirate captain's mouth is like a noose drawing tighter around my throat. "Why a little boy named Peter became so jealous of infant twins with a connection to Neverland like his own that he left them abandoned in a strange world? Or why you later returned to steal away her brother?"

Nibs comes around the mast to stand on Claire's other side.

"Yes," he adds, "or why don't you tell her why most of the other Lost Boys and I were forced to join Hook after you nearly destroyed one of our own?" His eyes flash like a fierce lightning storm.

"Why didn't you tell her who you *really* are, Pan?"

My mouth goes dry, and I'm scrambling, scrambling for some way to untie all these knots they've twisted. But how do you cut through a trap woven from truth?

Before I can even open my mouth, Claire beats me to it. Her voice is halting and rough.

"Is everything they're saying true?" Her dust starts to fall faster, darkening like the moody London sky.

I take a deep breath, inching backward. "I—uh—well, technically, yes. But I can explain—"

Her red eyes continue to stare through me.

"I've been trying for *so* long to defend you, to believe in you, but . . . I don't recognize this boy." She gestures to me, whole body quivering. "Did you really abandon Connor and me on Earth? Leave us to rot in a world where we didn't belong? Did you really take my brother? Have you been lying to me since the day I first met you?"

The gold specks of dust continue to grow gray and crinkle in the chilled air, plastering Claire's cardigan to her slender form and rocking her shoulders.

Hook and Nibs edge backward, but Hook watches Claire with rapt attention.

Her grief churns around her as clearly as the shadowy flakes of dust, but I'm not about to back off. I have to get through to her somehow, before she snaps and does something we'll all regret.

I lift my hands slowly, taking a half step closer, watching as the darkening sky dissolves into the haze whirling around her.

"I—I didn't realize what I was doing when I dropped you both off on Earth. And when I saw you in Kensington, I thought you'd never believe me if you knew who I was. Please, just let me—"

"No more excuses." Claire's voice slices through me like a blade, but her eyes are filled with an ocean of aching, overwhelming grief. "I—I need to think."

Specks of her darkening dust hitting the deck and leaving tiny burn marks. Does she even know she's doing this?

Surprised murmurs waft over the crew, and Nibs is staring at Claire like he can't believe his eyes.

I ignore the flecks of dust that sting my face and sidle a little closer.

"Just hear me out, Claire."

She lifts her head, her expression partially hidden by the thick tangles of hair falling over her tear-stained cheeks.

"How can I believe anything you say? And what I do know now"—her voice breaks—"is worse than I ever imagined. You didn't just steal my brother and lie to me—you're the reason we were orphaned in the first place. You're why I've spent my entire life as an outsider, a freak."

Her lips are white, and her churning dust thickens.

The pirates draw weapons, but their cutlasses will be useless against Claire's dust. They have no idea what could happen to this whole ship if she loses control.

The scent of burning wood fills my nostrils.

"Just take a breath, Claire. We can talk this out."

She just shakes her head. "You know, I actually thought I was . . ." She swallows. "I thought I was falling in love with 'Ben.' But I never knew Ben at all."

Her eyes go distant, vague, as if she's drifting away, distancing herself from everything and everybody.

"How can I trust you now? You've broken everything."

Her vacant stare says the rest.

I've broken *her.*

A volley of choice curses pelt through my thoughts, but nothing can slow the bile rising in my throat.

Claire begins to tremble again. Her dust crackles and darkens, shifting from a gray to obsidian.

Oh no.

It fills the air around her like a black storm cloud. The burning dust skims the deck, and instantly leaves a charred impression across the wood. Any deeper and it could singe a hole to the underbelly of the vessel.

The pirate crew starts to panic, scrambling to the edge of the bulwark, a few looking ready to dive overboard. But Hook doesn't even flinch, a victorious smile on his thin lips.

"Beautiful," he murmurs.

Claire's head drops against her chest, legs trembling. She's beginning to pull back into herself.

I'm losing her.

"Claire, I—"

Claire turns her back on me.

"I can explain everything . . ."

Even with her back to me, I can see her shoulders heave with a sharp intake of breath.

"Please. Go away. I can't think." Her voice breaks. "Oh, *Connor . . .*"

I can't lose her like this. I rush forward, to grasp her hand despite the whirling dust, despite the way it scalds my skin and stings my eyes.

"Claire, it's still me. Just let me—"

Claire pulls away. *"No more stories, Peter."*

Then her dust explodes in a massive, burning cloud that slams into me with the force of a cannon shot. I'm thrown backward in a haze of scorching ash.

35

CLAIRE

London, England

*B*en *is Peter Pan.*

Somewhere in the deep recesses of my mind, a part of me already knew. But I thought, somehow, he was different. That he was more Ben than Peter. That I could hold him, keep him like this. Like the Ben I wanted. That if I believed his tales enough, they would be true.

But it's all a lie.

Everything he said about me, the boys, about Connor—it was a lie. A lie that let him use me, use my kiss and my childhood and my brokenness so that he could get what he wanted.

Because in the end, Peter Pan only ever cares about himself.

And I'm an idiot for refusing to see that.

That twisting, shattered truth blazes into rage, and I let the anger erupt, crack my body apart, and send dust hurtling from my skin. The world dissolves into a dark haze as the flecks pour out from me, aching and shriveling and screaming the words my soul can't find the strength to say.

My dream was my darkest nightmare all along.

My whole world has gone up in ash—the person I was

becoming, the boy who saw me as more, the stories I'd believed, even everything I've learned about Connor.

No wonder my dust has turned to ash.

I'm angry at the lies. Angry at Peter for manipulating me. Using me.

Angry at *myself.*

For being so blind.

My fury begins to dissipate, like a raging fire running out of kindling, leaving only an empty, sour ache of grief. I can't stop the desperate sobs and the dust fades to a trickle as the anger fades and the grief fills into its place.

The haze thins and the world around me sharpens into focus. The *Jolly Roger* comes into view like a grim, windswept vision.

The ship is coated in ash.

The pirate crew huddles at the opposite edge of the deck, staring at me with expressions of mixed awe and terror. Several Lost Boys have sought refuge by climbing the rigging.

They're afraid of *me.*

It's like a bucket of cold water slamming into my senses.

I did this.

My body goes stone cold.

Where is–?

I frantically search the ship, my skin clammy.

Where is he? Where is he?

My gaze slams into a crumpled, too-still form lying against one of the stacks of crates. He's curled up in the fetal position, and there's something odd about his clothes. Swells of red and pink mingle with the singed green of his hoodie.

My legs nearly give out. I clap a hand over my mouth to force myself not to retch.

His skin is raw and blistered. Patches of his beautiful red-gold curls are charred, and blood splatters the deck. His chest rises and falls in slight, ragged movements.

Dear God—what have I done? What have I become?

My vision goes black, the world spins, and I can't breathe.

The anger that consumed me moments ago is nothing but a hollow echo. Peter didn't deserve this.

To be wounded by my darkness.

I'm destroying him, and I have no idea how to undo it.

I want to cross the deck to him—but I'm crumbling again, and more dust pours from my skin. If I draw closer, I'll only injure him more. If I move, I'll make it worse.

I clench my fists and try to force it back inside. To close away the shadows and quench the dust. But it doesn't work. I can't seem to conjure a single happy thought.

Even the pirates are staring at me like I'm a monster.

Maybe I am.

Despair weighs me down like it did when I lost Connor. When I gave up hope all those years ago and jumped out a window.

The shadows are back, and this time they're going to finish the job.

Maybe a part of me wants them to.

I hunch over the deck, fingers grasping at the grimy wooden planks. I curl inward, the overwhelming weight shutting me down, and I sense a prickle along my arms. It's just a sting at first, and then it starts to sizzle.

Burn.

I gasp. Through my tears I can make out tiny welts rising on my arms. *What?*

And then the sizzle becomes scarring, spiking pain that

bubbles my skin where graying flakes hit.

My dust is burning me!

Pain jolts through me, spiking blisters along my hands and face.

The inferno swirling around me only picks up. I gasp as more flakes sizzle over my shoulders and blister through my cardigan.

"Please! Make it stop!" My scream is frantic. The more terror fills me, the faster specks of acid scorch my arms in deep, raw blisters. I've felt pain before and have the scars carving across my spine to prove it. But this is much worse. "Make it stop!" I moan.

Panic darkens my vision, and my fingers go numb.

Burns flay my skin. Every raw nerve screams.

I've lost all control.

This is the end.

I'm so sorry, Connor.

Dust whips into my face. Tears sizzle from my clenched eyelids.

"*Help—me—*" The choking words are cracked and grainy.

"Oh, love, can't you see? Only *you* can make it stop."

Hook's deep voice is steady and cool as a blade. I pry my burning eyes open. Scorch marks and burnt patches mar Hook's meticulous scarlet coat.

He watches me unwaveringly. There's not a shred of fear in the pirate's expression.

A shiver crawls down my spine, but the fury of ashen dust whipping around me begins to slow.

Hook give me a dark smile. "You are *stunning*, love. Every part of this."

He lifts his hand, the curve of metal jutting from his crimson cuff. He steps forward to slice through the cloud of dust with his hook, the ashen flecks smoking against the metal.

Hook doesn't flinch. He isn't afraid.

The pirate captain continues. "Like your brother, you are shadow and light, power and fear, weightless and crushing. Don't sell yourself short, love."

His words settle over me like the faintest breath of cool air, skimming across my skin and softening the swelling burns.

But as if on an invisible tether, I'm drawn to Peter again. He turns his face to me, his glistening green eyes a sharp contrast to the harsh red welts peppering his skin.

Despite his pain, those eyes carry a depth I've never seen before—and a spark of something so determined that, for a moment, it wipes away everything else around us. Until it's just him and me.

Me and Peter Pan.

Peter who has broken so much—but Peter as Ben who showed me something I would have never known without him.

That my dust can shine.

Peter is moving his cracked lips, but I don't catch his words.

The Lost Boys drift closer to Pan. They send an inquisitive look at Hook.

"Please," I plead with the captain. "I need to know what he's saying."

Hook scratches at his beard and finally sighs.

"Well, I suppose we can give the little devil his final words . . ." His lips smirk as he nods at the boys.

"Thank you." I really mean it.

Hook waves the gratitude away.

A tall, lanky boy bends down beside Peter, listening as Peter speaks.

The Lost Boy glances up, bewildered.

"Broken wing? That's it, just 'broken wing.'"

The words catch in my memory. Peter gives me the faintest nod. I get it. I understand.

I squeeze my eyes shut and plant my palms on the deck. I shut out everything else. The noise, the looks, the fear—and the dust.

I quiet the chaos and think back to that moment in Kensington Gardens that feels like a lifetime ago. Just before I tumbled over the bridge and into the water, when the pixies were dancing around us—and I saw the little pixie with a broken wing.

And I'd watched, transfixed, as the wing straightened and healed.

My eyes dart back to Peter.

That magic in your veins means you have a choice, Claire. Lily's face flashes in my mind despite the fact she deceived me, too. But not about the most important things. *You were created for more than to bear the weight of your shadows—but you have to choose to no longer let them define you. You have to choose to let the light shine through the shattered pieces.*

Hope stirs in my chest.

Maybe this dust isn't a curse—but a choice.

There is light in me. And maybe it's more powerful than the shadows.

It has to be.

I open my eyes. "I am more than my shadows." The thick haze of dust begins to thin, churning slowly until it's nothing but a soft ripple. The black specks lighten to gray.

"There is light."

I hold onto that phrase like a promise, a hope. A happy thought.

I send thin ripples of pale dust skimming toward Peter. He lifts his head and gives a brief smile, his movements slow and painstaking.

He believes I can mend these shadows.

I just have to believe it too.

I close my eyes for the briefest moment and let that belief sink somewhere deep into my core, sprouting into a seed of hope.

"There is light more powerful," I whisper again.

The crew watches, wide-eyed, and I feel Hook's unwavering gaze on me.

I open a hand. Dust pools in my palm, and the crinkled white begins to soak up color. Begins to take on a healthy pink hue, and then tinges of yellow.

For the burns marring Peter's body—for Connor and every other child who has ever felt forgotten—for the pixies suffering because of the destruction twisting their home . . .

And most of all, for me, for the girl who believed she was broken but who couldn't see the beauty shining inside. For the person the creator of the stars made me to be.

"I choose light."

I lift my hands, letting the dust sift through my fingertips and slip away. It has softened to gold—and my skin is returning to its normal color. Healed.

Tears prick at my eyes. I would have never imagined my dust could do this. Could lift and, most of all, mend. Restore.

I take a deep breath and spread out my arms. Sparkling dust flows from my fingertips like a shimmering river. I stride toward Peter, light and warmth rippling down my body and across the deck.

If the stars could speak, maybe they'd say this is who I really am.

A girl of stardust and shadow, who chooses to let light heal the broken pieces.

36

PETER

London, England

The web of lies I spun for myself is burning, prying the skin from my flesh. I've had close calls before—nicked by a cannonball, an arrow in the shoulder, nearly drowned by some angry sirens—but I've never felt anything like this.

I curl up on the deck, forcing air into my burning lungs, trying to salvage any remaining strength I have. My body is being torn apart, my skin peeling away. I'm evaporating into a choking, shriveled husk. It's not just the welts bubbling my skin. The shadowed flakes seep deeper, bleeding despair and destruction.

Please, Claire. I can only hope she understood. Hope she can figure it out.

A cool, soothing flake brushes my shoulder, then another lands on my jaw. It soaks in and softens the pain. More land on my skin, easing the desperate burning.

It's Claire. It has to be. *Open your eyes!*

A cough wracks my body, and pain flares in my chest, but I finally get my eyes open.

And there she is.

Claire is gliding across the deck, floating like an ethereal creature, a sheath of glistening, gold dust coating her skin. Her dust pours out, faster and faster.

It drips down her like some kind of rippling, shimmering dress. Her hair is unbound, thick and full, those untamed curls float around her face as if caught by an invisible wind.

There's my Pixie-Girl. Cor, she's stunning.

Her dust pools around my body, falling across my shoulders and chest like a whisper. I reach for it, my fingers skimming the edge of the satin sheen of gold coating the grimy wooden boards. The dust flows over my fingers and down my arm, cooling the burns.

The pain begins to ebb.

It's working!

A genuine smile pulls at my lips, and I lift my head to look up at Claire. Her teary eyes warm at my smile, and her dust pours out even faster.

"Knew you—could—" I choke out the words. They're thick and coarse on my tongue.

"Is it helping?"

I manage a half nod.

She kneels beside me, reaching out to tenderly brush my forehead with soft fingertips. Her dust fills the air like flakes of sunlight caught in the darkening night. The golden flecks continue to fall to cover my fleshy, bubbling burns.

Claire notices the pirates edging closer. She waves them back.

The pirates mutter among themselves, glancing at Hook. The captain and Nibs have closed in even more. The captain doesn't so much as look at his crew.

Hook's expression turns as he glances between Claire and me. His cold gaze practically splits me open—but then his eyes look at Claire and they soften. He almost looks—triumphant. Pleased.

A shudder snakes through me.

"Give me room." Claire turns a piercing glare on the pirate crew. "You've seen what I can do."

I smile at the note of steel in her voice. I can't quite tell if it's a bluff or not—but Claire's threat gets the crew's attention, and they immediately shuffle back.

"That's my girl." Hook gives a low chuckle.

I'd vomit if I had anything left in my stomach.

Slightly and the other Lost Boys are perched in the rigging and clustering at the stern.

A trickle of glistening dust speckles my singed eyelashes. Claire leans over me again, hair dangling around her face, her brow puckered thoughtfully. She's so close . . .

A wild side of me wants to lean up and press a kiss to her forehead.

"Why are you looking at me like that?"

I give a little cough to hide the slight flush heating my already singed skin. "No reason."

She blows out a long breath. "You stupid, stupid boy. Why did you keep pushing me? Why couldn't you have backed away when you saw my dust darkening?"

I don't hold back my smile. "Wanted you to know I'd never meant to hurt you."

Her face pales. "But you did. Your lies hurt more than my own burning dust ever could."

My heart sinks.

"But even with everything you've done . . ." Claire reaches down to brush a fingertip over a particularly bad burn, letting dust drip from her finger and cool the ragged searing of the blister.

"I can't just leave you like this," she says. "I won't let my pain tear you apart. I have to save you."

Her words strike me dumb.

This girl is so different from anyone I've ever met.

She leans closer, hands on my arms, and her eyes close again as her forehead ripples in concentration. Her dust dissolves into my skin like water soaking into parched, cracked earth. I gasp, arching my back at the strange sensation but Claire doesn't let go.

Her dust continues to saturate me, rolling over in waves and spreading a strange heat through my limbs. I can breathe again.

I wipe a coat of dust from my eyelids, careful not to upset Claire's hold on me.

I can feel Claire's rapid heartbeat through her palms. The pain drains away, and with the raw ache gone, the warm hum of magic rushes in my veins—and it feels *great*.

I've never felt so alive.

Claire releases me and leans back. She rests against the stack of crates behind us. I get to my feet, raising my hands to stare at the unbroken skin along my arms. My lips part in awe. Even the thin scar that usually pokes out over my shoulder blades is gone.

No way . . .

I shove up my charred left sleeve and stare at my forearm. *Nothing.* The skin is healthy and clear—not a hint of the scars or calluses I've gotten over the years from tumbling out of trees or picking rock fights with the Lost Boys.

Wait. What if . . . ?

I scramble for the heel of my right trainer, the rubber sole misshapen and burnt, and chuck it off quickly.

"Peter, what are you doing?"

I flash her a smile.

"I think you . . ." I toss my shoe aside and balance on one foot to peer down at my heel. I nearly choke on my own excitement.

"*Yes*, you did! They're gone!"

Claire pushes off from the pile of crates. "I did what?"

I gesture to my heel. In the gleam of her gold dust wafting through the cool night air, Claire's eyes drop to take in the smooth, calloused lines of my foot.

"What? Peter, I don't see anything."

I grin. "Exactly. You didn't just heal my burns, Claire. You healed my scars too. Even the ones on my feet from cutting off my shadow. Cor, you're amazing!"

Claire's awestruck expression slowly dissolves into something I can't read.

"*You* cut off your own shadow?"

I drop my heel, letting both feet thud against the slick deck. "It's a long story . . ."

Claire turns away from me. "I don't understand anything anymore."

Hook is right there, of course. "I knew you could control it, love. Now you can go find your brother." He winks at her and bows, motioning to his vessel in a sweeping gesture.

"May I offer this ship and my guidance to help you make the trek through the stars? We have enough supplies to easily get us to Neverland, and I can show you the way."

Oh no you don't, you blasted cad!

I grab Claire's wrist. "Claire, you can't trust him!"

She pulls away.

"And you think I can trust you? Everything I thought I knew about Peter Pan, Captain Hook, or any of this is so messed up."

Nibs gives her a little reassuring smile when she glances his way. I *so* want to toss him overboard.

Claire crosses her arms, and immediately dust begins to

cascade from her skin and fill the air. "I have too many things to think about and obviously I'm not going to get any privacy here."

She lifts her eyes to the stars and takes in the open expanse overhead.

"Even a spark of light can ignite a night sky."

Her toes leave the ground and she begins to rise in a wave of gleaming pixie dust that draws a gasp from the pirates on deck. She gains speed, racing past the rigging and above the mast. Golden flecks pour from her skin as she gains height, shooting past the *Jolly Roger* to hover out of reach of the pirate huddled in the crow's nest.

She's flying. By herself, for the first time.

I can't help but grin as I stare at her.

"She truly is magnificent," Hook croons, clipping across the deck with that uneven gait of his. The rest of the crew surges forward, weapons glinting.

Without the threat of Claire's burning dust to hold them back, I'm an easy target. Or so they think. Traces of her gleaming golden dust still coat the deck and catch in my jacket. I can practically feel it coaxing me upward. I smirk at the angry crew as they rush me.

Ah ah ah! Not this time, chaps.

My heels leave the deck, and I crow triumphantly down at Hook's scowling mug.

"Trust me, little boy"—Hook spits out the last word—"this is far from over. For years, I thought simply destroying you would be enough for me. But I've been thinking too small. Playing too shortsighted of a game. I won't make that mistake again."

Hook's expression edges with a deep-seated animosity that makes the air feel metallic and heavy.

"I'm going to tear you apart piece by piece, Pan. Just like

you did to me and the woman I loved. I'm going to carve away everything you ever cared about until you are *begging* me to feed you to that crocodile." His lips curl. "Starting with Claire."

I flounder midair. I fight to latch on to a happy thought. A flood of anger wells up in me, and I spew several choice curses. "I'll never let you hurt her!"

I spin around and shoot upward, darting through the lattice of rigging, and find Claire.

I won't let him put her in danger.

I hover just below the Pixie-Girl, bouncing on my heels in the empty air.

"Claire?"

She ignores me for a long moment. Then she lifts her chin at me. The *Jolly Roger* bobs on the Thames far below us.

Pixie dust fills the air around her.

"You were right about one thing, Peter. I don't belong here." Claire gives me a wry smile. "Connor and I were made for something more. For years, I couldn't believe that. Couldn't find any beauty in my dust, in myself. But then, I met you."

Her sea-blue eyes glisten. I rise a little higher until we're at the same level, dangling by unseen threads in an impossibly large sky.

"You didn't see me as a freak. You said I was beautiful—and that changed everything. You became my happy thought. I needed you to learn how to fly."

Behind her, the bank of the Thames is hidden behind roiling mist, a chill drifting out over the swelling water.

"But I can't keep waiting for someone else to tell me I'm worthwhile. The light has got to seep deeper than that, or else I can't truly help myself or anyone else. I can't always depend on Peter Pan to fly."

I cross my arms over my singed green jacket, her words heavy in my chest. "You're right—you don't need me. Cor, you don't need any of us." I gesture at the pirate ship bobbing on the evening tide beneath us. "But you can't trust that blaggard. Hook isn't your mate—he's just using you to get back to Neverland. To get *you* back to Neverland."

Claire sighs. "Of course Hook needs me to get back to Neverland. He's never lied about that."

With a little sigh, she slides through the air, drifting to the right, away from the *Jolly Roger* and out over the rippling Thames. My pulse jumps as I catch sight of the dock jutting out into the water not too far from us.

"Hook is dangerous. He manipulated Connor, and he wants to tear me apart and—"

"He's the villain of the story—I get it." Her toes trace small patterns in the air dozens of feet above the glassy river. "But that's just the thing, Peter. It's always been what you tell me. Even when it comes to Connor—it's always been your side of the story. I need to find the truth for myself."

I poke a finger through one of the charred holes in my jacket sleeve as I follow her over the Thames.

"All right, well, if you won't listen to me—why can't you just let me take you? By the stars, I swear I'll get you straight to Neverland, no funny business. Give me a shot, mate."

"I'm not your mate, Peter." More flecks of dust speckle Claire's arms, clinging to her cheeks and spilling from her body as she slides through the air in a slow circle around me. "Do you really think after everything you did to Connor that I could just pretend like nothing happened?" Her words come in staccato, heartbroken notes.

"I may not hate you for what you've done, but that doesn't mean I'm going to just close my eyes and make believe everything is the way it used to be. I don't *know* you, Peter. And I'm not even sure I want you anywhere near my brother."

My eyes shoot wide—and I drop an inch. Then another.

I can't make her words fit together, make sense. My pulse thuds hollowly, a tightness clamps my throat.

No . . .

This can't be happening.

"We're so close—just let me help get you to Neverland." I fight to keep my voice light. "And then you can heal the island, and we can all be proper finished with this whole mess."

Claire's expression falls. "Wait—you mean so I can get to Neverland and save my brother. *Right?*"

I gulp, pulse pounding like I've been backed into a corner. Still, lying didn't work out well for me last time around.

"Ah—aye. But first, we have to figure out how to help you heal the island."

"Heal the island?" Those blue eyes spark. "You think I can heal Neverland? Like how my dust healed you? Is that what this has been about all along?"

Her face hardens. "This whole time, your priority wasn't helping me find my brother—it was me fixing another of your messes."

I rake a hand through the thick hair clinging to my forehead. "I do want to help you get to Neverland! But it's all a bit complicated."

"Things always are with you, Peter." Her voice trembles. "This isn't about what I needed. It's all about *you*."

I open my mouth, but Claire shakes her head at me.

"You live in a fantasy world, Peter." Claire's eyes are wet. "You

live in this made-up place where you can do whatever you want
and don't have to bother with how it may hurt others."

My mouth is dry.

"But this isn't Neverland, and the rest of us can't live like that."
She bites her lip. "*I* can't live like that."

I plummet a few feet toward the water below before catching
myself. My lips part, and I stare up at Claire, but I can't speak.

This can't be happening . . .

Claire lifts her hands, her dust holding her suspended, a few
feet above me.

"I never had a childhood, thanks to you. And unlike some,
I can't spend my life running from what I've seen and what
I've done."

Her words plow into me like a punch in the gut, and I
spiral backward.

"Claire, don't do this . . ."

"You've already done it, Peter." The words burn.

The dust suspending me flickers. The icy river is only a few
feet below, its murky depths reflecting the blurred stars overhead.
I claw at empty air, trying to force myself higher, trying to draw
on a happy thought—but I can't think of a single one.

"Claire!" I press all of my desperation into her name. I reach
out, aching for her to reach back. "Just give me one more chance,
Pixie-Girl."

"You have so much you still need to learn, Peter. So much
growing to do. And I have every hope that you will get there. But
I can't be the one to help you." Claire's lips tremble. "There are
just so many lies . . . lies I don't think you even know you've told."

She sinks a little lower, but still doesn't reach for my
outstretched hand.

"I need to find my own way."

No! It can't end like this.

She draws a ragged breath. "How can I trust you to guide me through the stars when I can barely stand to say your name?"

A cool breeze drifts across my skin.

"Goodbye, Peter Pan."

Despair fills my chest like concrete, and suddenly the pixie dust around me disappears, like the lights of a thousand pixies blinking out.

I fall.

My body rockets downward, the world ripped away. Claire hovers in the air, spun of stardust and silhouetted by the dark sky behind her. Her hollow expression is the last thing I see before I hit the water.

37

CLAIRE

London, England

I'm done waiting.

Conviction burrows deep into my heart. I pause midair, looking down at the Thames reflecting a kaleidoscope of stars. Peter's head finally breaks the surface of the water. I inhale a breath of relief—and exhale a sigh.

Shock and despair fill Peter's water-soaked features as he stares up at me. Peter's beautiful lies can't define my world anymore.

It was never about helping me with my missing brother.

I need to find Connor.

Determination wrapping around me like the veil of pixie dust, I glide through the air and descend toward the pirate ship.

My feet hit the deck, dust skimming out around me, floating across the worn boots of dozens of men hurrying around the vessel, once again loading on any last crates and preparing for cast off. Dark expressions glint toward the edge of the Thames where they must have seen me drop Peter, causing victorious snarls to ripple through the crewman.

My eyes turn to Hook. He gives a slight nod.

"You've never needed that boy. You are more powerful than you can imagine."

He looks past the edge of the ship, to the pallid silhouette of Peter bobbing in the murky waves. "What is it that you truly want, love?"

I swallow around the lump in my throat. Hook may be a scoundrel, but our interests seem to be aligned. Since I met him in his estate those weeks ago, he has offered a single bargain—to get me to my brother.

And while I can fly through the stars, I can't navigate them. I need a guide.

A part of me wishes I could confide in Tiger Lily, ask her to guide me to Neverland. But the tribal princess herself admitted that she doesn't know her own way home. And if I reach out to Lily . . . Peter won't be far behind. They're a package deal.

I meet Hook's silvery eyes. "Is your offer still open?"

The pirate captain gives a low chuckle. "Of course, love."

I cross my arms. "This doesn't mean I'm joining you. I just want to get to Neverland. Nothing more. But, in order to even consider it, I'd need certain . . . guarantees."

Hook's grin slithers wide. "Name them."

"Privacy and safety." I glance at the ramshackle crew scurrying around the vessel. "I want you to promise me that my safety will be upheld the whole trip."

Hook nods again. "Of course. I swear on my own life that you won't suffer so much as a scratch while on board my fair vessel. In fact, you can stay in my cabin. With the lock and key, of course."

He gestures with his intact hand at a red-painted door of the captain's cabin, tucked away on the tail end of the ship.

I bite my lip, liking the idea of having a secured cabin but still uncertain of how *easy* this all feels.

"How do I know you won't just tie me up again?"

Hook's beard twitches. "I am a pirate after all, love. But I promise that I will do you no harm and simply guide you to Neverland. After all, you are our best chance of getting the *Roger* home. And, as I've said, I know what it's like to lose someone to Pan." His expression darkens. "And if there is anything I can do to prevent that from happening again, I'll do it."

I draw myself to full height. "If I ever feel threatened—you've seen what my dust can do. I also won't hesitate to jump ship. I'll take my dust and leave the *Jolly Roger* and its crew to plummet through the stars."

"I would expect nothing less."

The pirate captain lifts his hook and gently traces the curve of my cheek, his lips twisted in an odd smile.

"You are a force to be reckoned with, love. And if any of the oafs on board this vessel don't realize that, you are more than welcome to burn the skin from their bones."

I'm not sure if it's the mental image or the careless way he says the words that repulses me more.

I step away from his reach. "That's not exactly what I meant."

His silver eyes gleam. "Oh, don't underestimate yourself. I certainly don't."

I flick salt-streaked curls out of my eyes and rub my arms.

"Ah, it's getting cold out." Nibs clears his throat, speaking for the first time since I landed on the deck.

He shrugs out of his jacket and offers it to me. "It'll just get colder the higher we go."

I take the jacket and sling it over my shoulders. It carries his warmth and smells of sea and earth.

"Thanks."

Nibs flushes and gives a half nod. He presses a fist to his lips, and then speaks in a low voice. "Claire, we really do just want to help you get home to Connor."

"Aye, let's get you home to your brother." Nibs slips into the background as the captain addresses me. "Do we have a deal?"

Captain Hook lifts his curving metal hook for a hand and extends it toward me, like an open palm. An offering.

The sounds of the ship go dull and distant as I study the pirate standing in front of me. For the first time, I know how to use my pixie dust to make the journey—and I'm no longer afraid of myself.

So, I take a deep breath and reach out to place my hand around the steel hook. My voice is steady as I meet Hook's eyes.

"Yes."

And just like that, the lost girl with pixie dust in her veins strikes a deal with the storybook villain.

Before I can even take my hand back from Hook, a loud roar pierces the air.

The sound hits the ship like whiplash, wrenching around and stirring the entire crew into motion. Shouts fill the air, and several pirates race toward the port side of the ship, facing the dock.

The air is rent by another echoing growl that is vaguely familiar and the heavy thud of something pounding across the wooden dock toward us. Something big. Really, really big.

I'm swept up in the melee as the rest of the crew and the Lost Boys dash to the edge of the ship. Nibs pulls me along with him.

"You'll want to see this," he says.

I peer over the bulwark with the rest of the motley crew as a massive form emerges from the mist sweeping across the shore. Large paws with dark, shaggy fur and elongated claws thunder over the docks. As the creature steps out into the moonlight, I gasp, unable to believe my eyes.

The beast is easily the size of an elephant. It has massive paws and thick fur that looks so dense that it could withstand a bullet or a blade. Strong shoulders and a sloping back taper into a thick, coiling tail that flicks through the air like a whip.

But the sight of its head is what really seems a nightmare, wide red eyes, ears cocked at the top of its skull, and a large muzzle that snaps open with row upon row of teeth.

Two familiar people are tucked behind its massive head. Jeremy and Tiger Lily—and they're *riding* it.

The creature stops at the edge of the dock, rearing back to unleash a roar that rattles the *Jolly Roger*. It paws at the dock, looking like it's ready to leap for the ship and tear into the frightened crew. For a moment, the creature's attention sweeps to Peter still treading water. He's swimming as close to the *Jolly Roger* as he dares without getting slammed against the hull, and he doesn't seem the least bit worried about the beast.

But the pirates around me sure are.

"Cast off, men!" Hook shouts. He shoves past a Lost Boy with curly hair and takes my arm. "We must leave now, love. There's not much time."

I continue to stare at the massive beast on the dock. "What is that thing?"

"'Tis a Neverbeast, love. And if Jeremy has unleashed it, it means they're here to stop us." His voice is suddenly urgent. "If you want to save your brother, we must leave *now*."

I'm still trying to take in what I'm seeing with Jeremy and Lily riding the massive Neverbeast, the tribal princess gripping her staff. I can't make out her earth-brown eyes, but I can sense her focus fixed on me.

I look at the crew climbing through the rigging and hastening to prepare the ship for cast off. To sail off into the stars.

Then my eyes slowly go back to Lily and Jeremy. And, finally, to Peter. The people I once considered friends. Family, even.

But my real family needs me.

I place my hands over the ship's railing. Purpose fills in all the places that ache at those I have to leave behind.

I'm coming, Connor.

My eyelids close. I block out the swell of the Thames hitting the *Jolly Roger's* hull. Block out the image of the Neverbeast and its riders on the docks. Block out the cursing and boisterous voices of the crew behind me. Block out Peter.

Block out everything but me and the stars.

I let the dust free and send it cascading down my skin and spreading from my touch. I can feel it skimming across the bulwark and filling the deck at my feet. It flows from me and spreads out in wave after wave. Rushing faster and fuller than it did even when I was trying to heal Peter. It's as if a reserve deep inside has been unleashed. It spirals from my chest, warm and evocative and right.

This is what I was missing when I flung myself from that two-story window those years ago, nearly insane from the grief of losing Connor. I didn't understand it then. I thought the scars meant I would always be grounded. But the scars, the doubts, the weight . . . they don't truly matter. They can't crush me anymore.

I can soar.

The ship pulls free of the water, rising from the Thames, even before I crack my eyes open. Flecks of gold are a glowing, gleaming cloud that fills the whole ship, coating every plank of wood. The pirate ship is bathed in light. It spills up the mast and tangles in the skull-and-crossbones flag dangling from its top.

The air grows cooler as the ship continues to ascend, drawing away from the world below, leaving mist and trees and asphalt and cityscape.

Around me, the crew has stilled, gasps and low murmurs of awe filling the deck.

Hook is close beside me, an approving smile on his face. "That's it, love . . ."

The ship continues to rise through the air, aiming for the sparkling stars. I take one last peek downward. The group on the dock is almost too distant now to make out any expressions.

But my breath still catches as I take them in—Jeremy, standing beside the Neverbeast, the London Police Officer who gently guided me toward someone who could explain my dust.

Lily, at the edge of the dock, as if she's ready to dive in after Peter. She's tall and steady, gripping her staff in one hand. The closest thing I've ever had to a best friend.

And finally, Peter, still floating in the water. Peter, who taught me to fly, taught me to see my dust as a gift. Who risked himself to help me, even when my own magic had turned to poison.

Peter, the boy I let steal my heart.

The boy who still has so much to learn.

We're rising faster. Seconds later, all of London stretches out in a vast blanket of arching spires and light and bustle. A city that had held hope when I'd nearly lost all mine.

Hook stands silently beside me, eyes soaking in the city dissolving below us. Nibs is at my other side, so close his sleeve almost brushes mine, and even though he's looking away, I can tell his eyes are shining. Before long, several other Lost Boys and pirates crowd in too, peering over the edge of the ship for their last sight of a world fading below.

I lift my eyes to the stars patterning the sky above us. I spy two particularly bright ones and fix my gaze on the second to the right, feeling the ship gaining even more speed. Several pirates grasp for the railing as the wind whips past us, but I don't let my focus waver.

The stars beckon, drawing me onward.

Toward Neverland.

Toward my family.

Time seems to slow and speed up at the same time in the strange journey to the island of dreams. The world is enveloped in a spray of color and laughter and childlike dreams.

I open my eyes to a forever journey that is over in a blink.

I cross to stand at the edge of the ship again. Only this time, I'm not staring down at the darkened globe of Earth—but at the curving silhouette of an island in the middle of the stars. It's surrounded by water and gleaming colors that I never knew existed.

Even the air here feels new.

My heart pounds as the ship draws closer and closer to the island suspended in the stars like a jewel nestled in a crown. And despite the strangeness of it all, despite this world that I have never set foot on . . .

Here there is hope.

The magic in my veins has begun to hum along with the starlight. The rapid cadence of my own heartbeat pulses in time with the song of this whimsical island resting in the stars. Calling to me. The soft melody that fills every fiber of my being and makes my soul dance because—just maybe—I belong in this world.

In this Neverland.

"I'm here, Connor."

38

PETER

London, England

*S*he's gone.

The Thames is icy and heavy, weighing down my jacket and seeping into every inch, but I hardly feel it. All I can do is look up at the sky.

I stare at the gaping emptiness overhead, where she was only minutes ago, willing her to reappear. To come back so that I can warn her about what truly awaits in Neverland. But I'm too late.

Much, much too late.

All that's left is a hollowness that soaks into my chest, forming a vacuum there I've never felt before.

When I close my eyes, it's all still branded across my thoughts—the image of the *Jolly Roger* aglow with pixie dust, Claire beside the pirate captain at the helm, bathed in gold and boldness. The ship was a streak of gold that sailed across the stars one minute—and then blinked out of sight. Proof of everything Claire is capable of. Everything she is.

Without me.

My arms have gone heavy from treading water, and numbness seeps up from my toes.

It's not the first time I've been abandoned by a Kenton.

Instantly, a flash of an angry, icy-blue gaze lances across my memory, like a brief stroke of lightning that ignites a dark room you didn't want revealed.

No, not now!

My fists curl. I don't want to see this. *Can't* see it. Not with the realization of everything this stored secret holds for Claire.

Everything it holds for me.

This is why I refuse to let the memories in, and I couldn't tell Claire. Because if I remember what I did . . . I'm not sure I'll recognize myself anymore.

The lad I've become.

Just like that, the headache starts again, stampeding at my temples. A flood of memories hammering at the back of my skull.

My arms pinwheel, and I claw at the roiling fathoms around me, gasping for air. *No! I won't see this!* My teeth chatter, eyes burning, nostrils filled with the thick dampness of the Thames.

But the little boy is there again. Salty, windblown blond hair, playing by the sirens' lagoon. Glancing up at me, trusting. As if he'd follow me anywhere.

Until everything was torn apart.

I grit my teeth to stunt the deluge, but glints of memory still snake through.

I see snatches of faces and scenes and places echoing through the frigid, dark water around me. Glimpses of Neverland and the echo of children's laughter. Alluring, ferocious sirens. Stoic tribal warriors.

Claire will soon see it all. Or at least a broken reflection of what it once was.

And if he has his way, he'll break her too.

My legs curl and my arms go stiff. I begin to sink, body immobile from the ache spiking through me. There are the snatches of his voice, as the memories do their bloomin' best to rip me apart. This one is worst of all.

But I won't let it in.

Just as I am able to force my submerged body into motion again, I hear a loud splash. Something churns the water, paddling toward me.

A massive, dark shadow slices through the Thames.

What is that?

Before I can react, the Neverbeast is upon me.

Oh stars. Don't tell me—

My head breaks the surface and I'm inches from a massive face with rows upon rows of teeth grinning down at me. Dripping fur slicked and eyes gleaming. There's some kind of thick leather collar around its neck.

"Ah—nice doggy . . ."

Its massive jaw splaying rows of teeth reaches for me. I utter a short cry, but instead of becoming a Neverbeast snack, the creature clamps its mouth on the edge of my jacket, scooping my hood up.

I'm dumbfounded as it cranes its enormous head, lifting me so that my torso is above the ripping flow of the Thames. And then it starts to swim toward the distant dock where two blurred figures are waiting.

"'Ey! Take it easy!" I splutter at the mighty creature. "This is my good jacket!" At least, it used to be.

The water funnels past in white threads as the Neverbeast paddles toward the dock. The mist-soaked figures come into view, and the next thing I know, Lily and the Guardian are reaching for me. They drag me out of the frigid Thames and dump me onto the rough-hewn dock.

I hack up water and the numbness wears away and cold seeps in. The shivers start.

"Here." Lily crouches in front of me in her long, brown jacket. She helps me to remove my own sopping jacket and slip into hers. I nod a chattering thank-you.

Pulling my knees to my chest, I sit hunched on the dock and look over to Jeremy Darling, who is standing a few feet away beside the dripping Neverbeast. The collar of his dark blue coat up around his sharp jawline, and his icy-blue eyes regarding me with curiosity.

"Well, if it isn't the Guardian." My voice is hoarse. "I'd almost forgotten about you, mate."

His expression darkens.

Spoil sport.

But it's not just Jeremy who looks stoic as a statue. There's a heaviness about Lily next to me, leaning on her staff.

"Lily . . . ?"

"Just tell me one thing, Peter." Her eyes are filled with harsh, pooling tears. "Tell me that Claire did not just join *Hook* and take him and all of her magic to Neverland—without us?"

My throat closes up. Hearing it aloud makes it more real.

Her voice catches. "Tell me we did not just lose everything?"

I can't.

A shiver sweeps over me. "Maybe I can fly after her? Maybe I can still stop her—"

"How?" Lily is almost frantic. "Even if the pixies weren't so weak, this will only make them more afraid to come anywhere near us if that means crossing Hook, now that he has what he wants." Lily's hair falls over her eyes. "Even if you could get to Neverland . . . it might already be too late."

I cringe at the depth of sadness in her voice. I've never heard the unshakable warrior princess this unnerved. This hopeless.

Jeremy clears his throat. "I can get to Neverland."

Tiger Lily and I both turn to stare at him. "What?"

He straightens his navy jacket. "Yes, I have a way to help one person fly to Neverland. But I don't understand what the urgency is. You've always had your problems with Hook, what makes this any different?"

Lily toes a black leather boot against the chipped planks underfoot. "It's not Hook we're worried about."

Jeremy's eyes narrow. "Then who?"

Lily looks at me pointedly, and instantly that blasted headache is back. Gaining momentum. Stars, this has not been my blasted day.

"There are . . . other things at play in Neverland," she says.

"In Neverland?" Jeremy blows out a long breath. "Never mind, I don't really want to know. What happens in Neverland—your magical feuds—those aren't my concern. I have enough to manage here. I came because you said Claire was being kidnapped, but she clearly left of her own choice. Whatever you decide about Hook, I can't be involved."

And just like that, the Guardian turns on his heel to stride away, taking with him whatever key he has to Neverland.

Cripes, I hate his guts.

"For once, couldn't you break your own blasted rules?"

Jeremy just shakes his head as he crosses the dock, heading for the Neverbeast pacing nearby.

"You're leaving? Just like that?" Lily shouts after him as she jumps up. "You know what, Jeremy Darling?"

Electric, sizzling anger is sparking across the tribal princess's features.

She's furious.

"You are a *coward*." Lily flings the word at him as she storms across the dock toward Jeremy. "You claim to be a protector who keeps peace. But you're just a coward who won't commit to either side of this war." She lifts the weathered spritewood staff in her hand to point it at him. "And mark my words, Jeremy— this is a war. Regardless of how much you try to ignore it. If you don't do something to stop Hook and the others, they'll come for Earth. And then you won't have any London left to protect."

He stops mid-step. Beside him, the towering Neverbeast's hackles rise.

Lily isn't finished. "That girl? Claire? She's not just anyone. There's magic inside her unlike anything you've ever seen. And right now she is sailing toward the only other person who is as powerful as she is—and he is a bigger threat than any of us can imagine."

Jeremy slowly turns to face her. "Go on."

Lily thuds her staff. "I honestly don't know how we fix this—but I do know we have very little chance if even the man called the *Guardian* won't help. Together, we might have a chance. Especially if you know how to get at least one of us to Neverland." Her expression is stony. "But if you keep riding the fence and refuse to pick a side . . ." She lifts her chin. "Then the few good people left will probably lose the last thing they have in an attempt to stop Hook—*their lives*. You really want that on your conscience?"

Dang, Lily.

Jeremy's aloof expression begins to crack, understanding and uncertainty and a hint of shame showing through his gray-blue eyes. He speaks slowly. "All my life I've been taught that by standing immovable between two worlds I was protecting both. But maybe . . ."

His words hang in the air several deathly seconds, and he fingers the golden ring on his left hand.

Then Jeremy Darling lifts his head to stare straight at me. "Maybe it's time this Guardian wrote some rules of his own."

Brilliant! It's about flamin' time.

He gives Lily the faintest smile and then crosses to the Neverbeast towering behind him. He scratches behind its silky ears and then reaches for the leather collar strapped around its neck. He unclips the binding, pulling the massive piece loose, and starts toward us. "I've kept this for years in case the day ever came that I needed to return to Neverland."

He slides his hands along the inside of the collar, the part pressed against the Neverbeast's fur. A latch clicks and there, lying in his palm, is a thin vial filled with glowing, golden dust.

I'm at his side in two steps and reaching for the dust. "Cor! That's brilliant. I can leave immediately, find Claire, and maybe stop them before they reach Neverland—"

Jeremy makes a guttural sound between a scoff and a chuckle. "You really think I'd let you anywhere near Neverland unchecked? For all I know, you started this whole thing."

"*What?*"

I must have heard him wrong.

I'm Peter Pan. This is what I do.

Lily looks at the Guardian. "Peter may be our best option. He knows how to navigate the stars and—"

Jeremy waves away her words, eyes piercing through me. "I need to know you'll do the right thing. I need to know you'll really try to fix things. You have to prove to me that you won't choose to be the typical selfish Peter you've always been."

I stand a little taller, fists on hips. "I'll do whatever it takes."

His eyes glint. "Then tell me the truth. All of it. *Who* are you so afraid of?"

The headache slams into my temples with such force, my legs nearly give out. I grab at Lily to stay on my feet.

I hear Tink's screams, like shattering glass.

But the screams aren't the worst of it. It's the hollow laugher that echoes behind them.

"Peter, what's wrong?" Concern etches Lily's face.

Jeremy starts toward me—but I jut out a hand. "Stay back!"

He can't help. No one can.

Except maybe me.

Because I'm beginning to think that maybe these memories aren't as connected to Neverland as I thought. Yes, the island's magic allowed me to forget the darker things. But perhaps the painful resurgence isn't triggered by a twisted Neverland— but by me.

By one specific incident I'm doing everything I can to ignore.

But maybe I can't . . .

You live in this made-up place where you can do whatever you want and don't have to bother with how it may hurt others. Claire's words lift in my thoughts, cutting through the pain for an instant. *But the rest of us can't live like that.*

I lift my gaze from the weathered dock and up at the star-streaked sky.

Maybe she's right. It's not just about me anymore—this is

how I save Claire and everyone in Neverland. By facing the dark shadows I want to hide from. The ways I've treated Lily's tribe— or the time I left that batch of sour, rebellious Lost Boys to die in their own trap they'd set for me. And the countless other scars and wounds I'm responsible for. Things I never cared about because they didn't hurt me.

But I care now.

And maybe—by letting in, by owning it, by trying to fix what I've broken—I can be *different* from my father.

I take in a deep breath, look up at the waiting Guardian.

"Connor is the one who's destroying Neverland. He's become a monster—and I think I made him that way."

Connor is not the brother Claire remembers. He's not an innocent little boy anymore. Maybe he never was. Maybe she just loved him so much, she didn't see the shadows.

Flashes of Connor's blond hair and blue eyes flit through my head as I stop pretending. Stop trying to ignore what happened. What I did to him.

I let it in.

All of it.

And as the memories crash over me, I gasp against the pain. My knees buckle, and I collapse to the deck. I can practically hear it again—the crunching echo of the island splintering apart. I envision the broken boy who tossed Neverland into a cacophony of monsoons and earthquakes far more savage than I ever had.

And then I see Tink. Flittering at my heels as I fled—until she was thrown to the side in a harsh wind. And he caught her, laughing wildly as he ripped her wings from her spine—and then tore the little pixie apart.

I had to carve my own shadow off my heels to escape his hold.

Had to flee the island, bruised and bleeding, just to survive.

Between gasps, I shove words out and Jeremy's and Lily's expressions pale as I speak. "When I left Connor and Claire on Earth as babies, I had no idea how connected to Neverland they were. And that the island would dim without them there. So I went to find them and bring them back—but only Connor believed me." My shoulders jerk, wracked with pain. "I stole him out from under Hook's nose and took the lad to Neverland."

But I hadn't known that the boy wasn't an innocent. He'd seen things that I couldn't even fathom.

I clutch at my head, but as I talk, the pain begins to lessen.

"Connor never fit in with the other Lost Boys. And once he'd tried to share why to me . . . explain what had happened." I can picture his tearful expression, so vulnerable as he opened up about the tears in his soul. "But I didn't know how to process any of it. What to even say." And like the selfish child I'd been . . . "I told him to stop crying. Told him that boys didn't cry. Told him to stop being a baby and just . . ."

Just . . .

I grab at the chipped wooden deck until the splintered wood makes my fingertips bleed.

"I told him . . ."

And then I spit out the three words that make my insides so violently churn:

"Just grow up."

I double over. But the pain in my temples is ebbing, fading.

I had wanted to snatch back the words the minute they came out back then. The minute my father's voice poured from my lips.

But it was too late. The damage was done.

I wipe away the sting blurring my eyes. "It broke Connor. He hated me for that. He went on a rampage, nearly splitting the island in two."

Not that I blame him.

I hate me for saying it.

And I've been running from that knowledge since the minute I crash-landed here.

Lily gently bends down to place a hand on my shoulder, quietly finishing the story for me. "Connor was fearsome enough that even Hook obeyed him—and then forced most of the Lost Boys to join his crew. They give Connor whatever he wants and are too terrified to cross him. And now he wants Claire. Who knows what he has planned for her."

Shoving hair out of my eyes, I pull myself to my feet. My voice is steadfast.

"I may be the only person who can talk Connor off the ledge I set him on. Or at least tell Claire the truth and help her. Maybe together we can fix this beastly mess I created."

Jeremy studies me for a long second, then nods. "All right. Somehow I don't think you're lying." With a hint of a smile, he reaches out to press the vial of pixie dust into my quivering palm. "I'll believe in you, Peter Pan. Go save your island."

My hands close around the vial. "You know, you're not so bad after all."

Jeremy just shakes his head.

Holding the vial of dust tight, I take a deep breath. I let the crisp air wash over me and gaze at the sky.

The warm tug of dust in my hand beckons my feet to lift off the ground—to make the same trek I've flown a thousand times.

I'm going to do it.

I'm going to face the shadows and rise above them.

I turn back to Lily and Jeremy. "I guess this is it."

Jeremy nods again. "I guess it is."

He checks his watch. "I should be getting home. Lily, you're welcome to join Tansy and me when you finish here. We can discuss what to do moving forward and can provide for you here in the meantime."

A grateful light comes into her eyes. "Will do."

Jeremy turns back to me. "We're relying on you, boy. Don't mess it up."

I give him a jaunty little bow. "Me? Never."

He rolls his eyes and then turns to the Neverbeast that has been pacing restlessly behind him, planks creaking beneath its weight.

He reaches for the hulking creature's muzzle, stroking it affectionately, not seeming the least bit worried by its massive figure. "Ready to go home, boy?"

Its coppery eyes look too big for its face.

It's almost cute.

If you can ignore the teeth.

The creature shakes its head, sending more water droplets flying, opens its maw to yawn—and begins to shrink.

Its body gets smaller and smaller and smaller, ears flopping over, tail shortening, fur growing more sparse and silky. And then, before my eyes, I watch Jeremy Darling's Neverbeast turn into a *dog*.

The mangy, scrawny mutt that's always yipping at the officer's heels.

I blink at it. Well, that explains so much.

"Atta boy, Nar. C'mon, let's go." Jeremy rubs the dog's head.

With a last wave at us, he turns and they saunter off together.

"Well, you'd better leave soon if you want to catch the *Jolly Roger.*" Lily's eyes are glistening.

And all of a sudden it dawns on me . . . I'm doing this alone.

"Ah, you'll find a way to meet me there soon enough." My voice is rough.

Lily gives me a quick hug.

Then she clears her throat and removes a wrapped parcel out of her jacket. "It's the sandwich I got earlier this morning, before Claire went missing. Looks like you'll need it after all."

I take the food and slide it into my back pocket. I smirk down at the tribal princess, tousling her hair. "Looking out for me as ever, Lily."

"I'm proud of you, Peter." Her voice breaks again. She looks about to say more but doesn't. It's more than enough. She gives me a last little hug and takes a step back. She smiles, white teeth gleaming. "You can do this."

My jaw tightens and my eyes smart. "I won't say goodbye . . ."

She inhales deeply, blinking back tears, and nods. "I know you won't. I'll see you soon."

"See you soon," I echo.

And then Tiger Lily smiles once more and raises one dark hand etched with silver constellations to point to the star-streaked sky overhead. "Go do the impossible, Peter Pan."

This is it. No more hiding. No more pretending.

Time to face the shadows.

I stride to the end of the dock and pause a moment with my bare toes hanging over the edge of the wooden platform. Light splashes of water cool my feet.

Lifting the glass vial, I uncork it and pour a little pixie dust into my palm. The golden flakes slip through my fingers and begin to speckle my clothing, filling the air.

I lift my eyes to the stars, a glimmering map of light written across the sky, and make a promise on the second one to the right. I will bring the light back to Neverland. I will remind the island of dreams and wonder and magic just what it means to rise past the shadows and chase after the stars. I will win Claire back.

Time to fly.

ACKNOWLEDGMENTS

We made it.

The whimsy-filled book in your hands is the culmination of years of fierce dreams and tenacious hard work. If I could, I'd whisper to my younger self, an intrepid teen staring out of airplane windows as she flew across the world, always moving and never quite feeling like she fit in: *it's all right.* Those big dreams and your childhood in the jungle and unique perspective—they'll one day fuel a story that, at its core, is about stepping into the light of where you belong. And it will resonate. In the end, that will make all the difference. We will make it.

I dedicate *Dust* to you first, reader. Thank you for supporting me. For giving me a voice. I hope you've enjoyed the ride—we're only just beginning.

To my family: We've traveled the world ten times over, and we've always done it together. Thank you for believing in me. Thank you for lifting me when I was too weak to stand. I love you all so very much.

To RJ and Orrie: For seeing me. For believing in me. For everything. You both are the Tiger Lily to my Claire.

To Joanne, Sharilyn, Hadassa, and Kezia: Thank you for being my oldest friends, for being the wind under my wings, for cheering with me and wrapping your arms around me when I wept. I would never have made it this far without you.

To Aleigha: Your precious and brave, brave soul is such a light. Thank you for all the boxes of sunshine.

To Veronica: You deserve all the chocolate cake in the world. Thanks for being the best alpha reader and the biggest Dust fan.

To Ashley: For emboldening the light and hope of pixie dust, and being such a dear, supportive kindred spirit. Also, for sending the best Spider-Man GIFs.

To Steve: My agent, my publisher, my friend. For taking such very good care of me and this story. Working with you has been and always will be such an honor.

To the Enclave team: Lisa, for loving Peter as much as I do and so deftly polishing up this novel. To Trissina and Jordan for going above and beyond with marketing and doing so much to help get this story into readers' hands. All of you blew me away. Thank you for pouring your best into this little Peter Pan story.

To Lindsay, Sarah, Morgan, and the rest of my Enclave author family: It's such an immense honor to get to call each of you my friends and publishing family. So proud of the roads you're paving.

To Nadine, Sara, and Mary: The three of you have been my heroes since I found out that YA fantasy was a thing. Getting to call you my friends and learn and grow alongside you has been such an enormous privilege. I love you all dearly.

To Brett, Jaquelle, Josiah and Marita: Thank you for all the ways you have supported my journey. It's such a joy to get to be on faculty for the *Young Writers Workshop* alongside you.

To Alysia: For trusting me to do Peter justice.

To Emily: For being my Story Sensei and my favorite fellow Smallville nerd.

To Becky: For understanding soul-stories and loving my Pete.

To Desiree and Katie: Your editorial feedback on this story helped to bring Peter and Claire's story to life beautifully. And your friendship has made my life all the better.

To Shan and Jill: For being the queens of storytelling and supporting me ever since I was a young teen at a writers' conference not quite sure what I was getting myself into. I want to be you when I grow up.

To the writing community, my Starchasers street team and the YDubbers: There are more friends than I could possibly name who have supported and guided me along this journey. Thank you all, from the bottom of my heart.

To Tessa: For being the first person to give my stories a shot. I will always be grateful.

To J. M. Barrie: I'm rather fond of the book you wrote. Peter and I thank you.

To my Jesus, the first and the last, the Ever One: Thank you for holding my heart in the dark times, for setting the stars in motion, for bleeding in my place, and for giving me a hope that never fades.

ABOUT THE AUTHOR

Kara Swanson writes stories about fairytales and fiery souls. She spent her childhood a little like a Lost Girl, running barefoot through lush green jungles which inspired her award-winning Peter Pan retellings, *Dust* and *Shadow*.

She is also the co-founder of the Author Conservatory where she has the honor of teaching young writers to craft sustainable author careers.

You'll find Kara with her toes in California sand as a SoCal resident, belting Broadway show tunes on weekend drives to Disneyland with her delightfully-nerdy husband, or chatting about magic and mayhem on Instagram.

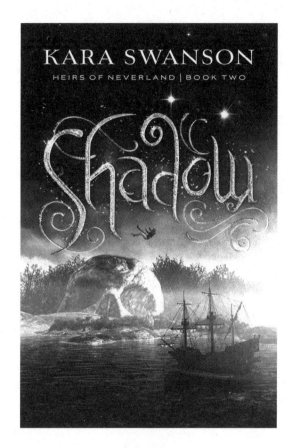